# LUMMOX

BROADWAY EDITION

# LUMMOX

by
**FANNIE HURST**

**P. F. COLLIER & SON COMPANY**
Publishers                              New York

LUMMOX

# LUMMOX

Nobody quite knew just what Baltic bloods flowed in sullen and alien rivers through Bertha's veins—or cared, might be added. Bertha, least of all.

She was five feet, nine and a half, of flat-breasted bigness and her cheek-bones were pitched like Norn's. Little tents. There must have been a good smattering of Scandinavian and even a wide streak of western Teutonic. Slav, too. Because unaccountably she found herself knowing the Polish national anthem. Recognized it with her heart as it rattled out of a hurdy-gurdy.

In her carpetbag, an outlandish one with a steamship stamp on it, were a bit of Bulgarian embroidery, a runic brooch, a concertina with a punctured bellows and an ikon in imitation mosaic. Old world.

And yet Bertha had been born in a furiously dark sailors' lodging house in Front Street, where New York harbor smells of spices and city garbage rides by to the dump on barges. One of those frightening emergency births of rusty instruments, midwifery and a sinister room made more terrible by the travail of her coming. Of no particular father (although the China seas could probably have yielded up the secret of his rollicking lane), and of a dead mother.

She had died two minutes before Bertha was born. Annie Wennerberg, landlady of the sailors' lodging house, who reared Bertha those first dozen years of her life that were sopping wet with scrub-water and soft-soap, knew. Horrid scuttling rat-like things that Annie Wennerberg knew.

Born of a dead mother,
Secrets of the grave you'll utter.

That couplet could run down Bertha's spinal cord like a mouse.

"I don't know any secrets of the grave, Annie."

"You do. They're written on your face. You got a look in that wide place between your eyes like the sound of a clump of dirt falling on a coffin. You're as full of secrets as a cow's tail is of burrs."

Wildly, and with a coherence she could have torn open her throat for, Bertha wanted to tell Annie that her secrets, if any she had, were of life, not death. The knowledges that came to her in chimes from the dark forests within her where the trees could somehow seem to stand with folded arms regarding her and the air to be wisps of old sound. Snacks of melodies out of eastern Europe. Secrets that shimmered. But it seemed to Bertha that her tongue was merely the shallow pan for those few words at her disposal which rattled off it so hollowly.

It was so hard to talk. Words. Frail beasts of burden that crashed down to their knees under what she wanted to say.

How to convey to Annie Wennerberg that her mother had not dragged her down to the clayey secrets of the grave but had endowed her with lovely, bosky, dell-like secrets of life. Those were the meanings of the wide silence of space between her eyes.

"I don't know nothing about the grave, Annie—"

"You do. For two minutes you was in the grave with your dead mother—yah—yah—

Born of a dead mother,
Secrets of the grave you'll utter."

Bertha wondered. But not unduly. She thought so dimly, almost as if she had breathed on a mirror and reflection could not come through. For that matter she even felt dimly.

"Sometimes," she once said to Annie Wennerberg, "I feel like my skin was a thick piece of flannel, between the inside of me and the outside."

Annie's retort was a single vile word. They jumped off her lips constantly, like hop-toads.

But somewhere in Bertha's mists were ecstasies. She would sit on the stairs at night, and huddle over to the banister for the passing of a drunken sailor, scarcely conscious that his enormous clod of a mud-caked shoe was almost in her face.

She slept on a cot that crawled with vermin, with the beauty of repose on that face of hers which was said to look like the sound of a clump of dirt on a coffin.

Once, way back before she had gone to the Farleys, she had worked out "by the day" as the saying goes. Odd jobs. Cleaning an old rooming-house for new occupancy on very East Seventeenth Street. Corners to be scraped out with a knife. Scrub water that became livid. Stench. Two men had sickened at the job and quit. Yet Bertha, with her lips held very tightly it is true, scraped and scraped, until actually, standing there at the sink, poking webby stuff through the drain hole, chimes came through to her from the dark forest. The forest that was Baltic and western Teutonic.

Yet sometimes, because of these great inner reaches of her, even the chimes arrived to her dimly. Muted melodies. Wanting-to-be-born thoughts. Bertha's prisoners.

She liked, after her day's work was done, to sit with them. Little bells in lovely headache against her brow. Words.

"Lyric" was a beautiful word. Rollo Farley had used it to a young girl at dinner, who had listened to him with the nape of her neck stretched and her lips scarlet. It had come through to Bertha peering from behind the pantry door. "Lyric," a golden word shaped like a harp.

She liked to say it and feel it race delicately around her lips as if it were a high-strung little roulette ball in its bowl.

Sometimes she spat like a peasant, of slow reflection.

There was a sliver of kitchen porch and a pad of backyard with a magnolia tree in it, behind the Farley house in Gramercy Park. She had seen that magnolia heavy with bud six beautiful times. She had cooked for the Farleys six years.

In spring, after the great dish pan with the gray cloth drying over it was turned to the wall and the linoleum smelling wetly from her mop, Bertha would sit out there on the sliver of porch waiting the interim between dinner and light refreshments of sandwiches and fresh fruit to be sent into the drawing room at eleven. Would sit barefoot. They were strong feet, still warm and damp from shoes. Great pale spuds with muscular toes that could spread separately like a wine presser's, and were full of a predatory power to clutch.

She could almost breathe in with her feet. She liked to feel their bareness pat at the old cheek of earth. All the big-footed and barefooted women out of her Baltic and Teutonic hinterlands rebelled against Bertha's shoes. They gave her bunions. Bulbs that projected off her foot like a nose, giving the shoe, after one day's wearing, the profile of a mean old man. So she padded around the kitchen barefoot, when Mrs. Farley's invasions, or Helga's the housemaid, were unlikely. There was a wininess in their bare contacts. Breathers. Suckers in of the little vibratory messages that run across floors. Toes. The prehensile curving of toes around the branches of the dark forest. . . .

Once Mrs. Farley, sweeping through the swinging door into the kitchen, found her on her knees before the oven basting a Thanksgiving turkey, the soles of her bare feet upright and staring out from under her cotton skirts like lantern-jawed faces.

"Bertha, don't ever let me find you barefoot in the kitchen again. It's disgusting."

"Yah'm."

Submission was so easy. Shoes. They were part of the day and the day was like a garment fashioned by the employment agency; the lady of the house; and for the last six years by Mrs. Farley.

There is not much of Mrs. Farley in this telling. She paid Bertha twenty dollars a month (it was the day of the cable-car and there was some talk of a Louisiana Purchase Exposition to be held in St. Louis), clucked her tongue against the roof of her mouth when she told about it and said, "What's the world coming to?"

She was kind enough in a fusty way, wore invariable black velvet neck bands, saved twine, and gave every other Monday afternoon to the Tenement Hygienic Committee of the Human Welfare League.

Helga, whose back always ached and who kept twenty rooms swept and dusted, was expected to sit up for Mrs. Farley until after theater for the single process of massaging the wattles underneath the band of black velvet.

Bertha scrubbed and cooked from the servants' breakfast hour at six-thirty to family dinner at eight P. M. and often until eleven, when there were the sandwiches and light refreshments to be prepared.

Helga spat on the Human Welfare League pamphlets and gritted her teeth at them.

Mrs. Farley was also on the letterhead of an organization called The Circle for Housing Relief.

Bertha's room cowed under the roof of the finely austere house in Gramercy Park beneath a slant ceiling that was like a threatening slap. No heat unless she left the door open and the warm breath of downstairs came up. A bed with a short fourth leg and a spring that sagged like a hammock to the considerable heft of Bertha's body. A bureau rigged up out of a discarded desk of Rollo Farley's and a pitcher and bowl on a soap box. For six years Bertha slept up there with that slanting ceiling on her chest. But usually she was so very tired that her sleep was like a death and the slant a clod of earth on the grave of another day.

Bertha was a good cook. "A good plain cook," Mrs. Farley apologized in her invitations to the more informal of her dinner parties. But she could do curlicues in icing. Bone squab. Work with such esoteric ingredients as marron glacé, pickled walnuts, and capers, illuminate carrots into rosettes, and stir a fish sauce with just the tricky rightness of the tartar touch. Rollo Farley had a frail digestion. Bertha had learned to broil and coddle for him and knew just the turn of his chop.

"She's a great unresponsive hunky sort of girl," Mrs. Farley would recite of her. "Swede, I imagine, or perhaps one of those blonde Poles. But she's a good plain cook and knows Rollo's diet. Good as one can do nowadays. Does not run about either, as so many of them do. Too lazy I suppose. Justs sits and daydreams. But anything is preferable to changing and having to start on the rounds of the employment agencies."

Bertha had an equal horror of employment agencies. Shambles of sullen stock awaiting inspection. The lorgnette fusillade. The bitter shameless questionings, like an apple corer plunging down into the heart.

"What is that on your face? I hope it isn't a rash. Do you expect every Thursday out? You bathe regularly, of course? You understand that my cook always helps with the housework on the maid's day out. I've a half-grown daughter and cannot permit my help to entertain men in the kitchen. Newspapers are full of such dreadful things. Would you mind having your things fumigated before you bring them to the house? Can't be too careful. . . ."

So Bertha stayed on at the Farleys, and when she had been there six years Mrs. Farley gave her a cast-off opera cloak of sea-green chiffon. It was rather funny in a way. Bertha of strong sweat and hands that could entrail fowl at one tear, in sea-green chiffon. She never tried it on, it would have embarrassed her, but the green seemed to fill her attic room like sea. Beautiful sea, that instead of rolling and hurting like a prisoner in her heart, was here on the outside where she could touch it. The delicate fabric clung to the roughness of her hands. In its way that chiffon was like the Polish national anthem which she could hear so poignantly with her heart, or like the word "Lyric" which she could feel with her teeth when she repeated it softly to herself.

After that she began to watch through the swinging door of the pantry, the fabrics on the backs of women at dinner. Satin, Velvet that was like a silence. Once she found a bit of torn-off spangled trimming and put it in the drawer with her ocean. Stars. She had only to jerk open that drawer and they lay there, lit and waiting.

One night at a formal dinner to sixteen, there was an ex-ambassador, and she had two helpers from the employment agency, and so could sit at the crack in the swinging door between courses. Candlelight bending and bowing into crystal and silver. Calla lilies. Mrs. Farley's harp, a curve of gold beside the buffet. Little hissing pools of wine. Mrs. Farley's back was half bare, and it sloped down into a valley at the spine. An old sunken back. Not nice. Nathan Farley's bald head and face were very red, so that his white mustache seen from the crack in the swinging door was almost like a frothing at the mouth. His kiss might leave suds.

Locked up gargoyles of thoughts in Bertha for which she had no words, except those feeble ones which fell to their knees like the frail beasts of burden.

There was a very long and slender-necked girl at the table with cool lips and a head the lovely shape of an egg, the hair revealing the face like reluctantly parted portières. To Bertha, who felt but could not say it, the lovely ellipsity of that head was like putting an egg whole into your mouth and then feeling it slowly come out.

Rollo Farley was talking to her. Bertha had prepared an aspic jelly for him, skilfully camouflaged to resemble the fish course that was going its rounds on an enormous silver platter flaming with carrot rosettes. Fish disagreed. He slid his fork into the aspic, carefully anticipating the deception, but constantly face to face with the lovely oval creature.

Rollo was about Bertha's age. But his flesh much tenderer. The quality of breast-of-fowl. Fuzz of down on the back of his neck. Nervous hands as if the fingers were dripping from them like icicles. He wrote with them, using a softly whispering pencil all through the forenoon and sometimes long after the household slept. Once Bertha, dusting his small, book-lined study on Helga's day out, read from one of the sheets on his desk. Short lines leaving much of the paper white. Lines that rocked softly like a boat with a lateen sail. Rhythm. "Love. Rove." "Pagan. Raven." "Lyre. Desire."

Flash. Flash. Flash. A plunging opal horse and a jade terrific lion and a lapis lazuli centaur, riding round and round again into alternate view on the merry-go-round.

She had dusted the wide-margined paper with the click of flame color through the words. As if you opened and closed your eyes very rapidly. Had dusted it dispassionately enough, but her throat felt all rigid. Tight enough for tears. . . .

She was dispassionate now through the crack in the door. Except that the down on the back of Rollo's neck was so— so young. Heart hurting.

At ten o'clock the great dish pan was turned, the helpers gone, Helga whispering at the service entrance with the night watchman, and Bertha who had sweated, out on the back porch, barefooted and cooling in the spring.

A night the color of a frosted grape. The hoar of an invisible moon. The magnolia. Big silences standing still in Bertha. Silences that to be told at all must be told silently. . . .

The iceman had caught her that morning unawares, slapping his hand down on her square hips. It was the first time a man had touched her.

"Hello, Bertha, got the Yonnie Yump Ups this morning?"

"Go away, you nervy!"

"Say 'Yonnie Yump Up.' "

"Yah—you—get—out—"

Bertha could not say J. It melted in her throat. She didn't know the reason, but she looked the reason, Swedishly. The great broad face. Pitched-tent cheek bones. The square teeth and flaring lips. The nose with the flanges spread like the fat haunches of a squatting idol. Eyes like globes of clear water against blue sky, but occasional darts through. Goldfish flanks. Braids of yellow hair strapped around her head in bandeaux.

In her body bigness lay beauty. Godiva's gleam. Light breasts, the way the Greeks loved them, without sag. Long white line of femur. Hip rhythm. The touch of the iceman's hands, hours old; hunky hands that she had rejected, still lay on those hips, as if clay had hardened there.

It was pleasant to sit on the sliver of porch with the feel of hands through the cotton stuff and on to her flesh.

After a while Rollo Farley came out on the porch. He was dizzy. Wine. Heat. And his mother had warned him against the croquilles. The air was like a lady with a slow fan. Little stirs of it. Cool. The smell of magnolia. Almost immediately the little beads on his forehead went out like lights and his wrists dried.

"Hello, Bertha," he said.

She sat with her knees very wide apart in an enormous cradle and her hands hanging in it.

"Hul," she said.

He leaned against the wall with his hand back between him and the brick. Little noises under the silence. His shirt front, champing at a pearl stud. He slid his hand into his pocket. She could hear his nearness.

"Good God, what starlight," he said finally, looking up through the moon hoar and doing a sort of calisthenics with his arms until the cuffs shot.

She sat.

He said strange, beautiful things sometimes. Words. She treasured them as a lapidary his stones. Occasionally he addressed her as she dusted his books on Helga's day out, much as he might have a newel post or the terra cotta Chloe on his desk.

"Sonnet" was another dear word. He had used it to himself more than once as she tiptoed. A word to lay away in the heart. "Good God, what starlight." Anyone might have said that—and yet—

"Bertha," he said finally, addressing her as if she were his cigarette smoke, "keep close to life. Don't let them find your nerves—or your soul."

". . . or her soul!" Bertha whose being was a callous spot through which the soul could not quite hurt through.

"Your problems are husky ones, Bertha. To-morrow's menu. It will warm the stomach, but it leaves the heart alone. Keep close to life, Bertha. Cabbages are beautiful and only a little tougher fibred than roses."

Vaporings. He was twenty-five and a poet.

Close to life. What was that? Close to life. Her toes dug

down against the floor as if they would translate it for her. He looked down at their white movement.

"Why, Bertha, he said, "your feet are like two big white magnolias off our tree."

She loved that, but she wiggled her toes and said, "They hurt."

He looked again at their white movement. The toes wiggling now under his words. Luscious feet that listened to the soil and stole its secrets. A sublime kind of capillarity. Bertha feeling for closeness to life with her feet.

Thick white feet, yet begetting in Rollo thoughts too fragile to hold in even the facets of a poet's brain. Thoughts as fragile as the throat of the nightingale that sang outside the emperor's window.

Actually for the first time in the six years, Rollo looked at Bertha with his attention. Splay mouthed. High cheeked. Muscular toed. A soaking kind of peasantry that flowed into him and made him want to write it out again in a meter that was like the clump of wooden shoes.

And then he looked at her waist, where because she had sweated, it lay open. Hillocks of white breast. Flesh flowing like cream into them. Strength and length of femur under cotton skirts. Crouching, submerged, and silent strength.

"Bertha," he said, and touched her lightly on the throat with his poet's fingers. How she beat there. It ran up his arm in an ecstasy. "Why Bertha, how you beat—underneath the whiteness."

"I—I——"

"Rollo," called his mother from the euchre table, "your deal, dear. We're waiting."

"Coming, Mother."

She hated the going sound of his steps, each new faintness of them a stab.

But her dark forest was full of chimes. Words darted through the branches with the brilliancy of flamingoes on wing. "Pagan." "Appassionata." Brooks of the frozen tears of her loneliness began to flow. She was bursting of music and the sound of the jeweled words and she wanted to run after him and help him somehow into the largo of the charmed forest of her heart.

But he was already back at the euchre table and opposite the slim head that looked as an egg would feel if it came whole out of your mouth.

Out on the porch it was still again, except for the brook of the frozen tears.

It was very late. Pain in the back of her legs as if the muscles were screwing. After Rollo's return to the table there had been an extra round of euchre and extra wines. Three sizes of goblets to be polished. Mrs. Farley wanted them soaped, bathed, breathed on, and then shined into nothingness.

Even with the screwing pains, Bertha liked doing them this way in the stilly part of the night, with the family upstairs and going to and fro to bed. The warm suds squeaking off. The soft hiss of the towel. Crystal frozen out of thin laughter. A trayful of the polite, chittering things. With one stroke she could break them back into laughter.

Milk bottles to be placed in a row on the kitchen porch and the ice card to be turned. So.

The shine of magnolias that were no whiter than her feet. Rollo Farley had touched her; trolled four of his fingers along her whiteness. They had melted against her throat and down into her heart. White tapering roads, his fingers, in the dark forest along which she ran, calling. . . .

Then up the back stairs to her room. It hurt her to climb them. On the third landing she sat down and let down her balbriggan stocking to rub at the calf of her leg. It was good, that leg, something that she could feel in the round. It had dimension. Flesh. Muscle. Bulge. And when it hurt she could lay her hands to it.

She undressed in the dark, sitting on the bed edge with the door open for the warmed air of the halls. It was very simple. Waist. Corsets. Chemise. Smelling strongly clean of laundry soap. Twenty times a day she washed her arms up to the elbows with the great brown cakes.

As she sat with her waist half off and the knoll of her first shoulder shining through, Rollo Farley came to her door. His face was like a lamp. And hers. Two dim rounds of light, wigwagging. They lit the fog with the faintness of flame chewing along low wicks.

"I can see you, Bertha, because you are whiter than the darkness is black."

Her heart shied back and leaped.

"Go away," she said with her lips, but she wanted to turn on her forest like a music box for him. Wanted her flamingoes to fly, the sands of the jeweled word-particles to sparkle. He took her hands and she was ashamed. They were so heavy and lye-bitten and there were such white ones at her heart that she wanted to give him. Like his. Pale whispers.

"You don't want me to go away, White Bertha. Why— feel—you have a little heart in your throat. How it beats."

She began to cry inwardly. There *was* a little heart in her throat that beat up against her silence. It was terrible to be dumb. She could have shrieked, "I am all locked! You hear! Prairies are flowing in me and oceans and I am under them. Locked!" Words! Words! To be able to pour some of her jeweled sands on to the sensitive plate of him. She could feel the sands want to run into words and the words thunder into wisdom.

"You are so white, Bertha. To think that I never noticed. Deeply white, like the flesh of a magnolia." She felt her shoulder gleam and pushed it back into her sleeve.

"Bertha—don't——"

"Go away——"

Then he began shyly at her fingers, lifting them one by one. "Strong Bertha."

Strong Bertha indeed. Their heaviness sickened her. She wanted to distract him from their roughness to which the green chiffon always clung, and to tell him how the lanes of his slender fingers led through the forest, but what she said was, "Get out. I can bite."

"Then bite, Bertha." The dance of excitement along his whisper! It set her to trembling. "Your beautiful strength! Give some to me, White Bertha."

"Mrs. Farley will not have goings-on. Helga will hear. I will call Mrs. Far-r-ley—"

She gargled the name a little. He looked at her with her face flattened by darkness into a mere lily pad and her nearness flowed over him.

"You—who are you? I know! You are the poem of the

woman whose feet are rooted in the secrets out of the soil. You are—you are a——."

"Yes? Yes?"

"You are a—a tower of silence that is buried under some sea. I want to write you into great oxen words."

Her splayed lips tried, but were dumb. There was something she so terribly wanted to say to that. A heart hurt. To tell it would be like giving him a jewel.

"Bertha, you are like a tree when you tremble, caught in a windshake. Don't be afraid. Come to me—Bertha—close—."

Something had gone over to him. A wraith out of a door. The jeweled sands were pouring. . . .

"Bertha——"

"No—no—Mrs. Far-r-ley——"

She came down into his arms that had the sudden strength to hold her. His lips were on her throat, listening.

The days were as days always had been. Entrails of fowls to be torn out. Mud carried in on grocery boys' heels. "Lawk, spinach boiled down so!" Pots. Pans. The grease clogging the drain and sucking the hands. To be ordered:

> Bay leaves.
> Prepared flour.
> Dry mustard.
> Kitchen Bouquet.
> Silver polish.
> Pickled walnuts.
> Caraway seeds.
> Bottled capers.
> Powdered sugar.
> Tarragon vinegar.

Just time, fluted into days and nights.

Rollo had not come again. That was part of the precious-
ness. The once. The beauty of that hurt more than the
pain. Her yearning was proud of his not coming.

Trust Rollo to pause a little this side of satiety, teased, but
with the flavor high on his palate. Asceticism of keeping a
little lean with self-inflicted hungers.

She had dusted the terra cotta Chloe three of Helga's Thursdays out and he had not glanced up. He could pass her on
the stairs without seeing, and did. One night, at dinner to
ten, wine had warmed him again, and he came out into the
kitchen.

Bertha was tilting an enormous copper pot to drain it of
grease, two fowl shining in it on a device that resembled a spit.

He regarded her through the slippery vapors, her pallor
not unlike the nakedness of the fowl.

*The Cathedral Under the Sea.* He had written it—weeks
ago—that dawn! Hours and hours that he could scarcely
account for. The shaggy manuscript of it in a red portfolio
up in the third left drawer of his desk. A secret palpitating
saga that stalked through forests of iambic and hexameter
with the sullen tonnage of a boar. Jove—up in the third left
drawer—must re-write and show it to Beebe.

He went out into the yard for a magnolia. They were
asleep on the tree like birds with tucked heads. Her heart
waited. Disks of poured-off grease riding on the sink water.
Her fork stabbing the softening haunches that were already
running juices. The big silence standing stock still. Hope.

He came in with a bud in his hand that was like a live star.
It gave a little movement forward of a sleepy petal, opening.
She wanted that star for her darkness. Rollo! Like a hoop.

the silent calling of his name rolling through the lanes his fingers made in her heart and yet, when he passed on through the swinging door, there was that yearning of hers, glad to be again denied.

Baste! Baste! Feeding back into the fowls their own drippings. Celery to be sharpened at the roots like pencils. A fleck of baking soda in the peas to bring out the green. Finger rolls warming their toes at the edge of the oven and Mr. Farley's slice of gluten toast. Fancy! To be full of the invisible tears of the hurt of beauty all the while she was toasting old Mr. Farley's slice of diabetic bread. Hurting gladness.

It was not easy to be glad. Yet Helga was full of gladnesses that you could almost touch. Dimension and bulge to them, like the calf of the leg. The easy gladness of Thursday out. "He says to me and I says to him." Coney Island. "That night watchman's a helluva fresh guy, but I like him." Swedish Barbecues at Concordia Hall.

Gladnesses that were as easy as spinach. How to capture them the way Helga did? They ran away from Bertha like little mercury balls.

Once on a Sunday she had gone to a clambake at Knuts Grove, with the plumber's assistant who came to mend a water pipe. He had pressed her hips like the ice man, and made her run panting among the trees and beer kegs. Great big girls with Hogarth expanses of bosom had sat in rope swings and propelled with their legs until the flounces flew back and shouts went up to the accompaniment of forefingers scraping forefingers. "Shame—Oh Shame!" The plumber's assistant pushed Bertha. High. Higher. Balbriggan legs above laughter. "Let 'er go, Gallagher. Whoops—see! Oh—

Oh—that gal's all there!" Stabs at the pit of her. Helga's gladnesses these. "High! Higher! It's raining in London! Yah—oh Baby!" Eyes and wet grins all blurry with beer fumes.

Let the old cat die! The wooden seat tilting and her skirts higher and her screams full of panic. "I'll yump—let me out— yah—yah"—slapping right and left and her stocking and shin torn from the jump—"Yah—you—lunks—you got lice. Dirty —dirty—youse—dirty—"

She ran then, climbing over fences to find the street car line.

Gladness in the round. What were they compared to the hurting gladness of Rollo, passing through the kitchen with a breathing star in his hand? Baste! Baste! Celery to be sharpened. Baste! Then came the dishing up and the riding of the platters through the swinging doors on Helga's palm.

Later, much later, with her dish pan turned and the ice card out, she could see through the crack in the door, the two tables of euchre, and Rollo and the girl with the dark portières of low hair, left out.

An omission as graceful as the rest between the chords of a prelude. They were by a fire on a couch that fattened up around them. The star of a magnolia in her hair, as if it had simply whitened there. Rollo, nearing her, as he would do it, without seeming to stir. Fine fettled, both of them, his ears laid back as if to the wind; her nostrils, little pinks.

Puffs of talk. Silences made loud by heart beats. Her neck back from the imperceptible nearness of his breathing. Withholding her young body like an arched bow; his, trembling for the arrow.

They were so young. Crocus tips.

And Bertha, from behind the swinging doors, pinioned to

their moment, her heart trying to pull away from the spike through it.

She in there, who had so little to give and gave that little cannily. The lovely frugality of thin lips. Bertha back there with her riches, would have been willing to transfer them from her splayed lips to the thin ones that he in turn might kiss those riches off——

"Oh, Rollo—Rollo——"

He was feeling for the hair with the magnolia out in it like a star, but she would tauten back, and finally, on the flip of a despair, he went out and she remained thrust forward a little to the firelight, her smile flickering.

In the room beyond the portièred arch, the euchre tables were shifting. Middle-aged laughter. Silk *froufrous*. The firelight waiting for Rollo.

After a while he came back. There was a red portfolio under his arm. She reached out, but he withheld it and opening the shaggy pages began to read.

Slow oxen words plowing up secrets of the soil. Gleaming submarine words. Words out of jeweled sands. Heavy words that thundered into wisdom. The strange wisdom of the silence that stood stock still. The hexameter of the wide, white feet that the earth sucked unto herself in fond little marshes, as they ran through the forests surrounding the Cathedral Under the Sea. The song that was locked in a heart and hurt there. Rhythm. The fandango of sound. The saga of the silence of Bertha—there behind the swinging doors, hearing herself bleed into words. The brook of the frozen tears thawing upon Rollo's lips. The flamingoes flying——

The oval face was full of tears and so close to Rollo's **that** suddenly, over the red portfolio, he had it dry with his kisses, her body curving back and his curving over it. The flame of winding arms——

It was late when Bertha went upstairs.

She had polished and twisted twenty-four crystal wine goblets into nothingness. It was so with her pain. She wanted sullenly to twist it for twisting her. But it curved away. Nothingness.

It was good to set out the milk bottles. Six in a row. They were so there. Quarts. Bulge. Dimension.

The magnolia was quite naked. All autumn a circuit of excitement had been running through the house, ever since a Mr. Beebe, with a portfolio had interrupted the family at dinner and the mould of pistachio ice cream had come out uncut and steeped in its own melt. Day by day the plates coming out from the dining room were more and more nibbled and nervous-looking. The electric door bell with its batteries in the kitchen kept tittering. In the front hall the silver plate for visiting cards was high with them.

There were oatmeal cookies to be baked in daily batches now because Mrs. Farley, in the gray and jet gown designed for the Daughters of Confederacy annual luncheon, poured tea every afternoon out of a gold service that her grandmother had tilted in the same solemn drawing-room.

Half a dozen of Helga's Thursdays out had been commandeered.

"Fortheluvvaga, you'd think he was making his debutte. Little Lord Fauntlerollo has written something and it's a helluva sensation. One of those fresh newspapers guys slipped me something just now for slipping him up to the study. Fortheluvvaga, I could have tipped them off to that long ago. I've been emptying that trash basket of his writings for three years now."

"To write, Helga, is to make words into pack mules to carry fine thoughts on to paper—if I had the pack mules——"

"Pack mules! Ain't you enough of a pack mule yourself without wishing for some? Fortheluvvaga, a pack mule wishing for pack mules."

"Pack mules—that wouldn't fall down on their knees——"

"I knew a guy from Missouri once, sold mules. Spondoolaks! That baby carried four collars in his pocket to a dance and won his lady a manicure set every time he took 'er to a contest. Little Lord Fauntlerollo! Say, gimme a baby with liver and lights to him."

Rollo had written something. The white hands at Bertha's heart set up a fluttering. To write something was not to sprawl prepared flour and bay leaves on the order list. It was to paint into words and on to paper the submerged forests of the heart. Like transfer pictures that you wetted and rubbed.

More pleasant irregularities. Carriages at the curb and the family barouche at the most untoward of hours. Mr. and Mrs. Farley still rode out, with a conservatism that even then was beginning to be conspicuous, in an ink pot of a coupé drawn by two fat bays. Floundering, gasoline-gagged traffic banes.

Rollo, upstairs, smoking too many cigarettes and flinging out oaths to the visitors' cards that were slid under his locked study door. Old Mr. Farley, who came home to luncheon, cutting out newspaper clippings with his fork and reddening under what seemed more than his daily allotment of old port. The telephone a screaming cockatoo that had to be throttled a score of times a day.

*"No, Mr. Rollo Farley cannot be disturbed to come to the telephone. No, it appeared in four editions of New Poetry. Impossible to get a copy off the stands any more. Date of book publication December tenth."*

December tenth. A little knob of a day to stick out of the flatnesses. Bertha's hopelessness wound around it like a baby's finger. December tenth. She scoured a whole morningful of pots that day. Harsh bristles against stove black. Scoured because she was happy and was happy because she scoured. She was put away, one might say, like a Christmas-tree-ball. Wadded. Waiting.

It came. A black gusty December tenth of soot on the window sills, cold door knobs, and when she dumped her scrub water out over the porch rail, her bare forearms reddened and steamed. Winter. The magnolia as if a trumped-up bride made out of a poker had been stripped again down to the poker. She thought of it in bud, constantly.

The scrub water blew inward as she threw it, lashing her skirts to her legs. Time for flannels. She must shop new ones for herself at the Sailors' Supply Store down in Front Street, her first Thursday out. She liked them man-size with great ribbings at the wrists and ankles. They kept out soppy water.

She chose of their grossness as naturally as she spat.

December tenth was on a Thursday and Helga as usual was after her. "Fortheluvvaga, Bertha, have a heart. Gimme your Thursday and I'll do as much for you. I need stockings. Look at my heel hanging out. There's a fella down on Fourteenth Street selling them at the curb for twenty-nine cents. Gimme your Thursday, Bertha, you don't do nothing with yours nohow but sit and look at it. Aw Berth. I gotta cold on my chest. How is it they never seem to think the help's rooms needs heat same as the rest? I need a woolen shirt."

"Yah—Yah—you don't buy warm shirts, you buy thin stockings—all of you—nothing on the inside of you, so you hang yourselves with things on the outside.

"Inside! I got a floatin' kidney that's killin' me. I wish you had my backache for a day."

"That's an ache a plaster can reach."

"Yah, try to lay in bed one morning huggin' a plaster in this house and see where it gets you. Bein' sick by the clock. Hospital or get up. My idea of heaven is being sick and taking my time about it. Aw, Bertha, if you knew how my kidney's hurtin' and I need that shirt, gimme your Thursday——"

"Yah—yah—always the same. Graft. You got a nerve."

"Aw Berth . . . !"

"Yah."

So Bertha's Thursday out bequeathed to Helga and Bertha at dusting the study. Rollo's. She could stir the down on the back of his neck with her breathing as she rubbed at a chair. Shining ridges of book backs to be dusted. In waves. Thoughts that had found their way out and into the fragrant

prison of morocco. Jeweled sands poured on to paper. Fleck.
Fleck. Mahogany full of pools and one edge of a table into
which Rollo's profile sank—the nostrils, with a little rabbit-like
quiver to them, perpetually upside down. Slow-fingered firelight, like a neat little girl on a stool, tatting. The rug was full
of colors that were faint as her wisps of old sound. The
dust cloth, an old silk waist of Mrs. Farley's, clung to the
rough nap of her fingers and it hurt her like noise. A room
to be quiet in. A warm kind of a quiet, like a wool shawl over
the shoulders. The pencil whispering and Rollo's hand across
his brow like an eye shade.

"Ah me———."

Now, so! To lift that little pad under Rollo's elbow without an oath from him. There! Lawky, lawk. The rocking
horse blotter had a crystal knob. To reach that now, and to
polish it. Done! The stack of books at his right, half un-
wrapped. The flare of brown paper to be removed without a
creak. So! Two little stacks of slender books, rough-leaved
and in tawny jackets.

## THE CATHEDRAL UNDER THE SEA

BY

ROLLO FARLEY

The Cathedral - Under - the-Sea-by-Rollo-Farley-the-Cathedral-
Under-the-Sea.

Why, to fleck at them with her dust cloth was like touching a
bit of tremor. Her tremor. That figure of a woman on the
tawny jacket. Sullen and at a sea-edge, with the sand sucking
tight and eager about her ankles and the sky like a silence.
Jagged leaves which she opened shyly and with a stealth that
trembled.

Wide margins and little islands of printed words. Slow, pulling words. Arches of rhythm. The naves of her silences. The submerged grandeurs she had laid to his ear with the roaring shell of her heart. She had led him down the shelves of these pages, one night, her friends the soil and the sea-bottoms giving under their feet and sucking up softly about their ankles.

*The Cathedral Under the Sea!*

Lawk, she had dropped the book, face downward, so that the leaves doubled up and the ink pot tottered and she barely had time to save the spill and Rollo was savage.

"Damnation, Helga, leave off your puttering and clear out."

She had risen with the crumpled book to her like a hurt bird and the blood so furious in her face that it stung his eyes to hers.

"Oh, it's you. Of course. Thursday. Run along, there's a girl."

There were a few bank notes on the table, weighted down with loose change. His hand traveled toward them and then jerked back again, his attitude listening; his eyes toward their left corners listening; his dry pen quivering slightly as it, too, hung listening.

Those little book stacks on his desk that her eyes could not veer off from. Something of him—and of her—there. Herself on the outside of herself. The broken wing of a book in her arms. Their book. And yet he sat with his eyes in their corners, waiting for her to go.

"Rollo," cried out her silence, "I am the Cathedral Under the Sea. Don't you know me?" But all she said was:

"It bane all pencil shavings under your feet. If I could sweep them . . ."

At that his fingers where they propped up the pen relaxed to the page, his eyes sliding from their corners of unease.

"Not now, there's a girl." This time he reached for one of the bills under the loose change, handing it back to her over one shoulder.

Poor Bertha. An insistent sense of sickness that had been rising in her of late when she bent over to baste a fowl or scour a floor, came over her now, almost languidly. A dizzying kind of clutch, as if a pair of tiny hands were swinging on her heart beat.

"No," she said, standing back from the flutter of the bill. His eyes flew to their corners again.

"Leave me then. I am busy."

Standing there directly behind him, she forced him to look and her eyes were crucified.

"I want this."

The crumbled bird of a book. The bent page. The little islands of jeweled words margined in silence. The beauty of the silence of the Cathedral Under the Sea. Her silence.

"I want this."

And then when he did not answer and with his look impaled upon hers, she went out, dizzily, carrying the book, her broom, a floor brush, and a bottle of furniture oil.

Guests would be in to tea and there were oatmeal cookies to be made, but she dragged herself up to her room that was trapped under the two slants of roof. It was good to be up there on her bed. Suddenly and again that new and fantastic

craving irrelevantly had hold of her. That sense of bud; that
desire to behold the leisurely beauty of a bud opening. The
backyard magnolia was stark now. But to see it bloom!
Petals to bow back ceremoniously from calyx. A gesture so
fine that it took place between the battings of an eye. Often
and more often now, that sense of bud opening. Once in her
sleep the soft movement of a petal against the very walls
of herself.

A tulip twirling. That was her dizziness. She sat up to
shake it off. Oatmeal cookies to be made. . . .

And then in a flash, seated there on the bed edge, in her
silence, she knew! Knew it dumbly. That tulip twirling had
a heart and in that heart a child. Not his alone, like the book.
Theirs!

And her veins were torrents washing and carrying to the
bud the wisps of old sound and the whisperings of her friends,
the soils, and the messages of the chimes, goldily, and the kiss
of a poet. . . .

After a while she dragged herself downstairs. Mrs. Farley
was ringing. There were those oatmeal cookies to be made.

Marching days of rising in the iced dawn, when the air that
came up from the lower halls was frozen from open windows,
while the family lay deep under fluffy blankets.

Bertha slept with her windows closed, so that her room
embalmed the cold. It ran up her body in great flashes of
gooseflesh as she dressed. Once a week she bathed in a tin
tub the shape of a kidney. She carried the water in eight
pitcherfuls from a bathroom two floors below. The tin tub

wobbled as she stood shivering in it, the bottom denting in and out noisily.

Helga in the adjoining cubicle did not bother. She was a frail girl with cheek spots of red and at night she fell into bed, often in her underclothing and stockings, for the additional warmth and for the additional five minutes of sleep it gave her in the morning, because then she had only to slip into her black sateen and white organdie bows.

And for days at a time her bed went unmade. Once, on exploration bent, Mrs. Farley found it so, plucking very gingerly at the unaired cotton coverlet. Helga was summoned, and the house-man with a squirt-can of disinfectant, and scavengers were found nesting in the slats and Helga, with her nose very red from pinching it to keep back tears, standing furiously sullen.

"Disgusting. Filthy. Shame, Helga, upon any self-respecting girl. Dear, oh dear, not fit for a pig. What's that little greasy rag on the bed? 'Sore toe.' Ugh, what horrid things can happen to the servant class! Sore toes somehow don't happen to one's friends—ugh——"

And Bertha, standing at the foot of the stairs listening with one hand to her cheek, ached in her throat for Helga. She was so young and there was something so old about the days of dirty chores. They were like old witches and presently Helga would turn into one of them.

"I wish to God, Mrs. Farley, you knew how it feels to limp around picking up after you on one of them sore toes!"

Bertha knew, but meekly. Foot torture. The body tiredness at the end of a seventeen-hour day from stoking the coal range at six A. M. to placing the two shining apples and a silver pitcher of water beside the Farley black walnut bedstead at eleven P. M.

And Helga, who waited on table and answered door bells and washed up bathroom floors and emptied trash baskets and helped the laundress with the fluted pieces and sat up in the blue bedroom with the women's wraps during dinners and evening receptions and loved so to dance with the edge of her strength, knew too, but defiantly.

And that defiance created a servant problem.

Helga, who was shuddering now with tears, could not keep down her voice.

"You give us dirty holes to live in and expect us to keep 'em pink and perfumed like your boudoir. Some of the fine folks that come here to dinner oughtta get a look up here . . . they wouldn't have such a good appetite."

"Helga, you vulgar, horrid girl. I won't be talked to so!"

"Yes, you will. I'm a working girl, but I got my spirit. There's nothing right about the way the world's run nohow. Those that got the drudgery to do get the hard beds to sleep on. Those whose bones are rested from easy living get the soft beds —where's the right of it, I ask you?"

"Helga, you rude girl, if you don't hush, I'll call my husband."

"Call him. If the men knew the way women treat women in this servant game, maybe it would help us to get decent living conditions."

"Why, I never had a girl speak to me like this in my life. Every waitress I ever had in my employ left me only to marry."

"Yah, what's the use changing? Doing one's dirty work is about the same as doing the next one's."

"Helga!"

"You want us to keep clean, don't you? Like you. Well then, give us decent rooms and enough time to keep ourselves clean in. Take some of the show away from the front of the house and give your servants rooms that are fit to live in."

"My servants' quarters are as good as any."

"Yes, and that's no good. I got a floatin' kidney I have, and I won't lug bathin' water up two flights of stairs in six pitchers full for nobody, not even myself. Yes, a floatin' kidney, in case it ain't polite to have it in your society. Floatin' kidneys don't happen to your friends. Well, let 'em lug heavy platters like I do with their right side. Let 'em lug six pitchers of water—No siree, I won't take cold for nobody, bathing myself in a cast-off old foot tub that ain't as good as your poodle dog's, and the furnace heat not even piped up to the fourth story."

"That's no excuse, we take cold showers."

"Yah, because your blood's so sluggish from doin' nothin' that you got to do somethin' to get it goin'. We don't need to get our blood to circulating. The rich folks like you keep it circulating for us."

"No self-respecting girl would sleep on——."

"You want me to keep a pretty bed, don't you? Well then, gimme a decent one to lay on. You drag up here after all day and half the night on your feet and see if it matters to you if you get into a bed that's made or unmade. Nobody's got any pink satin covers turned back for me. We're in luck up here if there's enough servants' linen to give us a change once a month. When do you expect me to have time to keep my room like a sachet bag, Mrs. Farley? The eighth day in the week?"

"Look at Bertha, you rude girl. Immaculate. That proves how slovenly and ungrateful——."

"Bertha! Aw, she ain't human. She's a dray horse that's so used to pullin' she can't feel the harness. Bertha! The more

work you pile on her the less time it gives her to sit waiting for
time to pass. She's like a tomb, sitting hard on somethin' to
hold it down. Hit her on the bean and she'll sit there gazing
at the stars and not feel the hurt. I'm human. Bertha's a—
hunk."

And Bertha standing at the foot of the back stairs holding
her cheek in a gesture of compassion, heard.

Helga did not leave. Later, Mrs. Farley, who dreaded the
employment agencies, was willing to be placated and Helga,
shivering before the prospect of a luggage laden pilgrimage
through the icy streets, shoved her hand trunk which she had
started to pack, back under the bed, her sobs still jerking in
her throat.

A hunk. To be a hunk was to live deeply put away from
the sadnesses and the gladnesses in the round. To be a hunk
was to carry a heart the wonder of whose secret passageways
made everything on the outside, like Coney Island or quinsy
sore throat, or Mrs. Farley or twenty-nine-cent silk stockings,
seem not to matter much.

Not to be a hunk was also to crave a great deal for the things
on the outside to matter much. To want so terribly, as Helga
could, that extra Thursday out or dancing slippers with red
heels. To be able to want dancing slippers with red heels, that
was not to be a hunk!

All that day of the quarrel, while she washed down the
kitchen woodwork, prepared a clear broth and aspic for Rollo's
luncheon, and cleaned Helga's silver for her while she unpacked
her things, she rolled the word slowly over in her mind. A
hunk.

To be a hunk was to carry the secret of the life fluttering at her walls, without much discomfort. Somewhere, way back in the waste lands of her consciousness, women had borne child by scarcely more than pausing beside the plow. Bertha would bear that way, too. Peasantly.

And so the marching days and the marching weeks and presently the marching months and Bertha at lugging her bath water the two flights up, eight times. Heaving coal buckets from the cellar to the kitchen range. Four turkeys to be prepared for family dinner at Christmas, her clutch fiery from tearing entrails. At New Year's a baby lamb was sent from a Vermont Farley, and she drew it and quartered it and hid a bit of its wool away up in the drawer with the chiffon opera coat.

She made baby moccasins out of it without any great tenderness. The pattern troubled her and her underlip hung down with the effort of turning the tiny corners. But when they were finished one midnight, and patted out on her knee, a decision, began slowly to harden.

Rollo must know.

Winter was on its last lap. April soon and Rollo must know of the gift she was bearing. A fluttering of heart-beat at that. Irrevocably her time was nearing. April soon.

For two months he had been away. Winter flew at his chest and the first fury of a sleet storm had driven him to Florida. He was home again now and the city snow packed into corners was getting porous, and the family at a very private home dinner had enjoyed its first mess of spring onions daubed in salt and Mrs. Farley, a bantam with delight at Rollo's return, was constantly now, and unnecessarily, in and out of the kitchen to sip of his soups, and upon one occasion tiptoed out in black lace and aigrettes in her hair, to assure herself that the tenderest portion of mushroom-under-glass was for him.

Something slow and something vague was trembling in Bertha at each sight of Mrs. Farley these days. She dropped pans at the mere passing of her across the floor of the room above the kitchen, and on the night that she swept in from her guests in the black lace and aigrettes, startled, Bertha scalded her forearm in boiling duck grease.

"Bertha, you clumsy girl! See that Mr. Rollo has this large portion of the mushrooms. Dip your arm in flour and send the sauterne in with the fish course."

A secret and booming multiplicity of fears. That tight circle of faces in there around the dinner table. A closed circle through which Helga and a hired butler slid in the alien hands of service. Mr. Farley's face, as out of a Fifth Avenue club window, smugly. Dowagers sitting broadly and fat with security. The polite face of an explorer who had once killed his desert comrade for a water flagon. A lean face impaled on two collar points and engraved in the steel of the stock exchange. Another face soldered tightly into that circle of the icy beauty of frugal lips, skin too white for the blood to shadow, and hair drawn down like portières. Rollo's face with the singing look of choir boy in it; poignancy of young down on his long cheeks, lightening of his nervous nostrils.

Fear in Bertha as if the circle could somehow close in and throttle her. It could make her tremble now, the solidarity of those alternating black backs and white shoulders.

And then, with spring so perilously near, fear became puny in the face of imminence.

One evening, long after the family was quiet and the kitchen range cold, she sat and began to wait. There could be no more putting off. Rollo must know.

A rare evening of the family early to bed, Helga at the Second Avenue Dance, Hippodrome—Ladies Free, Rollo dining out. Bertha in the cold and tidy kitchen, waiting. The octagon-faced wall clock with the great separate ticks. The first generation of motor cars bleating their way dimly through the jam of city traffic, out into which she so seldom ventured. Tick. Tock.

About midnight she began to listen for the creak of wheels against the curb. Rollo would come home in a hansom.

At one o'clock he arrived and she was already in the front hall when his key began to twist in the lock.

Rollo must know, but it was as if she were bound and gagged to the mast of a fast moving craft and could not find the power to cry out to him when he passed—

"I bane waiting," she said on the top of the little noises he made entering.

He could take on the blue white of china under fatigue, and his lips were mauve.

"What the hell——"

She thought at first he was fuddled with wine, and then that it was the start of seeing her there under the dim hall light. It was a little of both. Wine went at Rollo with a rush. It befogged him, but politely. It gave him a caution of movement and a manner. He felt for the hatrack first, to be sure it was going to be where he intended hanging his overcoat. He was grandiose, and his evening shirt full of soft pools from the hall light. Very like a choir boy with tears in his eyes and very, very careful. He hung up his high hat so carefully that he caressed it. Not even the hansom driver had glanced at him twice.

He looked at Bertha as he had always done—since, through a haze of amazement and a little of the wryness of self-disgust.

He was conscious of a thickened-up fatty look to the center of her face. He has seen it in moon-hoar and in the plushy darkness of under an eave. A piggy little swollenness came out in this light, and her hips curved out with a flatulence that berated him for having been unfastidious. A great white cow. Uddery. Incredible. He must have been drunk. Damnably.

Gad, what a mouth, like a catfish gagging on the hook. And yet there had been a phosphorescence to her body whiteness up there under the slanting roof. That moment of her in his arms, when suddenly they were strong enough to hold her. The sullen booming of her heartbeats, like some faint ocean rolling and tossing over its treasures. Majestic dissonances. Aspidal choir of voices too remote to be heard, except with the touch of her flesh singing against his.

*The Cathedral Under the Sea?* To be sure, he had written it in the frenzy of that dawn with the lay of that great latent body of hers still along his. . . . That crouch of strength behind her silence. . . . But, ugh, great husky Swede! He *must* have been drunk—damnably.

"Bertha," he said, on the unwinding of his muffler and so casually that his words were like so many careful little tin coins dropping, "isn't it rather late for you to be about?"

The plating on his voice was something against which she suddenly wanted to hurl herself, smashing through it to those depths of his being to which she had the right now.

"I bane waiting—for you," she cried, and ran toward the

stairs at him as he placed his foot on the first step. "If you will please come up—to me, I will tell you something only for you. Please——"

He stood caught, as it were, in the motion of mounting the stairs, his hand softly white on the curve of banister between them. She could have crushed her lips to it and kissed her secret down against it, but she held herself trembling.

"If you will please, Mr. Farley—Rollo—come up to me—please——"

The lymphatic look of cow in her face. The string of gray wool scarf harsh against her neck. He hated the thought of her chapped hands unwinding it and catching on the wool with their briary surfaces. Her buttoned-up waist, concealing her whiteness where he had seen it one grape-colored night flow down into creamy hillocks of bosom, spanning her now, too tightly across the bust. How idiotically, nastily drunk he must have been.

"Mr. Rollo—come——"

"Shame," he said. "A great girl like you. You must be mad. Go to bed."

She was choking and nailed to the mast of her inarticulateness, he passed, and as he passed her, with his white hand riding up the balustrade, she came down on it with her lips, arresting him so that he jerked it back and shook it from him furiously as if a caterpillar had crawled there.

"Mr. Rollo—you should know it. I am carrying . . . your . . ."

"For God's sake," he cried, as if he could never have done shaking his hand of her lip prints, "don't you ever do that again or you'll have to go. Don't ever come near me. Bah. Here"—and from his pocket tossed her down a bill and while she stood watching it flutter he ran upstairs lightly. Then the sound of the key turning in his door. Lightly.

And suddenly it seemed to her that the silence within her was red banners and that she must scream them and tear them to shreds and she ran up the stairs after him, a flight of heavy thumps that ended in a stumble and, with her fists raised for a frenzied battering against his closed door, she crumbled up suddenly of black vertigo, into a heap there on the hall floor.

There was the bill he had fluttered at her, screwed somehow into her palm and with the remnant of her rage and her strength she began to tear at it with her teeth, worrying it like a terrier and spitting it out in shreds.

Dawn found her waiting for it, crouched on her bed edge, where she had sat five hours with her backache the shape of the stoop of her spine. The dawns were still very cold. They could come creeping across the house tops and lie wanly against her eyelids long before Helga's alarm clock ripped open another day.

There were some shreds of bank note on the floor. She picked them up and crammed them through the little hole in the pasteboard box that served her as hair receiver. Her light yellow hair was falling out in strands now, which she twined around her finger and poked away.

A flower stripping itself to divert the sap to the bud.

Three million dawns creeping over the sills of the vertical city. Bertha's a lonely iced one that she watched come up like an enemy. A thin dawn that magnified sound. The milkman crashing down four white quarts in exchange for the four empty ones. Her heartbeats galloping against her eardrums. Rollo must know. Rollo must know.

It was hard to move, because she was stiff from the hours of sitting in a curve away from the slant of ceiling, but at six o'clock she must be downstairs to start the range and the servants' breakfast. At seven, the three morning papers to be taken from the stoop. One for Mr. Farley beside his breakfast plate in the morning room. One on Mrs. Farley's breakfast tray beside her hothouse rose. One for Rollo who did not breakfast at all, softly, outside his room door. But this morning, his not to be delivered tiptoe as usual. To-day he must know. A whole string of quick rappings, too low to be heard by Mrs. Farley across the hall, but if need be, a rattling of the door knob, and then through the first slit of the door opening, her toe for a wedge, and in.

Oh, God, Rollo must know. Rollo must know.

What if Helga should notice? When Helga tittered it was like a mouse running up your leg. And Mrs. Farley. She began to cry with the sense of her growing hulk and fear. Cymbals of it crashing through her! Fear of Mrs. Farley and yet she came bearing gifts in the flesh of her flesh.

The tears lay to her cheeks and chapped there. She poured water into her bowl, plunging handfuls against her face and drying on her gray flannel petticoat. There were not always towels. After a while it was half after five and she could venture down, softly to save the creaks.

It was easier, somehow, waiting in the kitchen. Kindlier. But a chill smote her when she took in the milk bottles so that she sat down suddenly. The horridness of these mornings. The full-throated kind of sickness that could turn her whiteness sea-green.

But only for an instant. There were the coals to be hauled up from the cellar and the fire to be laid. The coffee mill locked in the vise of her knees and set whirring at top speed. Bacon to be parboiled and the servants' mess of warmed-over oatmeal softening its crust in the double boiler. The ice pan to be heaved sink high and emptied. Slops. Nibbled down asparagus ends smelling sourly down into last night's casaba melon rinds.

At half past six Helga came down adjusting the criss-crosses of organdie apron strips and tasting her lips as if they were bitter. She was swollen and her lids granulated with sleep, and she coughed with a certain pride in the depths of its croupiness.

She started her day tired. Bone tired. She could almost have gone to sleep standing there, croupily coughing.

"You've got a cold, Helga. Shame. Running to the dance halls and the gin parlors all night."

"What'll I do? Entertain the fellas in the drawing-room? She won't even give 'em kitchen room. Helluva chance for a fella with insides to him to want to cuddle a girl in the wintry breezes of Gramercy Park. The gate to that's even locked against us. Where does a girl get off, I'd like to know. It's either the gin parlors with them or sneaking them up to bed with her."

"Here's your breakfast. It'll warm you."

"Fortheluvvaga, warmed-over oatmeal again. I can't swallow the stuff. I wishtaga I could poke it down her throat, lumps and all, and learn her that the Lord didn't line her stomach no different than mine."

He lined stomachs and made the magnolia to bloom and He

sat on a throne drenched with Light.  Sometimes it seemed to Bertha that a little drench of the Light was on her.

Oh Lord.  Lord.  Rollo.  Help me.  Rollo must know.  Help me to make Rollo know.

"Fortheluvva.  This oleo is strong enough to walk.  Gimme a snack of little Lord Fauntrollo's sweet butter, Bertha.  This stuff don't slide down me no easier than it would down him.  Here Berth—where you goin'?"

But it was striking seven and down the length of hallway Bertha was already opening the front door.  Grayness of Gramercy Park.  Trees in bare black and rheumatic twists.  Fourth Avenue's lean, tall office buildings already breathing down in packs upon the little square of Park, wolfish to invade.

The morning papers in little huddle against the storm door.  Three.

She carried Rollo's upstairs.  It was very still outside his door.  It was as if, almost, the very door were saturated with a night of his breathings.  She could hurt it by twisting the knob.  If she rapped the panels might give a little under her knuckles, like flesh.

It was hard bracing herself for the string of quick low rappings, her toe set for the wedge in the opening. . . .

Imperative raps.  Rollo must know.  But her arm was too limp and the tears kept running down into her mouth and splotched right down on to his morning paper.

Rollo's paper.  She wiped them off with her elbow.  They had spattered a picture.  A woman's photograph looking up at her from the first page of the morning paper.  Long low portières of hair and a head shaped as an egg would feel if it came whole out of your mouth.

*"Miss Veronica Stedman Neidringhouse, one of the past sea-son's most popular debutantes, whose engagement to H. Rollo Farley, the poet, and only son of Mr. and Mrs. H. Freilinger Farley of Gramercy Park, is announced. The wedding will be one of the events of early summer."*

Suddenly the big silence standing stock still again. It was so hard to feel, except dimly, and all the little tumults and the little hopes and even the fears, were back now in their branches chirruping in a sleepy sort of dusk. A dusk that was stunned. A dusk in which a pain had died. It was good to be without pain and back in the dim quiet.

The newspaper now to be folded squarely over the tear splotches and left leaning so that when Rollo opened his door presently it would fall toward. It was merely a chore again. Part of the day's mute doing of mute things.

The oatmeal was scorching and her nostrils flared. It was instinctive for her to start to rush down, which she did, catching herself back by the balustrade.

Rollo must not know.

The morning was a grave and that moment outside his door a flower upon it. Everything was so simple because it was so quiet. She loved that, because it was the kind through which the chimes, if they would, might come through, goldily again.

Upstairs it was still cold, and when she stooped to drag out her outlandish carpetbag from under the bed, her breath was illuminated. There was not much to pack. A suit of the man-size underwear to be folded over bulkily. A pair of black buttoned shoes with scalloped tops. The green chiffon coat and the oddments of crystal stars. Balbriggan stockings.

Some sheet music that had come down to the kitchen from time to time included with the colored supplement of the Sunday paper. It was pleasant to ride with the eye along the ups and downs of the frozen rhythm. Her piece of Bulgarian embroidery. The concertina. A large greenish glass marble she had found once in a rubbish heap, a beautiful spiral of candy stripe down its center. Quite a wad of saved wages sewed into the pocket of a red flannel petticoat. Her bit of tremor, *The Cathedral Under the Sea.*

Poor Bertha, her face could look out so cleanly and whitely and as uncluttered as a nun's from the little three-cornered shawl she wore sometimes against neuralgia when she sat out on the bit of back porch. But in her slab of hat, with its trumped-up rose on a wire stem, it became broader than long in a comedy squat.

Then her cloak. A discarded black Inverness cape of Mr. Farley's, that she had bought back from the dealer who came semiannually, as he was going out the kitchen way. A black broadcloth that boxed her in squarely, the shoulders horizontal and two inches wider than her own.

There was a look of steerage about Bertha, who had never tasted the sea except from Front Street. A bit of Old World flotsam flung into New World jetsam and drifting along into fantastic amalgam.

On the other hand, Helga, who had actually come over in a ship little larger than a trawl, bareheaded, shawled, and with a bundle of strange foods wrapped in a Swedish newspaper, now wore high heels, half-silk stockings, and a small hat so American that it completely obliterated one eye.

There were no old sounds coming through to trouble Helga

and hurt of their imprisonment. Her heart was not a harp for them. Indeed, it was good not to be a hunk.

Helga had learned to bunny-hug in the Hippodrome Dance Hall down on Second Avenue, Ladies Free. Brilliantly lit egress from the long hours and the bearing down kidney pains. Pomaded men whose hands sweated through her shirtwaist danced there. She had gone to an hotel with one of them, sneaking in and up the Farley back stairs at five one morning with her shoes in her hand. He was a masseur in a Broadway hotel. A Swedish girl she knew had forced one to marry her that way. Frightening him with lies about a baby. Helga would go with her masseur again. Maybe if she were lucky she would "get caught." If not—if not, if one was clever like some, one could frighten a man into marriage. Helga was tired; bone tired and wanted a home. Oh yes, Helga had assimilated.

Her door was open as Bertha went out with her bag. Her bed unmade, the sheets still in the writhe of her tangled sleep. The halls were lighter now, the newspaper still leaning against Rollo's closed door. Mrs. Farley by means of a pink enamel bell that hung over her bed was ringing for her morning cup of hot water. Helga would pour it and carry it up on a silver tray. Now was Bertha's time while Helga was pouring.

It was rather strange going out through the front door and facing the Park from the eminence of the stoop. She was accustomed to emerge from the side entrance on a level with the sod.

It was six years and a half since she had changed places. Old dreads came flowing back. The Hungarian with short thick stumps for fingers who made her sign papers. Questions to be answered. Talk. New ways for old. You sat like a piece of cattle in a little fenced-off pen in the Intelligence Office. Waiting. Sometimes while you were being inspected, very closely, needles came out all over you and stung. Once a man had said laughingly to his wife, "Look at her teeth, too." That same woman had taken her directly from the Intelligence Office to her home. A handsome woman in a Persian lamb coat and lorgnettes, and the apartment on Broadway and Fifty-third Street was fine and new with a drawing-room hung in mulberry and light green. Apple orchards in June. But the servant's room was in the basement and half the floor covered with water that had backed from a drain. A kitten lay drowned in it. At midnight, without having undressed, Bertha took silent departure, traveling by elevated train down to the Front Street rooming house where her foster mother and a Danish sailor sat in a back room stewing in gin.

Old dreads. The lugging of the carpetbag into strange rear entrances. Strange pots and pans and palates. A family of rich Greeks on Madison Avenue had been kind, but the seasoning and the swim of olive oil sickened her. New waitresses to be encountered. They were a sniggering lot, often with filthy habits, such as drying the tumblers on the hand-towel, or sneaking up a bit of French pastry from the pantry to let it mould and draw vermin on a clothes closet shelf. One of them had once stolen Bertha's purse with her month's wages in it.

The thumbed-up old references to be dug up. And again drearily: "Every other Thursday out, you understand? Things fumigated. Grown daughter—no men in kitchen."

It was as if she had stepped out of the house into a swarm of these stinging recollections.

The postman was coming up the stoop as she went down, and she had almost to run and turn quickly to the east against Helga's imminent answering to his ring.

It was dirty with old snow on Third avenue, but there was the smell of melt in the air, and underneath the elevated structure the street ran with mud the color and consistency of a chocolate sauce.

The city, shuddering in its perpetual nervous chill of trucks over cobblestones, and elevated railroads, could always befuddle her. To-day it spun around her like a plate on a juggler's stick. Blurs of it.

Knut's Intelligence Office was on Second Avenue and First Street. She turned toward it. But no—not now—dizzy—where—what now?

It was suddenly easier to walk four blocks and board a bobtailed southbound car. A little sign swung over the motor-man. Front Street.

Annie Wennerberg. For twenty-eight years she had lived near bilge water in a street that wound back from the harbor as crookedly as a sailor's stagger. She neither knew the sea nor loved it, but its stench, with the salt tang strangely out of it, was in the hallways of her lodging house and she tasted it in the beard of stokers who kissed her when they were drunk enough. Drunk enough, because this side of bestiality even stokers were fastidious of her soot-filled pores and furious pockings. Tripe. There was that kind of sponginess to the cheek of Annie Wennerberg.

But to men glutted with sea and half daft with the stare of sky, there was land cheer in Annie's basement dining room, with the red bows wrapped around the throats of the two china vases on a shelf and where one could stew in gin slowly and warmly. Sailors could find letters waiting for them there, too, on the hall rack. Sometimes they were months, even years old, grimy with waiting and fantastic with foreign stamps.

On those brief and intermittent occasions when she was out of work, Bertha slept on a carpet-covered sofa in the basement kitchen. Curious rather sinister nights of great clod-boots walking none too evenly through the black uncarpeted halls. Sailor badinage in the dining room.

One night, a ship's dishwasher off a big twin-screw trans-atlantic, sleeping with five sailors in a second-story room set up such a howling of delirium tremens that an ambulance, clanging into the lane of Front Street, had borne him off finally, biting and wrestling with two internes, a policeman, and Bertha.

Front Street, rancid with sea sculch. Sailors with red threads in their eyeballs two hours after they had come ashore. The women in dreadful finery who preyed upon them. Men of all yellows. Malay. East Indian. Chinese. Javanese. Cooks. Stokers. Mates. Stowaways.

It was fantastic down on Front Street, but not to Bertha who had grown up in it. Annie, who breathed great gin-smelling bubbles when she slept. Public schools where the cross-breeding of white skin and slant eyes was frequent, and little boys and little girls knew horrible lurking things. At eight, Bertha had worn a hat pin under her waist against the bestiality of lodgers.

So when Bertha turned her face once more toward Front Street, she knew why. Annie charged her fifteen cents the night on the carpet-covered sofa. And no talk. Annie never cared enough to ask questions. Besides, year by year now her hearing was failing and she was usually pretty sleepy. Gin-soaked.

When Bertha arrived with her carpetbag, Annie was in the sort of combination kitchen and keg-room, sucking up coffee out of a tin cup, a bottle by.

"I bane outtava yob," said Bertha and showed her carpet-bag under the sofa.

"Fired?" asked Annie, who had not heard her.

"Quit."

"There's coffee," said Annie, who charged her five cents a cup and rose out of the huddle of herself, to remove a lot of dirty-looking rags from the sofa. A small exotic breed of South American monkey leaped out of them and skittered across the floor, making a noise like a boy running a stick along a picket fence.

An old Australian stoker off a fruit steamer who owned Annie, owned him, too. In the act of picking off the rags and cleaning the sofa of some of its debris, Annie suddenly began to limp, her hand back in a plaster over the small of her back.

"There's ten cots to be made up this morning, Berthy. Three freighters came in last night and they're sleeping all over them-selves upstairs. I'm breaking in two of the twinges, Berthy, and ten cots to be made . . . and the hallways, with me crippled up my back, rotting of dirt."

Sly old Annie. There were chores to be had out of Bertha, gratis, and she knew it. The last time between jobs, she had scrubbed three flights of stairs, the roaches scurrying over her hands. Bertha did not mind. It was easier than to sit and look at the furtive silence of Annie's house. She did not drink and the men knew she would jab them with hatpins.

"Hunky Dory," they called her, and "Milksop" and "Wench,"

and occasionally when an uninitiated one sprang out on her from a dark corner and with wet lips, she stabbed in deep and ruthlessly.

So usually in these intervals, she would work for Annie. Dirty chores, with her skirts pinned back, her feet bare, and her great white arms plunged to the elbow in dirty waters.

But not this time. "No, I bane going out," she said, stooping to unclutch the hand of the little monkey from the hem of her skirt and tossing him a small potato from a mound of them in the sink, "I got to go."

Annie began to sop bread in her coffee, chewing it along her empty gums. In her bloaty, befogged way she hated Bertha. Always had. She had cuffed her constantly as a child and the burr of an old couplet still clung:

> Born of a dead mother
> Secrets of the grave you'll utter.

Great silent clod of a Bertha, it was as if she were spreading her skirts not to reveal the bones of eternities of dead men's thoughts—lying bleaching on the fields of her silence.

"Slut," said Annie without glancing up from her cup. Annie's toad-like words, sometimes they jumped out in her sleep.

Strange that they had never more than jounced off Bertha, although all of her formative days had been lived in a hailstorm of them. Her body was like a white fog, surrounding the imperviousness of her. That, too, was why she could scrape drain holes to a sense of goldy rhythm. That was why she could go out now, with a word like "slut" hurled impenetrably at her back.

The sun was shining outside, and the air from the hay and feed store next door, full of warm fertilizing smells.

She stood irresolute at the door watching the little dribbly life of the street. A suit of men's jumpers dangling on a pole before the Sailors' Supply Store flopped like a man on a gibbet. A marine came out of a lean house and turned recklessly left. A few moments later one of the women of dreadful finery came out of the same house and turned cautiously right. A pair of handsome dray horses were led from a stable down a wooden incline to the street and stood there being harnessed. There were hoots from tugs and long-drawn whistles that seemed to leave a trail of smoke across the morning.

After a while Bertha began to walk. Without destination. At Battery Park where the city bows to the sea, she sat down on a bench. How it beat, that ocean, even in the trapped harbor, over its treasures. Bertha beating, too, over hers.

The day wore on. There were children shrilling up and down the curves of granatoid walks and clumps of shawled women and bearded men all very much concerned and fiery with foreign languages. A pier house kept disgorging little emigrant tribes from Ellis Island, their skins sun and wind beaten, and lugging, most of them, carpetbags. Like Bertha's. The tired yield of tired countries.

At five o'clock it grew chilly and because her legs were growing numb Bertha began to walk again, stopping at a caravan on wheels with a short ladder leading up to it, to eat two sausage sandwiches, washing them down with the East Side's favorite soft drink of celery tonic. The streets were lighted by then and she began to walk again, on and on. Poor streets made kindly by the glow from petty shops.

Bertha, who expected nothing, had lost nothing, and yet,

in the impotence of her dumb, hurting misery, she could have battered down closed doors for relief, jabbed at her arms and body with jagged stones, bitten down into her tongue, which she did and it bled.

It helped somehow to hurry along gaunt and boxed into her cape. To hurry and to hurry—alone, in her silence spangled with tears.

It was long past midnight when she finally rounded again into Front Street. There were drunks about, but no one molested her. On the contrary, they reeled rather away. Her face, fatty white, like jade, was so square, so riveted in its pain.

The hall was dead dark, a fitting lurchway for inflamed seamen. There was a seam of light beneath the dining-room door and a silence all corduroyed with snores. Annie and a Lithuanian sailor were asleep in their chairs, two bottles between them, her head and tongue lolling and he sleeping down into his beard. Sots. It was like looking in on a nightmare. Annie with her empty gums and breathing her bubbles.

It was dark in the kitchen, but without even benefit of the gas jet which was hard to reach, or the candle in a bottle on the sink, Bertha dragged the table across the door, barricading it and then piled it with an additional chair. The monkey leaped off the couch chittering, as fully dressed she lay down on it, spreading the Inverness cape for coverlet. He was a nervous little thing and sat huddling in a corner looking through the darkness at her with lit eyes. Amber tunnels.

"Yockie," she whispered, glad for those two phosphorescent disks in her darkness, "Yockie, yump up here." Finally he did, curling up in the crook of her elbow for warmth.

She lay with him that way all night, until her arms went numb and her fingers began to lose their sense of separateness.

But Jocko had ceased trembling and was asleep and to move would have been to awaken him.

Weeks of sitting six hours a day, in the railed pens of this and that employment agency, the wad of savings in her petticoat-pocket flattening. Long hours of women hesitating sometimes very long over her and then passing on.

One rather elderly matron in sealskin could not seem to get by her.

"You appear such a strong, clean European sort of girl. I'm sure you'll do very nicely. No. No. I can't seem to quite decide. I—well I don't know. I'll think it over."

A woman from Lexington Avenue dickered between Bertha and a Lettish girl at great length, finally deciding in favor of the latter.

A housekeeper engaging a new staff of servants for a Fifth Avenue ménage hired her in one breath and changed her mind in the next.

Behind the fatted mask of her imperturbability, a fear smote Bertha. The sisterhood's long nose of intuition was beginning to quiver at the flanges.

Then one night down in Front Street, Annie, brewing herself a stew of lamb neck and regarding Bertha, began to squint up slyly, a word that was horrible hopping off her lips. Then Bertha knew for certain. After all, it was to be expected. March had already turned the corner. The eyes of the apprais-ing women, focusing slightly, were beginning to suspect. And now Annie, soaked old hex, but wise in this from being a woman, dropping that hop-toad word.

"You bane one yourself," said Bertha back at her this time, trembling in her boxed cape, turning and walking out of the house. Walking and wanting again in her unassailed strength the relief of hurling down doors and hacking at herself with stones for the relief of pain. Rollo, help. Lord, drenched in Light, help.

Then again hours and hours of sitting in Battery Park watching the harbor waves, like lips, running out to the horizon to tell sky. Sky. The statue of Liberty pointing to it. Steamers hooting to it. Street cars crawling under it. Grass pointing toward it. A swimming sense of infinitude that drowned her finally into a state of quiet, and her pain went out like a match.

One day in a Delancy Street employment agency she obtained a job. Charwoman. Night work in one of those lower Broadway office buildings that house by day a vertical city of four thousand honeycombed, bumbling souls.

The woman with the drooping busts and machine stitched wig who conducted the intelligence office, had been sly about it.

"Say, for who sees you at night, you don't got to worry. In such a deserted office building like the Equitable, such a strong, healthy-looking girl like you should keep such a job until the last day."

Silent, tiled corridors, lavatories, elevators, and fire-proof stairs to be swabbed. Nights fitful with these mopping charwomen weaving their long strokes through the long, long corridors. A battalion of witches of Endor. Women with old pools of eyes that were gathering scum. Crooked backs. Empty gums.

At nine o'clock they met with pails and mops, an army

of the silent dead flitting through corridors and gathering up the footsteps that men leave after them. Ghouls preying upon the death of a day. At dawn they faded out again. Grayly. Gray into gray.

To Bertha, mopping, mopping through these corridors of the night, it was as if her scrub water, as it blackened, became alive with vibrations. Nervous floors still beating with men's anxious hastenings hither and thither. Whither? Squnching her mop in the bucket, the water crowded up thirstily around her wrists, like a mouth.

And then it was pleasant walking home before the city got its stranglehold on the day. There was a graveyard in lovely and impregnable tranquillity around Trinity Church, its silence louder than the typhoon of men that raged about it all day. Sometimes Bertha sat down against a headstone. Between two deaths. The little death before life that she was carrying. The tired death after life beneath the slabs.

Presently the death that Bertha had under her heart would be born into life. The little life of a little death. And under the slabs the death of a life. Life of death. Death of life. A cycle of perceptions twirling slowly in her consciousness. Not thoughts, just a slow kind of dizziness.

She dozed a great deal. Against the headstones. In parks. On the carpet-sofa in Annie's kitchen. Waiting. It was good to be working nights and rid of the fear of the sailor-infested darkness of Front Street. Days, with Annie bickering about, no matter how gin-soaked, there was more security to lying stretched out on the carpet sofa under the Inverness cape, Jocko trembling to her for warmth.

One night, swabbing up a tenth floor corridor of the Equitable Building, a pain smote at Bertha that caused her to cry out and clutch at herself, as if someone were trying to shove her off the top of a skyscraper. A leap of forked lightning that went through her like a jagged grin of steel. . . .

Twenty minutes later in the ambulance on her way to city hospital, her baby was born. Painlessly. So without labor that the internes joked and told about it at experience clinics.

A son. The music of the chimes goldily tranced in his eyes. Tranced there, like the candy strip down the glass marble in her carpetbag.

When Bertha's boy was two and one half weeks old she signed him away, sprawlingly, as she would write, "prepared flour" and trying, with her left fingers about right wrist, to keep her hand to the dotted line.

A lawyer with a brief case on the desk beside her sucked up with a blotter the symbol of her deed. Ellen Dike Bixby. John Kendall Bixby, Detroit, Michigan, added their respective signatures. A nurse from Bertha's ward stood by and signed as witness. The champ of a seal. More blotting.

"There," said the lawyer passing around the folded documents and beginning to buckle up his brief case. "That's that."

He was like a clamp on a coffin lid and Bertha wanted to cry out against him, but she only stood very still holding her document.

"Well, my girl, what you have done is very sensible. You are not in a position to provide properly for the boy and you are placing him in the hands of two very splendid and trustworthy people, who by legal adoption have just now become his parents. You are a very fortunate girl. Mr. and Mrs. Bixby can give him the refinements and the opportunities of a beautiful home and the best of educational advantages. So my girl, instead of feeling unhappy, you should regard yourself as the object of congratulations."

Her throat hurt from holding down moans. There were little red glass mulberries on Mrs. Bixby's hat. Such a pretty hat and her face was plumpish and fresh, and her hand constantly in sympathy on Bertha's.

"We will be father and mother to him, dear. He will never know the difference. You see this—to-day is the fifth anniversary of our—of our little one being taken from us. That's why your little one—ours—his beauty is so like—like—our— little boy's—was—"

"Go. Go," cried the moans in Bertha's throat, caught there like a log jam, "Go. Go."

Mr. Bixby had short clipped hair and carried a well-brushed derby hat and wore a tiny Masonic emblem on his lapel.

"Good-by," he said, and "Thank you and God bless you."

"Umph," said the lawyer and followed them out.

Then the moans came. Terribly. Once a dog, run over by a truck in Front Street, had moaned like that. The unwetted sobbings of one who does not know how to cry.

The little nurse who was left alone with her was kind and soothed her with chirruping noises, and poured some spirits of ammonia into a glass of water, which Bertha drank at a gulp and then smarted with tears. But she could not stop moaning and shivering, and kept sitting and clinging to her corner like a dumb animal that had been hurt.

Finally a young interne was sent for and he came in and gave her something brown and bitter, and although she had been discharged from the ward that day, between him and the nurse they led her back, chattering and shivering and shuddering, little streaks of foam out along her lips.

The nurse was very young and the interne, too, and Bertha's kind of story was very old, and so they did the properly sedative things, but their eyes kept curving around the dull reality of their charge for the wonder of one another.

All night in her bed in the ward Bertha lay shivering and huddling like the dumb thing that had been hurt. Then they washed a little spot on her arm with cotton and jabbed a needle in. There was no pain but after a time she lay back. . . .

Wonder of Bertha. The hems of her skirts were sour with bilge water and she had been forced to hold her right wrist with her left fingers in order to sprawl her name half legibly on the dotted line . . . but The Cathedral Under the Sea was of her and yet not hers. And now—her son, choir-faced, with the wisps of old music that were so lovely to her, tranced in his eyes—was of her and yet not hers—of her and yet not hers—.

Days with the old flow to them.

Odds and ends of jobs. For months she resumed the night work in the Equitable Building, but the crones were all sly-eyed when she returned and her finger tips began to split painfully. Besides, the days at Annie's were becoming not only intolerable but impossible for sleep, with Jocko chittering and skithering from keg to chair and Annie in a hunch beside the table and mumbling constantly into her cup.

When she had saved ten dollars she started in at the agencies again. The rows of mornings in the rows of chairs. At Rauss-

man's Intelligence Office on Fourth Avenue, they began to favor
Bertha, handing her out addresses and placing her in a conspicuous chair near the railing. She changed places so frequently and
the more she shifted about, of course, the more she yielded in
commissions. On again. Off again.

At kitchen work in a Broadway lunch room, they put her at
washing dishes, but the first hour she was dismissed by the proprietor who followed her to the door with his toes fairly lapping
her heels.

"Washin' the dishes in two waters. You're a fine square-head,
you are. Who do you think I'm in business for? The public's
health or mine—you get the hell out of here—"

It was all a part of the day. Her broad back without a quiver
to it. Like Annie's words, they jounced off and fell at her feet
like dead leaves, through which she walked, as if in the forests
of her inner tranquillity.

At another of these eating places the kitchens were small and
Bertha's bulk so dominant that she created a sort of pixie psy-
chology. Waitresses, by contrast made gay and delightfully
aware of their slim flanks, slid under her arms, giggling. One
little one stood behind Bertha and called, "Find me." She was
like some huge impervious Golem, all the pixies running
up her knees and arms to play and pinch and poke in her eyeballs.

After a week she left.

Then she began to hold out for domestic service, sitting stiffly
averted against demands for restaurant help or char work.

The elder daughter in a private family of six took her home
one day in an automobile, to a rococo brownstone front in West
Fifty-third Street. There was brook trout *au meunière* for the
family luncheon that noon, but the canned salmon, which she had

been obliged to pinken up with soda for the servants' meal, poisoned the crew of them, and Bertha, wretched from her own illness, was the first to pack up her bag and depart.

In a cream-colored renaissance home of stone lace and gargoyles in East Sixty-first Street the bed she was forced to share with the waitress was a three-quarter one and the waitress herself a large south of Ireland girl, with a scrofula running up her leg that was frightening.

Secret places of the household, these, that were never aired along with servants' bedding or the servant problem.

Two old gentlewomen with frail hands and cameo brooches and a house in Nineteenth Street that breathed dampness like a cave, asked all their questions simultaneously and engaged her in a breathless duet. It had been a large household once and there were rooms with workbaskets left open with the bit of colored embroidery half out of it, just as a beloved daughter had left it when her last illness tapped her on the shoulder; a half-written letter on a desk that a brother's death had interrupted. A home full of the reminders of the casualness of life. It was more like a half-way house. Some one had paused there to do a bit of colored embroidery. A child dancing through the interval between its birth in the south chamber and its death there, had left a muslin doll on the floor with its arm stuck grotesquely up. It was like walking between the slabs of Trinity. Grotesque stick-ups where there had been a life.

One night up in her room next to where the winter potatoes were stored, a thought smote Bertha that sent her bounding up from her cot and barefoot over the splintery floor to the window. Sure enough, there through the leaded pane, the spire to the Farley house in Gramercy Park was plainly visible. Pointing! There was no window shade, so she pinned her

flannel petticoat across the glass. But all night through the
flannel and her closed lids, the spire kept pointing. Pointing.

At dawn she laid the fires for the old ladies and left.

Raussman's again. Two weeks of sitting there through the
sullen mornings of inspection. There were only coins left in
her petticoat pocket, that rattled softly when she moved. Bertha
hated hunger. She could sleep on the carpet sofa at Annie's and
poke through drain pipes without much nausea, but hunger
slashed through her bulk like the blades of a great machine.
Foregoing the morning cup of five-cent coffee at Annie's was
an economy, but it made the day wavy. It rose up on all sides
of her and sometimes towards noon she dozed with its motion
and old man Raussman had to yank at her cape.

"Wake up. We ain't got no calls for sleeping beauties."

But one day he handed out a Riverside Drive address to her
on a dirty slip of paper. "Musliner. Two in family. Cook."

Mr. Musliner, a two-weeks-old bridegroom, interviewed her
in the kitchen and engaged her without parley.

It was pleasant at the Musliners. A bride had furnished it.
Creamy light of new woodwork and pale paneled walls. An
oval drawing-room in the fragile mood of Fragonard. Dining
room in marquetry and the panel above the mantelpiece another
bow to Fragonard. A pair of solid gold Adam urns. Grapes in
December. Crystal chandeliers tittering with light.

An entire corridor of little nonsense bedrooms in a hush of
rose taffetas and Canet beds *bouffant* with *point d'esprit*. Mrs.
Musliner's was a shell that curved her to it as if she were a
pearl. She awoke that way, a lovely pink one in its heart, with

the laces creaming about her. Mr. Musliner's, next to, but not adjoining hers, was in the same mood *mousse,* except with certain sterner concessions. No frothings. His bed cover was a pale gold brocade with a large diamond-shaped monogram in the center. Chiffonier mirror adjusted to his shaving line. An old-fashioned leather collar box, which sometimes crept out of a top drawer of certain of his cherished bachelor possessions, along with a smelly old pipe that violated the pale brocade scarf.

Mrs. Musliner would tuck them out of sight, her lips shuddering slightly as if her teeth were on edge. They could lift back like that frequently on those very rare occasions when she permitted herself to be alone. They were very, very rare. Always guests. Luncheon. Tea. Dinner guests in candle-and-flower-lit circle around lace over pink. Week-end guests, who nested in the little frilled rooms off the corridors and, night after night, some girl friend or other to share the lovely lace mist of Mrs. Musliner's bed.

Even Bertha's room, directly off the kitchen and facing a court darkly, could look sunny with the strip of new chintz on her washstand and a blue cotton bed cover with fringe. The housemaid and the waitress, sisters, had their room at the top of the apartment house.

It was warm in Bertha's room and she liked to sit in it evenings, barefoot and wide-kneed in the dark, with the door leading to the kitchen left open, its fine white porcelain refrigerator like a dim smile across the silence.

But a dim unvibrant sort of silence now, as if she were seated in the vacuum of a closed bell. All the little jeweled sands had run away. Sometimes she looked at them in the little islands of words that were margined so wide; fingering the leaves of her hurt bird of a book, which she kept wrapped away in the green chiffon cloak.

And the wisps of old sound. She had seen them, too, but not in the book. Tranced in her baby's eyes like the candy stripe down the center of the crystal.

To the pain of that empty cove of her arm where the small head had lain she had done horrid, unmentionable things. Sunk her teeth into the yearning flesh of it, leaving an inflamed crescent the shape of her bite. Rubbed one bare foot up and down against the other leg until the skin came off like erased blotting paper. Prayed to an inchoate God which she scarcely knew, except as a curse word upon Annie's lips. A hurt, beautiful word that could smoke in her heart.

But now the silences had come back. Not the old singing ones that had been vibrant as a black cat's arched flank. The merer silence of the inside of a bell.

And in this silence she was like a wound healing, the little line of the scar shirring up.

The Musliners were kind.

He did the ordering and was more frequently in the kitchen than she, who danced in only upon the gay occasion of candy pullings and every so often for the excited unwrapping of belated and excelsior-bound wedding gifts.

Shortly after he left in the morning, deliveries began. Great T-bone beefsteaks. Braces of wild fowl packed in hampers. Grapes in December wadded in cotton. Foreign-looking tins of caviar. Marron glacé. Chinese ginger. And especially for Mrs. Musliner, who loved littlenesses, plover eggs and palm-sized squabs with bones like toothpicks.

Once, that first winter of their marriage he brought her home, all cotton-wrapped in an enormous carton, an entire miniature farmyard made out of marzipan for the centerpiece that night at her birthday dinner.

She was like a child and bit off the head of a lamb with a squeak of delight. He tried to kiss her there at the unwrapping of it, because in her pink pearl kind of loveliness she was a phantom of delight to him. But she had a way of evading his wetted lips and their background of brown face, with a steely strength that the moment could seem to lend her.

Once when there had been only one week-end house guest and he had gone to his room, Bertha had seen Musliner softly knocking at his wife's door. Almost scratching like a dog.

"Erna," he whispered in the caressing way his brown lips had of saying her name, "Erna." As if the word were a puff of down. "Dearest. Please?" It was very quiet in the hall and her closed door like a tongue out at him.

Something like an ache for Musliner smote Bertha. He was so kind. Often in the fruit hampers was a bag of sweets tucked away for the servants and on Bertha's every other Thursday out, a dollar bill was left lying for her on the kitchen table. He was sensitive, too, in a way that hurt Bertha dimly. Once when she had inadvertently stumbled upon him, seated alone in the dining room with his head in his hands, he had jumped up redly, giving her a random order with a brusqueness not his. . . .

He would have jumped redly, too, had he seen Bertha seeing him as he knocked and tried the door softly.

"Erna—dear. You asleep? It's Ben. Please. Dear? I want to come in."

Finally he went back to his room, closing the door.

Bertha somehow, knew.

Doors. The long corridors of her silence were all nicked up with the sounds of them, closing.

One day, when May like a shy pink parasol was beginning to open wide and wider over the city, a lovely thing happened to Bertha.

The Musliners gave a picnic. Thirty guests climbed gleefully into a moving van especially upholstered in gay cretonnes for the occasion and rode fifteen miles up the Hudson to a grove, recently acquired by Mr. Musliner as an anniversary gift to his wife.

There were hampers of food and freezers of cream and cases of drinks and dozens of lemons and all the flimsy paper napkin and wooden plate paraphernalia dear to picnickers. Hundreds of sandwiches. Pails of salad. Cakes of every turn known to Bertha's hand. For two days Bertha and Julie the waitress and Lulu the housemaid buttered and sliced and wrapped in oiled paper and packed.

A set of white enameled picnic dishes arrived which Mrs. Musliner rejected as "spoiling the fun." Apples were dipped into syrup and impaled upon sticks. Boxes of marshmallows for toasting. Potatoes for roasting. Hammocks were packed into the van and an old upholstered couch upon which Mrs. Musliner reclined, once they had reached the open road, her guests in mock homage about her.

Bertha and Julie rode in front with the driver. How they chattered! Julie was a dark, nervous girl. Rather pretty in her waitress uniform, but sagged and run-down-looking in street clothes. She had been married once and upon the slightest provocation would display a scar across her neck to indicate where a jealous husband had attempted to cut her throat. When the driver saw it he tried to kiss her there and she lurched against Bertha and Bertha lurched against the side of the van and the open road rang with laughter. Julie's. The driver's.

And the rising merriment of the group behind. Bertha's laughter, too.

The day was so soft. Warmth ran up her legs. The driver reached around Julie's shoulder to pinch her and she reached across Julie's lap to slap him—plump in the stomach, so that he simulated pain, while really he was doubled up with guffawing.

From inside the van someone spied an organ grinder toiling up the road.

"An organ grinder! Come on in. Hey—you—stop. Come on in. Mucha mon! Comma to picnic. Mucha mon. See. Play for the queen on the dais. Come up—in."

And so the lifted, bewildered Italian dragged merrily into the van and the horse flecked onward with a whip that flashed into an S.

The river ran ahead to show them the road. Bertha had never seen a river. This one was quick and gay and on its way somewhere. Not full of lips like the harbor.

On its way to the grove. On its way to the grove.

"Looka," cried Julie, "all them rusty tin cans down by the water. Some tin can sports musta passed this way."

"Oh. Oh. Oh." Julie holding both her sides with laughter and the driver letting his lines slide to lean over and hold them for her, too.

"Look at that Bo over there in the field," he cried, cracking the S with his whip, "that ain't a nose on him—somebody fired a ripe tomater and it stuck."

"Oh la, la! Ripe tomater. Ain't he bloody? A ripe tomater. Go tell that to your rich uncle if his laughs don't come easy."

"Well, Square-head, it's your looka now. Looka now. Looka there. Looka quick, and tell us what you see—"

"He says, 'Looka quick, Bertha.' Come outta your trance

and look! Whadda you see? Look about you. Looka here. Looka there."

"Looka, looka," cried Bertha half daft with the lush smell of grass and of warmth, "looka those clouds—white—white clouds —little children up there—see—falling outta bed—"

"Oh Lord, that's a good one! Giddy ap, you gol-darn plugs you—little children falling outta bed.

> Oh lud, it's great to be crazy,
> It's great to be crazy,
> Oh lud, it's great, oh it's great to be nuts.

And then Julie taking up the refrain.

> "Oh lud, it's great, oh it's great, to be nuts."

The Grove ran out in a point to the river and would not let it pass, so the water went around it with a soft hiss. One tree grew almost horizontal and laughed down at it.

Little Mrs. Musliner, with her blouse open at the throat and whortleberry leaves in her hair, jumped astride it and beat it as if it had been a horse.

"Giddy-app—my trusty steed—swim me across the Hellespont!"

Bertha, tilting the salt water out of the ice cream freezer, stood almost waiting for the plunge and the sound of foam and the arrowhead line of the water parting before the tree stump whose leaves were a flowing mane.

A Young Fellow who dined frequently at the house snatched up a fruit knife from one of the hampers, clamped the blade between his teeth, and flew on the tree trunk behind her, balancing her against the shock with his hands on her light young hips, and the guests stood back and cheered.

"If I was little Musliner, I'd wipe up the floor with that young customer," said Julie, who was squeezing lemons.

"What?" said Bertha.

"Aw—you—hunky—you don't know you're on earth unless somebody stages an earthquake under you."

Suddenly Musliner came running down the turf, straddling the tree trunk, too, his little legs waving and too short even to dangle loosely.

"We're off," he shouted and dug with his knees into the spongy bark.

"Three's a crowd," sang somebody. "Who has the grace to stay home from the Hellespont?"

"Why I have," cried the Young Fellow, bounding off, and the red scorching through his fine tan.

"Now," cried Mr. Musliner, wriggling forward with his short fat knees, his hands coming down on the curve of his wife's slim young hips—"Now—we're off—alone!"

But suddenly Mrs. Musliner was tired. She climbed down jerking back from his touch. The wind and the May had gone out of her face.

"Come on," she said, "let us eat."

The meal was already spread on long wooden planks set up on wooden braces, but someone found a natural table of dog violets set out beside a little orchestra of waterfall and with great ado and much merriment the feast was moved up the hillside.

Under her breath Julie bitterly demurred. The climb was rocky and the running back and forth, from the hampers in the van to the remote spot on the knoll, twisted her ankles and strained her back and once, scaling the top, she fell and barked her shin and passed sandwiches over gay shoulders with her eyelids stung with the heat of the held-back tears.

But Bertha! With one heft of her arm she carried a case of wine, running with it lightly over the knoll. The dance up and the dance down. Ice cream freezers to be rolled up hill. She shoved aside the assistance of the driver and spun them in an ecstasy along the dark, damp flesh of earth. Rocks bit in through her shoes and she wanted to kick them off, so that her freed toes might bite them back. Rivers of strength seemed pressing at the dam of her body. She wanted the knoll to be a mountain that she might stagger, slip, and sweat up its flank, and the hampers to be kegs with the weight to bend her double.

The old Slav song of the women far behind her, who had worn the runic brooch, was so close to her consciousness that she wanted to sing it as she mounted the hill. The muted old concertina in her carpetbag, from dear knows what ancestral squatter in a peasant hut—she could have played it then; squeezed some of the locked-up ecstasies through it. She wanted to run. Feet were not mute—they tasted the sap of earth and bounded back vibrant with it as if they had drunk wine. The hillside. It cut her. It skinned her shoes and on the inside her toes curled, pushed against her stockings, and wanted out.

The wine ran in little pools. The Young Fellow, with his fingers for Pan's pipes, did an oafish dance around the table that was spread with wood violets. Someone tossed a great platter of the sandwiches high up and let them rain down again, splattering and scattering. Mrs. Musliner sucked at a candied apple and shot out her little red bib of a tongue at everybody, but longest and reddest to the Young Fellow, who touched the top of it with his forefinger and then pressed that forefinger behind his ear.

The sun, hot and high and prodigal, made great stains of light and shade. After a while groups and pairs began to shy off. One dark youth in eyeglasses stretched himself solemnly down the length of the table of dog violets, an empty wine bottle very tight in his clutch, and almost immediately fell asleep. Mrs. Musliner, side-stepping him gingerly, stuck a lilac spray upright between his teeth, so that it waved there to the tipsy wind of his breath. Then she and the Young Fellow squealing delight at this danced off down a footpath that turned suddenly and wiggled teasingly through some underbrush.

Even Julie and the driver had gone off and the organ-grinder lay asleep in a tree hollow with his body all up in a coil.

It was pleasant tiptoeing over the violets and wadding all the paper napkins up in a ball, and poking them out of sight in a hamper and stacking the wooden plates and scattering the crumbs and running up and down the knoll and clearing the forest back into its woodland quiet, so that the tinkle of the waterfall came through again and, except for those caught under the sleeping figure with the lilac spray waving in his breath, all the little violets lifted themselves up again as if after a storm.

Once, rolling an empty freezer down a steeper side of the knoll, she came upon Musliner, seated at the head of the trail that wiggled so naughtily off through some underbrush, and chewing a blade of grass.

"Well, Bertha, we seem to be the sole survivers of the party."

"Oh, Mr. Musliner, it's grand."

"Grand." A word as lonesome as a mountain and she wanted to tell him warmly about the lovely, green-lace grove of his and of the Slav song that ran along her throat wanting out, just as her feet running over the warm earth in their bluchers wanted out. "Grand." She could have bitten her tongue for some of its blood to flow into and warm what she wanted to say, but all that she had was "grand" and so she stood saying it and smiling at him with the lips which she hated because they were mutes.

"You're a good girl, Bertha," he said, looking at her with eyes that were hurt as if they had spikes through them, "you don't run off and shirk the job like Julie. Here."

He handed her a silver dollar. She took it and should have gone on trundling her ice cream freezer down the hillside toward the van, but somehow she didn't. She stood there, looking and wetting at her lips.

"Well?" he said. He was half seated on a tree stump, one leg dangling, and chewing and chewing the blade of grass along his front teeth.

Her gaze kept darting from him to down the little snake of trail and her throat kept tightening. She knew. He had worked very hard over this day. Her day. It lay now in a ruin around him, as he sat there chewing the grass blade his brown lips twisted as if it were bitter. In the tree hollow the organ grinder slept in his tight little coil. Bertha trundling the ice cream freezer down the hill. Otherwise no one left back. Not even Julie and the driver. Little bells of laughter through the trees. Bertha somehow didn't matter. For the life of him he could not keep his eyes, as if they were wounded in his head, from rolling a little toward that trail.

"I'll bring you a candied apple," she said.

She wanted him to be surly. It would have been easier then, for her not to be sorry, but he smiled and nodded no, and all she could think of to say through the ache in her throat was:

"There is an ice cream rooster left over and some Burgundy. You would like a nice cool glass of Burgundy?"

"No, Bertha," he said, "thank you, now you run along and clear up and don't you bother about me." But his eyes were traveling down the trail with hers, and finally he rose and came over to her, looking up at her from his squatness and with the brownish whites to his eyes very prominent.

"She's very young, Bertha," he said. "We must help her."

"I—want to—"

"Help her, Bertha. Never let her do anything that will make her unhappy. She is too young to see clearly ahead— you are a home-body—watch over her, Bertha—mother her."

Mother. That was a word that could twist her and make her want to bite at the cove of her arm, and yet, standing there on the hillside, hurting with this man's pain, it was as if something within her were spreading to cover a huddler. Actually, Bertha was two months younger than Mrs. Musliner, but so strangely older in the locked-up lore of the dim procession that peopled her silences!

Back in that procession, a young fledgling who walked in beauty and whose Sonatas had not yet been born, but whose melodies were to wind down through the centuries, had pursued a girl with flax-colored braids like Bertha's, across a plushy field in south of Hungary, capturing her finally and kissing her. At first she beat him off and then, because his lips were rich and his young head defiant, like a child's, it was she who held him. Broodily and close to her heart in the harvest moonlight . . . at dawn he was still singing softly to a great-great-grandmother of Bertha, troubled wisps of melodies that were not quite born to him yet—precious, groping old songs that were locked now in the heart of Bertha. Old Bertha, who was two months younger than Mrs. Musliner.

The sunlight bowed back out of the grove and the couples and groups came back tiredly and happily and hungrily out of the dusk. The driver built a bonfire and the Young Fellow unpacked the marshmallows and Bertha, with the water singing over her hands, washed the potatoes for roasting at the spring, and a full moon as dainty as an apricot came up between two trees.

Firelight on faces. Eager mouths with the teeth showing, hovering over just the right brownness of marshmallow. Low laughter. The grove crowding up around the circle of light. Mrs. Musliner, with her face in her palms and the reflected firelight leaping and falling in her eyes which had crybaby rims around them. The smell of darkness and the bleed of sap. Leaves, curling and burning to death with gestures of human pain. Over by the spring it was so dark that it seemed to Bertha that the evening was some great black cow standing there beside her panting softly, so that she could feel its sides breathe. Sweet-smelling darkness with a give to it like a cow's flank. The earth beside the spring was all wet with clear water and leaning over to rinse potatoes, she could feel the little sucks, greedily at her feet.

Warm, pulling, sucking earth that had teased her all day and over which her feet wanted to leap, free!

And then Bertha sat down, slyly, on a moss-tinged jut of rock, and picked up her skirts, and down came her great balbriggan stockings, wide-ribbed and the color of clay, and out sprang her legs. White urns in the gloom. The rip open of buttons. Little yawns of her empty shoes standing there on a dirt ledge. Squnch, into the slow pour of the good black mud that closed up around her ankles like a strong and hungry mouth.

Squnch. Squnch. Squirm of the pouring soil up between her churning, spatulate toes. She could feel it with the very pit of her. Warm. Black. Close. Her mysterious friend, the soil, whispering to her with those tight eager lips—it was difficult not to throw out her arms and shout—tear open her bulk of blouse where it cluttered her breast and shout—the curling, winding, whispering, kissing soil hugging her with its eager lips—she wanted to run—to run back barefoot along the plushy fields.

The organ grinder, dazed with good food and drink, began suddenly to grind out, in rapid spill from his hurdy gurdy, a folk song out of Ukrainia.

High cheek bones and velvet bodices that laced up in front. Red cotton skirts that twirled. Men in high boots and tight red sashes and fine mustachios that scratched! Sweat in hovels. Long low rafters, candlelight-scarred. Quivering hips. Waving mugs. Low of bulls and slow, hot smell of steaming dung heaps. Sweat and love and courage of solitary childbirth on wide moors. Strength of splayed Slav lips! Yeow, the ring of rafters! Yeow, the splayed Slav lips! Bertha with her arms outspread and a yeow that landed her squat on her heels out on a spot of turf that was stained with the firelight!

"Hurra! Look! Who is this? The cook! That's the girl. Give us a dance. Native heath, by Jove. Look at your Swede.

Muzz, spinning a goulash fandangle. Bravo, go to it—Yuiop—
I say!"

Spinning tarantellas with broad white toe for pivot. Swaying
hip rhythm, eyes slits, like wise smiling old buttonholes.
Hands broad on haunches and little bulge of bacchanalian belly
—Yeow—squat heels deep in turf, arms flung wide and half
wrenched from sockets! Leg out from under. Yeow—up
again on toe pivot—spin—spin—laughter over wild moors—
sweat in hovels—hot male hands on square-hipped girls—
scratch of mustachios against laughing, square-teethed women
—crones with the soil ground into their wrinkles. Sing,
peasant, sing, and swing the grinning scythe! Sing of the
strong fertilizing soil and the dung heaps that steam and
the crones that are wise with old lore and the women who
love, and who bear, and who weep, and the wide-legged men
with the necks like tree boles. Sing—Yeow—of meat and of
soil and of strength and of love—sing Yeow! Yeow! Yeow!

The hurdy-gurdy suddenly silent—Bertha with her arms
flung wide and half wrenched from their sockets. Toes in the
soil. Hair down. Her bosom where the waist had fallen open
gleaming and high.

Going home through the languid night it was Bertha who sat
next to the driver, his knee slyly digging up against hers which
she flung angrily back.

"Big girl. Good girl." He kept saying over and over again
under his breath without moving his lips.

She felt the tail of his glance slide over her bosom where the waist had fallen open and she clutched it closed and kept edging toward Julie, who was sullen.

"Before I'd dance for pennies, like a dago's monkey. What's the idea, giving a free show without an invite? I know my place, I do. They'd have showed you yours, if they wasn't all boozy as boiled owls. Listen to them now. I'm a self-respecting girl. I know my place. I don't dance for pennies. That dance was a give-away. You musta been born in a cow house where they dance all night and then grab up their pails and start to milking. That's old country dancing. I'm American. I know my place."

"What did I—do—Julie?"

"What did you do? Say, was it as bad as that? You musta had some inside information on the Burgundy. Made a holy show of yourself, that's what you did."

All the way home, edging away from the driver's horrid knee, the question kept spinning inside her brain, "What did I do? What? What?"

She felt so empty. As if all the strength had run out through her fingers and toes. A flask that had been drained of wine, that for years and years had been beating against its sides.

One evening in a winter that roared with blizzard, and snow-storms like plunging white buffaloes leaped before city traffic, there were dinner covers for eight at the Musliners, but no guests. Automobile wheels ground futilely in the hub-high ruts. Surface cars, shaggy with storm, stalled in their tracks. The streets slept standing, like horses.

In spite of Bertha skimming each new grease film off of the foods, dinner began to cloy, the entrée of creamed mushrooms darkening, the patty cases sagging as they waited.

With fever spots in her cheeks, Mrs. Musliner, in a bower of the tulle that her dress formed around her, kept rattling at the telephone, her urgent forefinger frantically up and down at it, but the wires were under the storm and only snow-hush came through.

"Central—you must answer—it's urgent—you must—hello—"

In his dinner clothes and very brown above the white of his shirt front, Mr. Musliner chided her in a little good-humored way he had.

"Well, little Snow White, it looks for once as if you must have dinner all alone with your old hubby."

Her smile up at him could be like a crucifixion—as if a tourniquet twisting in the very ganglia of her were forcing her lips to part.

"Central," she implored, working the hook up and down, "please—won't you answer?"

Through the little glass pane in the pantry door, Bertha could see him, bumbling about the rose tulle of her in the slow hitting fashion of a brown bee, his hand, wanting to touch her but constantly withdrawing, did pause at her throat where it flowed palely down into her bodice. It stiffened at his approach and a rib of vein came out.

Julie, peeping too, sniggered. He had a curiously sensitive blush. It came up, redly, as if he had heard.

"Central—can't you hear—you must answer."

He walked over to the buffet and shot out a swallow of seltzer.

"Afraid it looks like a quiet evening—alone, Little One,"

he said, with his words etched on his laugh like a design against thin glass.

She hung up the receiver, with the one vein still out on her pretty throat, and drew up her chair beside the lace, the flower- and the candle-spread table.

"Of course, Ben, it's just disappointing, that's all. Horrid old storm." She made a little *moue* and he looked at her adoring it, and then started for the vacant place beside her.

"Oh," she said and leaped backward—"I—they may come yet."

"How stupid—of course—they may—come yet," he said and took his accustomed place, remotely opposite, but his eyes, with their liver-spotted whites, eager for her through the little jungle of fern and pink roses of the center piece.

In the kitchen Bertha began to ladle out the bouillon. It made a clear little pouring noise. Like a thin cry.

A square of light from a window across the areaway could work its way into Bertha's room in a luminous plaster. Long after the electric bulb, dangling by a wire over her cot, was snapped out she liked to lie regarding the reflected glow.

A patch of warmth against solitude. A cave with a lit mouth. It was pleasant to walk through it and down into the aisles of doze. . . .

That night, the glow sprang sharply across the snow-packed areaway and long after she had crawled into her cot, she lay at this fantastic entrance into her sleep, dallying.

Little wisps of smoke rose off the embers of the day. Half consciousnesses. Six of the eight medallions of the salmon *mousse* were left over. That ridge of fear in a vein out across Mrs. Musliner's throat. The Farleys would have relished the salmon *mousse* creamed the next day. Not the Musliners. Sufficient unto the day the salmon thereof. The grapes he had brought her were wadded in cotton and in the upper section of the refrigerator. Would the salmon *mousse* taint them of fishiness? Snow. A wide, wide wilderness of it with humpbacks walking hidden under it and pushing it up into mountains. Drip. Hollow, pleasant rhythm, through the doze that made it difficult to awaken. Drip. Drip. Drip. That must be the ice pan flooding. It was so hard to awaken. Drip. Drip. Drip. Doors. The brown door that was Musliner and it led inward to a dwelling place of light. Drip. Drip. Drip.

And then in a crash through the light fabric of this doze, a pink little cyclone.

It was hard for Bertha to cross the hair line from her dim sleep to her dim reality.

"Who is it?" she cried. "What?" And sat up in the gilt darkness, two enormous braids of her tan hair hitting against the wall like rope.

It was Mrs. Musliner, in a nightgown made pinker by the flicker of her body through it, shuddering there on the floor behind the refuge of the door she had slammed and locked.

"Mrs. Musliner!"

"Bertha, hide me. Keep me here with you. Alone. Bertha, let me stay here with you."

She was trembling so that her nightgown went rippling along her limbs and her teeth and her lips were fanned dry with moans. And Bertha, Norse in her hulk, and in the great flannel undersuit and petticoat, stooping over the torn little huddle there on the floor.

"Mrs. Musliner—little baby—what is it?"

"Keep me, Bertha. Hold me tight. You will keep me, won't you, Bertha?"

"Baby. Little mine. You'll catch cold. You have bad dreams. This is no place for you."

"Let me stay. You're so quiet, Bertha. Let me stay here with you. It calms me. What are you hearing all the time while you work? What do you know? Bertha, tell me—what makes you so still—what do you know that I don't know—help me to know it too—help me be quiet like you—that dance—I remember—you know things that are beautiful and terrible— and yet you are quiet—help me, Bertha—I know so little— only that I am a bad, bad girl—and afraid—Bertha—afraid—"

"You poor little one—you bane walking in your sleep?"

"No. No. I'm not asleep. I'm not dreaming. I'm afraid, Bertha—keep me here with you. Hold me—don't let go— don't let him—get me—Bertha—"

She was like a child in a storm flung there against the rock of Bertha, crying there and clinging there and shuddering there.

"You little thing—you yoost shivering—you bane sick—I go and call Mr. Mus—"

She was a flash then, out of Bertha's arms, halfway across the room, her gown a quick ripple of silk about her body, and her arms out toward the window with a gesture of destination.

"Don't open that door! If you call him, I'll jump. I can't stand it if you open that door. I'll jump out!"

"Mrs. Musliner. Baby. Wait! I won't open it. You bane sick. I keep care of you. So. So. Here, in my bed—yoost shivering—yoost shivering—"

She carried her bodily, a curving petal, toward the cot.

"Don't let him get me, Bertha."

"Poor little baby. Here please, if you don't mind—on my cot —you bane chilled."

It was still warm there from the sag of Bertha's body. A nest of coarse bedding that grated through Mrs. Musliner's film of gown.

"Let me go get you soft blankets. Mine bane stiff like a board."

"No. No. Don't leave me, Bertha. I like it hard. I want it stiff—like a board. Like a cross. Like you. To hurt with the hardness and not have it matter. Don't leave me, Bertha, stay with me close. You understand, Bertha. He mustn't come near—I couldn't stand it. He's so brown. A brown dog scratching at my door. Scratching. Scratching—night after night—all these months. I can't endure it. To-night—I—it seemed to me—he had a key! I thought I heard him fumbling out there with one but—he wouldn't do that—would he, Bertha —he wouldn't do that?"

"No. No."

"But he kept turning the knob—and scratching—that terrible scratching—and then—something—that sound in the lock—like a key—hold me, Bertha."

"Oh, Mrs. Musliner—don't be afraid—"

"I am, Bertha. I am. You understand. He mustn't come— I can't stand it. Ever since we're married—I have managed so—never to be alone—never to be alone. I shouldn't ever have done it. They forced me. My father—family—money—he's so brown, Bertha—so terribly brown—brown lips—so good and so brown and so terrible. Help me, Bertha. You understand. You somehow—you—you cook—you understand."

Bertha did. Dumbly. Mutely. And in a way that wound like a cry around her heart.

"Poor Mrs. Musliner," she wanted to say, frightened by the wetted lips and inexorable eyes of the cyclorama, even when they only shone at her through the little pink jungle. Hers not to reason why. Nature's big impervious scheme for her had no concern with the shrinking of her flesh beyond that she must beget flesh.

"He bane good man."

"I know it, Bertha—that's what makes it so hard. Bertha— I want to go away—there's someone—Bertha, come closer— there's someone—"

"The Young Fellow," said Bertha, and looked at her and made deeper the cradle of her arms about her—"Oh, Mrs. Musliner—yoost open the brown door."

"I can't, Bertha. I've tried and I can't."

"Yoost lay and get quiet."

"You're so deep and still, Bertha. Like snow. I never noticed—before——"

"Shh-h-h, you little one. Don't shiver so. Let me go, yoost over there to the cupboard to get you my coat, it bane hard here——"

"I want it hard—Bertha—hard and cold—I'm bad—and it's cool and clean and meek to lay myself on wood—like you, Bertha—you're so meek—why are you so meek, Bertha?"

"I—I do not know."

"Hold me. You're so still. Hold me. I never noticed how deep and still you are. Ah, it's good. Hold me, Bertha."

She began to tremble softly into tears, the hard little rod of her body relaxing.

"I'm no good, Bertha. Why don't I die?"

"You bane very good, Little Mrs."

"He's good. I'm bad. He's so good to me, Bertha, I can't bear it. I can't bear him. His lips. Help me, Bertha."

Bertha, help her. Why, she wanted to. Bertha, who could pull webby stuffs out of drainpipes to the sound of chimes goldily, how she wanted to tell her of those inner secret solaces that rest in the lovely grail of the spirit! Yet all the words that would come were:

"He bane good—open the brown door—"

"Listen! There he comes. Down the hall. Don't let him in, Bertha. I couldn't stand it. Don't. I'll jump out the window first. Don't let him in. Don't let him in."

All the rigidity was back and she clung in a tense hammock, her knees braced up against Bertha, her arms up and locked about her neck. "Save me, Bertha. Save me."

To the convulsive rigidity of the small figure in her arms, Mr. Musliner's voice as gray and as flat as a moor came through the door:

"Erna."

She clung tighter, stifling her sobs against the hurting silence of Bertha.

"Erna. Go back to your room."

Frantic little sob-racked whispers. "Tell him, Bertha—I can't ever—can't, can't ever——"

"She's yoost a little nervous, Mr. Musliner. Maybe if you would please go away for a while—maybe a little later she—will come——"

"Never. Bertha, tell him for me—can't—can't ever—not to be angry—but—can't——"

"She says in yoost a little while, Mr. Musliner—if you will please go away, in a little while I will bring her back."

"No. No. No. I didn't say it, Ben—I can't—can't——"

"Take Mrs. Musliner back to her room, Bertha, and stay with her there—all night. I am going to my room now and inside of ten minutes I shall expect to hear her go into hers—and lock the door."

His footsteps went off into the same thin silence as his coldly thin voice, Mrs. Musliner shuddering down into a state of silence that was more like a faint.

"Come—Mrs. Musliner."

"No. No. No."

"He bane good——"

"I know it, Bertha, but so brown—so terribly, terribly brown——."

To find the words to whisper to her of the little vibratory paths that cut through the brown clay of externals . . .

"Yoost so the heart is not brown. . . ."

"I know, Bertha, but I can't find my way there. It's so dark —I've tried."

"Come, little Mrs., I'll take you. . . ."

"You can't. Nobody can."

"I can—little Mrs.——"

They sat still, crouched in the gold-powdered darkness, heartbeat to heartbeat. The sobs died down. Tears cooled and chapped little pathways along her cheeks. Bertha spread-kneed in her flannels, and the heavy gray petticoat. Barefoot.

"Oh Bertha—Bertha—so quiet—here with you. Hold me closer."

The Laocoön of them wound arm in arm there on the side of the cot. Colder. Later. Stiller.

"Mrs. Musliner——"

"Let me rest, Bertha, here with you—I feel so still. Stiller than I have ever been."

"It is already the ten minutes——"

"I—can't——"

"Come——"

"How——"

"With me."

She was like someone very quiet with a lovely kind of fatigue. Swoony. No remonstrance to the blanket thrown three cornered across her shoulders and the little journey, half propped against Bertha, through the chilled tile and linoleum of the kitchen.

At Mr. Musliner's door Bertha put up her hand and knocked suddenly.

"Oh God—no—not there—" cried Mrs. Musliner, and reared back.

"This is the way—little Mrs."

"No—no!"

"Yes."

"Oh God," cried Mrs. Musliner again, but suddenly she stood silent and waiting.

After a second Mr. Musliner opened the door. He was in a dressing gown that roped around his waist and his face seemed to look out brownly from behind the white mist of his pallor.

"Ben I—I——"

"She wants to come in, Mr. Musliner——"

"Ben—I—please. You. Me. My dear. Ben—may I open —the door—and come in? May I—Ben?" she said, and stepped with a little rush over the sill.

The door closing on them sent a little sigh of air out over

Bertha and left her standing in the river of the narrow hall's darkness.

Snow smother, as if the morning had taken a deep breath and could not let go. Almost the odor of Sunday, because not even the milk carts were able to be abroad and, opening the dumb-waiter a spiral of snow flew up like a jack-in-the-box and hit Bertha a good morning.

A white hearse of a day. Ice tesselated.

There were no breakfast rolls on the dumb-waiter and before Julie and Lulu came down to clutter up the silence with talk, she began to mix biscuit, squatting with the bowl caught between her knees, her fingers webbing up with dough.

Presently, early even for him, and cautiously, before the arrival of Lulu and Julie, Mr. Musliner came in. She wanted somehow not to have to look at him, and could feel the ox-blood color of her flush as she bent low over her mixing.

His shoes were brown with tan uppers and she could almost see in them a new firm planting on the ground as he stood there before her.

Pride of the male.

"Bertha," he said, and clearing his throat slid his hand down into his right pocket.

She wanted to help him and his scorching discomfort, but her eyes were glued as if by the dough and would not lift.

"Bertha—I—Mrs. Musliner is very much better this morning."

"Yah—so."

"A little nervousness last night—you understand. Over tired. Bad dreams—quite recovered this morning."

"Yah—yah—so—"

". . . closing up the place here and taking a trip to Europe for the change—nervous—needs a rest."

"Yah—yah—so? What?"

". . . might be easier if you would leave here immediately—before she has occasion to see you again. You understand—nervous condition—"

"Yah—yah—so—"

"Extra month's wages—references—good girl—but after what has happened, embarrassing for all—you understand—going to Europe anyhow—good girl—go now, before Mrs. Musliner awakens—good girl—extra month's wages—"

"Yah—yah—so—"

The day might have been a spark struck off clashing steel, so coldly blue it met Bertha.

Almost immediately her fingers began to ache around the handle of her carpetbag and she could feel the wire-stemmed rose on her hat thridding with still-cold.

It was like being awakened out of a warm dream. For a moment she could not place where she was. What next? Which way? Nothing to suggest traffic. A white nun of a day standing *impasse* to the march of the city.

An early bird of a boy, a demon with the joy of the storm, flung a snowball at her, missing her so closely that she could taste the whizz.

"Hello, Square-Head! Square-Head!" And then as the thin air passed it along and along after her as she hurried:

"Hello, Sq-q-uare Head— Sq-q-quare Head."

The wind had a long whizz to it. Zeouw! It raced around corners, so that it struck her broadsides and jerked her breath away. It rose up under her hat and set it on end like a plate on a juggler's brow. It sent up spiral snow ghosts in front of her and blew flurries of them into her mouth. It caught at her skirts and tore up under, chapping her knees. It tweaked her ears until the lobes were red and swollen and shiny. Zeouw! The Inverness cape went up over her head like an inside out umbrella and her skirts blew forward and the outline of her big legs sprang out. A gilt boot over a cobbler's shop blew down and grazed her by an inch. She was winded and twisted and the carpetbag hooked into burningly cold fingers when she finally staggered into a drug store. There was a pot-bellied stove with an iron fence around it. Her flesh began to sing. She cupped her hands against the warm, sheet-iron fence. All ten of her fingers, little bells ringing. Tears of cold, that the wind had lashed to her cheeks, started to thaw and run down. She began to fumble for her handkerchief with the ten bells of fingers that would not stop ringing.

The chemist, holding a measuring glass to the light and dripping into it a colorless liquid from a large bottle, glanced up and shrugged softly in his seersucker coat.

"Worst blizzard in ten years."

"Yah," she said, with her mouth full of the chattering dice of her teeth.

"Where you going? You won't get a train out of this town to-day. Worst tie-up in ten years."

"No. No. I got to go down to Front Street."

"Front Street? Docks, huh? You have as much chance getting down to Front Street as a duck has of swimming through snowdrifts."

"I got to go," she said.

He looked at her over his glasses. He had a Yankee face with a kick-up of beard.

"Where are you going, back to the old country?"

"Back? I've never been."

"Aint's you a Finn or something? You look as foreign to me as a samovar. Got some foreign streaks in you, I'll wager."

"Many—but I don't know—all mixed—."

"Melting pot—eh? Well, it's a bad morning to have going anywhere on your mind. Worst in ten years."

"I'm yoost changing places."

"Oh—housework?"

"Cook mostly."

"Whose firing a good, hefty girl like you on such a morning?"

"Not fired. I got references."

"Say, I have a customer over on Fifty-eighth Street needs a cook—worst way! Small family. Good wages. I'm putting up these aromatic spirits now for the old woman. You might take it over for me and size up the place. Want the address—good folks?"

"If you will please be so good—."

He ran his tongue over a label, smacking it on to the bottle. "No slip-ups on the way over. I'm taking a chance on you. My delivery boy wouldn't miss the chance of staying away for a snowstorm like this if he lived upstairs. Here's the name and address—."

She took the slip with her thick numbed fingers.

"Wall-en-stein—."

"Just around the corner. Tell them I sent you. He's the owner of the Sample Shoe Store on Thirty-fourth Street."

She felt it incumbent upon her to purchase something, her eyes roving along the shiny convex surface of a glass case. Rows of scented toilet soaps shaped like the bodies of birds and made to cut softly into the water. Perfumes. Bottle after bottle, the fragrance throttled down with white membranous hoods. Sponges with gaping thirsty little mouths. Things. Things that were sweet to the flesh. Bertha had never owned of them.

"I'll have that," she said and pointed down into the case. It did not matter.

"You don't want to buy anything," he said, and reached in for a cake of the soap, slipping it into her hand. "I don't want you to take something just to be polite. Have that on me. You're a nice girl. They'll be lucky to get you. Wish I could afford you for the wife. Don't forget the package."

She picked up her bag.

"Want to leave it here—in case—"

"Oh no," she said, "I don't mind," and curving her sore fingers again about the handle, went out.

The wind met her with a swoop and a yell, standing her hat again up on end. She bent into it, baring her teeth with the effort. The elliptical shaped bar of soap was in her palm. It had pleasant dimension. The smooth little blob of soap, shaped as an egg would feel if it came whole out of your mouth.

The Wallensteins, where Bertha was to remain several years, lived on the fifth floor. There were two middle-aged men in uniform in the lower foyer, and pressed leatherette walls with grape-and-leaf design embossed into them. What was really a small black onyx fountain in the center of the lower hall was kept filled with artificial daisies, and odds and ends belonging to the elevator men were surreptitiously tucked under the cotton moss.

The Wallenstein living room overlooked the heads of the buildings opposite and took in a fleeting view of Central Park with an etching of tree, a pagoda on a rock, and a round of lake with a swan boat floating upon it. A showy room of the shiny, overstuffed leather furniture of the period. Velour hangings with tassels. A handsome baby grand piano and a lamp with an openwork brass shade. Paintings in shadow boxes and, incongruously enough, to fill in the narrow panel of wall between the mantelpiece and door, a few Japanese prints which Mr. Wallenstein had once been obliged to take over as part payment of a bad account. Cool and thin with the fine calligraphy of a minute and apparently emotionless art. Bare-legged coolies full of little running steps. The span of many bridges. A plum tree, botanically wrong. A peacock, ornithologically wrong. Slant faces hung on like masks. Bertha liked to dust their impassiveness.

Evenings when there was not a poker party around the dining-room table, the Wallensteins lounged about this room in loose unexcited attitudes. Mr. Wallenstein reading the paper and yawning enormously with protracted shudderings as he turned the pages. He was a tall, heavy-set fellow, with very black hair parted down the center and set on to his head squarely, like a toupee. His small, straight mustache with the ends waxed up enhanced this squareness. When he stretched out in his long hypothenuse and hoisted the newspaper, he littered the entire center of the room, and to pass him, one had to climb.

Mrs. Wallenstein, on these evenings when there was no poker game, uncorseted herself immediately after dinner, the soft white flesh running down the hill of her body. She was very blonde, and wore her hair in an elaborate tier upon tier of puffs. These puffs, made in rows of three, four, and five, like hot buns, cluttered the house. So much as open a drawer and one crawled out at you and wound itself around your fingers in a webby, highly unpleasant fashion. Once Mr. Wallenstein slid into a row of them that had somehow dropped into his shoe, and forthwith had the noisy horrors.

Whenever old Mrs. Wallenstein found one, she picked it up gingerly, as if it were a mouse by the tail, and handed it in a scathing kind of silence to her daughter-in-law.

"Pfui!" was how she felt about most things pertaining to her son's wife. But she sat, too, in the living room with the pair of them after dinner. There was an arch of shadow where the lamplight did not reach. Old Mrs. Wallenstein liked to sit back in that, idle and brooding and with dry old eyes like prunes.

She had to have a hassock, because her feet did not touch the floor. Young Mrs. Wallenstein had a way of kicking the hassock savagely when her mother-in-law was not about, gritting her teeth with pain at her stubbed toes and taking a fierce kind of delight in that pain, and then kicking it again and again with her fancy tipped shoes.

Young Mrs. Wallenstein's shoes were eloquent. They were short-vamped, florid, and after even one wearing apt to tipple a little of run-over heels. Bertha was constantly at them with polish and cleaning fluids and vaseline for the patent leather. There was one pair of very high-heeled, slightly lop-sided champagne-colored ones with black jigsaw trimming. Mrs. Wallenstein never failed with her "pfui" when she passed them, smelling of cleaning fluid and drying crookedly on the window sill. There was something suggestive of blondely loose fat about their short vamps and run-over heels.

Old Mrs. Wallenstein wore square-toed, black bluchers with rubber insets, which she polished herself every morning and set on the fire escape outside Bertha's window to dry.

Her son, who was inclined to bunions, wore square toes too, but with the additional flourish of spats with the green or ruby of vivid hose above them.

Underneath the dining room table, their respective feet spoke volumes. The polished orthodox ones of old Mrs. Wallenstein on their hassock. The short-vamp, champagne ones. Wallenstein's rather stolid ones between the two.

Difficult, nervous meals of three kinds of silences. An old lady's aching one. A young woman's high-tensioned one. Wallenstein's tired one.

Sometimes it seemed to Bertha that the dining room of golden oak and swell of elaborate sideboard was filled with a gale of this silence, like one of those terrific arctic windstorms that old sea dogs dread because the water, in horrible phenomena, lies like glass under the gale too wind-beaten to lift a wave.

"Pass me the butter, Wally." Scarcely the phraseology to rock empires, and yet, when May Wallenstein said it, old Mrs. Wallenstein, whose skin was sapless at best, could seem to shrivel into the ancient parchment of the Torah.

She kept kosher. Valiantly. The forbidden combination of meat and butter might desecrate her daughter-in-law's board, but not the spirit nor the palate of the old lady. At her end of the table the sacred rituals of the *"fleischig"* and *"milchig"* remained unviolated. There was a shelf in the kitchen,

especially contrived by her son, for the kosher utensils and a
two-burner gas-stove in the corner for the personal and private
preparation of her orthodox foods.

May hated that stove and the little whisper of garlic that
hung above it.

"Makes me sick to my stummick to walk into my own
kitchen" was her frequent *sotto voce*.   "I'm Episcopalian, but
I'd like to see myself frying myself Episcopalian pork chops.
Good to their stummicks!  Oh, Lord!  Kosher is another word
for stummick-love."

And Bertha, hearing, would clatter pans and turn on the
spigot for the plunge of water into the sink, because sometimes
the undertones percolated to the old woman's dim ears and
then she had one of her smothering spells and spirits of
ammonia had to be administered.  On one occasion, Mr.
Wallenstein, in the midst of a Monday marked-down sale
of Oxford-ties had to be sent for, and all through the rush hours
was obliged to sit alternating between holding his mother's
hand in her darkened bedroom and pacifying his wife, who
invariably expressed her frenzy by throwing articles of clothing into a traveling bag and then strewing them all out again.
It kept Bertha on the jump, what with the hot water bag
for the old lady's numb feet and picking up the young one's
distracted articles of finery.

"No.  I won't be the one to go.  Why should I?  That's just
what she's laying for, to break up this house.  But she won't!
Not while my dress buttons up the back with tiddlywinks!"

The last was a favorite aphorism of Mrs. Wallenstein.  You
could hear it from the poker table:

"I'll raise you two bones.  You can't bluff me.  Not while
my dress buttons up the back with tiddlywinks."  Or over the

telephone to her sister, who clerked in the Sample Shoe Store:
"Tell Wally his mother is fixing him one of his sweet-sour
messes for his supper and to stop by and bring me home a
couple of chops for mine. I wouldn't eat anything sweet and
sour for no man. No siree, not while my dress buttons up the
back with tiddlywinks!"

A gay painted phrase like the little pagoda all lantern-hung
in one of the Japanese prints. Bertha liked it. Button up the
back with tiddlywinks! To be sure, May didn't button up that
way at all, but with much holding in at the waist and reddening
of the face, and exclamations like "Ouch, watch out, let me
straighten my shields first. A little elbow grease will help."

The fastenings were usually blobby velvet ones or hooks that
strained at their moorings.

To button up the back with tiddlywinks was to be gay as a
striped tent. It made Bertha feel gay somehow, just to repeat
it to herself; as gay as the day the river ran ahead of the furniture van to show them the way to the grove.

But, generally, there was little enough to feel gay about at
the Wallensteins, with May and her tantrums so quick on the
trigger, or the broody old woman who on Friday evenings would
light the candles in her room and keep open her door so that
the sound of her weeping came in little bleatings down the
hallway.

"She's putting on, putting on," May would sing-song, as she
lolled *en déshabillé* in the living room. She had a perpetually
hoarse voice, full of fog. "When I feel like having a good
cry, I go in my room and shut the door, and God knows there's
enough reasons around here for having a good cry. Evening's
diversion. God, how they love to cry. It's a wonder there's

not an Atlantic Ocean somewheres made up of noisy kosher tears."

"I wish you'd leave my mother out of your gab, May."

"Oh, you do, do you?" Well then, I wish she'd leave her gab out of my business!"

"Between you and your rows you two women are driving me plumb raving crazy. At least if I was the youngest I'd give in to an old woman—like my mother with only a few years left to live. I'd humor her, May. Honest I would."

"Few years. Long enough to have ruined my home for years! Few years! With her digestion for the greasy meals she eats, she stands a good chance of ruining it for many years to come."

"I won't stand hearing my mother talked about in language that's only fit for a bar-room. This isn't the Bowery. It's supposed to be a home where a man who's been on his feet all day can get a minute's peace."

"What about me? Am I entitled to a little peace in my own home, too? That old woman is driving me crazy. I can't get no friends to come to the house no more the way she sits out in the next room yammering to herself—I won't turn kosher for nobody's old woman. You married me for what I was and my Episcopalian hide is as precious to me as her kosher one! This isn't a home. It's a hell-house."

"May, you can't change a leopard's spots. My mother's old, and she's grieving herself to death over things you're too young to understand. She likes you, May."

"A lot I care if she likes me or not. Nobody could live in the house with her. The dusting don't suit and the cooking don't suit and the poker parties don't suit and the number of petticoats I have in the wash don't suit. Bertha is the first servant we've ever been able to keep in the same house with your mother and if that big lummox is human I'll button my dress up the back with tiddlywinks. . . ."

"She's the best servant we ever had."

"Yes, but nobody but a great, cream-colored elephant like her would stand for the old woman's butting in. She's got a hide not even your mother can break through. That's the way to be. Tough, so that they can stick things in you and you don't feel 'em. I'm sensitive. That's me. High-strung. I can't stand no yammering old hex in my affairs, and not get the jimjams."

"You eat those words that you just called my mother."

"Eat 'em? I'll spit 'em out, you mean! Hex—that's what she is. Hex!"

"By God—"

"All right, hit me! Hit me! Lots I care—go in there and cry some kosher tears with her—I can't help it because your father died—I can't help it because garlic makes me sick to my stummick—I can't help it because a penny don't look the size of a sunrise to me—hit me—hit me—but if you do, there'll be the greatest little smash-up around here this happy home has ever known—hit me—I'd like to see you try it, Sheenie!"

"By God—you—"

"Ah—ow—"

Then, to Bertha shuddering in the kitchen, the tormented frenzied tumble of him down the hallway, the slam into his room and presently the horrid distressed sounds of the violent sickness which these scenes never failed to induce in him.

Silence, with May lying swollen and wet-mouthed on the couch, and the bleating from the old woman's room whimpering down into sobs.

Virtually, it was Bertha who put the family to bed. Additional blankets to be laid out. Pillows fluffed. The hot water bag for the old woman's chilled spine. Ice for Wallenstein to suck. Spirits of camphor for the threat of fever sore on May's swollen lips.

Yes, generally there was little enough to be glad about at the Wallensteins.

In spring Bertha wheeled the old lady out in her rolling chair. She had a hip-bone complaint and except in the house, seldom walked. Bertha liked wheeling her out in the spring.

Usually because the up and down curbs were difficult, she trundled her directly to the park.

There was a tree there beside the lake with the swan-boats on it, that in April popped out in a delicate rash of leaves. It was down eight steps hewn out of a natural rock, and sometimes old Mrs. Wallenstein squealed at the tilt of the chair, but once down, there was quite a little dell, and a bench beside the water so that when one of the swan-boats moved the water ran up almost to the small front wheels of the chair and then backed off again.

Long, sedative afternoons with the old woman droning into them and Bertha, her hand joggling chair as if it were a perambulator, watching the light bend around the lake. In repose the look of tightness could seem to ease up in Mrs. Wallenstein's face like the flesh of a prune that has been dropped in water.

Faces like hers, strong-skinned, high-boned, and the eyes a little fanatical with love, had kept the storm-blown flames of the seven-branch candlestick burning down through the ages.

When Mrs. Wallenstein wept for her son she wept for Israel, and that is why her eyes could sometimes seem dry as salt beds with bitter residuum.

Often, talking through the quiet afternoon, her lips would try to shape themselves for words too heart-twisting for her to endure to speak and so she would cry them, her mouth writhing back from the gums.

"My boy. I don't care, Berthie, so much that she has stolen him from me, every mother who loses a son to a wife must learn such pain, but Berthie—she's stolen him from his faith— ain't that an awful pain, Berthie, to have a son stolen like a baby from his cradle out of his religion? Away from his God—to hers."

Here was that God business again. God—drenched in Light. Why was Mrs. Wallenstein's God a better God than May's God? Why was not the God who made May, the same God who made Mrs. Wallenstein and Bertha and Mr. Musliner and —and Rollo and even Annie Wennerberg? All this wrangling over your God and my God. God—drenched in Light. Or was God Light? Then why this groping in the dark? Julie, the waitress, had talked to her God along a string of beads. May Wallenstein went out on saint days to visit hers. Mrs. Wallenstein burned candles and kept her tongue free of the salt of swine in His name. One God and yet all struggling over Him. Tearing Him to pieces and setting up each his shred. Mrs. Wallenstein refuting May's Shred for her Shred. Julie's Shred to be whispered to along a string of beads. Your Shred. My Shred. Yet all torn off the divinely bleeding and omnipotent form of God—drenched in Light. To sit in that Light and soak it in through the pores—drowsily as the old woman talked—and talked on—through the spring-lit afternoons.

"A boy who was raised in such a home like his should go out of it to another religion! Not a Friday night in his life that he didn't see his papa and me light the candles for our Shabbas. I'm afraid to die. I'm afraid to die and leave him to face her God."

Silently then, Bertha would jounce the handle of the rolling chair.

"She's not right for him, Berthie. How I prayed with him that night he came home from the dance-hall where he met her, he should not go to such places—even before I knew where it would lead to. She ain't a helpful wife, Berthie—like I was to mine. I stinted. She spends. I mended and washed and ironed. She plays poker and eats all day, chocolates. My boy works on his feet fifteen hours and she spends it faster as he can earn it. He don't realize it yet—he's in love. It ain't nice to say it—but he's in love just with her body—no man can change his God for a woman's body—and have it last."

Talk—talk—talk—through the long sedative afternoons. Sometimes Bertha dozed a little, coming up to consciousness for snatches of it and then slipping off again, her head over toward one shoulder and her hand automatically at the little sedative jouncing motion.

"You should have seen, Berthie—such a little new suit as his papa bought him for *bar mitzvah*—to get *bar mitzvah* by us is the holy time when boy becomes a little man in his religion. His papa—how every night after supper, in the back of the store so sometimes the customers had to wait, my husband heard that child his *bar mitzvah* lesson. And for what? Such a blonde shixsa what don't do nothing except set him against his mother and his religion and throw out his money for him faster as he can make it. Thank God his papa didn't live to see it—maybe he blames me when we meet again—I couldn't help it, Julius—I tried—I prayed—I tried—I prayed—she got him with her white flesh, Julius—blonde flesh like he wasn't used to. When a woman gets hold of a boy that way—ours—not even his mother—or even his God, Julius—can hold him back—Julius—don't be mad—I couldn't hold—him—back—he's a good boy—but I couldn't hold him—back—"

And so on and on through the whimpering lips, until the copper band of light around the lake snapped out and with a great pulling and tugging and sometimes the help of a passerby, Bertha began to yank the wheel chair up the steps that were hewn out of natural rock.

Bertha's second summer there Wallenstein and his wife took a two weeks' holiday at a small lake resort upstate known as Becker's Point. May's second brother ran what they called "the pickle boat" around the lake in summer. A small provision tug which puffed about all day, dispensing from landing to landing, the tinned, the tabloid, and the compressed foods of the summer colony.

"You would rather have your vacation, Wally, by Fleishmans in the Catskills where you're used to it, but lots she cares where you get your vacation just so she gets hers. Her brother with his store on a boat! We're plain but substantial people. In our family we got our stores on streets like it is legitimate."

Wallenstein took his mother by the wrists and pressed his fingers into them until white areas sprang.

"For God's sake, mama, don't start anything with May now. I *do* want to go to Becker's Point. I need a rest. I'm nervous. Damnably nervous."

"I won't say anything, Wally, to her if I bust with it. I'm only saying it to you—I know how you like it at Fleishmans in the Catskills—"

"I'll send you there, ma—Bertha can take you—"

"Me? For myself, Wally, I'm satisfied to stay home and do a little saving. But that you should have to lay around such a *goy* place!"

"Ma, if I hear that hateful word from you one more time! I'm worn out—I can't stand it—I'm nervous—you hear—"

"All right, Son. Don't holler. Maybe I won't be here so much longer you should holler at me like that—if only I wasn't afraid to die and meet papa—"

He dropped to one knee, kissing her hand.

"Mama, mama, don't torment me. I love her, mama, and I —sometimes—I—I'm afraid—I hate her! That's torment for you—torment of hell on earth. To love a woman at the same time that you hate her!"

So that summer for two weeks of an August that glared down upon the city until it was as bleached and polished as old bone, Bertha and Mrs. Wallenstein had the flat to themselves.

Hot, motionless days and nights that seemed to sit still and brood like pyramids! For the time, Bertha slept on a cot at the foot of the old woman's bed. She tossed a great deal and a little moan ran through her light snores, and sometimes she started up with short, sharp cries.

"Wally! Don't let her! Julius! It's *pesach*—Wally—don't

eat that bread! Shiksa! A shiksa wife! No, no, papa—I tried—I begged. I prayed."

Often Bertha had to get up and turn on the light.

"You bane dreaming, Mrs. Wallenstein. See. It's Bertha. Here, let me fix your pillows—take a sip of water—so—there's nobody here but Bertha."

"I thought it was *pesach,* Bertha—when my people must eat only *matzoths*—the unleavened bread of God—and she wouldn't let me—Bertha."

"Shh-h-h, Mrs. Wallenstein."

"She stepped on them once," and up went the voice to the peak of hysteria that was so hard to quell. *"Matzoths.* God's bread. I can't ever forgive her that. . . ."

And so on and so on and so on through the burning deserts of these motionless August nights and sometimes, of sheer exhaustion, Bertha slept. Vastly. With her cheek crumpled up against her arm, the sheets thrown back from her body, and the great ridge of her uncovered legs magnolia-white in the darkness.

One dawn a withered leaf fluttered down upon the heavy torpor of Bertha. It was Mrs. Wallenstein's hand, plucking at her from across the footboard of her bed.

"Berthie!"

"Oh—what—yes, Mrs. Wallenstein."

"Berthie, I been called home."

"Where?"

"I want to go, Berthie. It ain't long now before I won't be here no more and before I go—I want to go back down there. It won't be so hard I should have to face Julius if first I can only go home."

"Why, Mrs. Wallenstein, you bane home—here."

"Here is not home for me. Get me my foulard dress and my bonnet. Quick! I want we should start before the heat of the day."

"But your son will not like it."

A sudden slyness came curling out in the old woman's face.

"No, he don't like it if I go, Berthie. It ain't stylish that his old mother should remember old days, but Berthie, please, take me home. I want more as anything to go. Only down by Division Street, Berthie?"

"Mrs. Wallenstein—you can't walk—"

"Look, Berthie—when I got ambition, see how I can walk—see, Berthie—please—"

And sure enough, she began to limp about, outlandish in her nightdress, with the rack of her old body shaking through, but her face thrust out ahead of herself, like a lantern.

"Mrs. Wallenstein—your son—I promised to take good care—"

She was slyer and slyer, her eyebrows running up into little peaks and her cheek bones and chin jutting out into points.

"He don't got to know, Berthie. Take me home, Berthie, before I die. I'm going to die—soon. I hear it at nights underneath my sleep. And you know what it is, Berthie, to hear things—that way. Because always you too are listening to something. I heard it again last night—take me home, Berthie, so I can get strength back to meet papa—I want my old home where we lived twenty years and where my boy learned his *bar mitzvah* lessons behind the counter—I want to go back—"

And Bertha washed the old face of its tear traces, brushed back the old hair into thin streaks that scarcely covered the scalp, and fastened around her the decent silk foulard dress.

The August day came out at them like a parched and coated tongue as they started for Division Street.

The wheels ran and banged, and a breeze that smelled of armpits and little babies, milk-soaked bibs and bedding that had been sweated into, blew through the street car. A breeze as curiously alive as breath.

It stood the little invisible nap of fine hairs on Bertha's forearm up on end in an electric little rash and it rushed against her ears, thick with words that could not form themselves out of the two dozen languages that the East Side exuded. A conglomerate breath, rich in nationalities and that would one day find voice. Bertha knew that rich kind of muteness. It beat up against her so.

At Canal Street it was as if the sidewalks ran shouting to meet them. It was hard to steady Mrs. Wallenstein against the dizzying swirl, because she was crying and through the dimness of tears wading her way eastward, her umbrella, which she carried as a steadying cane, waving out before her as if to clear the way of children and languid puffs of dirty newspaper and rinds and rinds of fruits.

"Ten years since I been home, Berthie. How I worked when I was a young woman down here to get ourselves out of it and now I got myself out of it how I eat my heart to be back in it. My boy was *bar mitzvah* down here. My husband made us a living down here. My happiest days in my life I spent down here with my people. Hurry, Berthie. I want to get home. It's two blocks only now. I want you should see where my baby was born—"

Old Mrs. Wallenstein. Suddenly full of young little running steps—two long raspberry ovals of color out in her cheeks, the foulard dress ballooning as she hurried. Tears. Tears. Tears. Thick lenses of them.

The house in Division Street was as lean as a witch. Human bodies, lax like pillows over sills, dangling and shouting from windows. That dingy and perpetual banner of poverty, the family wash line, kicking and writhing. There was a poultry store on the ground floor. Strong smells of chicken blood and hot fuzz, and on the high stoop, like a brooding conclave of the shawled women of the east, half a dozen old crones in white headkerchiefs and burning back deeply in them—deeply, burningly back, tired Old-Testament eyes.

Suddenly Mrs. Wallenstein's legs gave out under her. They would not climb that stoop. Twice, with Bertha's sturdy hand at her elbow, she raised her foot for the first step and twice her knees doubled under, until finally she crumpled up on the first step, leaning her face against the railing to cry.

"I can't go no further. I'm too happy. I'm home. This is my stoop. I don't know no more these faces, but this is my stoop."

And the snow of hot fuzz blew against her lips, and children, filthy with the fruit-rinds of the littered streets, gathered around, and the biblical old women with their peering faces and dead-leaf hands came down the steps, and Mrs. Wallenstein, laughing and crying, held out her arms to them and they drew back shyly.

Then came an avalanche of words. Words. A torrent of them that were new and alien to Bertha. Words that she had never heard before. Down off the chute of Mrs. Wallenstein's tongue they came, tumbling in Yiddish. Coals off a chute. Clatter. Clatter. And the circle of the old women closed in, and off ran the children, uninterested in just another conclave of the elders. And the sun grew hotter and higher and the din ground itself against the flesh like grime, and Bertha sat by waiting, while the whining voices of the old women, in a circle now on the lowermost step, wove on and on.

The heat was like a boil, gathering and throbbing into the head of high noon, and still the children shouted and the bodies that hung across window sills pointed and shrieked down to them. Pushcarts began to leak of their softening and rotting fruits; old men dozed into their beards; cats slept in the attitude of death, but with palpitating sides. A tailor sat on his ironing board reading the newspaper in which his half-eaten herring sandwich was wrapped, and played up and down on his small pocket piccolo, the thin grieving notes of the desert.

Oi—oi—the high quail voices of the old women—the dry old women past childbearing and with the dry eyes and the dry breasts and the dry tears.

Bertha began to walk. Banners waved. The banners of the flying gibbets of leggy underwear from high clothes lines. The jargon of Yiddish ran in a tide. More and more old women on hot high stoops. The life of the children close down to sidewalks with the rinds and the drip from the fruit carts.

Then suddenly Prince Street, little Italy, the women with the pot bellies of more and more child bearing, the men debonair with the blackness of hair and the whiteness of teeth. Curving scimitar of Chinese Pell Street, the shape of a mandarin's little-finger nail; skins the color of apricots. Much further down ran Front Street with its flotsam from the sea and still further down, West Street of the water pipe and fez.

Hot, disturbed breaths of alien climes, not soluble one in another, but all soluble in the new world. And out of the new world was one day to come the rich composite expression that struggled so for articulation.

The words of the jeweled sands.

The day was on the down side. Through the heat dance all the lean houses seemed to have wavy walls, and it was not easy to manipulate Mrs. Wallenstein back again to the street car. They had to let two of them pass because again the old woman could not quite bring her foot to raise for the step, but finally she made the hoist and plumped down inside with a burst of perspiration.

Except for the sighs which blew and blew off the twisted old crags of lips, she seemed to doze, with her fist plunged deep into Bertha's palm and throbbing there.

"You seen, Berthie—my people—those are my people—and his—our people. Berthie—who are your people?"

"My people?" She looked at her softly, the wide lips falling apart to smile. "My people? Why those are my people," she said, her eyes very blue and her lips fumbling to say more. "Those are my people. Out there. All. Everywhere."

It was the last time the old woman ever left the house. August roared on and Wallenstein and his wife returned. Bertha moved her cot back into the breathless room that opened off the kitchen, and the old woman resumed her long, motionless watches in the shadowy arch between the folding doors. Sitting

there during the long merriments of the poker game, her dry
eyes forever focused upon her son, they could seem to smear
into a single tearless and reproachful orb in the center of her
forehead.

"Gives me the jimjams—her sitting back there—" was another frequent *sotto voce* of May, her white flesh writhing up
and down under the large pearls and transparent chiffons she
was fond of wearing.

"Mama dear, don't you think you had better let Bertha take
you to bed—we're going to play a round of rudles yet and you
must be tired."

"I'm all right, son."

Once a guest, a Mr. McGuire, who was a frequent visitor,
swung around in his chair to her.

"Come on. Grandma, have one of these kosher ham sandwiches. They're kosher, ain't they, Wally—."

Oh. Oh. Oh. The poor dried prunes of eyes in Mrs.
Wallenstein's head. They seemed to have died there.

One January noon when there were pork chops snapping on
the stove for lunch, Mrs. Wallenstein was suddenly missing
from her rocking chair beside the window in her room. She
left there less and less now, and never without the hoist of
Bertha's arm.

"Mrs. Wallenstein—the old woman—she's not in her room.
I can't find her."

May was drying her hair in a great fan that spread in a
patch of cold sunlight on the window sill.

"She's not far. No such luck."

Sure enough, Bertha finally discovered her shivering and crying on the fire escape, where she had climbed with an agility that frenzy alone could have given her.

"Mrs. Wallenstein, you must come in from the cold."

"Let her stay out there, Bertha. She'll soon get enough of it, if she sees she can't spite me by one of her loony fits."

"Quick—come in right away. That is not nice to sit in the cold."

"I can't stand it. She should cut out my heart to get rid of me, but I can't stand it I should have to spend my days in such a household where my son's home is made every minute an insult to his religion. It's like my own heart was frying with them pork chops. Thank God his papa didn't live to see it."

Bertha coaxed her in, dragging her a chair for the step from sill to floor, and full of little urgings.

"There. Now. So."

"It would be better, Berthie, if I die to-morrow. Then I don't stand any more in my son's way or in my daughter-in-law's."

"No, no, Mrs. Wallenstein."

"It's not good, Berthie, a woman should got to stand between such a good son's happiness with his wife like I do. Only, Berthie, she ain't his happiness—he don't know it—but I do. A man who has to pay with his God for his love don't find no happiness. My poor son—he don't know which he should be first. My son or her husband. I'm in the way, Berthie. Nobody knows it better as I do. Berthie . . . never leave me, Berthie. . . ."

She needed Bertha so. Even the absurd fashion in which she pronounced her name was like a cry in the dark. A little winged sob that could beat its way and nest in Bertha's heart and hurt there. Sometimes at night, long after the lights were out, the cry would come through to her, and down she would tiptoe and curl up at the foot of the old woman's bed, ponderous as a mastiff.

Wallenstein was grateful. He had her come down to his shoe store on Thirty-fourth Street to be fitted for two fine strong pairs of bluchers, and as she went out with the package under her arm, he said:

"Never leave my mother, Bertha, and you won't regret it. She's a little peculiar in her ways and her ways aren't my wife's ways—but a better woman doesn't breathe—never leave her, Bertha."

"Yah—sure—never—"

Poor Wally. It was as if a wire cage had curved itself somehow about him, with the egress woven cunningly into the mesh. He was in and the two women with him, making a prison of what, with either of them alone, might have been a nest.

Bertha felt, dumbly, fiercely, the relentless pattern of that mesh, the angry tortured eyes of the three of them looking out. She wanted to reach and to fold them all to her understanding. Even May.

Constantly, as that winter dragged through, there were half moons in May's hand where the finger nails bit in.

"She-devil" was an expletive which smoked constantly on her lips. She said it with her pinkly pointed finger nails cutting up into her palms and her toes piling and her teeth grating. "She devil."

One day she ran from the luncheon table into the clothes closet in her bedroom. It was horrible. Because she bit at the empty sleeves of gowns hanging there, tore fabrics, jerked hangers from their hooks, trampled on Wally's dressing gown, kicked until she bruised her shoes and toes against the wall, and finally half collapsed in a hurricane of the garments she had pulled down about herself. "She devil. Old Hag. Matzoth face. Can't stand it. Sheenies. Both. Stingy-gut. She-devil."

It happened trivially. Something like this. About noon a fog had descended over the city. One of those gray smothers that roll in off the sea. There was something extremely cozy about the indoors on a day like this. Bertha prepared tea and fluffed up an egg omelette with a fusty sense of that warm indoor coziness.

May had been stacking chips for a poker party that night. She was playing practically every afternoon now, losing large sums which were the subject of heated controversy with Wally, and five evenings out of the week there were games at the house, too.

This day she wore a pink flannel wrapper and her hair was in curl rags that rose off her temples like a shriek. She had a headache, too.

"Got it too good," was the old woman's under-her-breath diagnosis of the almost daily ritual of cold compress or head-ache powder.

"Yeh—swell chance for any one to have it good with a tight-wad like you in the house." Also *sotto voce*.

Oftentimes Bertha, hearing, would sicken with a sense of futility that made almost the lifting of a pan from the stove too nerve hurting to be endured.

Lunch was a meal to dread with the two women alone, and without the intermediary influence of Wallenstein.

When May in the pink flannel wrapper entered the fog-swimming dining room, she switched on the lights, seven high-power ones in the colored glass dome over the table.

"Give me a tablet in a glass of water first, Bertha. My head's splitting."

Then old Mrs. Wallenstein came in, stiffly in her black percale house dress shotted with white four-leaf clovers, and carrying a bowl of thick black lentil soup which she had warmed from a specially prepared crock of it which she kept on the window sill.

"Say, May, since when has Wally got a stand-in with the electric light company? If I can find my mouth in the middle of the day, you should find yours with your younger eyes."

With a good humor which she valiantly tried to simulate for the trial of these noonday meals together, the old woman clicked out the lights again, just as May gulped down the headache tablet. The almost reflex action of a woman who for a period of thirty thrifty years had run her own home; and with that same reflex of a woman bound in turn to run hers, May, the fuzz of fog in a whirlpool of anger about her, sprang to the wall, clicking the lights back again.

"You dare," she cried with her lips lifting back drily off her teeth, "you dare to dictate to me when I can have light in my own house and when I can't!"

The old woman had a way of appearing to shrivel and to yellow under the lash of her daughter-in-law's tongue. She seemed to recede to a point.

"Is that the way, May, a daughter-in-law should talk to her husband's mother, nearly three times her age, and who didn't mean nothing but a little economy?"

"Economy my hind-foot! I'd like to see you or anybody like you tell me when I can have the electric light on in my house and when I can't. Not while my dress buttons up the back with tiddlywinks."

"Maybe, May, if you didn't know everything for yourself so well and would let an old woman three times your age help——"

"Not you. You can't tell me nothing I don't know already."

"I can tell you that a good dutiful wife don't squander her husband's money away on gambling debts and matinees——"

"You keep your gab out of my affairs. You've done enough damage in this house as it is. My husband is my business."

"Your husband is my son!"

"More's the pity."

The shuddering, sucky, ligament-twisting cry of the mothers of sons bearing them. That was the kind of moaning noise Mrs. Wallenstein made as she went down into a little huddle on a dining-room chair.

"Mrs. Wallenstein!"

"Let 'er alone, Bertha. I'm used to those bluffs. I've seen her topple over into those fake faints for years now. Temper, that's all. She's tough as tripe."

"Oh God, why don't I die."

"Mrs. Wally—she bane old——"

"Let her alone, Bertha, I said. Hands off. That's the trouble now. Her out there in the kitchen with you all day crying for sympathy. It's a good thing you're built like a rock-of-ages, with her on your neck all day or she'd have driven you away long ago, the way she did every other servant we ever had. I'm sick of it, I am. Wally's got to decide between her and me and pretty damn quick, too. I wish to God I could go off somewhere and live in one room and never have to clap eyes on the whole shebang again. He'll have to settle good and heavy on me too—mind you that. *Matzoth house,* that's what I call this. Well, thank God, I wasn't raised no matzoth eater."

"Belittle me. Belittle even my boy . . . the finest son a mother ever could be proud of—but don't make little my religion—don't make little my God because he is not your God."

"God! Who said anything about your God. Matzoth is what I said, and I say it again. *Matzoth house.* Two stoves. Two sets of dishes. Matzoth crumbs all over the house so I have to be ashamed to have company at my own table for matzoth. Matzoth. He likes 'em too—dips 'em in coffee. Once a matzoth dunker always a matzoth dunker. Can't change a leopard's spots. Matzoth is what I said. You hear! *Matzoth house!*"

"Julius, my husband! Wally, my son! I can't keep it shut up in me no more. I can't live here no more. To have to see, with every hour I live, everything what is sacred to me and to mine, made little. Papa, where are you up there—let me come to you. I'm alone—down here, and I'm afraid to leave Wally—alone—with no God—help me, Julius—help——"

May swung heavily into her chair.

"Well," she said, flopping the omelette which was cold by now to her plate and jabbing into it with her fork, "here is where I am let in for another pleasant lunch hour. It's a wonder I don't croak of *kosher* indigestion."

"I can't hear that word no more so abused! It's like salt in a sore. Oh—oh—oh—if not for my son, I would right away pack my things—why did he pull me up away from my people down there—these ways ain't my ways—those are my people— he should let me go back."

"Well, no insin-uations, but you can take it from me if he didn't always have you nagging him over to your ways, I could make him a darn sight happier than he's ever been in his life before. He'd be a live one, that son of yours—if he dared."

"That just goes to show! A woman with her thoughts on her home and her husband's interests and—and children—don't got time for such shennanigan talk like her husband should be a—a *live* one."

"You're going to ram that children talk down my throat once too often. I'll have children when I get good and ready to have children and not before."

"A woman shouldn't put her time for it, before God's time for it."

"If—if you weren't his mother and—old—I'd drive you out of the house for less than that."

"Why don't you? It would make it easier than I should walk out from my son's house on my own——"

"Well then—I do! You can't stay here day after day to devil the life and soul out of me. I won't stand it. I—now—you—go—!"

"God, papa—God—Wally—no—no—it ain't possible I should live to see it—out from my own son's home——"

"Yes—yes—out of your own son's home—driven out by the devil in you—yes—yes——"

"Oh, Mrs. Wally—she bane old—oh—oh—oh, Mrs. Wally——"

"And you! Square Head, you! Lummox! There's something about you gives me the jimjams. For all I know you're one of those still ones that run deep. How do I know you're not taking sides with the old woman and running to my hus-

band with lies! Go—the two of you—the quicker the better—
go—go—go—"

It was then, because the words in her throat were a mere
strangle and her hands were curved and spread out like claws,
that May ran screaming to the clothes-closet, dragging down
the garments in their avalanche of fury down about her and
gasping, choking, spluttering:

"She devil! Matzoth God! She devil!"

Toward dusk Bertha began to try to feed the old woman
soup out of a spoon that clicked against the square, porcelain
teeth that were twenty years too young for the gums.

"Can't swallow. Leave me alone, Berthie. I'm an old
woman put out from my own son's house. Where shall I go,
Berthie? No. No. I won't go. Nobody can drive me out
from my son who needs me and who has lost his God."

Forcing the spoon against the glassy teeth a sense of the race
indomitability of this old woman smote Bertha. Exactly as
she had recognized the Polish national anthem with her heart,
so Bertha knew this. There was no suppressing the mother
of Wallenstein. Oppress her, yes, but the light of the children
of Israel was like a camp fire in her eyes and would not be
ground out.

It was bitter to stay, and the lips of the mother of Wallenstein were twisted with that bitterness.

"The reason, Berthie, why nothing is so wonderful in a
woman's life as to have children, is because even to suffer
for them—to suffer for them is a blessing."

"To suffer—for—them——"

"But I don't wish it to no woman she should have such a knife in her heart like mine. Death is not the only way to lose a child. You should thank God, Berthie, you don't know what it is to give up a son of your own heart's blood——"

"Not know what it is——"

The brook of the frozen tears, she could feel them thawing and rushing up against her throat. Bertha who so seldom cried. She tried to hold them back, tensing her tonsils into a dam against them.

"Take the soup away—Berthie—I can't take it—you're spilling it on the sheet——"

How they pained, the pressing gorging tears. She was blind with them, and when she swallowed them down with her great strength, they ran back upon themselves and filled her with hurting torrents.

"Don't cry, Mrs. Wallenstein," she said finally, the words coming out evenly over her own inner hemorrhage of tears.

"Two babies I lost to death, Berthie—but not even such suffering was so bad as to lose a child to life."

"To—*give*—a—child—to—life, Mrs. Wallenstein."

"Hold me, Berthie, close—and say that over to me—over and over again—to *give*—and not to lose—him——."

"To—give—a—child—to—life. To—give—a—child—to—life. To—give——."

The old woman slept and finally there was dinner to be prepared and it was Bertha's day for scrubbing the kitchen floor on her hands and knees.

It was good, the great harsh drags across the splintery boards, pools of soapy water smearing before the brush, her shoulders sweating. Good, good, to sprawl for that reach under the sink, with her great legs thrown out like those of a swimming frog's, and her heart through the soft pad of breasts, beating down close where the tremors were. The little vibratory tremors. . . .

Great soapy circles. Pain that had dimension—pain the shape of her arm sockets. Singing knees and the pleasant relief of lifting one from the floor so that the sensation died down like suds.

Zeouw! Zeouw! This way and that, the water running a little after the brush, and the smell that was almost a green one, coming up between the boards. Water under her brush. She ground it in and in and in, back into the soil from whence at some time or another it had come and from whence it would come again.

At seven Wallenstein would come. There was dinner to be prepared. A round of roast the shape of a cord of kindling wood. Gristle ran through it. She cut it out as if it had been a nerve. A nasty hurting thing. It was good to be able to slither it out and throw it away in the tin pail under the sink.

Onions to peel. Tears. Light tears that seemed to leap from the outside and lay against the eyes. Not the inner pushing ones that tore the throat in their frenzy to get past. The smart ran up to her nostrils. Good. Good. She could rub her nose, thick, white and squatting and lawk, the smart was gone. Easy pain. The pull of her arm sockets. Easy pain. But to be able to tear open her throat—somehow—and get in at the torment there—the buried secret torments that had not dimension. . . .

Wallenstein would be home any minute now. Bertha had a sly little procedure before dinner. It was to draw together two of the most comfortable chairs in the living room, chummily, as if two women had been sewing and gossiping there during

the long quiet of an afternoon. And Wallenstein liked the little
first-hand attentions that May, in prime mood, would give him.
His slippers with the toes out, standing waiting. A glass of
orange juice on the table beside their bed.

The look of strain and of drain would run out of his face
when he walked in on evidences of what might indicate that a
day of rare tranquillity had rolled over the household. He was
quick at these perceptions. An overturned hassock might mean
that May's toe had been stubbed in rage, or the sweetish thickness of an incense stick, burning up into garlic fumes, warn of
conflict before he had even fitted his key into the lock.

Bertha was particularly careful about the two chairs. She
dragged them together and they squealed on their casters.
They met his eye directly he entered. May was stretched
asleep on the sitting room couch, her cheeks still wet and her
lips, always with the sensuous look of just having been kissed
very hard, slightly, rather appealingly, apart. One of her
hands trailed to the floor and there was a pale scatter of freckles
on her arm, great isolated ones, so large and far apart that
Wallenstein could run his lips up it as if it were a flute, kissing
them one by one.

But when he finally did turn his key in the lock, it was as
if May, deeply simulating sleep, had been merely lying on the
edge of it waiting, so quickly she pounced at him, the castle of
her yellow puffs down over one ear and her right eye dragged
upward from lying on it.

"May! My dear——"

"Yah, 'dear'—you'd better 'dear' me—leaving me shut up here
day after day with a lunatic. Well, you don't need to go no
further to hear her side of the story with her lies, lies, lies!
You can hear it right here from me. Either that old woman

gets out of this house—here—now—to-night—or I go! As God is my witness—I'm through!"

All the little wrinkles came running into his face like sand over paper and he tried to take her in his arms.

"Oh no, you don't! Not this time. A few smooth words can't make up for the all-day hell of living in this house. That old woman goes or I go! I couldn't stand another day of it. You've been a long time choosing, but you've got to chose now! I've tried. I've bit my tongue in two trying. But I'm done."

"Why, May," he said in the sedative tone that must have worn a little rut along his vocal cords from the repetition of it. "I know that Ma's not easy, and there's not a day that I don't think of my girl at home under conditions that aren't just right for her, but she's old, May, and she means well and—and good God, May, a man's mother is a man's mother, little eccentricities and all."

"No—no—we ain't going to argue any more, not while my dress buttons up the back with tiddlywinks. I've been over it all till I'm as crazy loony as she is. You got to decide. This time it's me or her. One of us gets out!"

His nose was like a blade, the nostrils sort of drawn in by the sharpness of his breath, and he stood under the hall light, growing paler and paler as the fatigue lines deepened.

"May! you've never been like this! Has anything unusual happened? My mother—how—where is she?"

"Oh no! Nothing unusual. Just the usual. That's the devil of it! Just the usual, but the camel's back broke to-day. There's no argument. There's just for you to decide which of us gets out." Her body was bent backward in a curve and her head dangling, as if it were a pale lantern weighing down the bamboo pole of her body.

He looked at her and at the shine of her flesh up at him through the lace of her bodice and the old familiar trembling seized him, but he dug with his nails into his palms and his words were all crowded behind his teeth.

"Well then by God—you go!"

It was as if he had stabbed her in the up-thrust of bosom she could always dazzle him with, because she threw out her arms and stood like a great open fan, with the finery of her sleeve drapes falling to the floor.

"Me!"

"You," he said, "yes—yes—you——"

"You don't mean that—Wally."

"I do," he said, still with the jam of words behind his teeth.

For the first time her body sort of unwound itself of its tight theatricalism and she looked at him with her mouth shaped to cry out, but it only quivered.

"If anybody goes out of this house, it's not going to be my mother. Get that! I may be low—but not that low. She stays here!"

"You heard what I got to say," she said.

"Yes, I heard," he said, and looked at her steadily and without the flicker of a muscle. "I heard."

There was a pause that was full of their breathing and then with a lightning gesture she darted out for his hand, but he was too quick for her.

"Wally!"

"No," he said, holding it behind him, "no, none of that."

She darted again and he looked at her coldly and smiled, holding himself on a little oblique that eluded her.

"That don't go this time, May. I'm at the end of my rope here. You have been called upon to make certain sacrifices. I know that. And I don't say they have always been easy ones. But that's part of this game of marriage. Learning to take the hurdles. You haven't taken yours. There's no argument here. Between two women, one of them young and able to take care of herself, and the other seventy years old and—my mother—well, if it's a case of one of them having to go, it's not going to be my mother! This is one of those deadlocks in marriage where there is no solution. A woman either gives in or she—don't. You don't!"

With his body thrust back from her, the words in her mouth were meal, and she knew it and suddenly, with a sinuosity that was rare with her, she had her arms about his knees and her cheek to him and her sobs coming, so that even through the fabric of suiting her warm breath reached him.

"Wally!"

He wrenched himself, but the vise of her arms was relentless, and so with his head held up and his body still tense he stood taut, feeling the tremor of her and finally the wet of her tears—warm—warm—against his knee.

"Get up," he said, with his head back and his body away from her.

"Wally—Wally—for God's sake don't—don't throw me off for her—Wally——."

"Off! Good God, what's a man to do—murder an old woman to get her out of the way of a young one—God—God—what mess have I let myself into! God—God—May—don't——."

"Wally"—her hands were up now against his waistcoat, so that the shape of them burned through, and his face, which he kept averted, was reddening, a slow red that ran down into his collar.

"You can't get me that—way—any—more——" he said, and caught her two hands by the wrists and flung her backward, but she was too quick for him again, and, as if from the momentum of the shove, she was back again, with her arms about his neck, and her lips which were shining with tears, straight and pat against his.

"No—No—May—none of that—no—I say—oh——"

Suddenly it was quiet, and when he lifted his head she was crouched in a cradle his arms made for her and the tears were running heavily down his cheeks.

"I'm tired," he said, crying frankly and daubing his eyes with the back of her hand, "—dog tired" and sank down on a chair in the hallway and she dragged up a stool, an outlandish one on the four curved horns of a bull, and her arms were about his knees again and her shining lips always close enough for him to feel the breath.

"You love me, Wally—I love you—what's the use—you can't give me up——"

He beat his knees.

"God. God. Was ever a man in my plight? I can't give you up. Well, where does that get me? I can't give her up, and the two of you together are making my home a hell. I'm cursed *with* you and I'm cursed without you. God, God, was ever a man in such hell? I'll be the one to get out—by God—I'll end it—I'll be the one to get out——"

"Wally—Wally, that won't solve anything. That will bust it up for all three. I've got a way out for us. Wally, it's the old woman. I tell you she—she's got to go!"

"And, by God, I tell you, no! My mother doesn't pine out her days alone in a rooming house——"

"No—no, Wally, you don't understand. Why I— you think I'd let her pine out her days in a rooming house? The old woman's sick, Wally. Her mind's sick. The old woman needs a hospital—a fine sunny big hospital where they can take care of her——"

"My mother's not sick—she's—she's old—she's orthodox and she believes so strong it makes her eccentric—she's not sick——."

"She is, Wally. Any doctor would say so. You don't see her all day in the house like I do. You're making me live with a lunatic, Wally."

"You—take that back!"

"You don't know it. But I do. She sits all day talking to herself. I'm afraid of her. I wouldn't ask you to throw her out, Wally. I'm telling you she's got screws loose. She can get violent any time and then you *will* have trouble. There's institutions. Fine sunny clean ones. She ought to be committed. It's the only way, Wally—to save her—and to save us. You want us to go to hell over a—a loon? Lots of people go crazy on religion—the old woman, Wally—has screws loose— it's against the law not to give her medical treatment—there's plenty places, Wally—fine clean places where they don't even know they're in that kind of a place where she can live in peace and we can stay here in peace. Wally, are you going to throw me over for a poor old woman that's lost her mind? I tell you she's crazy, Wally. What'll you have out of it if I get out and leave you here with a loon? You got to support me. No man can get away without doing his duty to me. You got her and you got me any way you look at it. If one of us got to go, the poor crazy old lady ought to be the one. Get her in a—

an—asy—a—hospital, Wally—and that'll leave us here—in our home—together. Wally—poor, tired Wally—home alone—here with his May."

His head fell down against the little cove of her shoulder and he could feel her warm kisses through his hair, and finally when he looked up with the stricken eyes of a St. Bernard dog, the tears ran down over his words.

"I can't give you up, May. My poor mother—she's sick—she needs the best of care—best—institution—she's sick—and she's got—to—go——"

Tears. Tears. The dining room looked crazy through the blur of them, and setting out the salt cellars and the vinegar cruet Bertha could scarcely find the table. It waved up at her. Tilted. Ran in little ripples that the tears made. Tears. Tears. The old woman——

She ran down the hall. It shot off in a little ell and on the slant of wall was the door. The door that was between the old woman and the knowing. The bitter knowing that must presently creep toward it and under it like a terrible tide. She crashed through the door and stood trembling in the center of the room.

The night light was burning and the old woman flew up in her vast walnut bed with a cry.

"Wally—who? Ach, Berthie, how you frightened me. I must have been dreaming. My Wally. My Julius—Berthie—it ain't nice you should rush in so on me. You've made me a pain—here. What is it, Berthie—nothing ain't wrong—Wally—home yet? Nothing ain't wrong?"

"Why—no—Mrs. Wallenstein—nothing—I yoost looked in a minute—maybe you want something?"

"No—I—Berthie—you shouldn't rush in so—a pain here—from the fright you gave me—such a pain—my heart—ach no—Berthie—I can't lay down—it's a knife in me—you frightened me so—my heart——"

Her face was so little, and back in the frill of her cap a pointed sort of receding look had set in, and she writhed up from the support of Bertha's arm, against the pain of lying back on the pillows.

"My drops—quick, Berthie—my drops. I—you shouldn't have frightened me—quick—my drops from the doctor."

There they stood, the little colorless phial of them on the table beside the bed. Five of them. Bertha knew how—drop-drop-drop-drop-drop—into a tumbler.

"Berthie—please——"

"No, Mrs. Wallenstein—no—yoost—lay still—— No, not any drops this time—sleep—sh-h-h—no drops—sleep."

"I—my drops—pain—I—I'm so tired, Berthie—hold me—you frightened me so—I was dreaming—my boy—she didn't get him—away from me—she tried, Berthie—I dreamed—but she didn't—he wouldn't—my boy—he stuck to his mama—she's old—she's in the way—but he stuck—why don't you give me my drops, Berthie? I—he stuck by his mama, Berthie——"

"Yes, Mrs. Wallenstein—he stuck——"

"I—I was never so tired—my drops—you should give me my drops—dark—Berthie—yes, Julius—tired—he stuck—my boy—to his mama—didn't he, Berthie?"

"Yes, Mrs. Wallenstein—yes——"

"—tired—my—drops. Wally—oh—God—ouch—oh—oh—ah——"

A sudden lurch forward in Bertha's arms, so that her torso rounded up and left an arch of space between it and the bed.

It was hard to unbend it, because the body had stiffened, and with her cheek to Mrs. Wallenstein's heart, Bertha pressed, pressed gently until the little attitude of convulsion had straightened. It was so quiet there with her cheek to Mrs. Wallenstein's dead heart.

A doctor folded the brittle hands. Little gulls skimming the old breast. The preliminaries of death were set in motion. A soul had been set free and mortals were solemn. Almost immediately the shades somehow were down and there was a new odor. The odor of death.

May had gone out like a flame. Her face seemed suddenly very small between the two enormous blobs of pearl earrings, and she had pinned up the flowing sleeves so that she had the plucked, necky look of a fine bird that had lost its feathers, revealing the long pores of dingy flesh.

"Poor Wally. Poor Wally."

He looked at her through tear-scalded eyes that did not see her at all.

"My mother—my poor little mother—gone without a word——"

"Lots of them go that way, Wally. My old woman died in her sleep——"

"God—God, what her poor little life must have been here alone in this room—nights. Mama forgive me. Mama, forgive me."

"She was a good sleeper, Wally. I used to hear her snoring

and always tiptoe by the door. I was always careful not to wake her."

May, craven with death.

He looked at her with his eyes full up with misery, and kept repeating over and over again his phrases—"Mama forgive me. Poor little life. I knew what you suffered, mama. There wasn't an hour of the day or night it wasn't over me. I did it. I did it. Mama, mama forgive—why did you leave me——?"

"Wally, you've got your May. Poor, poor Wally, don't cry—ain't you got your May?"

He kissed her wildly, his wet lips smearing over her cheeks and the twisted, crazy look in his eyes.

"Help me—help me to bear my remorse. I used to snap her off. I never had patience with her. We left her alone when we went to the country—alone here—she might have died like a dog—she did die alone—like a dog—alone——"

"No, Wally. No. Bertha was with her!"

"Bertha! Then why didn't she give my mother her drops? She let her die like a dog. That's what the doctor asked—why didn't the person in whose arms she died, give her the drops? Murderer—where is she—get out—where is she—I want her to get out!"

And Bertha, carrying down through the gloom of the hallway the seven branch candlestick for the foot of old lady Wallenstein's bed, stood hearing, her face picked out in light above the pointing flames. A white face, floating in shadow and shining out of the darkness that poured around it.

A clear, prophetic face above the seven lights.

It was then, gazing upon her, that Wally turned on his wife and struck her three times on the very cheek that his lips had smeared. "Mama," he screamed, "forgive me," and smoking hot off his lips came words that had long since lain dead like dried roseleaves in his memory.

שמע ישראל האלהינו האחד

Then he turned around on May.

"You go," he said, with his fingers curling inward to form little cages, "go—go—while God gives me strength not to kill you. My mama—my God—my darling, heartbroken mama— you made me a traitor to her—you—you—you! Go—go—or so help me God—if ever I see you again—God strike me dead if I don't kill you."

"Wally—for God's sake—don't—don't! Let me loose. I'll go, Wally. Leave me go, Wally—for God's sake. You hurt! I'll go—Wally."

After a while it was quiet in the house. There was still the little frangipani scent of May in her room, where she had fussed about in the hysteria of packing. It followed her trail along the hallway as she backed down it in terror, her little valise, with a twist of lace caught in the fastening, held out before her. Then the hall door—and out.

Quiet. With the light from the seven candles burning against the transom and out palely into the hall, and Wally silent in there hour after hour, cramped up against the bedside of his dead.

At midnight the first Mourner sprang up. One of the Old Testament women off the stoop in Division Street, and from behind the closed door, when she slid in beside Wally, her cry went down like a rapier into the heart of the silence. A cry that stuck there to the hilt.

Toward morning when the Mourner dozed in a rocker at the foot of the old woman's bed, Wally, who had never moved from his crouch at the headboard, sprang up suddenly, his hair torn down over his face, but his eyes clear.

"Bertha," he called, and ran out to the hallway and into her room. "Bertha—you—you knew! Bertha—you cook! Bertha — Bertha — come — back — Bertha — I see it now — Bertha——"

At that moment, in a dawn that ran thinly along the edge of the roofs, Bertha with her carpetbag hooked to her fingers was walking. East. A wettish wind, the wind before the dawn, blew her all forward. Her skirts. Some strands of her paling yellow hair and the terribly dilapidated old rose on her hat.

There were no pedestrians. Not even milk carts yet. Only Bertha, walking before the wind.

Annie Wennerberg was on her back. Tied in a knot there on a cot of a rheumatism that made bulbs of her knuckles, and swelled up her legs as if they had been great goatskin water bags.

It was horrid, coming out of the clear morning, to walk in on her, tucked way back in the lurking room she shared with the Australian sailor when he was in port.

An iron shutter from the warehouse next door blocked the window, so that it was dark and the jet of gas burned in there all day and kept the smells warm. A sickening, stinking room, with Annie knotted into it as fast to its walls as a fungus.

And Annie in all her knots of pain, looked fat—a swollen fat that was the color of the goatskin water bags.

There were several pillows in their dingy tickings stacked behind Annie's back, and a gray blanket wrapped around her legs that were as lifeless looking as an old bundle. Jocko slept up against them.

A child of about fourteen, with a three-cornered face and a three-cornered shawl spanning her little shoulders that were held in as if from the shivers, was spreading a thick paste along a bit of cloth. Antiphlogistine.

Bertha knew. The poultices like those she had made for Annie when she herself was a child! And the cry that met Bertha as she entered. She knew that, too. A whinny.

"I'm sick as a dog—lying here nine weeks come next Monday. My joints won't untie. Nobody to do a turn. You're a lunk or you'd look in on a body year in and year out. Me that raised you and fed you when your tongue might have been hanging out for want of a home. Clean me up—Bertha. There's eight cots upstairs walking away with themselves, and only this brat doing the work of 'em. There's a fruit freighter of boys in to-morrow—clean me up—Bertha."

And so that morning, with her carpetbag and coat on a chair in the kitchen, Bertha moved Annie out of the hot, unaired nest of her blanket, rubbed her with a liniment the doctor from the clinic had left, combed out the gray dribble of hair, and got her back somehow into the knot that was easiest for her to lie in. Poor Annie cried out at Bertha lifting her ever so gently from her huddle, and the little girl's shoulders shivered narrower together, and Jocko let himself be dragged along with the blanket sooner than uncurl out of his warmth. Annie wanted gin terribly and screamed for it. Its acid was what was burning in her joints, but at noon she finally fell asleep, shuddering and groaning. That afternoon, on her hands and knees, Bertha washed down two of the dirty flights of stairs, did the unmentionable chores of slops and bedding, turned over a drunken sailor on his cot, and washed open his grit-bound eyes.

For eleven months, while Annie slowly untwisted and the swelling went down, Bertha scrubbed these floors, tended the twenty cots, and helped countless drunken sailors to bed by pulling off their heavy shoes and piling them, like great lolling sacks of potatoes, underneath the thin gray blankets, sometimes hoisting them upstairs by the armpits, with an occasional boost of her knee from the rear.

One boy died up there one night of delirium tremens. No one could get hold of his arms to twist them behind him. Bertha did finally, squatting on his head as if he were a fallen horse, while a sailor sat on his feet and still another on his middle. He was a Scandinavian with a thin blond beard and a neck as lovely as a woman's. With his wrists tied together he lay back in Bertha's arms. She held him across her lap, he kicking and plunging his shoulders this way and that. It was horrible to feel his great body fling back against her knees and the strange foreign words flying on flecks of foam from his lips. She began to croon to him one of the Polish melodies that she knew somehow with her heart. He turned his eyes to her, and watching the little beating movement her throat made as she sat singing there in the dirty gas light, began to grow quiet. She unloosed his hands. Finally, when the ambulance came he was asleep, with his cheek to her heart and one arm about her neck, like a child. Dead.

Months of these fantastic, sailor-infested nights. Night after night of brawl after brawl. The slapping of hands against the walls of the narrow hallways from the lurching this

way and that.  Little yellow seamen with eyes that could seem
to hang in the darkness of those halls long after they had
passed through it.  Slant gashes.  The squawks and cries of
men bestial in their sleep or dreaming of thirst and typhoon,
mutiny and sudden death.

The lowing of steamers.  Enormous cries, as if a strange
breed of sea cattle were swimming in with the tide.

Wide, impersonal nights that the sense of the nearness of
the sea could make seem vast and booming.  And all these
little men of every clime groping in its enormous darkness,
dreaming their puny bestial dreams into it, cowing away from
the stars, most of them, on their bellies up there on Annie's
cots, their lids granulated and their breathing sour.

Chita, the little slavey, came every day.  She was one of
fourteen children in a Minetta Lane tenement and she was as
wiry as Jocko and as quick upstairs and down.  She never
ran her errands but rode her way, curled up in a little
cocoon on the back of a truck and dodging the driver's each
crack of the whip.  She could sidestep a blow from Annie with
one beautiful curve of her little body, and once she ran up
Bertha's great flank, for all the world like Jocko, and turned
a double somersault down off her shoulder.

In winter her hands bled from chapping and her little nose
was horrid and her eyes grew into great disks as her face
became smaller under the pinch of cold.

Bertha bought her a reefer and mittens at the Sailors'
Supply Store and hemmed her two muslin handkerchiefs, which
she bunched into dirty little wads, and immediately lost.

She was as incessant as a buzz. Quick, capering, noiseless on her feet. Never actually ill, but always with the head colds and her little arms so skinny that it hurt to see them strain to lift a pail.

This was little Chita who came, as that slow damp winter wore on, to live in the big, dim shadow of Bertha. She was fourteen and Bertha, who knew what the sailors could say in their bestial dreams, kept her close.

It was not a cold year, only sullen and penetrating and full of soot. Bertha and Chita were covered with it. It blew in on the plumes of smoke off the harbor tugs. The furnace belched it out at them. Chita's little face was like a feeble light behind her mask of this soot and, looking in a straight line down her own nose, Bertha could see the black marks, smeared along the flesh.

Sometimes the sailors sent Chita out for stogies or tobacco or beer. She was greedy of the pennies and foreign coins they threw, sometimes sucking them up under her tongue all day and holding her mouth grim and tight when Bertha tried to pry in a finger to force them out.

A long winter that, more like a cloudy November dusk. Annie knotted into her bed and looking out through the door of her room, which she always kept open, upon the two of them moving so tirelessly upstairs and down, at slops, scrubbing until the wet stench rose, and when a fruit steamer or a freighter came in, running with the gray blankets and the pillows.

Chita feared Annie and the vituperative words. She seemed to shrink and the disks of her eyes to become larger. Annie's hands were too crippled to strike her, but all the same she

would quiver back, her arm dodging up before her eyes, and
the great bony bulbs of her knees clicking together.

But in the shadow of Bertha it was safe. There she could
play around with Jocko, herself so curiously like Jocko, cheat-
ing on the job outrageously. They would start, she and Bertha,
at the opposite ends of a floor, scrubbing toward the center,
only Chita never arrived. She liked to sit in a huddle and rock
herself, arms locked about her ankles and chitter—chitter questions at the great crawling hulk of Bertha as she came scrubbing toward her on all fours, her arm plunging from the socket
and sweeping its great circle of dirty suds.

Darting, steely little questions that she threw like knives
in mumblety-peg, landing them straight up.

"Bertha, b'Jesus— Whozee? Huh?"

"Jesus? He was a man, Chita."

"A man nawthin'! He's God."

"He bane a perfect man."

"Bloke, you! God wusn't a man. God, he had curls and a
white dress."

"Yah—He—was drenched in Light—that was his white
dress."

"Bloke, you! Light ain't no white dress. Silk is. That's
you!" said Chita and slid out with her palm a splash of greasy
water from her scrub pail upon Bertha—"that's you—drenched
in slop."

Bertha boxed her then, roundly against the ear, so that the
little imp, strung on her wires of legs, jumped and dangled.

"You bane a—a bad rowdy—brat—."

"Bertha—drenched in—slop—."

She looked down to fleck off some webby stuff that had clung
to her gray woolen skirt.

"Slop cannot drench—like Light!"

"What light?"

"His!"

"Aw you—square head—there ain't no light."

"Aw you—curly head, there ain't unless you see it."

Sometimes Bertha kissed her, right down into the riot of short curls that rose off her head like the suds of a shampoo.

But Chita was nervous and vicious from being afraid. Once she bit Bertha on the lips until they bled.

"Bloke, you fooled me—diden you? Bloke you! I thought you wuz gonna hit."

Chita had black and blue marks on her arms and down her lean little legs. Usually when she came to work in the morning she could display new ones. Not without pride.

"Me mudder give me this one. Me old man. Me brud! Look at 'em and make a snoot, Bertha."

The sight of these blue and green bruises, burning there so sullenly along the tan little limbs of Chita, could cause Bertha's lips to fold back in a quivering ejaculation of sickness. That was a "snoot."

"I don't know any snoots, Chita."

"There, bloke you—you're doing one now a snoot like there was somebody sticking a knife and fork in you and then cutting you up in little bittsa pieces——"

Chita was fond of the torturous phrase. She liked to devise them. Her father's favorite threat to her was, "I'll brekka your leg."

"Bertha, what if somebody 'ud cut off Annie Wennerberg's head and cook it with cabbage."

"Chita, you think only bad thoughts."

"Me brud stuck a pin in my wrist once, all the way in."

"Poor Chita."

"If I was a jackknife I'd cut all bad people's eyes out——"

"Poor Chita—it bane terrible bad for you with your people——"

"I'd slit a Chinaman if I had a butcher knife."

"Chita!"

"Looka, he gimme this—me old man—he pinched—look—make a snoot now—look—ouch—don't touch."

It was a savage-looking black and blue mark on her shoulder, and one day it began to fester and Chita, a little stoic for pain, started whimpering and reaching up her lower lip to suck in the tears.

Squatting in their puddles, as they scrubbed toward one another down one of the pitch-black upper halls, Bertha, who had grown bold in words with this child, began to piece out a story to soothe her.

"Don't cry, Chita."

"Hurts.   Hurts."

"Poor little Chita your tears are falling right in the scrub-bucket——"

"I hurt so, Bertha——"

"Sh-h, don't cry, Chita.   Once upon a time, there was a good little girl like you——"

"Me?"

"Yah.   She cried too, little Chita, because her wounds they hurt."

"Pinches, like mine."

"Yah, pinches."

"An' bloody sores—I got bloody sores, too——"

"And bloody sores——"

"And she lived by the ocean——"

"The Cunard piers?"

"No—no—out somewhere—old countree—a gray ocean—with rocks——"

"Old countree. Naples is old countree——"

"It was lonely by the ocean. Sometimes she cried much."

"No mudder—no brud?"

"Nobody. Only wind that tore her and rain that wet her and snow that froze her."

"No bread? No spagett'?"

"Sometimes a fisherman out of a boat on the sea brought her fish——"

"A beau——"

"N-no—yoost—a man."

"Did he like 'er?"

"She—could—clean—fish——"

"Ugh!"

"But that was yoost ugly to her hands and she did not mind."

"Phew!"

"She used to cry—sometimes because it was so beautiful—the rocks and the sea—or so lonely—the sky and the rocks and the sea—so big—like she felt inside of herself—big——"

"Big as—New York?"

"Yah—she used to cry—right out of her heart—into the waves—yoost like you cry into the bucket—and whadda you think?"

"What?"

"Her tears got folded up in the water of the waves and one day a little girl way off in New York——"

"Me?"

"Yah—took a drink of water and whadda you think was in the drink of water?"

"A bug!"

"The tears—the beautiful tears that the lonely girl in old countree had cried because the sea was so lonely and the sky and the rocks and the sea—so big and—and heart-breaking and——"

"She drank 'em—the same tears——"

"Yah—and whadda you think?"

"What?"

"When she drank 'em—the little girl off in New York——"

"Me?"

"Yah—they began to boil inside of her——"

"How——"

"Just boil—and swell—like waves—and she was all full—of the sky and rocks and the sea and the heart-break and whadda you think?"

"What? She busted!"

"She began to sing, Chit—the tears inside they were hurting —and she began to sing—all the beauty of the sea and the sky and the rocks and the—loneliness and the heart beauty— wasn't that grand, Chita—and from all over the people came to hear her—the most beautiful singing in the world all filled with the tears that were shed by the sea——"

"Was that me——"

"Yah—I guess so and——"

"And the girl in the old countree?"

"Oh she—I dunno—she——"

"Didn't her beau——"

"Yah—her beau—the fisherman, I guess, came one day in the fishing boat——"

"And was she glad?"

"Yah—all her tears—the beautiful tears—were gone and she went with him then——"

"To clean—the fish?"

"To—clean—the fish."

"I'd rather be me—with all the people in the world coming to hear me—than cleaning fish——"

"I dunno—Chita—I dunno——."

The upper hall was full of the black twilight and Chita in her puddle had scarcely scrubbed her way forward at all. It was Bertha who had come scouring down the hallway toward her. They met on all fours there at one end of the gloom. Chita with her little bright eyes shining in amber tunnels like Jocko's. The hulk of Bertha.

"Kiss me, Bertha."

"Oh Chita. Chita."

Something hateful happened. On Dearborn Street near Front was a pretty brick house, conspicuous for its undilapidated shutters and polished doorplate. Bertha passed it upon those rare occasions when she walked out. It was next to a meat stall, where she went to buy lamb-neck for stew. Annie's favorite dish. A small meticulous house with something of the narrow-shouldered air of a lady missionary. The little white ruching of front steps. The pious precisions. The exactitude of window shades like eyelids discreetly lowered for prayer. That polished doorplate! It has a habit of moving along sedately before Bertha's eyes to the meat stall and back again.

Society for the Prevention of Cruelty to Children. Society-for the prevention of cruelty to children.

Chita's tan, taut little body with the blue spots running up her leg. There was even one on her tiny, lovely breast. A lurid, frightening purple. And Chita's eyelids were peculiarly red at the rims and her feet inflamed looking, probably merely because she loved so to dance, but her toes were all curled under, in a prehensile fashion.

Bertha liked to rub them warm, until the blood circulated, and to anoint the bruises with the many different liniments she was lavish at buying. And the reefer! To unbutton it from its warm fastenings when Chita arrived in the morning and to button it up snugly in double-breasted fashion when Chita went home at night! Sometimes as it hung on its peg all day Bertha would button it there, and then unfasten it again. Chita's little reefer. Chita.

So resolutely, she kept her head away from that small polished sign. But even so, it was screwed to her eyes. "Society for the Prevention of Cruelty to Children." She scrubbed floors through it, she stirred stew of veal through it. She saw Chita through it. She shook open a gray blanket to make up a sailor's cot, and there it stared up at her. Society-for-the-Prevention-of-Cruelty-to-Children.

Then the something hateful happened.

There were three freighters in and the men were sleeping two on a cot, and floor pallets were to be made up, and all morning Bertha had been hoisting mattresses up the narrow stairway, even Annie, who could walk a little now, hobbling as far as the foot of the steps with an armful of pillows. Chita was like Jocko and Jocko like Chita. They scampered over banisters. Slid downstairs and rode up on Bertha's shoulder. Only with Annie about, one had to be very spry, and by noon Chita had made sixteen cots and filled all the wash pitchers. Usually

Bertha filled these for her, but Annie's eyes seemed to have the power of turning the corner of the upper halls, so Chita lugged and tugged alone and her breath came very short, and the red rims around her eyes seemed almost wet with blood.

The men began to swagger in on sea legs. Rum. The smell of it ticklingly through the hallways. Annie back in the keg room now, whacking her knees with the best of them.

"Chita—you bane tired, poor baby. You can rest now. I will do it for you."

"They hurt," said Chita and rubbing her arms began to cry. She never cried to Annie.

Bertha rubbed them, the little bony fragile things, and blew on them with her strong, hot breath. The room was in appalling disorder, the sprawling cots, the mounds of mattresses, the dirty waters of yesterday gathering scum in bowls. Thirty cots to be made and already the seamen, lurching as if the world were a deck beneath them, were sprawling in, loony with land.

One came in on her tussling with her man's task of getting mattresses laid, a Scandinavian whom she knew by the name of Tor. He was one of the troublesome ones, and he swung his arms around her waist, and she shoved him from her with a force that sent him backward, down on one of the half unfurled mattresses, and almost immediately he was asleep and she dragged him to a corner, and there he lay for twenty-two hours, like a dog, snoring.

And then suddenly, while she was dragging these mattresses into place, Bertha missed Chita. Chita who danced so nimbly in her shadow all day and ran up her shoulder like Jocko.

"Chita," she cried, and jerked the pillows this way and that as if she might have been a kitten, hiding. "Chita!"

There should have been nothing frightening about Chita bounding off that way. But suddenly the silence seemed to have a little pulse to it. It beat in Bertha's throat. And so she ran about the long ward-like room, peering under pillows and mattresses for all the world as if she were looking for the kitten.

"Chita!"

In the hallways was the hot pulsing silence too, except down in the keg room there was laughter; crazy, skating laughter.

"Chita!"

There was a closet at the end of the hall, almost as large as a room and with a skylight. It was filled with such miscellaneous old refuse as a broken chair, leaky pails, the Australian sailor's lambswool jacket, bottles, brooms, and a rusty gas stove.

Somehow, the door to this closet seemed to blow out at Bertha like a woman's skirt. She opened it. There were Chita and a young Italian sailor off a fruit ship. He had a face like a carved almond. Narrow. Slit. White. And his fingers were quick and caressing over Chita's little body, as if she had been a harp, and there she lay back in his arms, her eyes, usually as quick as Jocko's, suddenly like fresh and flowing waters that had been dammed. Stagnant and a little heavy with mud. Chita lying back there, drugged-looking and with her agile young limbs tranced. Chita—Chita lying back there with her stagnant-looking eyes and her dancing limbs that were suddenly full of a dreadful kind of languor.

The sailor oozed away. Literally. Because under Bertha's very eyes, he was gone, leaving Chita on the chair like a doll that had been cast there, along with other broken things.

"Chita——"

She began to whimper and dodge back.

"Diden do nawthin'——"

"Come here—to Bertha——"

"You can't hit me—you're not me mudder."

"Bertha won't hit you, Baby. Chita—come—to me——"

But Chita was still afraid, and it was almost like luring Jocko, to unlock her tight fingers from the chair arm, and draw her out of her tight crouch in the corner.

"I diden do nawthin'—lemme alone."

"Chita—little Chita."

It was dead in the old closet. Stale smelling. For an hour Bertha held Chita there, in her big, man-sized arms. Close. Pressing her little boniness against her breast, while the beat of her heart pounded through.

Below the men were swaggering in now, outlandish with their packs and bags of luggage, and downstairs Annie's voice, shouting for Bertha and shouting for Chita, kept screaming out oaths between greetings.

"Bertha—was I almost being bad——"

"Yes, Chita. Terribly. Terribly bad."

"I won't no more, Bertha. My Bertha. You're cryin'——"

"For you, Chita."

"No, Bertha, I'm gonna be good—Bertha—what's that on your insides? A heart—it's ticking—like a clock."

"For you, Chita."

"Tick—Bertha—for me——"

She fell asleep, and finally Annie's oaths died down in the hullabaloo of arrivals, and the great empty barracks of a room with the unmade cots and the half-furled mattresses stood waiting, and the skylight over the closet turned taupe, and down in the keg room the shoutings rose and somebody must have overturned a tray of glasses because a crash splintered the silence and, under cover of it, Bertha shook Chita gently awake and buttoned her into her reefer. It was dusk and she walked home with her down to the mouth of a filthy street on the lower West Side.

"Good night, Bertha—my—Bertha——"

"Good night—Chita—mine——"

She watched her scamper down the street, nimble once more as Jocko, and up into the black mouth of a tenement.

The way back was through a district of torchlit pushcarts and the flicker of pale wastrel faces. There was a waving light before the meat stall. The meticulous little house with the narrow shoulders of a lady missionary stood out of the glare. Neatly. The shutters were closed, but there was a fan of lit transom above the door.

Society for the Prevention of Cruelty to Children.

Ringing the bell above that small sign, a tear meandered down to the corner of Bertha's lips.

It was noon of the next day when they came to take Chita. She was washing the iron grating of a ground-floor window, the grotesque bulbs of her knees rubbing and shivering as she reached.

Bertha lifted back her wisp of furiously sooty little panties to show the purple smears. A cranberry of a little man rubbed his chin and said "M-m-m-m" and a young woman in an alpine hat opened her notebook.

"Chita—these bane good people here—to help you."

Suddenly the little monkey-like focus of Chita's gaze seemed to slide right down the bridge of her nose and up to Bertha!

"Cops!" she cried and sprang back.

"No, Chita—good people——"

"Cops! You dirty snitch. You got the cops on me—the plain closes bulls—you dirty bloke—I diden do nawthin—he was a dago sailor and he gimme a dime—that's all—you dirty square head—snitch—the lord hates a snitch—me brud'—he'll knock the stuffin's out of you—snitch you—dirty square head snitch—I'll sick me brud' on you——"

They carried Chita struggling between them into the little enclosed wagonette at the curb. A light tan omnibus with curtains at the window of the rear door.

"Chita," cried Bertha, and stood there with the tears raining down her cheeks, "Chita—mine——"

"Bloke—you—dirty—snitch—bloke!"

Against the little window of the rear door of the omnibus, her simian little furious face with the Jocko eyes and the twitchings of rage grimaced back at her.

"Bloke—dirty snitch—square-head—hate yuh—lunk——"

Chita who had loved so to listen to the tick of Bertha's heart. Chita. After a while the face became a blur.

Chita——

The window gratings were only half washed. The pail was still there.

"Chita," cried Bertha and plunged in her brush. "Oh God —my Chita—gone——"

Rub-a-dub-dub. Scrub-a-dub-dub.

Annie paid Bertha twenty dollars a month, when she paid it. Usually during these bedridden weeks of Annie's, there was a household deficit which Bertha dug down into the pocket of her gray flannel petticoat to meet.

The wad with the rubber band about it, which had a friendly way of hitting against Bertha's leg when she walked, was very light now.

At the Wallensteins' it had fattened out into quite a roll of soft dirty bills. Her wants were so meager. The Sailors' Supply Store filled them mostly, and a sliver of a shop on the Bowery where the kind of flannel waists she wore, flopped on hangers outside the door.

But invariably in the end, one way or another, Annie wormed away these little savings, so that her intervals of unemployment had a frightening way of draining her petticoat pocket. Frightening, because somehow that wad, hitting against her when she walked, meant a pad between her and she knew what! The women one passed at night with dragging hems and twitching faces. The crones picking out of refuse boxes and asleep in doorways. The girls in dreadful finery soliciting along the wharves.

That hit-hit against her leg. It could seem as if someone were walking in step with her.

Then one day the wad petered out into a mere handful of change, left from a dollar bill with which she had purchased a bottle of sarsaparilla for Jocko, who loved to drink it out of the bottle and rub his little belly.

A shudder went down her back. Ninety-five cents in silver. The hit gone from against her leg. The women one passed at night with the dragging hems. . . .

There was new management at Raussman's. An unctuous Bohemian with a pimply face sorted out the human stock. All the young girls sat in the front row with their big red hands like beef-steaks on their laps. The older women were placed against the wall. They seemed to sit hugging themselves underneath their jackets and sighed a great deal. Some of cold, because the gin fires had gone out. Some of fatigue, and some of an unutterable hopelessness that pulled down their eyelids like window shades. There was considerable traffic among the young girls in the front row. The alert Bohemian was kept busy between the telephone, the passing out of slips, and the arrival of clients.

The assorted display in the front row was in a constant state of change, as if someone kept plucking bonbons from a box and almost immediately the little fluted container would be replaced with another.

The row against the wall did not change much. The faces were grimmer and the slow frieze of them would sit sometimes uninterrupted throughout the day.

Bertha found herself in this back row of the waiting faces, most of them flecked with fear. Not Bertha's. Hers was so big and so pale. Like a light. It burned roundly and patiently through the greasy twilit days at Raussman's. But after several of the futile ones of waiting, there were just twenty-five cents left in the petticoat pocket.

Then she began to buy newspapers and pore over them. It was November and the parks were old and gray-looking and newspapers ballooned up in the wind unless you sat on one end and nailed the other to the bench with your palm.

## HELP WANTED, FEMALE

Columns of it, yet the dread of going the rounds. The women aggrieved with the servant problem, who asked abashing intimate questions, and weighed out the weekly consignment of second-grade butter and eggs for the help. The women aggrieved with the servant problem, who provided kennels for sleeping and railed at high wages for the fourteen-hour day. The dread of starting those rounds. Help Wanted, Female.

The park benches were strewn with discarded newspapers, turned almost invariably to the classified advertisement page. Sometimes a little oblong had been torn out with a hair pin or penknife. One day in City Hall Park, poring over one of these left overs, this one burned up at Bertha from its little enclosure:

> Wanted: Practical nurse to assist governess in care of five-year-old boy. Must be well trained and efficient. References. Apply W. Bixby, 3450 Madison Avenue.

It was a rowdy of a day. Whistling, prankish winds that flew up under capes and rushed newspapers along the curving walks of the park. A pecksniffy little gale that filled the air with dust and paper. Pedestrians hustled before it and the benches were pretty well swept, except for one or two hunches of men asleep under their hats and the hoppings of sparrows aiming for empty peanut hulls. And Bertha. She sat forward, her torso a little oblique as if someone had placed a broken urn there on a slant, and the look that she had lifted up from that newspaper insertion, pinioned to her face.

The city ran past her. Dived into subway hoods. Clamored over cobbles. Honked, whizzed, banged. Park Row had just spewed out a red-hot edition and the newsboys' howls ran high.

It was strange to be there in the midst of life when the heart was as dreary as a moor. Wasteland down which she could see herself stalking, brooding and terrible with the tears that were dry and sobs that were silent. She began to walk. It was very far. The city blocks streamed behind, one after another. They were so full of life. But the moor gathering around her heart, it encompassed her.

The house on Madison Avenue was as handsome and portly as a park statue of a gentleman in a frock coat. It had an air and a gracious, portentous dignity, as if any moment the double oak doors might swing back and someone important and lovely sweep down the fine curve of stone steps. Candlelight would gleam on old silver in such a house and the kettles in such a house would be of polished copper that swelled what they reflected. Fine, drum shaped kettles, that would draw the juices out of fowl.

The curtains were frilled net and did an elaborate crisscross in the center of the long windows, and then drew back to reveal the shoulder of a chair or the dim loveliness of marble statuary. A child in such a house could, if he wanted, peer out of that little open place between the curtains. He would probably leave five fingerprints against the pane. Spudgy little fingerprints that would polish off with a dry cloth. But there were no fingerprints against the panes. They were very shiny. Peer as she would with the corners of her eyes as she passed the house, up the block, down the block, there were no fingerprints against the panes.

It was easy to pass and repass. That is, if one kept shoulders bent into the wind as if with destination. There was a constant trickle of pedestrians along the fine wide avenue. One swung back and forth with the little tides. No stopping to stare, of course. Just that tail of the eye, ready!

It was a block of portly houses. Of great wide windows and curving stoops and motor cars at the curb. There were several ways of not passing up and down too often. Walking on the opposite side. Appearing to stand at a corner for the traffic to pass. Strolling around the block and loitering a little along the way.

Not even the smudge of a sprawled little palm against the window pane. How precious had there been!

Once a young woman entered the trade entrance. She had a click to her broad heels and there was a gleam of starched white under her long blue cape. The door was opened to her only the fraction of an inch and closed again, gently. She went away on heels not so clicking. Bertha, passing, could have touched her.

Almost immediately after, a big heavy-busted woman, with hair on her chin and also in white uniform that crackled under her cloak, rang the bell. Bertha knew her! A Mrs. Mahaffy! She had once tended the senile grandfather in a private house on Lexington Avenue where Bertha had cooked for a month. "Hateful Mahaffy" the waitress had called her. She was always fussing around the kitchen with trays, mostly her own, and had let the old man fall in his bath one morning, for which she was dismissed. Her arms were pock-marked too. The waitress had stumbled across a little nest of hypodermic needles under her mattress after she left.

Hateful Mahaffy!

Passive Bertha with her slow, white face. A sudden, a new, an aggressive rage laid hold of her. A frenzy that made her want to tear and strip and choke. She started after the largely undulating figure of Mrs. Mahaffy, but the one inch of door had already been opened and closed to her, so that they met on the sidewalk.

"Save yourself the trouble," said Mrs. Mahaffy, "the place is already filled."

She had a horrid kind of voice for a woman. It seemed

to want to boom because she had hair on her chin. Then she recognized Bertha.

"Wasn't we in a place together once? Lexington Avenue."

"Yah——"

"Well, you're in wrong here. Practical nurse is wanted. Big automobile moguls from Detroit. Just moved here. New-rich. Give me the new-rich every time. They got proper respect for their servants, and not too much for themselves. Well, stung here, but they're engaging a new staff in that big brown house over on the corner. Want to come with me?"

"No," said Bertha. "No."

"Well, you always was good company for yourself," said Mrs. Mahaffy and stalked off on a diagonal across the street.

Hateful Mahaffy, who, they said of her, pinched children, and had let the old man slip and break his hip. To think that hateful Mahaffy, with the boom of voice, might have gained custody over the child within that house.

Or someone like her might already have been hired! Or someone worse! Fear flashed through her. Flash after flash of it. Then again the swelling anger. Mrs. Mahaffy. She pinched children. She started across the street, striking into her solemn golem trot, her lower lip pursed out.

Mrs. Mahaffy had disappeared. She hurried a block after her, her stiff Inverness cape blowing out from her, and her face thrust out ahead.

Mrs. Mahaffy. What had she to do with it? Do with it? Why, there was a child over there in that house—five years old—who made it unbearable that any child should be pinched.

She hurried. Mrs. Mahaffy had disappeared. After a while she began to cry. Slow ashamed tears. The house looked soft through the blur of them. Almost as if you could poke in a dimple through the wall with your finger, as you could in the cheek of a child.

A man in shirt sleeves and a black apron came out of the service entrance and began to polish the brass doorbell. He was shaved to the skull, and his neck was fat, and he danced up and down from the knees as he rubbed. A gay feather duster stuck up from his rear hip pocket. He whistled. She could not tear her eyes from him. His jouncing legs and the little jelly-dance of the fat along his neck! Perhaps as recently as an hour ago—ten minutes ago—five—he had passed the five-year-old child in a hallway. That gay little duster might have flecked a chair that he had sat upon.

The excitement of that! It ran like a fever through her. She stood and looked at him. Just stood there in front of the house and watched him rubbing the bell. After a while he turned, because the irises of her eyes must by this time have been like hot disks on his back. He had a face of loose fat and the jowls fell in pleats like a spaniel's. A soft face that you could mash up softly with your hand like pie dough. Ugh.

She began to walk and he followed her by swinging his head around to glance over the other shoulder.

Perhaps so recently as an hour ago—ten minutes—five—he had passed the five-year-old in a hallway——

He winked.

Slowly and with the horrid sensation that she could softly mash up his face into pie dough, Bertha winked back.

"Fine day for a walk," he said, and sucked back his words and made a noise like a kiss.

"Yah," she said and lifted her lips back off her square white teeth to make a smile.

He was chewing something and he spat, quid and all, on to the stoop of the house adjoining.

"Big 'un, ain't you?"

"Me? I dunno——"

"Ticklish? Slk-k-k-k-k," he said, and made a sound between his tongue and his cheek. Nasty. Frightening.

"Naw."

His face was shaved, but the day's stubble of beard was out, and when he rubbed it you could hear the bristles scrape.

"Good time?"

"What?"

He bunched up his mouth again with the little hissing, kissing sound. Someone lowered a window with a slam. He flecked open his polishing rag and began to rub at the bell again.

"Wait for me a few minutes down at the drug store on Thirty-ninth. I'm off at five. Big 'un, heh?"

She moved off. That face of old dough—ugh!

It was horrible waiting. It grew dusk and she shivered and her tongue thickened and her distaste kept welling. But her feet stood rooted, sullen, there. Waiting. The ruby urn in the drug store window lit up and threw a stain on the sidewalk. He came, looking stuffed into his coat, and his derby hat sat high on his head like a rocking chair. He was short. She had not noted how short. Why, she could have almost leaned an elbow on his head and rested her cheek comfortably upon her palm.

Silly Willy.

Idiotically enough, that transpired to be his name. Willy. She was never to utter it without the aftermath of a little chime in her brain. Silly.

His soft mouth slid around so in his face. It was a little

sunken because his molar teeth were gone. Slk-k-k-k-k! He was always making that noise between his tongue and his cheek and making a boring gesture with his forefinger, Slk-k-k-k-k. He met her that way.

"Slk-k-k-k-k, you're a husky one."

"You bane a *little* one," she said with elephantine coquetry.

"I'm little," he said, "but oh my," and beat himself upon the chest.

"You bane short and I bane long, heh?"

"That's me! Little but oh my—is what they used to label me in Winnipeg."

"Oh, that bane a big fine place."

"Winnipeg! She's a dream. There's a little city with a gizzard. I was born there. My boss comes from Detroit. You know him? Ever been in a Bixby Six? That's him. Every third time you bat your eye a Bixby car runs past you."

"You bane house-man?"

"Yeh, but I don't live in. I got a room. Good time?"

"It bane a big fine house. It's a fine big family?"

"Big family! There's him and her—fine as silk—and a kid —the little devil is five——"

"You—know—him——?"

"Little devil—let me so much as be washin' the window of his nursery and he gets me down on all-fours for a ride on me back."

"Your—back——"

"To-day, if anybody be askin' you—I can feel his little heels in my shins yet——"

"You!"

"Slk-k-k-k-k! I live over there—near First Avenue. I got a room."

"He rode you—to-day——"

"He's a card—kicked my shins——"

"Will he ride you to-morrow——?"

"Mebbe."

"You like me?"

He threw up a killing glance from under his rocking-chair derby and poked her under the cape with his forefinger.

"Slk-k-k-k-k."

They turned down a crosstown street that ran toward First Avenue.

Willy's room was over a garage where a great mercantile establishment kept its regiment of trucks. It was large, with one end filled with traces; the body of an old horse-drawn delivery wagon and some old leather harnesses that smelled.

The front part of the room had a bed and a chair and a table and a small stove the shape of a snow man. Bertha hung some muslin portières up one day. That cut the room in two and shut off the wagon top, with a red star and R. H. Stacy and Company painted across it. This seemed to move the chair, the table, the bed, and the stove into a cozier propinquity. Otherwise, it was rather an awful room. It stood there cold and mean and bare all day, scarcely more than a kennel, waiting for the occupants who called it home, to creep back into it at night.

Willy usually came first. It was a straight cut cross town, from the house on Madison Avenue. Bertha's hours were more irregular. Her work took her far and wide.

Once, during Christmas holidays, an agency on East Twenty-third Street which kept her constantly supplied with day-work sent her, along with a staff, to clean a schoolhouse on East One Hundred and Ninety-second Street. It was ten o'clock before she climbed to the room.

Willy was asleep on the bed with his shoes on and his derby hat over his face. There was no fire and no supper. Willy could cook. He had always lived off like this in a room with a bed and a stove. But with the advent of Bertha an atavism cropped out in him. The stove might be laid, but unless she struck the match, there was no fire. It was easier to be cold and hungry and lie on the bed with his derby over his face, waiting.

"You're a lunk," Bertha cried one night and hit him across the soles of his shoes with a poker, as he lay stretched and waiting on top of the bed.

"Then get out," he said, and turned over and dozed off until the fire began to crackle in the round little belly of the stove and the strong smell of tripe stew to wind through the room.

He was vicious, but in the small ways that a terrier can be vicious. Yappy. Snappy. But the crack of a whip could curl his legs under him and make him slink. He had the mind of a child. Colored picture cards amused. He could not drink, and what he chewed was tobacco substitute, and his pockets were filled with bits of bright glass and twine and pencil stubs and old screws. Even his vices were not man size. He was sly and he was a thief, but he stole only pennies and doll's eyes and no one in the Bixby household could call a penknife or scratch-pad his own. He was constantly filching the smaller coins from Bertha's pocketbook. Coppers. She could feel his hand steal under the leather cushion that was her pillow and would lie there in the darkness with her eyes wide open, looking at the dim white smear his teeth made across the darkness when he laid them bare in his effort at stealth.

Silly Willy. He was not even a man. That made it less horrible, even while it made it more horrible. She slept on the other side of the muslin curtain, on the long leather seat of the old delivery wagon. It made quite a couch. Only her feet dangled off, and she could crowd them in if she drew up her knees. It was almost private, except that he liked to peer through to see the gleam of her hair. Unbound it fell in a slow cascade of heavy, solemn, taffy-looking yellow.

"Get out! Sca-at!"

He didn't always, and had to be pushed out like a hateful boy. She despised him and was never free of the feeling that his face was boneless and made of dough, and that by the pressure of her palm against it something terrifying and featureless would be left there before her.

And yet when Bertha came home from work with her pulpous brown butcher's package, and her arms stinging from lye water and the sockets aching, sometimes she could not run up the stairs fast enough, skinning her shins and stumbling in her haste.

Willy would be there. Silly Willy. And he could show her the very spot along his back where the boy had straddled, riding him horseback and kicking into his shins. Once he had come home with the skin on his arm torn. The boy had flecked him too hard with a whip. Bertha washed it and kissed it. Kissed that wound on the hairless arm of Silly Willy.

It was easy to make him talk. A sack of little cone-shaped chocolate drops would accomplish it, or a new screw driver, or a roll of adhesive plaster. Any little tinkery thing. And because he was sly, he would only answer Slk-k-k-k-k to her questions until she produced the bribe. It never bothered him to know the why of her trembling interest in the boy. He just was silly and would talk for a cone-shaped chocolate drop.

Sometimes at the Bixby house, instead of his emptying ashes or washing windows or polishing brass, they would detain him in the nursery on a rainy day to play those straddling floor games that the starchy nurse could not manage. Silly Willy could amble on all fours for hours. He would buckle on a leather harness that had bells, shake himself and roar, and the boy, straddling his back, would kick with his heels and shout.

Silly Willy was good at these games. He played them sincerely and with the mind of a child.

Sometimes the boy stole down to the furnace rooms, where Willy kept fires banked, and looked with solemn pools of eyes into the red maw of the boiler. He had rather a frail, choir-boy face with long cheeks and very straight yellow bangs which came down to his brows. He could stare into the fire until the black irises almost crowded out the blue in his eyes and his cheeks began to redden. He liked fire. It fascinated him. Infuriated him. He would contemplate it, then catch up a broom and ride hobby-horse astride it like one possessed. Usually Willy followed, more feebly, on a second broomstick.

His nurse or his mother usually precipitated this and Willy on his springy knees would wabble back to the fire, to feed it, to sit in its red stain, and to chuckle.

Sometimes in good outdoor weather or with the family away, there would be no sign of the boy for days, for weeks. That was dull for Willie. He liked to play. But Willie was sly.

For a bag of the chocolate drops or a screw or a ball of twine, he would invent the day's encounter with the boy. Nothing very ingenious. Willy's imagination was a feeble affair. Just a sort of refurbishings of oft told tales.

Bertha did not mind. No sooner had they sat down with their dish of dinner steaming up between them, than her hand made its insidious curve down toward her pocket.

And then without any particular preamble Willy would begin: "He's a devil for fire. He is. Gets his owl eyes full of it from staring and then goes crazy with it. He's a fire horse. So am I. We're a team of fire horses."

"Willy—that's a dangerous play!"

"Dangerous! You got to straddle your horse tight. That's all. Hold 'im in—is what I tells him—hold 'im in and you're all right."

"Is he strong enough to hold 'im in?"

"Naw. That's where I come in. Slk-k-k-k! I rein him up!"

"Willy—tell me again—what does he look like—the little boy?"

"Didn't I tell you—again and again and again——"

"Yoost once—more, Willy."

"Is it chocolates? Gimme."

"What does he look like?"

"He's a boy—he is, with eyes and hair——"

"Yellow, Willy? His hair bane yellow—like mine?"

"It's yellow all right."

"He's a big boy, Willy?"

"I showed you on the wall—he bane that high."

"That was last week—he bane bigger now?"

"Aw—not quick—like that—gimme what you've got. Chocolate?"

She handed him the sack of cones, for his dessert.

One evening over the strong smell of their kidney stew he screwed up his eyes at her!

"I give him one—to-day."

"What?"

His eyes looked sly and almost at once that frightened her. "What—Willy——?"

They disappeared as if dough had crowded up around two raisins.

"Willy—one what?"

"One of my chocolates!"

She rose up sudden and threatening as an apparition, her two arms towering as if they would crash down upon him, and he cowed in his chair with his mouth fallen open.

"You gave him from those——"

"Yeh——"

"He ate——"

"Naw—we put it in the fire. It melted up. Get away. You!"

She came down from the great towering gesture of her wrath, which he interpreted not at all, and her fingers unclenched and the blood went back into her face. She shook him then, by the scroff of his coat until his head bobbed loosely.

"Don't you ever—don't you ever again—give him those ten cent cones."

"Stingy-gut, Slk-k-k-k-k—I only gave one——"

"Never. You hear, Willy. It bane bad for the boy. You —you'll get fired. Make him sick. I'll bring you chocolates for him. Not your kind. Chocolates for him——"

"Yeh, we're fire horses."

Chocolates for him! She could not sleep that night. Her feet kept plunging off the end of the seat and sometimes she sat up in the leather-smelling darkness because she breathed too fast and felt crowded.

She bought a dollar box the next day. A red paper affair with a dog and a boy on the cover. Stale bonbons that had lain in the incandescent glare of a Third Avenue window for weeks.

The boy never received them. Bertha did not know, but he had been in Asheville, North Carolina, for three weeks with his foster parents. Willy ate the chocolates beside the glow of his furnace, popping them whole into his mouth.

Willy had slacked. Shamefully. He no longer paid the rent for the room, eight dollars a month. Bertha did. The first time she did it because he wanted a tool chest for seven dollars and eighty-five cents in a First Avenue show window. After that he never paid anything. Bertha didn't demur. It was too precious, coming home in the evening to Willy who that very day might have been galloping like a fire horse for the boy.

Tools. They grew in a pile. His complete earnings, forty dollars a month, went into them. He liked to sit and polish them. Test the ductility of saws, run his plane around the floor for the curl of the shavings. There were boxes of nails in assorted sizes. Screws. Gimlets of every graduated variety. He could bore with them for an entire evening into a bit of plank or the flank of the old delivery wagon top. Bore and bore with a little mousy sound. He liked that best. Slk-k-k-k-k! He never made anything. Only bored and sawed and piddled.

Sometimes Bertha sewed. Made the muslin portières. Patched his denim house-jacket.

Usually she was so tired evenings that to the sound of the mousy borings she fell asleep behind her portières. Day-work was draining. It was like undergoing the dreadful preliminaries of a new job each morning.

"You can put your shoes there under the sink and there's a chair down in the basement where you can hang your hat and coat. You don't go stocking-footed, do you? Gracious, that agency is getting the limit for day-help. Here's a pail and a mop. You can scrub this whole courtyard in a morning, if you're spry. My former girl did it before she got consumption. If that drain there backs water on you, ram your arm down."

Day after day of it. Day-jobs where the residuum of dirty work was apt to lie waiting and accumulated. Wet, sloppy, puddled days. Cold, gaunt houses about to be occupied. Public buildings with rooms full of the stench of neglect. Once, at a fishmonger's, scales clung to her arms. Shining fish scales that hung to the flesh like burrs and would not wash off. She scrubbed at the faucet, and suddenly panic of them, the wet, slimy things, seized her and she screamed. The fishmonger, enormous and stained and with a mallet for pounding down codfish steaks in his hand, came and plucked off a few of them for her and laughed, and then, because her arm was white and firm, kissed her with wet, fish-smelling lips. She struck him with his own mallet by jerking back his arm until he hit himself in the head, and in his rage he struck back and she went home discharged and with a blue welt coming out above her cheek bone.

Cold dirty days. Then hot days, equally dirty.

That way the months swung around and, through the poor silly eyes of Willy, she beheld the boy grow older.

And as the eyes of Willy became sillier, and the face around them more and more horridly doughy, Bertha, who hated him, was glad. As he receded more and more into childishness, he played with the mind and the heart of an innocent. Sometimes, on spring evenings, after his supper, he joined the street boys at baseball or swapped some of his shiny screws for chinies. Bertha, sitting up behind the window curtain, would watch him. Carefully. He was kind to children.

He had come to hate her in a sly and secret kind of way. He was cunning enough to know she paid the rent and bought the meat for stews and that, by grace of her, the stack of his shining tools grew high, but there festered in him, day by day, the desire to torture her.

The same impulse, doubtless, that led him to delight in tearing off the wings of flies. Or perhaps dimly she was to him the badge of his impotence, and so he smouldered against her and hated. He had never been a man, and yet the pangs of impotence made him more horrible than he might have been with desire.

He liked to grimace at her with every torturous twist of feature he could connive. To awaken her by hanging over her couch with his face all drooly and loose of feature like an idiot's, and his hands drooping loosely from the wrists so that they swept her face.

The horror of this made her wild. She would tremble for an entire day from the start of waking up to this loose, drooling face of Willy's. He was devilish at these little abuses. One day he brought the window sharply on her hands as she leaned over the sill, so that it made her finger nails blue. He

never failed to scratch down deeply into her palms if he had
occasion to take anything from her, and one evening he wanted
to hand her the red hot poker and when she saw the ruse and
held the hand behind her, he brought it down on her shoulder
so that it singed her waist and the flesh.

But he was kind to children.

There was only about one way to deal with him. To slap
him. Usually, with his ears boxed, he could be trusted to trot
over to his tools and begin to plane or bore. Sometimes the
cartwright's child next door would come to play. Together
they would set up the racket of carpentry. Particularly with
the plane, improvising mustachios and fierce whiskers out
of the shavings. Sometimes he carried a handful of the
shavings to the boy.

The mystery of the will to live. Not a morning but what
Bertha knew the terrible reluctance of awakening to reality.
She came up out of sleep with a struggle, fighting off another
day; turning her back to it and lying there sick with its
imminence as the muslin portières began to lighten. To come
out of sleep so enamored of it that to feel the lids lift back
from the eyes was torture. To die a little every night and
yet fear the beauty of death more than the starkness of life.
Sometimes when Bertha came up out of sleep, fighting and
sobbing against the awakening and the grimacing face of Willy
hung over her terrible with reality, the impulse to throttle herself back to sleep seemed too strong to withstand. And yet
that wink of dawn against the muslin. The tiny vibratory
messages of life that were waiting to run across the floor when
her bare feet would swing down to it. Ah, that will to live.

The little runs of life at her from all directions. The cartwright in his shop next door was already striking sparks off

an iron bar. She could hear the deep-throated sledge hammer. The mystery of the will to live. The mystery of the cartwright's arm, that could make the iron boom. And so morning after morning she rose, and wrapped the gunny sack she wore for an apron into its wad of newspaper, and trotted off to the agency that seldom failed to have a day's assignment awaiting her.

Days of rub-a-dub-dub. As if the floor of the universe were an enormous penny to be scoured and polished, and the emblem on the coin was the face of the boy.

Almost three weeks of the November of that year were so sleet riddled that the city seemed merely glimpsed through bead portières. Horses danced on their haunches and smote sparks. Shrubbery was embalmed under ice, and urban trees stood like fountains whose ornamental waters had frozen as they curved.

That year the Inverness cape fell literally to pieces like "the one hoss shay." An uncompromising death. The weave simply would not hold the thread and the patches fell off in scales. She bought a reefer at the Sailors' Supply Store. It buttoned about her warmly enough, but it reached only to her hips and the cold got through to her legs and, worse than that, the sleeves were too short and too tight and the armholes cut her. There were always red rims on her flesh where she had strained through the harsh prison of this reefer, and at the very first wearing a seam at the shoulder opened in a grin.

Chita's reefer had been like this one, only smaller. It was hard to disassociate reefers from Chita. Sometimes, buttoning it up, it was almost as if Chita's eyes popped through the buttonholes with a wink. A row of Chita's hard, bright, suffering little eyes down the front of her jacket.

Ah me—Chita——.

Lashing its tail, November plunged on. It was pitch dark at six in the morning and sometimes after their breakfast of tripe-stew and strong coffee she had literally to take Willy by the wrist and lead him to his corner. He cried when it was cold, like a child, and would run along the sidewalks wringing his hands as if they would fall off, and crying and whimpering with the pain.

Bertha hated him for this. Once he came home with a red welt across his neck where the boy had stropped him soundly as he came in crying one day with the cold.

Bertha knew why, exultantly. He hated what she hated. Sniveling, mewling Willy.

The agency opened at seven. First come, first served. For almost a week the water froze everywhere in the pipes and there was no work. One of these days she was put at swabbing out the lobbies and lavatories of a theater, where the water was hot and plentiful and plunged out from the faucets in great clouds of steam.

She had never been in a theater. This one was on Broadway near Twenty-seventh Street, and its lobby was already bombastic with the sunrise of the cinema. Promises in lithograph. Empyrean ecstasies in three colors, of girl-cheek to boy-cheek. That swoop of the senses to a woman's figure with her dilated eyes upside down, as she hurtled head first off a trestle. A circus for the emotions here, the human heart their trapeze.

All the forenoon she swabbed the tiled floors, worming with her rag in between the feet of the little groups that stood before these posters of escape. Snow-caked shoes. The feet of the city. Gay feet, old feet, young feet, tired feet. The square little feet of children and the bulbous feet that had grown lopsided with the journey. Skulking feet with soft soles and eager feet with kicked toes. Little girls' feet with tassels and the feet of a crone wrapped in gunny sacks. Derelict boats. In, out, among those feet all forenoon. The feet of the seekers after surcease from reality.

After noon an attendant with a festoon of gold braid across his breast, threw open one of the baize green doors. The feet began to turn into the theater. Eager pushing feet with little runs to them.

After a while Bertha was sent inside, too. There were lavatories to be swabbed.

It was dark there and flesh smelling and slanting. To Bertha, as if she were walking down an incline into the drown of phantom plush. She floundered and her pail made a ringing noise and that brought her up suddenly, behind the curtain of a box. . . .

Square gem of light mounted on facets of darkness. A green field flowing gently toward her, and a child with a handful of flowers plucked up out of that field turning to smile at her with lips that the darkness sped up against hers, pucker and all. Silence that began to throb like the felon that sometimes attacked her third finger. It was the organ rumbling up into a prelude. A chord came through like a wave breaking. She slid in. The music of the chimes goldily—

Then the lettering. It was difficult to follow, because she

picked out the words so slowly, mouthing their bathos aloud. Glitter of jeweled sands that sped across and ran away.

### TRAVELOGUE

"Within Easy View Of Vesuvius, Sorrento Lies Dreaming In The Sun. Note Donkeys In Distance."

Quiver of hills. . . .

"In Capri The Italian Takes His Best Girl Out Riding In A Sail Boat. Better Than The Subway, Isn't It?"

To ride in a slim sailboat. . . .

"Sunset in Venice."
"Lake Como's Twilights Are Deep Purple."

There on the outside of herself, a twilight the color of her silence. Grays—with the purple bleeding in. She cried out at its passing——

"Shh-h-h-h——

Mountains next. And after them a magnified view of a rosebud opening. An intrusion almost, to behold this slim thing bowing with life. Once petals like that had kissed the very sides of her being. She began to cry. . . .

Next, a love story. A shoddy sop to reality. A man and a maid worrying at their emotions like terriers. Scurrying little field mouse motions that live on chaff.

And yet to Bertha and the rows and rows like her sitting there in the darkness, it was as if they had been kissed on a bunched-up mouth by love in a brown velveteen smoking jacket and prettified eyes. Stinging vicarious sweetness. . . .

Lights. The pale froufrou of shifting audience. Of course —lavatory floors to be swabbed. The water scurried in little pools before her brush.

All the way home, while the sleet flew at and bit her, she kept smiling. "Lake Como's Twilights Are Deep Purple." Herself on the outside of herself.

At one corner, a taxicab skidded within an inch of pinning her to the curb. Oaths. A blur of faces, fatty looking with curiosity. A policeman brushing the water and ice off the flank of her reefer. The taxicab driver had a zigzag of cut on his face from flying glass. Red through the glassy fog and he sopped it against his bare hand, great fellow, and was sick.

She stalked on, big, boxed and smiling, the bulk of her displacing the dance of the storm.

"Lake Como's Twilights Are Deep Purple." To think of that! The deep winey purple of her forests.

Banners. Banners. Banners. Streamers of them from roofs and poles. Little licking tongues of flame curling out. The ripple and snap of them was a pleasant dazzle. Even the cartwright had a two-penny flag in his window and a photograph of Roosevelt pasted flat against the pane.

That was the occasion. The return of Roosevelt from African adventure. The city fluttered, knife edges of stone softened into waves by the dance of pennants; the street a fluted alley of them.

Willy, vociferous as ever over his tripe stew, was wild to be off.

"The parade will pass the house. Me and the boy—you watch—we'll be in the window!"

"Willy—he'll be in the window?"

"Sure. We got broncho caps. I made them. Slk-k-k-k— Roosevelt—he shoots lions. We'll be watching for him in broncho caps."

He was sly, he was excited, and he jumped up and down again, until he choked on his coffee and was horrid and she left him there.

It was delicate June in the streets. Pink and blue sky and awnings with stripes. The bazaar of the city in spring. Bertha was due for her weekly day's work in a rooming house in West Fortieth Street near Eighth Avenue. Her feet were so loth. Again and again she dragged them toward Eighth Avenue, only to turn back and eastward toward Madison. In two years, with the exception of those days when the water pipes were frozen, she had not failed a day's assignment.

Flags kept snapping. The air was May wine. The city ran of excitement. Quickened steps. Pennants. A great man was coming home. The boy at the window. There would be a boy at the window to greet him.

The window! Her feet kept trying to walk on resolutely. Seventh Avenue. Eighth Avenue. Finally, it was no use. She turned back and began to run a little, with the quickened city. Clumps of people hurrying and dragging children by the hand. Curbs and balconies and wagon-tops began to blacken and one truck filled with chairs rattled by, to shouts and squawking horns.

It was hard not to run. Madison Avenue! The jammed curbs. They were three deep. And the sidewalk was a little groove between walls of buildings and of human flesh. The blazing balconies. The fluttering windows! A window of *the house* was black. She could not look. She stood on the opposite curb, and with the tail of her eyes she knew that a window of *the house* was black! But she could not look. For the life of her, the life of her, she could not look.

Blare! A curve of music through the sunlight. Brass. Bright. Screaming. The street a metal strip. A major domo came over the top of the hill. Everything ran toward him. The fluttering. The sway of the crowds. The blowing hair from the heads out of windows. The shouts.

She stood wedged, her elbows pinned to her hips. The window. She could not, could not look, but the tail of her eye kept tattling. There were heads and halves of bodies out of it. Flutterings. One head was very bright. It caught the light in pools, like the silver ball of the major domo. She fainted a little standing up there. Just let go, and the crowd sustained her of its denseness.

The pulse of the living wall that held her—it sang against her—it wakened her—she leaned out—the major domo was stalking past. Roosevelt then, standing up in a motor car and flashing and bowing, with the light on his spectacles and his teeth and his cheek bones. *There* was a man who felt the little vibratory messages run in and flashed them out again, broadcast! He was like a magnet with them and the nap of the crowd rose up to his passing! Cheers! He stood as he rode, always smiling, and always with the light on his spectacles and his teeth and his cheek bones.

Smiling! Bowing! Bowing to the window! Bowing to the window! Her eyes would not lift, but the tail of her glance kept knowing. The Colonel bowing to the window. The Colonel and that very bright head that caught the light in pools.

The crowd began to loosen. A disintegrating snowbank. It was frightening to feel the support withdraw. The Colonel had passed. It was easier to move. She was going to look. She had found the strength to look. It was hard to breathe and to swing her heavy burning eyes just a little upward—there!

But the heads were withdrawn and someone was jerking down a shade. The window stared over at her blandly. A slap in the face.

All the little flutterings had run out of the street. The asphalt flowed in a stiff river up to the peak, over which the major domo had come up shining. The houses, the brown, proper, hateful houses that could look so closed, had bowed back into themselves. She kicked in the impotence of her despair, against the stone trim of one of them, stubbing her shoes and her toes. It was hard for her to cry. The sobs came through her throat slowly and inflamed it. But for blocks she walked weeping them, dryly.

Her boy shining up there in the window. Her boy upon whose face she had not dared to look.

Willy was building something. The small mousy noises of his boring seemed suddenly to have destination. Sometimes an hour or two after she had fallen asleep on her wagon seat behind the curtain, Bertha would wake up to the sound of hammering. For the first time something was taking shape under his tinkerings.

"Willy, what are you making?"

"Slk-k-k-k-k!"

"Huh? Tell me, Willy."

"Slk-k-k-k-k—wouldn't you like to know?"

"What is it, Willy?"

"Puddintame, ask me again and I'll tell you the same."

One evening, however, the object took shape as he puttered at it. A box with hinges and a little padlock and various little compartments inside for irregular shaped objects. That same evening as Bertha rinsed off the dishes and ranged them in their poor array above the faucet, he painted it a bright green and with a surprising ingenuity for him, finished off with a large yellow polka dot on the lid. This dot seemed to punctuate the finality of his achievement. He could not keep his hands off the box there drying beside the stove, touching it every few moments for the assurance of drying paint, going through the ludicrous pantomime of carrying it before him like a page. In the bit of broken mirror above the faucet Bertha watched him. Silly Willy.

Suddenly he came up behind her, making the boring sound between his tongue and cheek that went in through the back of her ear like a gimlet.

"Slk-k-k-k—a tool box! I made it. Slk-k-k-k. It's for him. To-morrow is his birthday. I made it."

Birthday. The birthday of the boy! The clang of an ambulance through the mauve of a dawn. The incredible warm little bulb of a head in the crook of her arm. The music of the chimes tranced goldily there on the outside of her. The birthday of the boy. To-morrow! Why, it must be—yes— the hurrying, hurrying years!

She put on her pancake of a hat with a new and skiddering rose she had fashioned from a bit of ribbon. There were forty-five cents in her small black pad of a purse.

It was spring again. The lovely quality to it of a petal to the cheek. Somewhere through that night as it traveled, buds had dozed into it, cozily. Even the city could not entirely dissipate that smell of garden. Faces on stoops, dim lily pads lifted to the warmth. The thin high clink of water running along gutters. Children with dry noses. The open doors of shops and the musk smells of winter pouring out of them. The delicate mist with the lavender in it smeared with the soft gold of lighted show windows. Show windows! The blocks and blocks of them. They were beginning to blink out as Bertha roved them. Flimsy painted toys, with the glue bleeding out of the jointures and forming scabs. Stale candies in glass jars and powdered with city grime. Sticks of wood. Lumps of glucose. The abominable makeshifts of poverty.

Up and down a score of city blocks, not a toy, for ten times the forty cents in her pad of purse, worthy of the birthday of the boy.

The curve of lavender in the evening; that rill of beauty clinking in the gutters. Something as tender as these for the birthday of the boy! She could have cried, and did on the homeward turn.

Willy was asleep. There was a darkish mound of him on his cot, and a white night flowed in and filled the room with light the pallor of a bridal veil. That dreadful room, and its green box with the yellow polka dot drying by the stove. Willy face downward and clutched into his pillow, with his silly heels up. And yet it could be the color of moon, that dreadful room. Clear and cool and strewn with bridal veil. There was a gift for you! To capture that color of moon into a balloon that might burst with a pop in the heart of the boy.

She sat behind the muslin curtain, her mouth moving for the words that could bring this frail thought out without shattering it into the blunt grunting things she could say.

She began to undress, the white of her body climbing up out of the muslin underthings. Great ox-like pallor. The slow rhythm of her arms rising and falling. The two enormous and clankless chains of her hair. The whisper of sliding into the boxy whiteness of the coarse, clean nightgown. It stood off from her like a little bathhouse, her calm, spatulate feet moving about under it.

The birthday of the boy! She sat on the edge of her carpetbag, wrapped in the gray blanket that presently she would spread along the leather wagon seat and roll herself into. The unbleached muslin portières on their crazy draw string of twine blew in as if they were animate and wanted to nudge her. They towered and were alive in the white darkness and seemed to breathe back at her. The tears in her heart, like the clink of the clear water in the gutter.

The birthday of the boy! Even Willy could bear him gifts. The pad of black purse lay on the carpet bag beside her. Hateful symbol of the shopkeeper's hand crawling down into the glass jars for the glucose lumps! That was the limit of her purchasing power for the birthday of the boy! The glucose lumps or the painted gimcracks.

She slid down finally with her cheek to the carpetbag. It had a give to it that was friendly. Its nap cut softly up into her flesh. The tears rolled down and made a smell of must, as when she scrubbed too near a rug. A familiar smell that she dozed into, and cried into through the doze. It was still the lightish night when she awoke. There was a red triangle on her wet cheek where a sharp edge had cut up through the carpetbag. She awoke to the small pain of it, pressed there by the sharp edge of the concertina in her carpetbag. The outlandish one with the steamship stamp upon it. Old World.

She fell at the straps of her bag. The concertina! It bulged up at her there from a background of the lovely ocean of Mrs. Farley's cast-off evening cloak. Silver ends to it and a silver label engraved in a Russian phrase:

## ВЕСЕЛИС ДИТЯ ГАРМОНИКА ИГРАЕТ ДЛЯ ТЕБЯ

The little grin of white keys. The waffled sides. They were broken at the creases, but there were some little fugitive notes. She knew them. They ran upward as the keys sank down in a little delighted crescendo. La-dee-da-dee! La-dee-da-dee! She made a cave of her body over the pretty bleat. It ran up. It ran down. And then there was a way to skip in the middle that made it seem like a mournful dawn in a valley and another way to skip at the end that made it seem very glad. Four beautiful tender little ways to play it.

She fell to polishing the silver label, breathing on it and rubbing it with an edge of the green chiffon. It was a lovely chore, polishing, dusting down into the tiny crannies with a broom-straw wrapped in a bit of tissue paper, and every once in a while, down, deep, under the cave of her body, greedily away from the ears of Willy—La-dee-da-dee!

A spring day came up over the roofs. She dressed in its early chill, her fingers bungling as she buttoned with too much haste.

She came out from behind her muslin portières bearing her gift shyly.

"It bane for the boy—his birthday," she said, and placed the concertina on the table beside the plate of hominy she had fried and dished up for him. "My gift."

"Say, say, a little old accordion! That's a good 'un—where'd you dig that little old accordion up? Say now—Slk-k-k-k—won't he like that!"

"It bane from me—Willy—he won't know it but—it bane from me——"

"What'll it play? A tune?"

She could not keep her fingers from fluttering over it.

"Don't be rough with it, Willy."

He broke the sinuous fluted case, his head cocked and his eyes in their corners.

"La—dee—da—dee——

"Say—won't he like that! Me and the boy—we'll give a concert down in the furnace room—slk-k-k-k."

He could scarcely wait to strut off, the green box and the concertina crowded under one arm and tipping him lopsided.

He started off, his little pot belly leading and Bertha after him, until at the corner, under the elevated, their ways parted.

"It bane from me, Willy—he won't know it—but it bane from me."

"Slk-k-k-k——"

It was Saturday, Bertha's day for the kindergarten floors of St. Rose's Parochial School on Ninth Avenue.

The water ran in wide pools and her arm went in big swoops after it. There was a rhythm to each stroke.

La-dee-da-dee.  La-dee-da-dee.

The house in West Fortieth Street near Eighth Avenue was tall and thin, and small grill work balconies, mere pretenses, swelled out slightly from the two first-floor windows.

They were fairly neat windows, with a hideous *jardinière* containing cotton palms in each. Day by day they stood there revealing, between the tiresome lace curtains, the brown and yellows of the bulbous *jardinières*. The three upper stories were all closely drawn, dark green shades blotting out the look of dwelling and leaving something tall and thin, blind and a little sinister.

Every Wednesday morning when she arrived, Bertha was given a pail and brush and put to washing down the hallways and the four flights of stairs. A curious odor of lysol and scented soap drifted about in the stale silence of these corridors, a nub of gaslight burning at each landing. Sometimes in swabbing the woodwork, a flare of the dirty scrub water ran under the padded stair-carpet. Then the musty stench arose.

There was something mysterious about these halls. Occasional women in kimonos scurried from room to room and laughter and voices sometimes beat against the closed doors. But for the most part they stood black and silent and orderly. Sometimes there were big footsteps ground into the carpets and broken bits of glass, women's elaborate garters, and evidences of unsavory revelry strewn about the stairs, but Bertha's

day was invariably long and black and narrow. The four
floors of airless hallways to be swept; woodwork to be washed
down; banisters to be rubbed with furniture oil, and the four
red gas globes with warts blown into them to be unscrewed,
rinsed in warm water, and readjusted.

Mrs. McMurtry, who walked without sound, supervised all
this. She was very prim and very slight, and her lips had the
thin, unkissed look of triumphant asceticism. A man's hand
could have spanned the width of her shoulders. She wore
keys at her belt, a black alpaca waist with a standing collar
without ruche, so that there was a red rim around her neck,
and when she paid Bertha her two dollars and ten cents every
Wednesday evening, her thin dry fingers high-stepped gingerly
away from too close contact with the currency. She was about
forty and had let that forty come, grayly.

One Wednesday morning someone in the third-floor-back
must have been very ill. There was a sweetish, etheric odor
in the house, and Mrs. McMurtry hurried back and forth with
ice packs and blankets. A narrow black doctor with a narrow
black bag oozed up through the halls. A group of the kimono-
clad women gathered at the end of the hall, bleating like
frightened quail. One of them had left her door open. The
room was papered in light red, the drawn shades were green,
and four of the jets on a very ornate center chandelier were
burning. An imitation tapestry of nude Leda and her swan
hung over the mantel. A man was seated on the side of the
wide bed, bending to lace his shoes. Mrs. McMurtry, passing
with a bowl of cracked ice, leaned in to close that door hur-
riedly. Then she shooed away the girls. They scattered like
doves off of crumbs. One of them, trailing the edge of her

light sateen kimono in the pool of Bertha's scrub water so that
it slapped against her bare legs, glanced down with a kick and
an oath.

It was Helga.

Helga was so thin! And pretty. A delicate, convalescent
kind of prettiness, as if she had been ill a long while, and her
hands had whitened and her skin softened and her eye sockets
were like enormous pans with a jewel in them. This soft-
handed Helga whose wrists used to crack open from chapping
and bleed until she cried!

"Helga!"

"Fortheluvvaga! So help me—it's the lump! Bertha!"

Pretty, pretty Helga, with her brown hair frizzed and her
face full of pink light from the sateen kimono. Bertha on
her knees, with her hands dripping the sloppy water, could only
sit back on her heels and stare her fill.

"Helga, you remember me?"

"You're the square head from Farley's. You're the quitter
walked off one breakfast time and left us cold. If it ain't old
Berth!"

She began to cry, for all the world like a convalescent too
weak to know quite why.

"It's old Berth—still scrubbing."

"You're so pretty, Helga—that way."

"And you're so white, Berth. Still like a white old tomb,
you, sittin' on the world, listening to it."

"You don't work no more, Helga? You're so fine. Helga—
Helga—you ain't——"

"Yes—I am ! Oh I work all right, I work! Come in my room."

"Mrs. McMurtry won't like that!"

"The hell Mrs. McMurtry won't. I don't owe her nothing. She does all the owing there is around here. I don't owe her nothing. Not even an apology."

Helga's room was papered in light green and there was an atrocity of a great green satin bow, sprawled like a spider, pinned on the lace curtains. The shades were drawn against the relenting spring sunshine and the gas jets sang. A brass bed and a base burner and a carpet with an enormous floral wreath crowded up the room. Between the windows was a full-length repetition of the tapestry of the nude Leda and her Swan.

It was somehow a horrible room, the kind Willy was fond of looking at through the lenses in the Fourteenth Street nickelodeons. You half expected girls in corsets and ruffled panties to be sitting about smoking cigarettes.

"Helga! Helga!"

"Why not? Whose got the right to stop me, I'd like to know? I've slung my last pot for the privilege of keeping the slanting roof of somebody's garret over my head."

"This place——?"

"Yah—yah—what do you think? A convent? Don't look so holy or you'll sprout a halo. Sit down. Oh, I know all your Sunday school gab. You're afraid to touch me. Your scrub water has made you clean and I'm unclean. I know— the line of talk. You're clean with slops and me I—I'm dirty with stinkin' perfume—you don't need to touch me——"

"Why Helga—Helga—come here—kiss—me——"

Suddenly Helga began to cry again, the tears of physical weakness.

"I know what I'm doing. Pretty damn well. Where did I get off? Nobody's ever yet answered me why I had to get up at six, every tooth in my head rattling of cold and my back aching from a lumpy cot, so that four hours later a thin-lipped icicle that never done nothing for this world except get herself born into it right, could step out of her soft bed into a warm bath and then to her hot breakfast that three of us had been three hours bustling around in the cold dark getting ready for her. Not much!"

"How long, Helga, since you quit the Farleys?"

"I couldn't stand the young one! Rollo's wife. There's the one finished me. I stuck it out two years after she came. There was a hell-cat for you. The kind of a house-devil that wakes up with her eyes glued shut and can't straighten herself out into a presentable creature until along about noon when the society stuff starts to begin. I know 'em—the smooth-faced kind with the smooth-parted hair and the pecan-shaped faces. There was a woman could subscribe to a charity ball with one hand and pinch an orphan with another. She led me a merry hell for two years I won't soon forget. And Rollo—that poor piece of white meat! He can thank God he made himself famous writing a book before she copped him. He'll never write another. He's married to one that takes all and gives nothing. She couldn't inspire a man to write an entry in the butcher book."

"Why did you quit, Helga?"

"One month she had the old woman dock me for a little old terra cotta statue I knocked off of Rollo's desk, dusting it. She said Rollo had written his greatest poem in front of that

little terra cotta on his desk and that no money could repay it,
but she was for learning me a lesson. I learned her one. There
was ten coming to dinner that night and me on second-floor
duty. Well, that dinner party had to slide out of its fur coats
and powder its noses alone that night. I quit!"

"And this?"

"I got to thinking, that's all. All back doors and slop cans
for some—front doors and canopies for others—no reason—
just happening that way. God couldn't mean it like that. And
what if He did? He was God. I'm me! Little! Weak.
I get so tired, Bertha. Nobody gets so tired as I do. My
floatin' kidney. I love to sleep so. It's a sickness. I can't pull
out of it. I ain't strong, Bertha. I couldn't—I—I ain't strong
and white and all on the inside of me like you! Lye water
hurts my hands! Slops stink. It eats my heart to have to
peek through the swinging doors at the good things of life being
gobbled by others that ain't earned 'em as much as we have.
That's why I'm here. I thought maybe—God—I thought
maybe——"

"Maybe—what?"

"Maybe some of the easiness—was coming to me. There—
there was a fellow—you remember—while you was at Farley's
—Joe Dike, the little plumber that always used to kid you about
sitting and listening to the oleander tree grow. Joe liked me.
I never made no bones, Bertha. I wanted kids. A two-by-four
of my own somewheres and kids. That's all I ever asked out
of it. Joe, he strung me along a while after you left and then
—he quit. It used to go against his grain not even to be allowed
to sit in the kitchen. He had self-respect Joe did. He didn't
like courting in alleyways and elevated trains. I—didn't have
nowheres except to sneak him—up. That's where I lost my

chance, Bertha. Joe liked me while I was straight and used to talk marrying, but when he seen me up there in that dirty hole —living like a rat—he—I—aw—after him—I didn't—care—that's all. I don't care now!"

"I care, Helga."

"You! Lots anybody cares for me. But I fooled 'em. I fooled 'em—I—got a place—now—I—got a place now—to invite 'em in!"

Suddenly Helga, whose prettiness was drawn back from her face as if someone were pulling her by the hair, fell forward in a pink sateen huddle against Bertha.

"And now the worst of it is, I hate them, Bertha. Some day I'll kill one. Their mouths. Their ugly wet mouths. McMurtry sends me the slobbiest ones. She hates me, because she knows I hate her. They begin coming as early as six— mouths all loose and wet that slide around in their faces like something alive crawling over them! I'll kill one some day! Help me, Bertha. Where can I turn to? Where, oh God, where?"

Then Mrs. McMurtry came in. A neat little, black little engine without a puff.

"What's this?"

"I spilt a bottle of medicine and she wiped it up for me."

"Go back to your work, Bertha."

Out in the hallways the twilight was like smoke. It wound and it thickened and it flowed around the little nubs of light. The waiting webby water in Bertha's pail lapped on to her wrists as she plunged them into the pail again. Clung there.

At six o'clock Mrs. McMurtry paid her off. The two one dollar bills again and the ten cent piece.

"Next Wednesday, Bertha."

"Next Wednesday, Mrs. McMurtry."

Going downstairs she crowded up against the wall to let someone pass. He had a wet mouth. Like a live thing crawling across his face.

ometimes in summer, Willie went away with the family to a square house by the sea. Bertha knew it well from the picture post card view of it that he kept tacked up over the table. The edge of the vast smooth lawn was walled into a fortress, against which the sea plunged in a fury of spray. A row of imported poplar trees, straight as young boys, bisected this sleek lawn into an Italian garden on one side and a cleared area of playground for the boy on the other. There was a swing with an awning; a small wooden chute-the-chutes, carefully railed, and by scanning with the eye almost touching the card, tiny croquet hoops and pegs could be discerned against the turf, which undulated along, supple as a caterpillar, until the sea brought it up, sheerly.

There was something terrifying about that rebuffed surf, as it showed up on the post card, bending back with spray. Terrifying thought of the boy bounding down that springy sod with the wind in his face and the thwarted sea full of its licking tongues.

Often at night Bertha awoke trembling with that fear. It helped somehow to have Willie there with him—and yet—just silly Willie—and the leaping, grinding, gnashing sea running up to the feet of the boy.

So the summers could be long, even cruel, except that it was pleasant to have the muslin portières drawn back and never to feel the skulking putterings of Willie, or to waken to the grimace which he loved to hang over her pillow. The room could be very hot. It seemed to pant at night, as if the long scorching trail of the day had left it exhausted. Warm breath stole out of its walls. The leather wagon seat was hot to the touch.

One August evening she dragged the old thing to the window and lay on it there, where she could lift her face to the sill every little while in the hope of a fugitive passing breeze. It was horrible. Babies cried and died in that welter. The bare, tossing little limbs were sprawled on the stoops and fire escapes. She could rest her chin upon the sill and look out on the litter of them and on the mothers whose arms were filled with the hot, sick droop of prostrated children. The tired senile infants in the thick of their battle with the tenements. The secret exultancy of Bertha. An exultancy that could burn in her like wine.

Puling, mewling sons of the mothers whose arms were rich with them. Bertha's were empty. So empty that sometimes, for the relief of tangible pain, she would wrap them around her body until the hands clasped in back, for the ache of the pulling sockets. Those mothers out there who thought that their arms were rich with the mewling and puny sons. Bertha's were empty, but her son was in a white square house by the sea, where the nights blew in life-giving with salt, and a green lawn flowed all about him, growing and shimmering so that his swift boy's feet might beat it down. Tormented exultancy of Bertha!

Sometimes Helga came. She was only half a Helga now, so slim, and the indoor pallor made her very lovely. Until she spoke she was delicate as an old perfume and then her voice came out of this frailty with all of its old husky quality. The same berating Helga who could box an iceman's ears or shrill down Mrs. Farley over the strewn mass of her slovenly bed.

Her slippers. They were so pretty. Slim with tall heels and buckles of bronze beads across the instep. Twinkling feet. And a pleated silk dress with a skirt that opened out in a fan. And there was money in her purse. You could see the green of the bills through the gilt mesh. More than once her impulse had been to leave some of these bills with Bertha.

"I suppose if I was to give you a ten spot, you would sprout a sanitary halo and tear up the dirty stuff."

"I got enough. Day work is good."

"Yeh,—you got enough. Smoked fish and a horse blanket. Oh, I know. Even you are too good for prostitute money."

"Even—me——"

They seldom lit the gas. It cost, and besides in the heat it was unbearable. Sometimes, with the silk dress spread around her in a great flower, Helga sat on the floor with her cheek against the sill, her dry feverish face thrust up for a breath of air. Bertha, barefoot, upright on the soap box that served as the room's second chair, and a bit back from the window, the dark silence thick and luxurious to her as sealskin.

"Fortheluvvaga, why don't you say something? You give me the jimjams. I'd sooner have you say what's on your mind than sit there like you was sitting up on top of the world brooding over it. Whadda you keep looking at me like that for? You ought to set yourself in a gilt frame with some candles burning up to yourself. It's my funeral—not yours——"

"And mine—Helga—to see it go bad—with—you——"

"I'm nothing to you——"

"Nothing—and everything."

"Huh?"

"Nothing."

"Bertha—who are you——?"

"Yoost—me."

"Well, whoever you are, I won't be saved, if that's what's on your mind. I know the slick ways of the savers. Words. Words. Words from the teeth out never saved anybody. I know them. I hate a professional thin-lipped saver like I hate the ripple in a snake—I know what I'm doing, I do. Saved for what? Saved for going back to scrubbing somebody's pots and pans in somebody's kitchen? That's a helluva life, ain't it, to want to be saved for? You or any of the professional savers got a swell chance to save me from that."

"That—don't matter——"

"Yeh—yeh—I know! I know! Dishwater don't need to soak through to the soul. I know the line of talk. Well, it soaks through me! Makes me sick with the meaning of living. If there's got to be pot slingers for ladies who breakfast in pink silk boudoirs, then all of us on the kitchen side of the door ought to have been made with machinery inside instead of hearts and souls."

"Somebody has got to——"

"Well, that don't make it no easier to be one of the pot-slinging somebodies. If you've got a heart and a soul, then you're going to ask questions about what made you one of the somebodies on the kitchen side of the door, instead of on the pink silk side, and if you ask questions it's a helluva lot of satisfaction you get. Somebody's got to sling the pots. That's about all the answer anybody has been able to give me yet. Oh, it's all right about being too deep down inside yourself to mind the scum on your hands. Maybe you can pull a dead rat out of its hole like you was picking a lily, I've seen you do it, but

I'm one of the human ones. I'm glad I done what I done. I'd do it all over again."

"Helga——"

"I've nothing to be saved for. I've worked in the kitchens of the good ones and the bad ones and it don't make it any easier. Going around the alley way for someone whose heart is made no different than your heart and whose soul wasn't made in a special heaven. Yeh—I'd do it all over again—and I hate 'em, I tell you—hate them—I hate them—their wet slippery mouths——"

She fell down into the huddle then of the accordion-pleated silk skirt, racked with the sobs she had not the strength for, and she had to be cooed and soothed out of what seemed almost delirium. Cooed and soothed as if she had been a child. Bertha's.

It was raining in a soft, fast whisper. The first September gusts fanned sprays of it through the open window. A tin spout dribbled. It was an evening for placing a growing plant on the window sill. The gusts came stronger and full of rain. Finally the window had to be lowered and then the fine fizz went after the pane. An evening with a sense of hurry to it. Pedestrians hurrying with slant umbrellas. The waiter from Tom's Eating Place across the way, hurrying into the Crescent Billiard Parlors with a covered tray. And how the soft rain did hurry. It had a melody. Bertha dried her cup and plate to it. Sleet—te—tee! Sleettee—tee! Sleeeeeee!

The twilight was a little mouse, and the rain full of tiny scuttling feet. The old cup and the plate with a V chopped out, shone in a pale, jagged grin when she set them on the shelf.

It was hard to light the gas because the matches were damp. There!

Someone was coming up the stairs. In clumps. It was Willie, home from the three months of country. There was the rocking-chair derby, with a little rill of water dripping from the gutter of the brim, and a large newspaper bundle of his belongings throwing him a little lopsided.

"Slk-k-k-k," he said, and stood in the doorway.

She flew at him and took his wet hat and shook it and dragged the soap box for him up to the stove, so that he sat down in an immediate exudation of steam.

"Willie—the boy—you bane home again!"

He was sullen and held her off with his elbow.

"Don't shove. Don't shove."

"I won't—the boy?"

"Don't shove——"

She poured him a cup of the still warm coffee and he drank it gulping and sighing and staring, with the rims of his eyes stretched and contemplating the red doorway to the stove. There was something irate and dozy about him, like a man who has been jerked out of a nap.

"Willie—you—the boy?"

He began to swing what was left of the coffee around in the cup. He made a game of it. Swinging and swirling and then he threw it down his throat at a gulp.

"Ah"—he said—"Hell."

A dart of fear shot through her.

"Willie—the boy—quick—the boy—my boy?"

She had him by the scruff of his neck, so that he came up loosely like a sack of potatoes.

"Scat you! Crazy!"

"Willie——"

"Aw let up. I'm out of a job," he said, and sat looking groggily into the door of the stove.

"Then the boy—all right——?"

"Whadda you mean—all right?—All wrong!"

"Willie——"

"All wrong for me. They're takin' him to Europe to-morrow. For two years—maybe five. Leaves me flat of a job. All of us. There's a dirty trick to play on the staff. Not even opening the town house this year."

"Europe—the boy——"

"Yeh—all of a sudden the staff of us, except the old woman that learns him his books, gets notice. Could knock us down. Taking him to Europe to study the piano. Beat that! The boy's a great one for piddling on the piano. Nobuddy notices it much and then all of a sudden—Europe. And where does that leave us? Out of a job. And where do we get off because they're taking him to learn the bloomin' old piano? That's what a fella gets. Stays after hours to play with the boy and in the end it's the boy that costs him his job."

"The—boy—plays—the—piano?"

"Naw, he plays the scissors grinder, in case you didn't hear me the first time I said it. Piano. You get me? Piano."

Suddenly Willie leaped up, the grimace he loved to hang over her couch on his face. The vicious, drooly, half-wit mask.

"I know! You! You done it! You gave him that damned concertina! That was the beginning. He never played before then. That got him started. He couldn't leave off that damned thing. They kept making him play it for company. Had him down standing on the dinner table one night at a party, showing him off on that old accordion. Then they got him a new one, but he wouldn't leave off with the old. The one that you sent him. That's what got him started to fumbling out tunes all day on the piano. That dirty concertina. Yours! You lost me my job, sending it to him, and now you owe me my living for starting it all with your old concertina!"

"Willie!"

"You! God damn you." He lunged and struck her on the right cheek bone with a loud cracking sound and then, as the other cheek swung around from the impact, struck her again on the left, shambled downstairs and went out.

A little scarlet tear of blood began to trickle down toward the corner of her mouth. The taste of it was sickish, and the flesh began to flame up around her eyes. Waving purple flags.

She stood with her lips fallen apart in what might have been a smile. "You started it all with that damn concertina." Ecstasy of that! It made it easy not to faint through the waving purple and to walk over through the muslin curtains and there, from behind the overturned wagon-top marked in a red star and "R. H. Stacy and Company," to drag out the old carpetbag and pack it with unfumbling hands.

The rain had ceased. A warmish night was left that was soft as an oyster and felt clammy to the cheek. The street lights went down in corkscrews into the sidewalks, and when you glanced up the heavens were all moving with the hurry of low clouds. And yet the murkiness parted like a curtain. Bertha's feet were so swift and her face thrust ahead like a blade cutting. A lovely, draped kind of a night, through which she could pass to the swish of her own tingling blood. Street cars clanged angrily and almost touched her as she darted. The carpetbag hit softly.

The balls of her feet were part of this business of being glad. She felt big and silly, jiggling along on them. It was hard to keep the lip down firmly over the teeth. It kept quivering to smile. Sometimes the street ran in darts of color because of the bonfires underneath her eyes. Bonfires of exultant flame.

The petty shops and the soiled look of poverty began to peter out. The tenement badges of fire escape and clothes line, of prowling cats and strewn gutters, left off suddenly after Lexington Avenue, and by the hair line of a bisecting street, the respectable brownstone march began. Blocks of solemn, riveted, stare after stare. The monotony of the desert, captive in city streets.

In the well-to-do aridity of one of these crosstown blocks, as she worked her way zigzag toward boarding a car for Front Street, a pair of women walking ahead turned in at one of the ornate stoops. A street lamp burned before it and its reflection ran up along the wet steps in yellow shafts. In this light the quick, avian face of one of the women spun around upon Bertha and she grasped her companion by the coat sleeve.

"I tell you, there is a good girl leaving a situation. I know the look of them. Neat as a pin. There is no harm asking."

The second face was hung on delicately. Like a pear.

"'Tilda, how can you? It's not only an insulting thing to do, but in a city like New York it isn't safe. Come, dear."

"I've picked up some of the best servants I ever had that way. That is how I found Aggie one Saturday morning, right off the corner of Madison and Fifty-first Street. She reminds me something of Aggie, too. New York or no New York, I know a good servant when I see one. Say, you—girl——"

" 'Tilda !"

"Say, you!  Come here, please."

"Me?"

"Yes.  I merely wish to ask, you don't mind, I'm sure, if you are leaving a situation, or if you happen to know of a good cook or housemaid, who does want a place?"

" 'Tilda !"

"Paula, if you don't like it I wish you would go into the house.  I know what I am doing.  My daughter thinks it shocking because I stop you in this fashion.  You don't mind, do you?"

"No."

"Then do you wish a place?"

"Yah——."

"There, didn't I tell you!  Thank goodness, I am sufficiently strong-minded to follow my own intuition and ask for what I want in this world when I see it.  Are you a cook?"

" 'Tilda dear, if you must have this out, at least take her into the house and don't air the transaction to the entire neighborhood."

"Don't mind my daughter.  You know how young people are about doing anything a little off the beaten trail.  Come into the house.  I want to talk to you.  Never mind the servant's entrance, although that's what I like.  A girl who instinctively knows her place.  Come up the front steps with me.  I'll talk to you in the front hall."

The front hall was cold, with a wainscoting of white marble and there was the duenna touch of the black lace of iron grill work across the door.  A cold stately lady of a hall.  An alabaster Mercury lunged off the newel post and thrust up a lighted electric torch. A Baluchistan rug swayed a little under the feet in a springy turf.

"That's right, Paula, you go upstairs. I can talk much more freely with you away."

"You always did have and always will have your own way of doing things, dear," she said and disappeared around a charming curve of balustrade.

Her mother had the nervous intimacy about her of being always about to pluck a thread off of someone's collar or to moisten her handkerchief with her tongue and rub off a streak of soot from some nose.

She sat Bertha down with a pluck at her collar, on the lowermost step, plopping herself opposite on a Spanish marble bench.

"Don't mind my children. They get provoked at me because I insist upon doing things my own way. I said to my daughter as we passed you at the corner, 'There is a good strong girl for someone. There is something about her. I can tell a good girl when I see one.' Ordinarily I keep a laundress four days a week, a cook, a housemaid, a second girl, and a chauffeur, but since Aggie, the excellent cook who was with me for years, was obliged to leave, I haven't succeeded in engaging a staff that satisfies me. But that's one thing about me, when my staff is incomplete, I can pitch in and take a hand myself. Are you a good cook?"

"I bane good, plain cook."

"Of course. There never was one who wasn't a good, plain cook, to hear her tell it. Well, we are four in family, although one of my children is away most of the time. I have three young lady daughters and I am perfectly free to say that the girl who gets a place with us is fortunate. I am extremely active about the house, and I expect my servants to treat me with the same consideration that I give them. Do I make myself clear?"

"Yah."

"References?"

"Yah—I——"

"Don't take them out. If they contain anything bad you wouldn't show them to me, and if they are good I can find it all out quickly enough for myself. You're not a gadabout, are you? I always contend that a girl's chief interests should lie between her kitchen and her room, just as a business man's lie between his office and his home. Simple pleasures now and then if she will, but I give my girls nice dry rooms and I expect them to appreciate them enough to avail themselves. Now I am willing to give you a trial if you are willing to try us. I pay forty dollars and expect my money's worth. Yes?"

"Why—yah——"

"You see, I do not even ask you why you are leaving a position at this hour of the night. I depend solely upon my own judgments. I like your looks. What are you? German? Scandinavian? Pole? No? Well, it doesn't matter, you seem to be a little of everything. That isn't a black eye you are getting, is it? Well, that doesn't matter, either. I hope you haven't any kind of vermin or any bad habits. But if you have I will find them out quickly enough for myself. You look spick and span enough to suit me. I have my breakfast at eight-thirty. Downstairs. I'll come up and awake you at six. This way, please, and I'll show you up the rear stairs to your room. Don't bump your head on that slanting ceiling. I take one sliced orange, two three-minute eggs, two strips of crisp bacon, two level tablespoons of coffee to the cup, three slices of dry toast for breakfast. My girls have coffee and toast in their rooms. I have no waitress or second girl at present, but help from the agency comes in by the day. Nuisance. Don't bump your head on that slanting ceiling. Have you a friend—your type of girl, who wants an excellent position as waitress? I would be willing to engage her at once."

"Yah—maybe——"

"Here you are. I don't say my servants' quarters are palatial, but this much I can say for them. They are dry."

"I have a friend, maybe. Helga. Not right away but maybe some day."

"That is good, but first we shall see how we get along. Put your things down there. As my grandfather used to say of his stables, good dry floors, fresh water trough, add a little fodder to that, and no man or beast could ask more! No, don't look around for an alarm clock, if that's what you're after. I am the alarm clock in this family. There is your bed. Lie on it."

Such was Bertha's initiation into the house of Mathilde Oessetrich.

It was the tempo as much as anything else that tired you so. The household ran. Upstairs. Downstairs. From room to room. And even from kitchen to dining room, when there was no waitress, and usually there was none. Bertha ran, too, slapping her way breathlessly through the swinging doors, dishing up the foods with her tongue caught between her teeth and her spoons flashing.

The reason was that Mathilde Oessetrich ran. She was heavy, but she ran upstairs like some one playing an arpeggio scale. She brushed her thin electric hair in a series of such rapid strokes that it stood off her head in spikes. She drained her coffee cup in three firm gulps, and with one gesture plunged into her gloves down to their very finger tips.

There was no way to live under the roof with Mathilde Oessetrich and not feel this shimmer of her haste. Her second daughter, Ermangarde, was nervous with it. Olga, who attended a school for social research and wore her hair short in the days when it was referred to as "docked," lived away from the strain of it in a studio in East Seventeenth Street.

Paula was meekest under it, probably because it had defeated her first. But even Paula, who at twenty-five had the pale silk hair of a baby and a pear-shaped face that dipped down over a swan-like neck after the fashion of Fra Lippo Lippi's ladies, had her retreat from it. The large, fourth-floor-front room adjoining Bertha's little cubicle. There was a grand piano in there. For hours, sometimes for days at a time, Paula would disappear into this retreat, the incense of her tender, lovely, ruminating music stealing out through the crack under the door. She played Schubert like a heart-ache and sang his tender *lieder* under her breath. Her playing beat softly against the wall of Bertha's cubicle. Schubert. The dithyrambic brilliancy of Liszt. Chopin, that could seem to make out of that lathed and plastered wall between Bertha and Paula at her piano, a fan bowing softly in the darkness. Sometimes Paula could seem, at her piano, a little mad. The glints, that were like steel spears, a vertical one in each of her eyes, must have made her play that way. D'Indy. "Eye of newt and toe of frog . . . like a hell-broth boil and bubble." And Debussy—lanterns the shape of gargoyles, swung on poles, nosing among the stars. . . . The sweet forest where Goland discovers Mesilande. . . .

Waving tonal wall, between Bertha huddled there on her bed and Paula, with the vertical spears in her eyes.

There was a day's end for you. Evening after evening of Paula on her side of the wall. The wall that could sway like a lantern, or bow like a fan. . . .

It made the days themselves easier. You ran all morning, chiefly because Mrs. Oessetrich ran behind you. Calling you off of one half-completed task to begin another and creating in the great square kitchen an uproar of slamming doors, rattling tins, and the thin high clatter of her constant voice.

*"Get me the brown sugar, Bertha. I am going to make some of my panocha for the suffrage bazaar. What's that? Never let me see a spot of rust on the aluminum pots. That's one thing I am particular about. That girl does not eat enough to keep a bird alive. Here you, little delivery boy, never walk into anyone's kitchen in muddy boots. That's a certain sign of a slovenly character. If Miss Olga comes this afternoon, Bertha, while I am out, tell her that I expect her to be here for eight o'clock dinner to-night when her Aunt Mary and her godfather Oessetrich are here. My brother-in-law likes his sauce to leg-of-lamb very minty. I won't have her ignore the family in this fashion. She is already sufficiently out of favor with her godfather as it is, on account of her extreme ideas. Oh dear, not that way. You must beat egg whites as if you meant it. Elbow grease! Oh dear, run up in the library, Bertha, and see if I left my glasses on the desk. Is that Miss Ermangarde going out? Run up and bring me that small bag on my dressing table. I want her to exchange those tan walking gloves at Alberg's. Quick. And, Bertha, tell Eddie I want the sedan here in an hour and that Miss Olga will use the big car this afternoon to take some of the girls from her vocational guidance class out for a drive. I don't know how a boy who thinks as slowly as Eddie does, can make a successful chauffeur.*

*Hand me the telephone book, first, Bertha, I want to look up that caterer on Madison and Fifty-second—her godfather Oessetrich likes pistachio."*

The afternoons were easier. In the sedan with the haggled Eddie at the wheel she shopped and visited, matched up samples of silk, sought out seamstresses, interviewed at the employment agencies, sat on hospital and suffrage boards, stormed in upon Olga's aloofness in the Seventeenth Street studio, and about every hour found out a telephone to jangle up the silence she had left behind her.

*"Hello—Bertha, that you? I forgot to lock the linen closet. Do it. If Madam Gerbhardt calls up, tell her I have an extra seat for her for 'William Tell' to-night. 'Bye."*

An hour later:

*"Hello, Bertha, that you? Anybody call? Who? Miss Ermangarde? She what? Won't be home until six. Well! If she calls again, Bertha, tell her that I do not want her spending her afternoons down in that Greenwich Village atmosphere and that I expect her to come directly home from her drawing lesson. Fix caper sauce with the fish. 'Bye."*

That was how the days flew before her. Shooed like a flapping flock of tormented hens.

Sometimes Ermangarde exploded into little crying rages that made her very flushed and appealing. She was nineteen, thickly built, but with a square kind of Teutonic prettiness. Thin, badly arranged hair, but her gray eyes made extremely peculiar and intent by a fringe of thick black lashes. Under stress the pupils swam out into fine black areas.

"Mother, Mother, Mother," she cried one Sunday evening, jumping up from the tea table just as Bertha was trying to pass the lemon and the waffles in two directions at the same time. "Don't direct Bertha to pass fifty things at once. It's not humanly possible to bend six ways, even to your will. Don't! Don't!"

"Hear, hear," said Olga from where she sat cross-kneed and a bit back from the table, waving her cigarette in its long meerschaum holder and watching the smoke from under almost closed eyes. She had the same Oessetrich squareness, enhanced by the Hans Memling medieval look to her hair, the good gray eyes, the skin inclined to be muddy, and she wore tweeds, thick, expensive, and unbecoming, and a stiff white shirtwaist with cuffs which made the expression of her hands broad and masculine. The nails were unmanicured, but clean and square, as if they had been pared with a knife.

"Oh, it's all very well for you, Olga. You live away from the strain of trying to keep up with Mother. I notice it became too much for you! The pretext of your nearness to the School of Philanthropy doesn't deceive anybody. Stop driving us, Mother. Stop expecting the rest of us to keep up with you. Stop, dearest, stop!"

Mrs. Oessetrich popped one of the little German *simpfkuchen* which graced these Sunday evening tea times whole into her mouth and washed it down with a generous gulp of strong black coffee. She was crisp and entirely unassailed.

"Sit down and finish your meal. Eat some of those stewed apples. They are good for you. And, Bertha, always see to it that Miss Ermangarde has her bottle of tonic on her breakfast tray. Sit down, Ermangarde, you are getting pimply."

At that, of course, an entirely crushed Ermangarde left the

table, crying bitterly down into her hands, Paula, whose long pale face was always thrust forward like a flower eager for dew, turning after her.

"Mother, how could you? What a horrible kind of ridicule, and you know what a nervous state she is in!"

"Exactly. Self-pity is at the bottom of most neurasthenia."

"Oh—oh, why is it that the members of a family feel privileged to treat one another with a cruelty they would not exhibit to the merest stranger?"

"Nonsense," said Olga, reaching forward to knock off her cigarette ash and leaning back to watch the smoke. "Napoleon was very clever in the way she handled that case of nerves."

"Yes, Olga, it is easy enough for you to encourage Mother in her high-handedness, and call her Napoleon, now that you have up and cleared out. You forget that you used to be the nervous wreck of the household before you up and took the bull by the horns. It is a simple enough matter for you to drop in once a week from Seventeenth Street and view the situation with amused tolerance. But you know Mother as well as we do. You know that no one in this household is entitled to a will of her own except Mother."

"My dear Paula, you talk as if will power were a gift, like music or painting. Will power can be developed like muscle."

"Oh no. Your will power, Mother, isn't normal any more than a giant's muscle is normal. Yours is crushing. You— you've crushed me with it. Crushed me with it as surely as if you had steam rolled me. You crushed me with it the day you let—Harrison walk out of this room——"

"Now, Paula——"

"You did. You did!"

There was something so stricken about Paula. She was as

white as a handkerchief left lying beside waters that were being dragged.

"Paula," said Olga, who had risen, white too, "if you want to make me physically ill, then go into that all over again."

"I'm sorry, Olga."

"You poor weak child of mine. Is it possible you don't see yet that what I did for you was——"

"I'm sorry, Mother. Please. No more. I—only that question of will power coming up. I—I know so cruelly what—oh, what is the use of deceiving ourselves? Mother, this young fellow Wells who is coming here to see Ermie—you're not interfering there already?"

"The idea! As if one could even take him seriously."

"For heaven's sake, Paula, stop dramatizing an incident. The bare fact of the matter is that Ermangarde indulges in a nervous chill because the mater asks a big husky girl to pass the lemon and the waffles at the same time. You—Bertha—your shoulders are pretty broad, aren't they? I've an idea that you understand General Napoleon pretty well."

"Yah, Miss Olga."

"Bertha is a good girl. A bit slow but a good listener. There is an old German saying my father used to be fond of. It translates something like this. 'He was strange with the wisdom of his ear to the ground.' That reminds me of Bertha. Bring in some hot waffles, please."

Paula's pale face, with the brow shaped like the upper bulge of a pear and the thinning but pretty hair drawn so tiredly from it, was still quivering and there was a beating vein in her temple.

"Olga, while you are here, won't you talk to Mother about this servant situation? It is impossible for one girl to carry the work of this household with only the wretched assistance of day help."

"Well, Paula, Mother hasn't been able to keep help in the twenty-five years I've known her. What is the idea of unearthing the family skeleton at this time?"

"Shh-h-h, Bertha doesn't need to hear this discussion. I remind myself of the English government. I let my children talk revolution from their soap boxes to their heart's content and in the din of their mere words I sit back and run my sane and conservative household."

"Paula is right, 'Tilda, either you ought to give up the house entirely and go to a hotel like the Savoy or the Plaza, or learn to curb your personality sufficiently to make it endurable here for the average servant."

"Bertha is a jewel, but she is the only one we ever had who could sort of seem to rise superior to Mother's domination."

"What is she, anyway? A Pole or a Swede? Sort of a Sacred Cow from the look of her."

"She'd have to be, to be able to endure it here."

"Nonsense, she is a great serene peasant girl with that slow kind of strength that makes an invaluable servant. She is one in a million. I'll wager she is the only servant in New York in cotton stockings to-day."

"I tell you, Olga, 'Tilda is so strong herself she doesn't realize it, but it isn't fair to expect this household to run along with one servant."

"One servant. What is the matter with you? I do the work of five."

"Exactly. That is what makes a driving machine out of you. The average servant won't and doesn't have to stand being driven. There is another side to the servant question, you know. Silk stockings! Isn't it sufficient that they have to wash our pots and pans for us—carry slops—are we to begrudge them even the silk stockings of life!"

"Hear. Hear."

"The average servant, Mother, won't——"

"Oh, tush, tush, with the average servant. The average servant doesn't interest me. I am not an average person."

"But Mother, we are average girls! Can't you see the cruel sapping thing that life in this house has come to mean? Father —frankly ran away from it——"

"There is neither taste nor justice in that remark."

"Olga has left."

"School of Philanthropy——"

"I find what retreat I can—since—since—Harrison——"

"Paula!"

"And now—little Ermangarde! Don't blame her for running down to what you call the 'Isms' of Greenwich Village, Mother. Don't blame any of us for—retreating. You're a general, Mother—Olga's right—a Napoleon—we're only——"

"I am what is best for you all, only you don't know it. Thank God, though, my skin is thick."

"But to get back to the subject, Mother. It is unendurable that a home, I mean a house, like this must be run without servants, because of your tyrannies."

"What is the matter with you? Hasn't Bertha been promising us a house girl for sometime past? That Helga, a friend of hers."

"Why, we need at least five servants, Mother. We cannot even keep a butler. You know that yourself, Olga. You know how you used to storm every time a butler or a parlor maid left. Well, Mother hasn't had but one servant in this big barn of a house all the months and months that Bertha has been here. . . ."

"You can't change a leopard's spots, Paula."

"Well, you girls must confess that this dreadful leopard mother of yours is always willing to go on the dissecting table, for her family to further discuss the immutability of those spots."

"Your spots are too like Mother's, Olga. That's why you've —escaped, I guess."

"Nonsense. My rights are merely the inalienable rights of the eldest."

"Then, in heaven's name, what are just the inalienable rights of being just a daughter? A Terrible Meek—like me."

"Submission, my darling, is the terrible lot of the meek."

"Or disaster. . . ."

"Oh, God," chanted Olga, extending her legs and yawning with a crackle of mannish shirtwaist, "deliver us from the evil of those who have our welfare at heart."

"He *has* delivered you," said Paula and regarded her sister with eyes that were a little humorous and enormously tired.

"Come, come," cried Mrs. Oessetrich jumping up, "something tells me there is a hiss behind all this patter. I have tickets for Professor Hartwisch of Brooklyn Institute on Bismarck the Man and Myth."

"But, Mother, I loathe Hartwisch."

"Nonsense. Bertha, run upstairs and help Miss Paula with her wraps and tell Miss Ermangarde that my masseuse will be here at eight o'clock to give her a treatment for those pains in her shoulders. If Mr. Taggart telephones while I am gone, tell him I will be in his office at nine o'clock to-morrow morning on the matter of those mortgages. Hurry, Paula, Hartwisch

begins at eight. Bertha, oh Bertha—dear me, what dull ears—
Bertha, bring me down my moleskin cape. She's a good listener, but I have come to the conclusion that she only hears
what she wants to hear."

"That's why you have been able to hold on to her all this
time, 'Tilda."

Mrs. Oessetrich cast quick, bird-like, and adoring eyes upon
her eldest.

"You're impertinent, darling," she said.

Yes, that was the secret. To inure oneself to Mathilde
Oessetrich until she was like a great old tower bell ringing
out over a moor that had not even a parish to summon.

Ding. Dong. The words beat up against Bertha so dimly.
For years she was to move through the tinny clatter of them,
*ding, dong,* around her head in a flock of dissonances.

Butlers and parlor maids simply would not remain. Agencies
were indefatigable and newspaper advertisements brought scant
response. It was as if some invisible symbol of a chalk mark
were against the Oessetrich portals. But there were always
the fugitive day helpers, and in a way Bertha preferred it so.
It left her the sovereignty of the servants' quarters, and the
lovely evenings that Paula wove along the keys. These
evenings made the days seem merely like briary little paths
down which one must run to meet them. Cool dim gardens
of Paula's music. Schumann. Schubert. Brahms. Mozart.
Paula played Mozart as if the keys were little wounds that bled.
Lyric exaltation—morose mysticism of Richard Strauss.
Salome. Electra. Monstrous flowers of fancy. Conflagra-

tion of discord. Fiery particles. Boiling darkness. Then again, so tenderly that it was hard to bear, lacy loveliness of Chopin. Beethoven. Appassionata Sonata.

Booming names that Bertha had never even heard. Deathless masters of the deathless tonal torrents. Deathless masters— but one of them had strolled with the girl with the flax-colored braids like Bertha's, across the plushy meadow and at dawn had lain singing to her the troubled wisps of melody that were not quite born. The wisps of old sound. . . .

Dudley Wells was the wavy-looking young man who was coming to visit Ermangarde, wavy because his clothes seemed always too large for his nervously slender body. He seemed to shrink from contact with them, so that his trousers ran in little ripples along his legs and air currents got somehow up under the back of his coat and flapped it mildly.

He wrote poetry that looked on the page like the first footsteps abroad in a snowstorm and edited a slender sporadic magazine that was printed on arty deckle-edge, butcher's paper.

### The Whisk Broom
Published Every Once in a While.

The two collections of his poetry which Ermangarde kept jealously on her own desk were thin, too, ascetically bound in cardboard, and with the verse stepping in a stark sort of straggle down the page. One of them had its back broken from frequent opening to the same page; a strange page, with words gleaming as if a lapidary had tossed them willy nilly.

There was a copy of *The Cathedral Under the Sea* on that desk, too. It lay there so casually, sometimes open and face downward. It could throb through the dust cloth. The slender volumes, one titled "Lanterns" and the other "Sal Atticum," were very thumbed and even wept upon.

Ermangarde and her titillating secret! Dainty little hours of sipping into these books like a bird on the brink of a pool, but she would thrust them beneath a cushion if Bertha came in to dust, or she heard her mother's footsteps, and on the evenings that Wells came to sit stiffly beside her, on the pale brocaded couch in the enormously gold and brocaded drawing-room, the pink would come out in her face hours beforehand, quite effacing the muddiness.

Mrs. Oessetrich trod the delicate lay of the land between Ermangarde and the none too intrepid Wells, with spiked and characteristic boots.

Ermangarde, a frightened child at the frailty of the lovely thing that was newly hers, cried, and tried to stave her off.

"Mother, if you would only leave us be! Don't come tramping into the drawing-room on us that way, vivisecting him with your lorgnettes and calling him 'young man.' He's too sensitive. The things you say, 'Tilda, they make the room shiver, as if— as if a truck were rushing through. It's not so much what you actually say, but the way you say it, dear. So matter-of-factly. I—we—he isn't interested in your Ethical Membership Drive or your Single Tax theories. At least, dear, not when you tramp in on us—that way. So terribly matter-of-fact that somehow—oh, I can't analyze it—but it makes us feel ridiculous —futile—just sitting there. Mother, won't you please not make us feel so——"

"So what? Pish. I hate mooning. It's servant-girly and park-benchy."

"Mother!"

"Never did it in my life. That's one thing I can say for your sister Olga. Faults aplenty, but a matter-of-fact head on her shoulders."

"But——"

"Marry, if you must, when the proper man comes along. Nature is sly and catches most of us in the end, but don't piddle! Don't waste time on that absurd game of falling in love with love!"

"Mother——"

"I hate puppy love. It nauseates me."

"Dudley and I——"

"Dudley. Is that his name? His name *would* be Dudley."

"It is too bad to have to inform you, dear, that you are speaking of one of the foremost poets of the younger school."

"What school? Kindergarten?"

"Oh, Mother, you are the cruelest woman I ever knew. You've a way of making everything seem absurd. You—you could make Confucius seem ridiculous."

"He is."

"If you must know it, Dudley is the only human being I have ever known who—who—has shown me the way out of the hard crust of myself into—into—beauty—I—if I have the courage to use a sheer word like 'beauty' before you."

"You use the word 'beauty' like the child you are."

"You don't know any kind of beauty, Mother, except the beauty you can see with your mind. You're all mental."

"Thank God."

"You have never felt the sweep and surge of——"

"You are so callow that it is positively embarrassing to have to see it happening."

"I——"

"Very well, let your pale-faced poet with adenoids sweep you and surge you and see where it will land you——"

"Mother!"

"You say he edits the *Dust Broom*."

"The *Whisk Broom*, Mother, you know it isn't the *Dust Broom*."

"I beg your pardon, the *Whisk Broom*, of course. Well, you let one of those ninety-pound fangle-dangle poets around Greenwich Village do your sweeping and surging with his whisk broom and——."

"Mother, I know it is impossible to get the better of an argument with you. Only don't ridicule us, dear. Dudley is so—so sensitive. Don't make us feel silly and immature and drifting just because you are so sure and level-headed and both your feet so firmly planted on the ground. Let Dudley become more accustomed to us, Mother. I—Mother, you see, Dudley, he's nothing but a boy, dear, a sensitive boy—too sensitive to withstand your blasting kind of ridicule—if you could be a little understanding with him—with us, dear—Mother—don't drive off Dudley!"

"Well, if an old woman like me can drive off a suitor——"

"You can, Mother. Don't make me hark back to—to Paula and Harrison again—but if it happened with a hig, hale fellow like Harrison—why—why everything about Dudley, Mother, is too sensitive not to wither under your methods. Even his feelings for me. They would be the first to go. Not because he wanted it that way—but they would wither, dear. He will start by dreading you and then dreading me because I am your—'Tilda dear—can't I make you see just a little, the delicate fiber of a boy like Dudley?"

"I understand too much as it is."

"No. You can't. You don't. That's what frightens me so. You can't. Why even Bertha—that great, white peasant girl out there in your kitchen—why there—there is something about her comes nearer to understanding the frail, delicate, tremendous little trifles about life—than you, Mother—really."

"My two feet are on the ground."

"So terribly on the ground."

"Get out and interest yourself in things that matter. Suffrage. Social work, like your sister. What about that course in economics that I even agreed to take with you at Columbia?"

"I loathe economics. . . ."

"Well, you expect your share of a big fortune some day, don't you? If you do, learn how to take care of it first. Learn the history of coffee before you inherit your coffee plantations, learn——"

"Coffee doesn't interest me, Mother, any more than——"

"It doesn't? Well then, trust that Whisk Broom fellow to take care of you in the manner to which you have been accustomed. If you two young people are really serious, stop mooning and go off and get married and start on your own."

"Mother, you know we can't do that for a little while, anyway. Dudley isn't a money maker. He wouldn't be himself if he were. Mother, you—you've so much. So enormously much. That is one of the sublime uses of money. To make it easy and possible for genius like Dudley's to grow and expand. Mother—if you would!"

"Would what?"

"Would—I—somehow, I—we girls—not one of us, Mother, has worked out her life very happily, yet. Olga is only insulating herself with her bizarre way of living. Poor—poor Paula—and——"

"Paula!"

"Oh I'm not saying that Harrison was the man for her in the worldly sense of the word any more than—than perhaps Dudley is for me—but since—but since it happened that way with Paula—I—sometimes I fear for Paula, Mother. Her eyes. They can look so big and glassy after she's been locked up there for days and days playing to herself. I—Mother, we are none of us happy girls. Wouldn't it be almost like a symbol of the turning of the tide for all of us if Dudley and I—well—it—Dudley's proud, Mother. We would have to do it so delicately. As if he were granting us the privilege. And that's what it is—isn't it—to make the creation of beauty possible? I—if Dudley had me—Mother—he doesn't quite realize me yet, but he would. He would. If Dudley had me—and leisure—if we could make him feel that in permitting us to give, it is he, not us, who would be conferring favor——"

"Oh I see," said Mrs. Oessetrich, her laughter like a burst string of dropping beads, "my dear, clever second-born, the idea being to prevail upon our whisk broom poet to overlook the crassness of the offer and agree to live upon the bounty of a mother-in-law, whose only excuse for being is that she apologetically may keep the poetic hearth-fire burning."

"No—no——"

"Surely, my offspring, a plan to warm any parent's heart! Do esoteric poets accept anything so crass in payment as coin of the realm, or is there a more subtle way to cast gold-dust before the whisk-broom suitor?"

Ermangarde let her head roll back as if she had been wounded.

"That's the trouble with mooning," said Mrs. Oessetrich. "It makes fools of the best of us," and went out, sidestepping Bertha, who was on her knees waxing the floor.

The woolen little polishing-pad made a soft, hurrying, whispering noise and the floor began to gleam in pools and you walked on your knees and squatted under the piano and stole in between the legs of chairs.

Suddenly Ermangarde, left in a heap on the couch, thrust out her hand, and Bertha, her own smelling of floor oil, took it and held it there until the black wing of a December twilight came in through the brocade window curtains and Ermangarde slept in such a tense little ball, that in order to unhook her fingers, Bertha had finally to lift them off one by one, like burrs.

In the center of Bertha's brow the hair ran down in a peak. One spring that peak began to whiten. Ashes of roses. It was curious and a little bit sickening, seeing the white push its way through the yellow. The dainty hoar of a first frost and yet, with the immemorial gesture of women, Bertha sat before her bit of mirror plucking the new white hairs and spreading them sadly along the back of her hand. It was many a day before the new pale tinge came really to be noticeable, but the lovely jonquil braids that she could wind three times around her head were Bertha's vanity and she wept at their passing.

Something new, too, and subtle, was letting down in Bertha. The slowing of the engine. New tirednesses. Strange flushed lassitudes. The plunge of her arm from the socket was no longer straight as the drive of a piston. It broke at the elbow. It was still easy enough to drag heavy objects with the hoist of a man, or tear at the entrails of fowls with the old fiery clutch, but sometimes in the eternal upstairs and downstairs the knees had a sense of giving way. An absurd, empty, tickled feeling, as if they had each gone off into little faints. There was nothing to do but wait then, holding on to the balustrade until the strength flowed back into them.

The old lunge that could drive a keg halfway up a hillside; that fling of the wrist that could squeeze a mop dry at one turn —something had gone with the imperceptible, the pussy-foot years. Jonquils. That plunging bison sense of excess strength.

And the din, the din of Mrs. Oessetrich. Sometimes the clatter of it made Bertha want to cry. That was because she tired more easily. The years were at her, but she called it neck-ache and bought a bottle of liniment.

It was impossible to spend the every-other-Thursday-afternoon-off, indoors. Mathilde Oessetrich was at you like a woodpecker.

"Bertha, since you are not going out this afternoon, I wish you would help me take an invoice of the flat-silver for the insurance company." Or: "Bertha, how can you sit there doing nothing even if it is your day off? Boil up some suds and wash the crystal chandelier in the drawing-room. And be careful, those pendants are the finest cut-crystal."

There was no lock on her door and the imminence of these invasions made her sit stiffly away from the back of her chair, fearing them. So willy, nilly, on her every-other-Thursday afternoon, Bertha went out.

There was no place much to go except that Thurn's Department Store on Fourteenth Street had a sheet music department, where they crashed out the popular selections of the day on an upright piano. There was always a little swirl of excitement around it and sometimes, if you lingered on the edge, through the din and the clatter something sweet came through.

And then one day, Mrs. Oessetrich sent her down to Arrow-maker's department store to match some curtain net. That was a place to know! You could walk all of every-other-Thursday afternoon in a tropics of satin brocades and little wisps of fugitive perfume, and at three o'clock an organ played out into the din and made it throb like a heart. Then you could walk upstairs, the great stairs that were as vain as the arch to the neck of a swan, and across an aerial bridge that led from a Doge's palace into the dim Persia of the Oriental room, where the rugs burned in strange, flameless fables across the floor and squatting gods sat drowsy with centuries. Sometimes the doors to the auditorium were open and no one cared if you slipped in and sat down while the melody smoked out of the organ pipes. . . .

But then, gradually, Helga began to commandeer these afternoons. She waited for Bertha in a drug store on Madison Avenue. Sometimes they went to a motion picture theater or, if the weather was fine, walked in Central Park. Strangely enough, for Helga, who was loquacious, there was very little talk. So little that often they walked the wind-swept rectangle of the reservoir in silence, their faces thrust ahead for the slap of the gale and Helga's pretty fur scarf standing out stiffly behind. Hand in hand. Helga liked to worm her palm up into Bertha's as a child would, and then she had to take running little steps to keep up. Bertha's strides were so long. Sometimes, keeping up with her, Helga's breath began to come in gasps and tears of effort popped out in her eyes. Tears that she seemed to like to flagellate herself with, because she had to hurry with three steps to Bertha's calm, unconscious one, until the blur before her eyes and the pain in her side made the neat cinder path around the water a morass, through which she began to stagger. Then they would sit, still hand in hand, on a bench and watch the day wind down into dusk. No talk, chiefly because when Helga began and her lips started to shudder at what she had to say, she had not the strength, and had a constant, a neurotic fear of fainting out in public places; and so they sat silent or coaxed the squirrels or watched the children tear past on roller skates and sometimes Bertha had little drony bits to say of the Oessetrichs.

"Oessetrichs. Oessetrichs. I know why you are always rubbing it into me that there's a good opening for a second girl, there. I know!"

"I was yoost mentioning it, Helga."

"Ah no, you wasn't 'yoost mentioning it.' You're one of those workers in the dark. It's not what you say. God knows where you got the capacity for saying what you don't say. Well, lay off—don't you worry about me."

"I—won't——"

"Well don't! Save it for the second girl at the Oessetrichs if they are ever able to get one that's fool enough to stay."

But one Thursday evening long after, Helga sagged down so when they came to their parting of the ways at the Madison Avenue drug store, that Bertha had stiffly to hold her up by the arms for fear she was going to fall.

"Helga?"

"You got me, Bertha. I—can't go—back—there. Mc-Murtry—the mouths—I can't go back. Take me, Bertha—do they still need me—second girl——"

"I bane promising Mrs. Oessetrich I would get her a second girl. You."

"I—I—never thought you would get me."

"Come, Helga."

And so the Oessetrichs acquired a second girl.

That was a winter to be remembered. Sometimes at night if Bertha so much as threw herself across the bed for an instant before mustering up the energy to undress, there she lay all night, prone, her heavy shoes riveted to her feet and her clothing lumped clumsily between her and complete rest.

To find the time and the strength somehow, so that it would seem as if Helga herself had done it, to scour the pantry sinks. They were of German silver and Mrs. Oessetrich was inordinately proud of them. To beat the rugs for Helga's general cleaning day and keep for her the enormous drawing-room pier glasses and the crystal chandeliers and the bathroom fixtures glitteringly bright. To scurry upstairs with the fire logs when Helga sank down crying with them on the cellar stairs, and pile them outside the library door, so that all there was left for Helga was to trip in and stack them in little pyramids beside the copper scuttle.

It sapped you, not only the work of that, but the strain of that, and then all the old querulousness was back in Helga. As the pretty sheen to her hair dulled and the tips of her fingers began to spread and the nails to break, her eyes sort of dimmed, as if two little lamps had been hurried out of them and evenings up in the room she shared with Bertha, the din of her talk beat down the sound of Paula's playing and the wall was never a fan bowing, but of ochre and green wallpaper, with one flap of it hanging down and showing the naked plaster.

"Well, now you have me here, what are you going to do with me?"

"No, Helga, I—didn't——"

"Oh yes you did. You had your heart set on getting me here two years before I give it a thought. Old Napoleon told me so herself. The first night you was working here you promised to get her your friend Helga for second girl. You got me here, you know you did!"

"Yes—Helga——"

" 'Yes, Helga.' Well, I'm being a good girl. I'm back lugging the wood to toast somebody else's toes and eating off the kitchen table what's left off the dining room table. I'm back. I'm the servant problem again. The problem without a chance. You have a thick hide, you don't feel like I do."

"I feel——."

"Why, we ain't even got organization. The hodcarriers got that much. We can't tell the truth about the kitchen side of the door, because we ain't got the voice of organization. What's the answer? The women who hire us call us an ungrateful lot and who is there to answer back? Me? I got a fat chance getting listened to, ain't I? Ungrateful! Ungrateful for what? That's what I want to know. . . ."

"Helga, shh-h-h—Miss Paula——"

"There's nobody to get up and explain for us. The men don't know. They get all their information from their women. That gives us a helluva chance, don't it? And who is to dispute it all? We can't. We ain't got the voice or the language. Nobody writes pieces or prints articles about us from our side of the fence. We're not interesting. Who wants to see a show about a servant? Who hears anything about us except from what the women who hire us have to say about us? God help a woman whose reputation depends entirely on what another woman has to say about her. Well, it's that way with the

servant problem—every other kind of labor gets a hearing.
We don't. The public is satisfied to take the word of the
women who hire us. It's easier. Leave it to the public to take
the easiest way!"

"Yah. . . ."

"What kind of an angle on us do you think Mrs. Farley or
Mrs. Oessetrich give when they get up and spout about the
servant problem at one of their finger-roll-and-chicken-salad
club meetings?"

"Helga, shh-h-h——"

"Yes, I said it. What do they know about us, except that
we are fourteen-hour-a-day machines that mustn't balk
or break down, or we get ungrateful? Ungrateful for
what? Oh, God, tell me what? Ungrateful because my life
is chained to a sink. What's Ermangarde Oessetrich done to
make her so much better than I am that I got to make her
bed and pick up her silk nightgown after her? What's she
done that makes her the waited on and me the waiter on?
Oh, you got me back. But deep down in my heart I know
it ain't worth being good for. I'm like a kid sleeping on the
floor. I can't fall outta bed because there is no place to fall.
See? That's me. I lose if I win. There's a helluva lot of
fun in a game like that. I lose if I win."

Words. Words. Words. They beat about the little room
in imprisoned flutterings. Evenings of them. Weeks of them.
Eternities of them. Sometimes Helga fell asleep almost in
the midst of what she was saying, and had to be undressed
and tucked in between the scrawny covers.

She loved that moment of bed. The evening was like a nest
to her. into which she crawled drowsy with the sense of her

safety. Sometimes she sighed out and closed her eyes and snuggled her palm very deeply up into Bertha's.

"I'm safe here with you, Bertha—never let anybody—get me. I'll work. I'll pick up her nightgown and clean her shoes —my side—that's what kills me—but keep me safe—Bertha —McMurtry—keep me safe, Bertha——"

Then it was easiest to get her to sleep. She was like a child. Relaxed.

About once a month the von Schlegels came to dine. He was president of the Turnverein National Bank and also had enormous coffee plantation holdings. She wore a diamond necklace entirely concealed by the fold of fat at her neck. Hans von Schlegel was one day to die at his desk of a stroke. He was already purpling.

One evening at a dinner to the von Schlegels, Ermangarde, who wore a light blue taffeta dress sown in pearl passementerie and her hair in two little round mats of braid over each ear, burst suddenly, and apparently apropos of nothing, into such a fit of weeping that between them, Paula and Bertha had literally to carry her upstairs.

The meal proceeded stiffly through, and Mrs. Oessetrich did not leave the table. For an hour she and von Schlegel computed compound interest, with Mrs. von Schlegel nodding and breathing down on her bosom so loudly that the lace swayed. But after dessert she went upstairs, holding her heavy green satin gown up about her as she bent over Ermangarde, all her folderols of bead and bugle trimmings dangling. The Oessetrichs dressed like that. Sharp hard colors. Laid-on trimmings. Zouave jackets of spangled net. Appliqués. Not even the girls dressed wisely. Olga, to be sure, had her somewhat mannish, modish manner, but her tweeds were thick and her expensive felt hats had a dowdy droop. Mrs. Oessetrich loved parrot green. It covered her like a shellac, and her chapped-looking arms and bosom rose out of it and made her as brilliant-looking as a cockatoo.

"What is this? Don't you feel well, Ermangarde? Bertha, go downstairs and send Helga into the drawing-room with the coffee and liqueurs."

By this time, Ermangarde, her storm of crying over, and lying wanly in the crumple of blue taffeta dress, opened her salt-bitten eyes.

"No, Bertha, don't you go. Stay here. I'm sorry, Mother, I must have been a little hysterical. I didn't mean to. . . ."

"Does anything hurt you? Are you ill? No? Well then, bathe your eyes and come downstairs. The von Schlegels want a little bridge."

Paula, who had been sitting at her sister's head, looked up at this, her eyes the curious blue of flame burning along the top of cognac. Thin flame through which you could see the clear empty bottoms.

"Why, Mother! Ermangarde can't go downstairs any more this evening. She's had another nervous chill."

"Nonsense. A lovesick chill. A little self-control is the best kind of treatment. It makes it extremely awkward——"

"I'll go down, Mother, in Ermie's place."

"Very well. I suppose it will appear no more peculiar to have Ermangarde up here in a love trance, than it would be if you were to remain upstairs mooning with your music."

"Mother. I——"

"I suppose I may as well reconcile myself to a neurotic family of girls. Bertha, when Miss Ermangarde is finished having you hold her hand, I wish you would hasten downstairs. That girl Helga, for some reason, becomes a perfect moron when you are not about. If you need anything, Ermangarde, you can ring," said Mrs. Oessetrich, and bounced out, slamming the door.

But at two o'clock that morning, with Bertha still holding her hand, Ermangarde drifted off into such a gale of sobbing that Doctor Ehrenfest, the family physician, was finally called and the aroused household scurried through hallways in kimonos and soft slippers. Lights were blazing on all floors and Mrs. Oessetrich in a padded house gown, and her head in a fury of crimpers, was pale as china.

"Come now," said Dr. Ehrenfest, who had assisted the three Misses Oessetrich into the world, "we must get to the bottom of what is troubling this child. Love affair? Out with it, Ermie, you can't fool your Uncle Ehrenfest."

But the squirt of morphia into Ermangarde's left arm was already carrying her off down strange rivers, her closed lids quivering and her cheeks, down which the tears had stormed, lashed and blanched-looking. Paula, at the head of Ermangarde's bed, kept her head averted because she was crying.

A silent, eerie little group. Bertha, crouched there beside the bed, because Ermangarde's fingers were tight as wire around her wrist and would not let go. Paula with her queerlooking, blue-flame eyes. Mathilde Oessetrich, china-white and a little frightened, standing there at the footboard and gazing down on to the bed. The professional-looking face of the doctor beginning to pucker wisely.

"Mathilde, have you been up to your old tricks of taking captaincy of another daughter's soul?"

A long sob forced itself through Paula's clenched lips.

"Nonsense, I suppose it's her appendicitis pain again."

"No, the child's case doesn't diagnose that readily. This appendix seems to be up under her heart or in her brain. We can't cut to find this pain. We have to probe."

"That is mid-victorian. Girls don't do it any more. Swooning off at love affairs. Pish."

"Ah, now we are getting at it. Then there *is*——"

"Oh, Ehrenfest, you're an old granny. Always have been. Suppose there is. It just isn't done—it isn't nice—prostrating herself in this fashion. Dramatics, I call it."

"The child hasn't prostrated herself, Mathilde. She is in a state of nervous collapse. We must get at the source of this thing, and see what's to be done before she comes out from under the influence."

Paula turned her eyes upon her parent.

"Tell him, Mother."

"Tell him? Tell him what? This is abominable. Having my children talk to me and of me as if I were a criminal."

"Tell him, Mother."

"Tell him that the only normal strong and capable member of this family is myself?"

"Tell him about Dudley."

"Well, then, Ehrey, I suppose I am to confess to you, like a culprit parent, that Dudley Wells is the occasion of Ermangarde's brain storm."

"The author?"

"I thought the incident was closed and forgotten when he suddenly ceased coming here about a month ago. That is the sum total of it, so far as I know. But if that is the cause of Ermangarde's brain storm, I beg to be excused. I am going back to bed."

"Mother—that isn't the sum total——"

"It is a blessing I have a sense of humor to fall back upon. If ever a woman has tried to rear her daughters into self-sufficient, independent women, capable of swinging the great fortunes which will ultimately come into their hands, I have. I brought a great fortune into my marriage and, if I do say it I have managed and enlarged it with the clearsightedness of an entire corporation. I have tried to rear my girls toward that ideal of self-sufficiency. I have tried to inoculate them with a realization of their own social and economic integrity. I have——"

"But, my dear Mathilde, nature is——"

"Bah! Nature is a trickster. Let the weak succumb. If my girls must marry, let them use the same judgment and discrimination about it that I expect them to use in the management of affairs not so vital to their well-being. Nature tricks the weak. Gray matter, not passion, rules the strong. You've something of a sense of humor yourself, Ehrenfest. It should afford you a real laugh. Me of all women! Even Olga, I hear, is having herself psychoanalyzed in quest of her particular sex complex. Ermangarde here in hysterics because of a poet who wears a size fifteen collar, and Paula bemoaning her girlhood away because the man she fancied herself in love with had the good judgment to take himself down to Porto Rico and——"

"You drove him!"

"Ermangarde! 'Tilda! Not that old argument now, please!"

"But she did, Ehrey! She did! She drove him down there just as surely as if she had pursued him every inch of the way. Ridiculed him down there. Harrison wasn't made for that swampy coffee country. . . . It was like sending him to his death . . . a subtle, terrible way of doing it."

"Paula, you don't know what you are saying——"

"I know I don't, Ehrey. I'm sorry, Mother. I guess I—I am queer, Mother, just as you say I am. So queer that— that sometimes it frightens me—frightens me so that I cannot stand by now and see my little sister—Ermangarde—clutching on so to those illusions you are snatching from her. Olga is trying to fight her way clear. I don't matter any more. But Ermie! Mother, don't try to standardize us all according to your ideas of strength and efficiency. We are more like my father must have been."

"That's what I'm struggling to save you from, if you only had the good sense to know it."

"We are not the strong, fearless captains of women that you want us to be. Not even Olga! Let us be what we are, Mother. Don't break us all with your will."

" 'Tilda, these are stern words for your daughter to have to use."

"It's Ermie, Ehrey, that gives me the courage to use them. She won't talk about it, not even to me, but Mother has driven Dudley away, too. He hasn't been here for weeks. Mother, hasn't it meant anything to you, Ermie's face, those weeks while Dudley was coming? Her new prettiness, Mother?—you —why—why that girl there—Bertha—that servant sitting there holding Ermie's hand has been more to her these weeks— kinder—more understanding. Mother, Ermie's stubborn. She's been going about with Ewald ever since Dudley left. Don't

drive her to things like that—or worse. Ewald isn't the man
for her to be spending her time with. Mother, change your
attitude to Dudley. Bring him back. You be the one to take
the initiative. Oh Mother, give her what she wants. What is
the result of what's happened? Our Ermie, sneaking around
with Spencer Ewald, a married man twice her age. Mother—
make things right."

"Mathilde, Paula is right. There is a time for everything.
The time has come for you to give in to Ermangarde."

"Sentimental nonsense!"

"You've a sick child there, Mathilde."

"Well, where is he? What has become of him? Who frightened him off? In my day it took more than a foolish old irate
parent to——"

Ermangarde stirred there on the bed then, and began to cry
through her tightly closed lids.

"Ermangarde, look up, child, it is your old hobgoblin,
Ehrey."

"Ermie, see, dear. It's Paula. Open your eyes. See, dear,
we're all here. Everything is all right. Mother is as anxious
as any of us for Dudley to come back—aren't you, Mother?
Aren't you, Mother?"

"Yes."

"See, and everything is going to be happy and lovely, dear.
Ermie, you don't have to talk, dear. Just whisper to us where
to reach Dudley. Mother and all of us want it that way. Let
go of Bertha's hand, dear. See, here is Mother's instead.
Tell us, dear, where we can reach Dudley. . . ."

For answer, with two great blisters of tears forcing their
way out of her closed eyes, Ermangarde reached under her
pillow for a little wad of envelope concealed there and, burying

her head under the bolster so that her sobs were muffled, handed
the bit of paper up to Paula:

*"Ermangarde,"* it read, *"your little notes make it so
hard. I have not seen you in all these weeks, well because,
and I should, I must tell you, one night something inside
of me just curled up and died.*

*"It seems too dreadful, for me, who dwells down where
the hem of your skirt touches, to have to be the one to
write these words. But somehow I must find the strength
to be brutal with the truth. Something, little Ermangarde,
killed the perfect thing that was forming between us.
Something too subtle and too cruel for me to analyze, but
toward the end, dear girl, I never put my foot into your
home without a dreadful crushing sense of the imminence
of the death that was taking place in my heart.*

*"Forces too enormous and too infinitesimal for us to cope
with were at work. The shortcomings were all mine, but
alas! there they were. It makes this letter a bitterer task
for me to be obliged to close it on a note of my own happiness. I was married yesterday to Rosemary. You remember the night we met her at the play. And that is just
what she is. Rosemary. A lovely sprig of it, and she has
turned life into a garden. We are sailing to-morrow for
the Madeiras. Ermangarde, try to remember me kindly,
as I shall always remember you, beautifully.*

*"Dudley Wells."*

After the three of them had read this, standing there shoulder
to shoulder and their breathing beating down on to the page,
Paula turned suddenly upon her mother, the blue flames, thin as
breath, leaping along her eyes.

"I hate you, Mathilde Oessetrich. I hate you. I hate you." And cramming her handkerchief up against the terrifying words, ran choking from the room.

And yet the very next morning Ermangarde was up and about as usual. There was something diamond-like in her brightness. Hard. Showy. She was even rude to Paula.

"Don't try to baby me, Paula. I'm all right, I *won't* stay in bed! Do keep out of my affairs, dear. I know what I'm about. I'm quite well. Don't interfere."

So Paula went back to weaving her hours of music along the keys and Ermangarde to the routine of her French and her drawing and her fencing and her singing lessons. And if once in a while she skipped a luncheon or a dinner for which there was no particular accounting, Mrs. Oessetrich held thin-lipped peace. There was that dry, diamond hardness to Ermangarde.

Every Saturday, Madam Lina Gerbhardt, Mrs. Oessetrich's lifelong friend, an enormous contralto who wore stencilled scarves and had taught Calvé, came to the house to give Ermangarde her singing lesson, and then remained for lunch. Ermangarde had a clear little mountain stream of a voice. Lovely in its middle register and with a thin fluty upper range to which she had climbed on years of Madam Gerbhardt's careful *arpeggios*. It was pleasant, during these lessons, to dust softly about the hall that led to the music room.

"Do—me—fah—doh—fah—sol—me—doh—ahh-h-hhhhh—"

Madam Gerbhardt's voice ran underneath Ermangarde's, booming it.

"Doh—me—fah—doh——"

Light-colored Tosti bubbles. Flying banners of Bizet. Richard Strauss.

Bertha liked these lessons. Once Madam Gerbhardt thrust two tickets into Bertha's hands. "Here, girl, there is a Ukrainian chorus singing at Carnegie Hall to-night. You should enjoy that. Go, if Mrs. Oessetrich can spare you."

Bertha went and took Helga. The seats were very far back and the faces of the chorus dim as dreams. The drony silence while you waited. The yellow slits of light. The Slav songs that were full of heart beat and the Slav songs that were full of despair. The love of a harlot. The death of a Moujik. Cossacks who chant at dusk. It was as if the heart were embers and the chorus were sitting in its glow. Love and life and the taste of the red lips of harlots and the running of rivers that are made of tears. There was one. It sang of the Volga. The Volga! Boatmen whose thighs were sweating and whose eyes were bulging from the drag. The pulling boatmen along the shore. . . .

"Come," said Helga when the intermission came. "Let's run along. These Polish wops give me the blues."

There was nothing to do but go. Helga could be so querulous. But up under the roof, all of the night rocked softly, like a river. The Volga. The Volga. Rushing of tears along with the tide and where men sang of joy in a key that was minor. . . .

One lovely spring Saturday when the breakfast room, where the family lunched, was wide open to the languid drift of spring, Madam Gerbhardt, who had been popping salted almonds into her mouth, chopping them sharply and then popping more, spoke out suddenly, just as Bertha was passing her the fillet of sole:

"Well, I see where Rollo Farley died."

"No!"

"Yes, didn't you read it in the *Times* this morning? It seems he spoke at the Poetry Society night before last, complained of feeling ill when he arrived home, took a sleeping powder before he went to bed, and never woke up. Oh!"

"Bertha, you clumsy!"

'It's all right, no harm done."

"Bertha, do be careful. She didn't ruin your sleeve with the fish sauce, did she? Bertha, Helga should be serving anyhow. I cannot understand why you insist upon carrying half of that careless girl's work for her—so Rollo Farley is dead."

"Rollo—Farley——"

"A greatly overestimated man. A one-book author."

"Yes, Mother, but what a book! I think that *The Cathedral Under the Sea* belongs to the esoteric group of really great poems."

"Pish. Free verse. Free-and-easy-verse. I hate faddism. The forms that were good enough for Goethe and Wordsworth and——"

"Have you read *The Cathedral Under the Sea,* Mother?"

"No, but I know what the entire movement stands for. You belong to the violent reactionaries if you permit two lines to rhyme. A couplet is about as out of date as an antimacassar."

"You speak precisely with the authority of one who knows nothing about the subject."

"At least, Ermangarde, I am not a reactionary in the way I permit my daughters to address me."

"But, Mother, you must admit that at least I speak with the

authority of having read the book. *The Cathedral Under the Sea* is a great impressionistic poem, not the mere dithyrambic prose that the free verse writers are dabbling in. Its metrical devices are as cunning as Masefield's effects of the rolling of the sea."

"Now, when you speak of Masefield——"

"Exactly, Mother, it is because you can appreciate Masefield, that I won't have you condemning Rollo Farley before you have read *The Cathedral Under the Sea*."

"Ermangarde is right, 'Tilda. Farley accepts technique without being tied to it."

"Of course he does. He does precisely what your Masefield does. He does what he pleases with his rhyme scheme between his first and his sixth or seventh lines but those lines hold the internal ones firmly together. Farley is not an anarchist. He's merely a Progressive. He dares to liberate form and language."

"Pish, you've read that somewhere."

"I've felt it, you mean. Besides I'm not bothered about form. Much of the beauty of *The Cathedral Under the Sea* lies in its formlessness—the formlessness of life. *You* understand, don't you, Madam?"

Madam, who had a pudgy, a square, an emotional hand, placed it to the left of her stencilled scarf and closed her eyes.

"Indeed I do. Any work of art, regardless of its form or formlessness, is great when it makes you feel that its creator has dipped into your very heart for his sensation."

"Precisely."

"That turbulent, inarticulate creature in *The Cathedral Under the Sea!* I can see her sitting there, beautiful-eyed and barefoot, in the forest part of the poem. You remember? Listening. I suppose to the music of the spheres. Hearing it, full of it, and yet silent with it. That is how I feel about so much that is beautiful and fragile in life. Full of it, bursting with it, and yet with no power to express it."

"Oh Madam, you *do* understand!"

"That is what I meant, Ermangarde, in our lesson this very morning. Lift the tones, or they will sink back into the pools of silence and remain unsung. Can't you understand, Mathilde, why we—why that one beautiful thing, even though he never wrote a line that amounted to a hill of beans afterward, can perpetuate the name of Rollo Farley?"

"I must read it for myself," said Mrs. Oessetrich. "I am always prejudiced in advance by a book which has created the furor that this one did. I've never been able to abide his wife. She was a Neidringhaus. Ethan's daughter. One of those Botticelli creatures who is all effect and little else. And how she has capitalized the success of *The Cathedral Under the Sea!* I actually think she sometimes believes that she wrote it herself. Her proprietary air. They were wretchedly unhappy together, you know. Services from the old house in Gramercy Park, I suppose?"

"Yes, Thursday afternoon."

"Well, I'm not going. I might have put myself out while his mother lived. Lucretia Farley was at least harmless and not an attitudinizing Mona Lisa. Bertha, get Circle 345 for me on the telephone. I'll be half an hour late for my bridge lesson at this rate. Paula, for heaven's sake, stop staring. You are getting the habit. If it is one thing I can't abide, it is light blue eyes that stare . . ."

"*The Cathedral Under the Sea*," said Paula. "I was just trying to think. Where—The Cathedral Under the Sea—I—know—her—from—somewhere——"

How curious, turning the corner, just as the bier, slanting, was being carried down the steps. The violet blanket, starlit with anemones, slid a little. Its fragrance stole out softly over the fringe of onlookers. They formed the aisle, these onlookers. The bier passed between them, across the sidewalk and into the hearse. The blanket kept breathing out fragrance. You wanted to faint into it. Sweet. Wistful. Tired. It rode on shoulders and rolled a little, that hoisted caravan of Rollo, and the sidewalk was a desert and the blanket a purple sky with stars and the end of the desert was Rollo's eternity.

Something rather sickening happened then and brought you back into the fringe of the onlookers. The bier was tilted into the hearse. It ran forward a little as if on casters, and two doors with silver handles closed and pinched your heart. The doors closing that way. Like shutting a dear book that had a filigree lock on it and turning the tiny key. The doors closing. The last line of a sonnet.

You stood in the fringe that made the aisle through which the bier passed across the sidewalk, with a place nicked out of your heart.

And then the hearse moved up and a carriage slid into its place, and down the steps, through the sweet breath the violets had left, came the mourners. Mr. Farley. It hurt somehow to look. The years had shrunk him up. He seemed shorter, and all the bombastic pink flesh hung now in pale little oysters of empty skin, and his legs, that had used to be fat and strutty, wavered now, and kept wanting to knock at the knees. It was horrible to see him feel three times with the toe of his shoe before he ventured the step.

With Veronica it was different. Her foot came down coolly and slimly just where she pointed it, and through the mesh of her veil you could see the pale ellipse of her face. Dim. But the features in order. The neatly closed lips. Careful curtains of hair. A griefless face. Dry and oval. Ascetic even of tears.

It made one proud. So burstingly proud to stand there on the fringe of the onlookers, rich with the grief that the face of Veronica was as barren of as a crag. To stand there rich and brimming with the precious sorrow of a love! Poor Veronica, who had no grief.

Gradually the carriages were filled. There were the explorer and the broker and the ex-ambassador and Beebe, only without his portfolio, who had interrupted the family at luncheon that day and caused the nesselrode pudding to go out untasted.

The women whispered and made little sounds like the glass icicles of a chandelier. The ushers brushed their white gloved hands together. It was all very cool and very tearless, and the carriages began to move off without more ado.

It was easy in the city to keep pace with them. There were long halts for traffic and the horses, never out of walk, lifted their hoofs with almost a rhythmic leisure. Clip. Clop. The wheels, slow hoops. Unflecked drivers' whips. Wide sun-washed streets, drowsy with spring afternoon, and the narrow black procession winding out along them. Bertha followed from the sidewalk. It was easy, block after block, but then up over the shoulder of an asphalt hill, the green flush of the country set in and the sidewalks left off and now you had to follow more quickly along the stiff frozen dirt road, but just the same you wound along behind, sweetly and deeply into the quiet. Clip. Clop.

The caravan of Rollo rolling rapidly now, out toward the sun's edge, and Bertha with her gift of grief hurrying after it. She could feel her shoulders spangled with perspiration. They had been so deeply white to him, like the flesh of the magnolia. He had trolled four of his fingers along her whiteness. They had melted against her throat and down into her heart. White tapering roads, in the dark forest along which she ran calling.

The first minarets of the cemetery came up over the next hill. Pale moonrises against afternoon sky. A white battalion of a city, there at attention in the spring afternoon. The winding grind of the gravel roads, and the creeping sweetness of the earth. You could almost taste it. How they ground and squeaked, those wheels, and the horses made great splashes of gravel, and the sentinel city stood unbowing as Rollo rode in.

The little pop-ups of anemones. There was a turned-over clump of them beside the grave, standing there on their heads waiting to be patted down into turf again.

There was a yew tree grew beside an urn. Quiet of that! It made the day seem to pause.

The group tightened up around the grave. Closed solidarity of those backs again. But down on the lovely slant of hill the yew grew beside the urn and it was pleasant to wait there in the freckled shade. It ran along Bertha and mottled her into the background. It made her the color of a sparrow in a tree.

The white and listening marbles. The hill might have been a tripod and the faint throbbing of the burial service a slow rhythmic incense stealing down among the headstones.

A poet was dead.

Long after the carriages had crunched down along the drive again, and the hearse, lighter now, and looking silly with haste had turned cityward, Bertha stole up to the hill. The sun was gone, and in between the serried ranks of the white battalions the light was the color of sabre steel. The stars, too, had that steely aloofness of a spring day turned suddenly dead cold. They were the very early stars, Mercury, Mars and Jupiter, who love in their seasons, to edge the day.

The anemones were back in place. They had been patted there with the broad side of a spade. They looked broken-necked and dying. But the mound itself was raw and brown and its breath came up at you like a sigh. There was a pillow of roses at the head. An empty bed. Rollo was gone. You could sit and weep now, unashamedly.

Rollo must know by now. Everything.

Strange Paula. Sometimes now, she did not leave her room for a week. She played a great deal, for hours, in the whispering fashion up alone in her room. Beethoven. Brahms. More Beethoven. And sewed too. Pink wispy things that grew into a pile and then were folded away in trunks between tissue paper.

"Nutty" was Helga's frequent and succinct comment. Her eyes could seem to water at the evidences of pale finery strewn about Paula's fourth floor room. She fingered the stuffs as if they were flesh, and once Bertha walked in on her posing before Paula's dressing mirror, a web of a nightgown, with two lace butterflies poised on the shoulder straps, held up before her.

"Why shouldn't I? She's just my age. The Lord gave me the same kind of flesh. I love it, too. Anyway, she's nutty."

"You mustn't touch anything of hers!"

"Why not? She's no better than me. She thinks what I out and did. What do you think is in the mind of a girl who sits here day after day making flimsies like these, when she isn't even going to be married? She is no better with her mind than I am with my body. Only she is protected from doing what nobody gave a tinker's dam whether I done or not. This poor little nut thinks she's making a trousseau."

"Why not? Maybe she is."

"Why not? Eddie the chauffeur told me why not. There's no man. He passed out. He wasn't much of a go-getter and old Napoleon sent him down to the coffee plantations and he ate a few fever germs. It's a phony trousseau for a spooky groom. Old Napoleon knows. She comes up when the stuff gets too cluttery and packs it away herself in the trunks. Haven't you ever seen Miss Paula stare when she does it? That kid's queer. She sits up here staring at what she's missed. Sewing for what she's missed and trying to play on the piano what she's missed. Only she's protected from going out after what she's missed. That's the only difference between her being good and me bad."

"Helga, put it down. Someone is coming. Mrs. Oessetrich."

"Bertha, Miss Olga has just telephoned from her Settlement House. It is Commencement day for the girls in her Vocational Guidance Classes. Those nice girls are being graduated into full-fledged milliners. She wants the two silver punch bowls. The big car is up for repairs and Eddie has Miss Ermangarde out in the sedan. I'll have to send you down with them in a taxi."

"Yah——."

"I do believe you are up here doing Helga's sweeping for her! What are you made of? Cast iron? Helga, you shameless

girl, you, letting Bertha carry your share of the work in this
fashion month after month. Get down the two silver punch
bowls, Bertha. Never mind, Helga, I'll put away those pink
things of Miss Paula's. The idea, Bertha up here doing your
sweeping for you. Doing the work for two. What is that girl
made of? Sometimes, I wonder. . . ."

The Vocational Guidance House on Christie Street had no
trade entrance. Only a neat front door, painted red. It stood
open, and it was all that Bertha could do to wedge in sidewise
with the outlandish bulge of her punch bowls.

The door to the left of the bare hallway was also open. What
had once been two parlors of a private residence were thrown
into one. It made a sort of small lecture hall, with a platform
at one end and rows of camp chairs facing it. An American
flag covered one wall and there were white Swiss window curtains and geraniums in bright blue pots and over the platform
the usual engraved, "Opening of the First Continental Congress"
and "Franklin before the House of Lords."

Odor of embalmed philanthropy.

There were three rows of girls seated on the platform.
Latin-looking faces beneath smooth, tamed hair and their
young bodies seeming to flicker under the prisons of the neat
blue skirts and white shirtwaists.

Blazing absence of blazing neckerchiefs and of blazing skirts.
Doused Carmens.

An audience with firm, dry, Anglo-Saxon lips sat along the
camp chairs and stared up at them. The safe, trained little
Carmens who used toothbrushes and knew now, with an
Anglo-Saxon finality, that a rose between the lips was not a

rose at all, but lechery. Olga Oessetrich was speaking from the platform.

It was easy to hear through the open doorway. Olga's voice was so clear. As clear as her face with the hair worn smoothly away from it. As clear as her hands, white square hands that came out boldly from the mannish cuffs.

It was pleasant just to stand there and peer over the great protruding armful of bowls. Olga, who when she came to the house, only sat about with her long indolent legs crossed and watched the smoke of her cigarette with her eyes like slits, here now, eager, and talking down into those careful-lipped faces with a fine young fervor.

Every so often a little patter of hand-clapping broke through and then she stood and waited, her arms folded across her flat boyish bosom and her glance sure as a shot down into her audience.

And then the girls with the Latin faces and the bodies like the quiver of flame began to pass one by one for the tubes of white paper that were bound with red ribbon. Olga handing them, one to each, from the pyramid of them upon the table. Each girl as she passed stood for a moment in the little area of Olga's words, flushed, and then sat down to applause. Slim sapling girls with smooth hair and stiff cuffs like Olga's. Oh, how you wanted to think it was fine . . . all the doused Carmens. . . .

Suddenly Bertha moved forward, so that her head protruded in. Olga's voice and the face of one of the thin sapling girls were so clear. . . .

". . . this young woman need feel no embarrassment as I dwell upon these facts of her early childhood. She is a glory to our institution, and those of you who have endowed us so generously in the past may well look upon this girl with a kind of pride that will inspire you to endow us still more generously in the future.

"Some gracious maternal scheme of things threw her into our midst at the age of fourteen. She has developed from the pinched little undersized waif she then was into a young woman who is prepared to take up her place in the world with dignity and self-respect.

"Chita Migulchi, I have the honor to award you the first honorable mention in your class and a diploma which registers you at our industrial bureau as a graduate milliner of the Christie Street Vocational Guidance School for Girls."

Chita! Chita! You wanted to cry, your throat was so warm and full. Little Chita with the Jocko eyes, but her face smooth now and the lovely pallor of nun's veiling. The well-brushed sheen of her hair. It was hard not to cry with the warmness and fullness. It pressed up against the eyeballs and made them dim. You kept pushing open the door . . . Chita. . . .

That made a draught and someone wanted the door closed. It swung to with a little nick. It left you standing in the hall, which had grown very dark, hugging those preposterous punch bowls and groping your way toward the basement kitchen.

There was something about Ermangarde's smile that glinted. She did it with her lips closed and with the merest lifting of their corners. It was a cold ray of a smile, that made you think of pale-flanked little fish swimming snugly under ice. Her open laugh never came through any more. She smiled constantly, but with her lips in their rigid icicle. You were conscious of the warm white young teeth behind them, but they never lit up her inscrutability. Sometimes her mother regarded her with small, bright, cockatoo eyes.

"Ermangarde, you are pale. A good tonic is what you need. Liver, probably."

"Oh no, Mother."

"Nothing to be ashamed of. We all have them."

"Don't worry about mine, Mother."

"Your father used to say that, too. But I found it more expedient to worry about his liver than about the execrable bad temper that could result from its moodiness."

"Your panacea for all mortal ills, Mother, the liver pill, has its limitations."

"Of course. Meaning that yours is the immortal ill. Well, I am not so sure that my despised little liver pill is not the best sort of cure for lovesickness too. Puppy-lovesickness."

"Mother!"

"Great pouting girl like you. Why, you should be on your knees for thankfulness that you found the fellow out in time. You have been jilted, only you haven't the sound judgment to know it. And here you are, eating out your heart because——"

"Mother, if you discuss it, I'll leave the house—I can't stand it——"

"I am no more eager to discuss it than you are. But you are sallow and you are enigmatic and you are dull. The few hours a day that you spend at home are depressing for the entire household, and, while we are on the subject, you have been seen here and there with Ewald. You are meeting him in public places. Now it must stop. He's a married man and was coming to this house with his wife, Helene Craig, when you were in rompers. It's disgusting and vulgar, and if it continues I shall call him up at his club and forbid him. . . ."

The little icicle smile of Ermangarde's was out.

"Don't forbid any more, Mother. I wouldn't, really."

"You're a sour, enigmatic girl," repeated Mrs. Oessetrich. "The world is yours. You have youth, wealth, and position, but instead of taking advantage of your great opportunities, you sit on the edge of them and mourn for the loss of something that you never owned."

"You mean for the loss of something that you never permitted me to own, Mother."

"Oh, how weary I am of the exactions of my faultfinding daughters. I must be younger than they, in spirit at least, because they all treat me in a fashion that makes me feel juvenile and incorrigible. Family ties and the vulgar wranglings of the household! I wish I were like the cook in my kitchen, free to——"

"You couldn't be like—her, Mother."

"What?"

"Oh—nothing."

The war years plunged in. The city turned the sallow green of khaki. Regiments poured through the streets. Flashing impersonal rows of animated scissors. Farm boys with callouses deep in their hands, marching off, to war on farm boys they had never seen. Great oxygen tanks of patriotism, generated in a hurry, gushed out volatile and inflammable from coast to coast. The phrase "Safe for Democracy" began to jiggle like electric signs before bewildered eyes. Dizzy with its euphony, men fell into regimental step. Thousands and thousands of scissors of them. The whole thing began to swing into a horrible motion like the slow acceleration of a voodoo dance.

Envoys crossed word-swords and all the little men began to run, and the red threads of high-sounding idealisms and patriotism to come out in eyeballs. The inflamed voodoo dance around the cauldron brewed on the table of paternal governments began to grow. . . .

That was the way the men went off to war, riveted with that paternal eye and inflamed with the generated oxygen, the generated phrases, and the generated idealism.

Sometimes they passed the house. Regiments of them. They were so young. Lean flanked. Time and time again Bertha drew down the sashes against their passing. Tramp. Tramp. Tramp-tramp-tramp. It was a horrible rhythm. The willy-nilly young men, steaming up hate.

Olga was in khaki, too. It gave her the sleek flatness of a fowl. Where the expensive tweeds had been clumsy, the khaki lay slick. Slanting shoulders, neat at the armholes and a pat little hat. It made her busy and important, all the hating. She drove a small khaki-colored ambulance around town. Everywhere. She was very earnest.

The world safe for democracy. The little women without sons began to bustle so. The sudden splendidness of making the world safe for democracy. It made you as important as you were in your own home, on general cleaning day. Sweaters to be sorted. Chocolates to be stacked in boxes and addressed for overseas. Sandwiches to be cut for canteens. Chest protectors to be stitched in the name of democracy.

Olga ran her ambulance with her lips straight and her eyes probing ahead and stern. The zeal of the women. Democracy.

Sandwiches to be cut. Chocolates to be stacked. Tramp. Tramp. Tramp-tramp-tramp.

There was a portrait of Beethoven hung in the dining room.

"Take it down, Bertha," said Olga.

Paula cried, as Bertha, steadied on a ladder by Olga, unhooked it from its moulding.

"That's absurd, Olga. What has Beethoven to do with this horrible fighting?"

"War is war."

"Exactly. War is only war. A matter of nations. Art transcends war. Art is the language of God and war is the barking of men. Beethoven is bigger than war. Next year there may be a new war and we may be in league with the very nation we are hating now. Wars change. Beethoven is eternal."

"Easy there, Bertha. Let me hoist. There!"

"Olga—don't——"

"Paula, don't be absurd! How can I ask those boys who are going overseas to walk into my mother's house with that picture hanging on the wall? Have you no patriotism?"

"No. Not that kind."

"You talk like a pacifist!"

"Perhaps—I am."

"Paula!"

"If it means loathing war sufficiently to bear the unpleasant brunt of being branded a coward, I suppose I am a pacifist. Yes, I am a pacifist! I loathe all this blind rushing pell-mell into a struggle arranged by the mighty minority and paid for with the lives of young men who are drugged on trumped-up ideals. I loathe war which destroys the internationalism of art for the puny nationalism of men. The maimed bodies aren't the worst. That's the easy way to hate war. The safe way. I—hate it just as much for the maimed souls that stay at home —to whom the noise of military brass bands is louder than the music of Beethoven."

"Paula, you are merely stupid and sentimental, but just the same those are dangerous, disloyal utterances. You're not well. Go upstairs to your music. I expect some service men here this afternoon for tea and dancing in the drawing-room. Don't make me ashamed to bring them into this house. Bertha, take that picture upstairs into the storeroom."

"Olga!"

"Paula, I know you're not well. But please, dear, never talk like that, even among ourselves. Do you realize that what you said, even though it may be partially true, makes you a traitor? A traitor to your country. Paula—look at me— a traitor——"

The word bit in like a little asp. All the way up to the storeroom, slanting the picture along the narrow stairways, it stung across Bertha's silence.

Paula, who loved Beethoven and wept his lyricism softly along the keys. Paula, who loved Beethoven more than she could hate anything or anybody. Paula a traitor?

Barney, the private night watchman, liked Helga. You knew it by her new slanting and birdwise look. For a long time there had been something shy about her. New silences. She was sweeter about the dull evenings tucked up there under the slant of roof. Sometimes she sewed and smiled or, if Paula was playing, let her head fall back against the chair and her mouth drop open softly. On warm nights, she stole out on the rear stoop for whispering moments with Barney as he passed on his rounds, and on snowy nights, the kitchen range was kept banked a little more than usual. But even after she had gone upstairs for the bit of sewing or to lie back lulled to the weaving of Paula's music, she always slid forward a bit on her chair to the knocking of the night stick. One. Two. Three. Slid forward with the lifted, eager look. Then Bertha knew. The silences were so telltale. Helga, who could suddenly sit neat-lipped and rather inscrutable all evening, and then wear the little smile to bed. It was hard not to tremble for that smile. You trembled more for it than for the garrulous bitterness.

Only once in a while there was a flash in the pan of the old Helga.

In winter she had to snatch her visits with Barney, whispering with him in the kitchen, the ugly gray dish cloth drying across the pan and the great blob of brown soap still soft and smelling from riding greasy water.

"Having to sit company with a fellow like Barney in somebody's kitchen! There never was a girl didn't want a place where she could punch up a few sofa pillows and turn on a pink lamp. A self-respecting man like Barney, and me with no place to entertain him but next to the kitchen sink. A real honest-to-goodness man like him."

Barney was like that. Honest to goodness. A scrub of rough red Irish hair. Enormous hands that fiddled with his hat. Bright blue eyes with wrinkled lids that he batted for all he was worth, and when he laughed his entire face focused in toward the center, until it looked like a shirred rosette.

And Barney could make Helga laugh. Jerky, immature

laughter and one night, when she had her head thrown back in merriment at one of his slow overgrown antics, he put out a shy big hand and touched her softly on the neck where it arched.

"You're like a little bird, there," he said.

She was broody after that and Bertha found her crying the next morning, because Mrs. Oessetrich had her at cleaning some high and difficult pantry shelves that aggravated the chronic pain she had in her side, and Bertha did them for her and later that same day she cried because she broke a porcelain bowl and Bertha took that brunt for her and that evening, upstairs in the pocket of the fourth floor back room, she broke out.

"Barney—likes—me."

"Yah——"

"What do you think he says to me the other night, Bertha, and touched me here—soft on my neck. 'You're like a little bird there'—I likta died, I wish I hadda——."

"Helga——."

"He's got an old woman. His mother. Eighty-eight. Keeps house for him. I know what's in the back of his head same as if I could see in. He don't come out and say it, but he keeps hinting. Wants to take me there. Wants his old woman to see me before she passes on. The way he said that one thing to me. 'You're like a little bird there.' I likta died. I wish I hadda——"

"No—no——"

"Yes! I could land Barney. He's just waiting until his old woman passes on. I could land him, but I wouldn't! A man like Barney to happen to me. Got him hook and bait.

And what do I do? Unhook him and throw him back into the pond. That's being white, ain't it, Bertha?

"Yes—Helga——"

The boys kept marching. You had to stop at street corners to let them tramp past. Tramp. Tramp. Tramp-tramp-tramp.

You scrubbed floors to that rhythm. You breathed in your sleep to it. And the boys with the wide clean faces and the calloused hands stalked and stalked, made drunk with the sudden ecstasy of being a foe. It made the leap in the dark a thing of glory . . . that spat of shot . . . across the eyes. . . .

Every week Olga held canteen in her mother's gold and brocade drawing-room. Rugs were dragged back. Furniture stacked, planks spread from chair-back to chair-back and then piled with pyramids of sandwiches and mounds of salad stuck all over with small American flags. There was a victrola for dancing.

Helga could carve charming sandwiches. Little hearts and spades and diamond-shaped ones made in layers. The boys gobbled them at one mouthful. But sometimes, when the pain in her side was gnawing from the hours of slicing and buttering and stacking, she made plain, square, ragged ones and Olga was cross.

Olga! Life spun for her those war months and for the little group of drab-clad girls who came to help on canteen days. The eager, hating girls. It was thrilling to hate! Thrilling to feed these wide-faced, clean-faced boys the catnip. It made them heroic and gay and debonair and careless, and full of a very fine fervor for fighting that foe unknown and that foe unseen. It made the fine, high-sounding war phrases shine.

It was easier somehow to hate, and to want to fight, with all
of the machinery for making the world safe for democracy so
busily in motion. The making of the gas masks. The measuring of the chest expansion. The cutting of the sandwiches.
The wearing of the puttees.

If you were a farm hand with those hands still callous from
the plow, and every night had slept in the socks and under-
drawers that you worked in by day, and all your youth had
flung forkfuls of fertilizer out over fields and spat in ditches
while you dug them, oh it was stirring and exciting suddenly
to be fed the heart-shaped sandwiches, one to a bite, and to be
danced with by all the Olgas, whose hands were white caresses
and whose eyes adored. It made you long for a thousand
thousand foes and a thousand thousand hates.

Busy days for Olga and the thousands of eager girls in the
service, who were wearing becoming khaki and beating the
tom-tom of the war dance.

Sixteen months of it and on the seventeenth Olga, her eyes
high with strange new fires, sailed on a transport.

It was all very simple. She bounced in one day with a jangle
of the keys to her studio, while Mrs. Oessetrich and Paula were
at lunch. A solemn little meal. Mrs. Oessetrich, with the editorial page of the morning *Times* propped up against her
tumbler, and eating, in her pecksniffy fashion, short quick forkfuls of an *omelette soufflé*. Paula, whose blue eyes were so
languid, almost a little stagnant now, as if something in them
had jammed and could not seem to flow on.

"Well, 'Tilda, I've popped in for good-bys. We're sailing
sometime between now and midnight."

Mrs. Oessetrich swallowed her portion of omelet, and brushed
her mouth with her napkin as a man would. Two ways.

"Well, that's that," she said, and pushed back from the table.

"That's *that,* Mrs. Oessetrich," repeated Olga, and smiled at her with the eyes with the bonfires in them and whipped a cigarette out of a soft pack of them in her khaki pocket and drew up a chair beside the table and crossed her long legs and drew a puff of smoke.

"Have some lunch?"

"No thanks, Mother."

"Umph."

"Say, Mother, I think you're immense." Olga's eyes were round when she said that, with cockatoo rims to them exactly like Mrs. Oessetrich's. They made her very much her mother's daughter.

"I suppose you feared a sloppy mess. Well don't worry, if I have tears to shed I won't prepare to shed them now."

"I'll write often."

"I suppose this is where I should break in with the usual instructions from moron mothers to moron offspring. 'Keep your feet dry.' "

"Don't you love it, Paula? Isn't she great?"

"And there is no use crossing a submarine until you come to it."

"Here's the key to the studio, 'Tilda. You won't mind, dear, keeping the lease for me. It's only a hundred a month."

"I hate waste."

"I know, dear, but it's such a mess, subletting."

"Very well. Give me the keys."

"Where's Ermangarde?"

"Out."

"Oh."

"Take good care of yourself, Paula. Now—now—please—no waterworks!"

"You know—my sentiments—Olga——."

"Yes, and the true pacifist drops his lamb's clothing in time of war."

"Not the true one. The weak one. He drops it because it is so much easier to fight than not to fight——"

"You're sick, darling. Take care of her, 'Tilda. Good-by, Helga. See that you don't elope with Barney before I get back and don't be a sly one and shove off all your chores on to Bertha. We know your system."

Mrs. Oessetrich stood up very straight, as if there were a rod up her back, and her eyes were sharp and darting and as dry as shoe buttons.

"Hurry, girl."

"Good-by, Bertha, you old Rock of Gibraltar. It helps somehow, knowing you're here—on the job. You—whoever you are—so long—old Bertha."

"Good-by—Miss Olga."

"Well, Mathilde, Paula—old dears—tell Ermie good-by and to cut out the Ewald nonsense. It's disgusting. My bags are out in the taxi. The meter will click me out of house and home. So long, dears. Everybody. You know the address. American Expeditionary Forces. Paris—S'long. . . ."

It was very silent, and for every mouthful of tea poor Paula swallowed a great vein came out in her neck. Her omelet and editorial finished, Mrs. Oessetrich rose and following her custom, carried the few crumbs in her lap into the conservatory to shake them into the aquarium.

"Order the car for three, Bertha."

But it was almost five when Mrs. Oessetrich emerged finally

from her room. Eddie started up from a doze at the wheel
as she swept out.

"Where, Madam?"

"Oh—why—just drive."

Her eyes were very shiny and the cockatoo rims quite pink.
And Bertha had to run out after her with her handkerchief,
which she had forgotten.

Ermangarde had not returned by nine that evening, but a
messenger brought a letter. Bertha carried it into Mrs.
Oessetrich, who was sitting alone in the drawing-room, tapping
her foot. The high chandelier flooded the room through
crystal. Once in a while a prism clicked.

"For me?"

"Yah—a letter."

"*Dear Mother,*" it read, "*by the time you receive this note
Ewald and I will be on a steamer bound for somewhere sunny.
There is nothing to feel concerned about. We are very happy
and are going into this thing with our eyes open.*

                              "*Ermangarde.*"

The old, the terrible, the shoe button eyes of Mrs. Oessetrich.
When she raised them to Bertha, they lay shattered in her
head, broken there as if they had been drilled through and
had cracked in a thousand directions.

"Bertha—Bertha—lend me your strength—Bertha—you—
where——"

She fainted out stiffly, like a doll. To revive her, you held
her very closely and very warmly to your heart, until its beating
seemed to beat into her.

The house stood in a great silent yawn. You found yourself tiptoeing through the halls, and the front shades had not been raised, except for general cleaning, in months. Paula played a great deal, but in the whispering fashion, so that if you took your pan of potatoes up to the top of the back stairs and sat there in the gloom to peel them, and to listen, half the time all you heard was the little sing to the silence.

Mrs. Oessetrich drove Olga's little fawn-colored ambulance now. She wore the khaki-colored uniform, too, only where Olga had looked jaunty, she looked stocky. Her waist curved in so and the jacket strained at the armholes. The natty little service hat, too, sat up too high on her head. You suspected some sort of an elastic-band attachment so that if she attempted to remove it, pop, it would snap back like a vaudeville comedian's.

She drove like one possessed. Meeting transports. Carrying supplies. Skiddering across the city at all hours on all missions. The von Schlegels still came to occasional dinners and Madam Gerbhardt rather forlornly, with Ermangarde absent, for Saturday luncheon.

Mrs. Oessetrich dined in uniform. Sometimes a summons came and she rushed off during the meal. There was never a moment of the day that found her passive. She tore ahead of the hours as if they were wolves and their breathing was on her neck, and all day long the relentless jangle jangle of her at the telephone. It ran along your nerves. It pricked you into a frenzy. Jangle. Jangle.

*"Hello, Bertha. I'm at a pier in Hoboken. Tell Helga I want the pair of Sevres urns in the drawing-room washed in warm suds and polished. And don't let me discover that you have done it for her. If—if that letter—or cable—if anything*

*that looks like a message from Miss Ermangarde should come,
you can reach me in the next hour at the Service Station—no,
never mind, I'll call up again."*

But that letter or cablegram never came.

More and more the lean, quick, waiting look of a bird came
out in Mrs. Oessetrich and more and more, Paula, who drifted,
almost it seemed without footsteps, down to her meals and
then back again to her piano and the soft silent sewing of the
pink things, came to have the look of sleeping with her eyes
wide open, and more and more frequently her mother shot out
at her with the "Paula, wake up. Don't stare that way. It
makes you look positively silly."

Then one day Bertha stumbled across her in the musty storeroom, seated on the floor beside the Beethoven picture, twad-
dling over it. Poor Paula, her eyes had the tranced look and
she was whispering to it, a little sillily.

The way that Helga happened to break one of the beautiful
Sevres urns the day she was put to rinsing them was because
in the very act of lifting it from its pedestal, she fell screaming
and twisting with the pain in her side. There seemed to be
no way to unlock her of the rigid convulsion there on the floor.
Paula came creeping down to her cries and could only stand
horrified. Helga writhing on the floor and beating off Bertha.
Finally, there was nothing left to do but call in the nearest
doctor. At five o'clock Helga was bundled off to a public
hospital in an ambulance. At six she was successfully operated
upon for appendicitis.

It was strange being up there alone again in the room under
the rafters. The silence flowed back and all the little sounds

and sings and noises stole out of their corners and seemed to sit about like tame mice on their haunches.

Helga lay in a ward, but there was a screen around her cot and a bride had sent her altar flowers to be distributed in the hospital, and there was a fan of white hyacinth on a table, and the afternoon that Mrs. Oessetrich and Paula came, they brought the inevitable and innocuous jar of calves' foot jelly, and that glowed like a drug store urn on the snowlit window sill.

The pretty Helga. Two days after the operation her cheeks began to pinken and the nurse brushed and braided her brown hair over each shoulder and out came the frail, fine, small-boned look.

She loved the warm, clean cot and the smell of hyacinth even through the iodoform and the luxury of waking only to coddle over again cozily on her good side, and when Bertha came to see her and remained all of Thursday afternoon, she had the proprietary air of the convalescent.

"See that good-looking fellow in glasses? He's my doctor. I'd give a dime to know if he's married. Say, look around the screen at that little blonde one three cots down. The one with the green circles under her eyes. That kid—poor kid—what does she do? Getting over an appendix and spry as I am. Nothing to get well for. Cries out some fellow's name all through the ether. What does she do? Last night while the nurse wasn't looking, climbs out barefoot on that little balcony, gives herself a snow bath and swallows a pneumonia bug or two. Dyin'. Say, it's a great life. See that ell over there. Maternity ward. Kid born there fresh every hour. Ought to see. Ever see a maternity ward?"

"Me—yah——"

"The interne, he's a little gone on me if anybody should ask you. He lugged one over to-day for me to see. Three hours old. Ever see a little hard-boiled beet of a kid three hours old?"

"Yah——"

"I want a white one. White as my hands. Look at them, Bertha. Three days in bed and that snow out there on the balcony has nothing on them for whiteness. You don't mind yours that way, do you, Bertha?"

"How?"

"Horny."

"Horny?"

"You're like one of those war tanks, you are. Pushing right on over the barbed wire fences without letting them even scratch you. That's because you're all on the inside of yourself. Like your body was just an ulster."

"Don't roll so, Helga. The wound. . . ."

"That ain't the worst. I got what they call on the soap box speeches in Union Square, a social sore. And they bring me calves' foot jelly for it. There's a laugh for you, old tombstone! I got a social sore and they bring me calves' foot jelly for it. . . ."

But the following Sunday when Bertha arrived she was a very subdued Helga.

"He's coming at four."

"Who?"

"Barney. I didn't ask him, Bertha. Didn't even know he knew I was here. I got a postal. You must have told him."

"He kept asking."

"I wouldn't have sent for him. If his old woman was to pass

on to-morrow and—and he wanted me, I'd never do it to him—
that's something, ain't it, Bertha? I want him. I could have
him. He would never find out. He wouldn't understand if
I tried to tell him. To him fire don't cleanse—it only scars
after you've been through it."

"Yah. Barney is not a wise man. He is yoost a—good
man——"

"That just about says it."

"Yah——"

"What are you staring at?"

"I—why you, Helga. You're pretty."

"This nightgown. So coarse! I'm a fright in it. They
give them to you like that in the wards. Ugh—and him coming
at four. Bertha—would you——"

"What?"

"It's a long trip back to the house, but up in our room, there's
a box of some of my little things. I keep it hid. There's no
telling when a girl's room can get pried into. There's a little
box of my things up on top of the wardrobe. You can reach
up and feel for it if you get on a chair. He's—coming at
four."

"But Helga, I thought——"

"I want to deck myself out, so anyways he'll know what
he's missing—I hate him seeing me like this. All he's ever seen
of me is around ugly kitchen things, in ugly kitchen duds.
Bertha—if I could just have those few things to deck myself
out in when Barney comes. As long as he's going to lose me,
he might as well think I'm worth losing. Will you go—Bertha
—will you——?"

"Yah——"

The package was behind the wooden frill of the wardrobe. Reaching for it was a difficult tiptoe process that made the chair wobble, and a shower of old dust came down on the shoulders of Bertha's reefer. Hurrying down the steep rear staircase, Mrs. Oessetrich popped out a sudden head.

"That you, Bertha?"

"Yah——"

"I thought you were gone for the afternoon."

"I came back for a minute."

"Did you go to see Helga?"

"Yah——"

"How is she?"

"Better."

"Do you think she will be well in time to be back for the dinner to my Ambulance Corps? It's a great nuisance getting help from the agencies."

"Yah—maybe——"

"You are going out again?"

"Yah—I——"

"Of course, it's your afternoon, but the von Schlegels are coming to tea and it would help if you would stay in and——"

"I cannot—to-day——."

"Oh very well. I dislike asking favors as much as I dislike being denied them. What's that you are carrying?"

"A box."

"That is rather self-evident, but what is in it?"

"Some—oh—I don't know."

"Bertha, I have never known you to be impertinent."

"Mrs. Oessetrich, I am not."

"Very well. If you prefer not to tell me I suppose that technically it is none of my affair. But even with a trusted

servant I cannot seem to get over my aversion to seeing packages carted out of my house. Of course with you it's different,
but just the same I dislike it. Hurry along, then."

For some reason, taking that long crosstown walk back to
the Tenth Avenue Hospital, Bertha's cheeks and eyeballs and
the hand that clutched the box began to burn.

Helga's eyes were too bright. She threw herself about the
cot while she waited and when Bertha returned, she was all
thumbs at the package and when the knot would not untie, she
lay back against the pillow and began to cry.

"I'm too weak. Help me, Bertha. I give myself the cotton-
flannel horrors in this hospital sack. Fortheluvvaga don't stand
gaping. It's only silk and it won't bite."

"Helga!"

"Helga what? Helga what?"

There was nothing to do then but to lift out the filmy white
crêpe gown with the rill of French Valenciennes, and slide
it on to Helga. She came up out of it like a flower, her
neck and arms suddenly lovely under the shy mesh of the lace.
There was another gown just as sheer in the box and oddments
and ends of ribbon and trinkety bits of jewelry, and the nurse
helped, too, and tied a bandeau of ribbon on Helga's hair and
fluffed up the pillows and finally there was something very doll-
like about her as she lay back tiredly.

"Dig down in the corner of the box there, Bertha, right-
hand corner, there's a little rose quartz pin will look sweet on
this lace. If there's one thing I love it's rose quartz, it's the
color of a girl's cheeks."

"Oh, Helga—Helga——"

" 'Oh Helga, Helga' what? I know what you're thinking. Well you're wrong. Maybe this stuff of mine dates back to—well, you know the days it dates back to—and maybe you don't. And what if what you are thinking is right? Well, what if it is? McMurty——"

"I—don't know—what I'm thinking, Helga."

"I want him to see me once, the color of something lovely instead of something reeking of brown soap. Give me that rose quartz. It's the color of a girl's cheeks and that's the color Barney's entitled to."

Barney came. He was shy about coming around the cot-side of the screen and stood outside twirling his hat until the nurse, who had directed him, had to come all the way down the ward again and steer him in, and even then he could not be brought to approach the cot, advancing one step and retreating two, his great figure in bulky civilian clothing, exhaling the cold snow smell of outdoors. The red of his face ran up under the red of his hair and mustache. He jutted it out fiercely and then sucked it in again.

"Look, Bertha, he's scared of me."

Persiflage and poor Barney. It fuddled him and made him blink.

"Look, Bertha, he's afraid I'm a doll in a box."

"It's snowing for proper," he said. "Just came up now in a flurry."

He had a voice that shook things when he spoke. The spoon in the medicine glass trembled. Helga laughed at it and cried right into the laugh and licked off a tear with the little pink adder of her tongue.

"Howdy—Barney."

"You *do* look like a doll in the box—laying there."

"I'll be going," said Bertha.

"Don't you be going," he said. "We'll be wanting you," and sat down in the creaky edge of a chair there beside the cot and drew off his leather mitts and unwound his muffler and blew on his hands. And blew and blew.

"You're better, ain't you, Helga?"

She raised her bare arm in a half wreath over her head.

"Lots you care."

He blew and he blew.

"I couldn't come before, Helga. I been in trouble. Sit down, Bertha, we'll be needing you. My old woman died, Helga. Dead and buried this day week."

"I better be going," said Bertha.

"Wait, you, Big One. You know how to help. . . ."

"What?"

He leaned over to touch Helga shyly, where her throat throbbed.

"I want to carry her off from here. Home. There's bedside weddings. I've read of a many of them. To-morrow, Bertha, we'll do the fixings. Helga?"

Helga lay so white and still. You could almost see the heart of her seem to stir the rill of the Valenciennes. And her eyes were closed and the brown braids lay in ropes against her pallor.

"Helga?"

"I better be going," said Bertha.

Outside it was snowing in sudden loose flakes that spat you roundly on the cheek. It snowed up in merry little geysers. Slantwise and down your neck. The whole street blew forward like the frilled petticoat of a frantic lady. Your hat. Your heart. Your breathing. The wind lashed at them so and froze the tears to your cheeks. . . .

Something had happened. The screen stood huddled closely about the cot. A white interne came out with a tank. Oxygen. An electric bulb on a flexible stand was bent away from the bed, so that its light flowed down into a pool on the floor. There was a cruel rasping noise against the grain of the silence. It made you cold all over like the jerking back of a hangnail against the direction of the flesh. You stood outside the screen and listened and trembled. The noise was Helga, breathing.

There was something on the chair. It rose and fell. It was Barney's back as he sat by the cot side, all curved forward with his great empty hands between his knees and his eyes like empty cups.

The pink was gone from Helga's face. It was as if some one had held up a transparent finger before a candle and then blown out the flame. The laxness of the hand. It hung down like a lily on a broken stalk. After a time the dead old eyes of Barney swung toward the drift of hand. But without seeing. He only looked. Crowded hurting corner, filled with the little gale of Helga's breathing. The curve of Barney. That twisted neck of the lamp and the bulb that glared to the floor.

"What is it?" said Bertha.

"Pneumonia," said the nurse, and put Helga's hand back under the coverlet as you would a flower or a letter.

"Oh—Helga."

"She was coming along so nicely. She must have become delirious suddenly during the night. The second case of the kind in this ward in one week. They found her out there in that little balcony standing in the snow. Just in her flimsy nightdress. Barefoot. She must have been very sly about it. The night nurse had scarcely turned her back. I've never had a patient do it on me. Let me touch wood. Of course, they all say that I'm not only careful, I'm fanatical. It's double pneumonia. Of course some do rally, but—poor child—you're her nearest relative—or friend——."

"Me? Yes, I guess."

"You can stay and wait if you want."

"Yah—please."

"Has she ever been a mental case?"

"How?"

"A nervous history, I mean."

"Why I—dunno."

"It must have been sudden insanity or hysteria caused her to find her way out to that balcony. Second case in one week. I always say ward patients should be kept in ignorance of such accidents. Dangers of auto-suggestion."

"Oh, Helga—Helga——"

The white rose leaves of Helga's eyelids. One of them seemed to Bertha to crinkle at one corner.

Barney beat his big hands loosely together as they hung between his knees. His big hands. His empty hands.

She seemed to know with her smile that he was there. It lit once toward him and she tried to reach out her hand, but it just drifted along the bedside and hung loose, and he kissed it and put it back under the coverlet as if it were a small dead bird.

"Oh God," cried Barney in his voice that seemed to have the

mustache growing right on it. "There's no meaning to your wisdom. That talk is bunk."

"Yes, there is—meaning—somewhere——"

"To you maybe, Big One, but not to me. . . ."

"Maybe."

At dawn Helga began to slip away. She tried to keep the little thread of the smile on her lips but such a foolish sniveling thing was happening.

The years were like water surging her backward.

It was at Mrs. Farley's and she was coming down one cold morning, adjusting the criss-cross straps to her apron and tasting her lips as if they were bitter.

"Fortheluvvaga" was the last thing Helga said before she died. "Warmed-over oatmeal again. This oleo is strong enough to walk. Give me a snack of little Lord Fauntrollo's sweet butter—Bertha——"

The boys kept marching. Barney, who was forty, came to say good-by. It was odd to see him. Barney, who was forever bringing all the stray cats on his beat to the back-door for the leavings. Sometimes there were three or four of them standing around him, with hopeful vertical tails and meouwing up into his face. His brick-red, open fireplace of a face. Barney, all bristling now with new phrases which he wore as cockily as his puttees. "To hell with the Kaiser. Dirty Huns."

To hate was not so different from to love. Barney had discovered that. Only it was difficult to steam up the hate. Tramp. Tramp. Tramp-tramp-tramp. It was strange to see him with his fine square back and the curving seams, walking

off down the street after the good-by.  His shoulders were very
ferocious looking and pedestrians made little respectful detours
to pass him.  Barney, fine and fighty and hating enough to be
patriotic.

Even Bertha bought a Liberty Bond.  When Mrs. Oessetrich
was not driving the ambulance she stood on the steps of the
Treasury Building or the Public Library and sold Liberty Bonds
and collected Red Cross funds.  A stretcher was laid along the
sidewalk.  The money rained down on it.  Give.  Give.  More
stretchers for more maimed bodies.  And the frightening part
of it was that you gave.  Gave because the piece of cheesecloth
bunting snapping in the breeze made your eyes hot and your
heart hot.  Bertha gave.  It was hard for her to pass one of the
stretcher things and not drop a coin.  The terrible futility of
those marching little scissors-like men.  You knew it deep
down in your heart and hated the hating.

Bertha could sometimes sit upstairs in her room, big and
bitter and inarticulate with it.  Paula, who never played any
more, since the Beethoven.  Olga, gorging the little scissors
men with the aniseed cakes of stultification.  Barney, who was
tender to kittens, marching away with the places for cartridges
corrugated along his belt.  Mrs. Oessetrich baiting in the public
square.  And yet the bunting.  It made your tonsils tighten.
So hating the hate, Bertha gave.  Dropped the twenty-five cent
pieces on to the stretchers, that there might be more stretchers,
and bought a one-hundred-dollar Liberty Bond.

Bertha with her Liberty Bond.  It was engraved on tough
beautiful paper and scrolled like a bank note.  Sometimes she
sat and looked at it with her lips a little finicky and folded

back from her white square teeth. A wise old Chinese smile.

Even the delirious, banging day of the Armistice the smile persisted. The faces of all the little hurrying. scurrying people were so merely guzzled. So merely victorious. An oppressor had been laid. But somehow you trembled. Old hates for new. . . .

There was no evading it. Paula's queerness. For two weeks there had been no way to induce her to leave the fourth-floor room. She clung to it like a bit of ash blonde moss. It seemed to embarrass Mrs. Oessetrich, this timid, this astonishing, this not quite rational tenacity of Paula's. She hated even Bertha's knowing it and what went on between mother and daughter usually happened behind closed doors. Paula sat on her little sewing-chair and just faced her parent when she coaxed and cajoled and threatened, and would not be pried out. It was dreadful for Mrs. Oessetrich. Placed her rather in the position of luring a wild bird out of ambush with crumbs. Once she even tried to force her, but Paula's teeth went together with a click and her fingers clenched down around the seat of the chair, and frail little Paula, who looked as if Fra Lippo Lippi had painted her; frail Paula who loved Chopin and the miniature melodies of Mozart, there was no budging her. Not so much as an inch. She gritted her teeth and sat. Just sat.

Bertha used to tiptoe in with her meals. She would eat for Bertha. But sometimes it took an hour. Spoonful by spoonful of the broths that were tilted up against her teeth, and then the slow difficult gulps of muffin or of shredded meat. They were the hardest. She had a way of looking at Bertha over the top of the spoon. Those eyes would hang in Bertha's darkness. Disks of hot blue light.

Something of a sequence was taking place in Paula's aching brain. That was the plain fact that was so embarrassing to her mother.

First the trousseau things. Then the yards of maline veiling which she would pin to her hair and let trail off behind. Mrs. Oessetrich burned the veil one night in the furnace so that the house smelled with it.

And now Paula's sewings for the hours and hours in the little chair were all doll size. Baby things. It made the red fly up into Mrs. Oessetrich's face, and behind the carefully locked door, she went into long, low-voiced pleading conferences with Paula.

But it was no use. The piano remained closed and day after day Paula sat and sewed the small things.

Dr. Ehrenfest came. She only laughed at him, her large blue eyes seeming almost to cover her face and at the slightest approach in her direction, her hands locking down over the sides of the chair.

Down in the drawing-room, over the tea things that Bertha was spreading, Dr. Ehrenfest kept stroking his slim point of beard.

"Well, 'Tilda, let us face our facts."

"I have never been the one to dodge them, Ehrey."

"I think the only thing to do right now is to call in Lauer on this case."

"Dr. Emil Lauer the—the——."

"Yes. The neurologist."

"Then Paula is——."

"It may be only a temporary neurosis. But right now, Lauer

is our man. He has that splendid place out at Hill's End. It may be just what Paula needs."

"You mean—— "

"His sanitarium. I consider it one of the best in the country."

"Don't mince words with me, Ehrey. Dr. Lauer's place is a private asylum."

"I can't see that calling a spade a bludgeon helps matters."

"I hate minced facts. I can swallow my dose undiluted."

"Well, then, I want a psychopathist like Lauer in on Paula's case."

"All right. All right. I'll have another lump, Bertha. All right."

But her face seemed to shrink, the cheeks to recede, leaving the frontal part with its avian thrust even more leanly forward.

"I've seen it coming. 'Tilda, since—— "

"Since Harrison, of course, you mean."

"You cannot suppress every normal instinct in a high-strung girl like Paula and expect—— "

"Harrison was not the man for her. He proved it by what happened subsequently."

"What happened subsequently might not have occurred if—— "

"Suppressed desires, Freudian pish. Paula has been indulged in every possible manner except in the case of Harrison Gage."

"She pleaded to go to Europe that next winter, if I remember."

"Well, she studied music at home, didn't she? The best that money could buy was hers."

"What is this seems to be on her mind about Beethoven or

Mozart or one of them? She cried to me a little up there just now about Beethoven."

"I don't know, I'm sure. There was some discussion a few days before Olga sailed about that print of Beethoven that used to hang in the dining room. That must in some way be fuddled in the poor child's brain. Olga wanted it down. It seems silly now, but during the war in some devilish way, it sounded rational enough, and there was an argument. Olga felt rather firmly about it. Finally Bertha carted it up to the storeroom. That's all there was to it. Up to that time Paula had been working on the Sonata Appassionata. It seemed to upset her. Bertha, get down that print of Beethoven that you carried up to the storeroom that day and hang it back in the dining room."

"I—please excuse—I hung it back there yesterday."

"Presumptuous! The kind of thing I very much dislike. It merely happened to be all right in this case. Don't let it happen again. Bring Dr. Ehrenfest some fresh muffins."

"There's a strange woman."

"A priceless servant and yet sometimes—so strange—so strange—that—that——"

"What?"

"I—don't—know——"

You stood in the pantry and shivered and put your hands up over your ears. Your teeth were on edge and the entire surface of your body hurt.

They were taking Paula. Dr. Ehrenfest and Dr. Lauer, and a nurse in a cap like a charlotte russe case. Little Paula, whose bones were squab-like and who was the faint color of ashes of roses. Her strength terrified you. She did not want to go and you knew as you stood hurting all over the surface of you, that she was biting and kicking. Then you stole out to help, but you were trembling so and somehow you did not want Paula to know that you knew.

The strength of Paula. She would not be carried. And so she sat and crouched, with her terrified hands flaming white at the knuckles and twisted around the rungs of the banisters, and her eyes the lovely troubled Ophelia eyes. The blazing, blazing, flame-blue disks.

You cried with your heart. It was not to be borne. The carrying of Paula kicking and screaming down those flights. The streamers of her sobs. The streamers. . . .

"Paula," cried Bertha and ran up the steps toward her cowering at the banisters there.

"Bertha, Bertha," sobbed Paula, and uncurled her fingers, "they're taking me down off the wall. They're taking me up to the storeroom——"

"No, no, Miss Paula, they're taking you to make you well."

"You knew, Bertha. You used to sit on the steps and listen. They took him away from us, Bertha—you remember—I cried. Olga—the feeding of the men. The mad little men who hated Beethoven. They took him away from us, Bertha——"

"No, no, Miss Paula, he's downstairs in the dining room where he used to be."

"Where?"

"Come, Miss Paula, with Bertha."

"Where?"

"To a house in the country where you are going to get well."

"They took—him away—from us. You used to peel the potatoes. I could hear them fall in the pan. You listened——"

"Come, Miss Paula."

She went down the stairs and out of the house like a child then.

"Good-by, Bertha—they took him away from us—but I knew —you knew——"

"Good-by, Miss Paula."

She sat up as stiffly in the car as a doll, with blue Ophelia eyes, and let them seat themselves in a sort of dreadful battalion around her.

"We knew—we knew——" she said to Bertha, who was left standing on the sidewalk.

Upstairs in her bedroom Mrs. Oessetrich sat rocking herself. Rocking herself in a straight chair.

The house was like a tomb. It stood all day, listening. Upstairs, downstairs, and the old pulling pains at the backs of Bertha's legs. It was difficult without a second girl. They came and to the trip hammer of Mrs. Oessetrich's tongue they left. Insolently, most of them, and usually in the midst of a half-swept room or with windows flung high and the curtains pinned away for thorough cleaning. It was not much better with the day-help. They never came back the second time.

But after the Armistice, the agencies began to feed them out again.

Sullen men who did outdoor work and washed windows in their old army coats.

"Two dollars and sixty cents a day! What's the world coming to? Don't have that dirty-looking fellow in the old tan coat come here any more. I dislike his manner. There is something so bolsheviki about him."

The old tan coat was a doughboy's, grimy beyond recognition.

He was one of the scissors men and had been stoked up on sandwiches from hands as fair as Olga's. The bolsheviki look was the two dollars and sixty cents a day recompense for a badly gassed lung.

Laundry work had gone up, too. "It is ruinous. Three dollars and ten cents. Why, a family could live on that in the old days."

But not in the new. The new purged days since the war.

"Give her my Venetian point tablecloth to launder, Bertha. Tell her to be sure and use tepid water and a warm iron. It cost two hundred and fifty dollars before the war. It has to be done scallop by scallop."

Three dollars and ten cents a day to iron Mrs. Oessetrich's two hundred and fifty dollar Venetian point tablecloth. Scallop by scallop. Somehow if you looked at it that way—three dollars and ten cents for the eight hours of standing on the granatoid floor of the laundry was not so very high. Scallop by scallop. . . .

Bertha's wages had been raised to fifty dollars. The bulge in her petticoat pocket was growing again. Helga's funeral had depleted it for a while. Helga, who loved to be snug and warm, would have hated to lie in an untufted casket.

But with the raise to fifty dollars, the little hit-hit began again. It followed her all around the house. The stilly house. The listening house. The waiting, brooding, silenced house.

You looked forward to Monday nights because of the recreation of all the crystal chandeliers set blazing then and out came the solid gold plate that was kept wadded in cotton in the safe in Mrs. Oessetrich's boudoir.

Monday night was opera night. The Oessetrichs had subscribed for the same first tier box for fifteen years. The

Oessetrich little girls had grown up to those seats, so to speak, until gradually their feet had reached the floor and their heads shot up over the backs. Paula had kept the programs. They were in a stack up in the room. The lower ones all yellow.

Usually now the von Schlegels and Madam Gerbhardt or Godfather and Aunt Mary Oessetrich came to dine on Monday nights and then went on to the opera.

Mrs. Oessetrich in her shining expanse of hard colored satin. The beautiful diamond necklace, mounted very clumsily on red gold. The bugle and passementerie and crystal trimmings. The heavy incrustations of bead embroidery. She glittered and she clinked. You wanted to ring her as you would a bell.

Small but complicated dinners with a helper in the kitchen and Bertha in her rôle of waitress, boxed into a black sateen uniform that spanned her between the shoulders, and the white organdie turnover collar that seemed to jut out her cheek bones and give the wide area between that startling clarity of a nun's.

One evening there was to be a new opera. Madam Gerbhardt had the score. She sang snatches of it at dinner, and before the wraps were brought, she sat down at the concert grand piano in the drawing-room and played off pages of it. Coq D'Or. Tickling golden nonsense.

Oh, but you wanted to strut and stick yourself out in front like a fat king and hold off the gold platter with the excavated mound of pistachio pudding and rollic with it as if you had stepped down off a playing card. Fat, mad king.

Coq D'Or. You wanted Madam Gerbhardt to sit there in her upholstered-looking blue velvet with the cut steel buttons down it, and play them all out over the piano. All the lively little Coq D'Or people who resided in the foolish heart of the opera. The kings and queens and the jacks and the jokers off the playing cards. The little streets down which they swarmed over cobble-stones and the houses with waving crooked sides like the bend of a concertina. Crazy houses with a jester's cap on the peak, and a bell hanging down over one window. You could see them as you strutted out with the pistachio pudding. Purple sky like a bruise. And all the ladies had long thin necks with hooks in them, like swans'. They were the queens of the playing cards. And all the kings had little bellies and strutted. Coq D'Or. It made you merry and it made you foolish and it made you see the new-fangled bewilderment of a sky the color of a bruise. Hoodlum music that ran the wrcng way off the keys, like the Chinaman in the subway who read up and down off his newspaper. Tra-la-la-la-la—lalala. Lawk, you had almost stumbled with the solid gold platter of the pistachio.

"Bertha, bring the wraps."

Yah—yah—the silly queen.

"Bertha, see if the car is at the door."

Yah—yah—the silly queen with the hook in her neck like the plumbing underneath the stationary washstand. Coq D'Or—pouring golden nonsense. . . .

And the talk. You learned if you listened as you passed around the platters, charmed glittering names. Marguerite. Ophelia. La Navarraise. Sappho. Santuzza. Thais. Heifetz. Tosca. Caruso. Sembrich. Friedheim. Pederewski. von Buelow. Hoffman. Elman. Wieniawski. Ysaye. Charvet. Charvet.

One evening at dinner Madam Gerbhardt said something about this charmed and glittering name, that hung in the memory like a Christmas tree ball.

"Charvet is only a boy. They say, by the way, he is American. Without a doubt he is one of the foremost pianist composers of the day. Have you heard him this season, 'Tilda?"

"No."

"The moon-haunted fashion in which he played at yesterday's concert! He must have the heart of a woman, the brain of a poet, and the valor of a man. Ah, Charvet—there is a new master for you. Charvet."

"Ah, Charvet"—you tiptoed out with the platters. "Ah, Charvet." To be moon-haunted was to live with an opal mist about one's heart. Bertha knew. . . .

Go. Go. Go. Mrs. Oessetrich started out early as usual, but in the excellent quality, badly fitting tweed now instead of the khaki, and in the place of the fawn-colored ambulance, Eddie was out at the curb again, usually with the small sedan.

Difficult as it was to keep the tall house from swooning into its silence, somehow she partially accomplished it with the bang-bangings of her comings and goings. The telephone. The telephone.

*"Bertha, if Madam Gerbhardt calls, tell her I will be glad to use those tickets for the Vatican Choir at Carnegie Hall to-night. Tell the carpenter when he comes, to meet me at Miss Olga's studio, I want him to build those flower boxes before she gets back. It's beginning to rain. Have those three trunks in the storeroom, with red stars on them, dragged out into the hallway by the time I get home and I'll spend this wet afternoon unpacking some things for Miss Paula. Dr. Ehrenfest*

*call up?  Any mail?  Nothing from Hill's End?  Paris?  Miss
Ermangarde?  Look at the postmarks.  No cables—Paris—
Miss Ermangarde?—sure?  Oh—well——"*

There never were.

*"Well, I'll be home by two.  If the awning man comes tell
him to wait."*

Hammer.  Hammer.  Hammer.  Mrs. Oessetrich fighting
the house's silence.  Awnings went up as early as April.  Gay
orange ones with blue scallops.  The old-fashioned little dressing room adjoining Ermangarde's bedroom, with the built-in
wardrobe and the stationary washstand, was torn out and a
shining rink of a bathroom installed.  Hammer.  Hammer.
The rippling, striped awnings and then one day the entire house
front lit up with new window shades.  Festooned silk ones that
shirred up with the soft rush of a laugh.  The piano in Paula's
room had been tuned and stood open.  Smiling. Waiting.
But Paula never came.  The door always stood open, too.  But
you never looked in.  Somehow the smile of that piano could
seem more like a grin.

Then this happened.

Those three trunks with the red stars on had been dragged
into the hallway that faced Paula's room, before it turned off
into the ell that led to Bertha's door.

All afternoon, while a slanting rain flew at the roof, Mrs.
Oessetrich puttered up there among Paula's things.  Bertha,
waxing the newly installed hardwood floor in Paula's room
could glance out into the hallway and see her stooped there
with her dry shattered eyes roving among the dry things.
Paula's little things.  Paula loved little things.  There was a
whole trayful of the kind of trinkets that amused her.  Jade

elephants. Nubs of chrysoprose and malachite. Carved intag-
lios. Cat's eye trifles and chalcedony. Rock-crystal hens. A
silver filigree shrine the size of a thimble and wrought with
amazing detail. There was a Christus with the ewe lamb, hand
carved out of the yellow eye of a topaz. Green jasper amulet.
A little girl's pocket-book, red lined and fashioned out of two
shells with Niagara Falls written across it. Shoes. The soles
a little thinned in the delicate way that Paula would wear them
down. Letters. A tray of them sorted in stacks. The curious
rain-tapped silence and Mathilde Oessetrich with her eyes that
still had the look of the cracked shoe buttons.

Paula's tray of letters. There was something so faint and
pale about them. They seemed to rise up in the vapor of a
sigh.

After the waxing of the floor there were potatoes to peel and
the great red eye of a roast for dinner required larding to make
the juices run.

You picked your way down the back stairs, carefully, to save
the squeaks.

The afternoon drew in the silence like a poultice.

The red roast when you larded it with the stripes of suet
swelled up around your finger clammily, and with the heart gone
from the meat, out came your finger from the hole with a sucky
little pop. The house felt like that. It flowed around you so
coldly, with the heart gone out of it, and the pop of the rain
drops—pop—pop——

Finally Mrs. Oessetrich came down into the kitchen. Her
skin was all dry, like a fowl's, and it was beginning to wattle
at the neck. She was much thinner. It made everything about
her lower. Her waistline and the sags underneath her eyes.

"Bertha," she said, and sat down on the edge of a chair, "has anyone had access to the storeroom besides you?"

"No."

"You have always followed my instructions and permitted none of the day help in there?"

"Yah——"

"Sure? Think carefully."

"Yah——"

"Well, something has happened. Bear in mind that these questions I am about to ask are disagreeable ones, but they must be asked."

"What?"

"Bertha, there has been a systematic rifling of things going on in the storeroom. Trunks have been pried open. Articles are missing. There is a leak in my household."

"A—what——"

"A thief."

"You mean——"

"I mean that articles of Miss Paula's that I have been putting away from time to time in trunks, during the period that she has not been—so—well—have been stolen. Two of the trunks have been pried open with hairpins and articles of more or less value are missing."

"You mean——"

"I mean nothing until I have gone further into this matter. You are still a trusted servant. Now come upstairs with me."

The sickening process of that. Bertha, to whom things were so trivial, suddenly quivering before their omnipotence.

Paula's trunk *had* been looted. All the neat little stacks of her lovely handiwork were in swirls of confusion on the trays. A pasteboard box had been gouged at one end and its contents dragged out. A hairpin had got itself twisted about the lock and a hurried hand had left it there.

"You can see for yourself, Bertha, someone from the inside has been at work. Can you think of any explanation for these rifled trunks?"

"I—no——"

"This amounts to more than petty thievery. There were beautiful silk garments here. Some of them imported and some of them beautifully made by Miss Paula herself of the sheerest materials."

"Yah . . ."

"I was going to take some of them to her at the san—hospital. She will be shocked when she comes home and learns what has happened. Her things. Paula loved things. Why, there were three white crêpe gowns on this tray that I remember distinctly packing away. Beauties, with yards and yards of real Valenciennes that her godmother had especially made for her in Valenciennes."

"White *crêpe de chine*—real Valenciennes."

"Just see! Oh. Oh. This box torn open and a rose quartz brooch that was very precious to her—Harrison's—a gift to her from a dear friend—stolen. Who has dared?"

You just stood and felt your nails dig up into your palms, and your lips were so heavy. You kept trying to move them, but they would not lift.

"I intend to get to the bottom of this—regardless."

"Mrs. Oessetrich——"

"Why Bertha, you are crimson! Bertha?"

"I—you see—yoost remembered—yoost thought——"

"Just thought what?"

"I—I——"

"Answer me."

"I—don't—know——"

"Bertha !"

"It isn't possible. Not you. The most trusted servant I ever had!"

"But Mrs. Oessetrich, I——"

"So this is the mystery of you."

"I——"

"You strange white creature, you. This is the meaning——"

"I didn't know——"

"You thief! I never in my wildest dreams would have suspected you. Who knows what systematic process of stealing has been going on all these years under my very eyes."

"No—no—no !"

"Paula. My daughter Paula who trusted you. Who loved you."

"Please——"

"Thief! I shall call in detectives."

"No—no—please—I didn't know——"

"I too trusted you. I respected you. Oh, I cannot believe my senses."

"Mrs. Oessetrich, I only——"

"What nonsense has been talked in this household about you. Miss Olga who always insisted that you had the soul of a poet trapped in the body of a peasant. The soul of a thief!"

Dumb Bertha standing there with her lips all shirred in like an old woman's and her eyes down. It was horrible keeping her eyes down. It made her face a bonfire around them.

"Come upstairs into your room with me. I intend to go to the bottom of this"

The ignominy of that. Standing there with her arms huddled

up and her eyes seeming to suck back into her head like raisins into dough.

The opening and closing of drawers. Each dragging time the wood seemed to run against the grain of her flesh and leave her shivering there with a sense of splinters plunging horridly into her. Jagged little needles.

Open. Shut. Open. Shut.

"What's that, in there?"

"Yoost my aprons."

"And that heavy thick stuff?"

"Yoost my nightgowns."

"Umph. You were clever enough to dispose of what you took, I see. Why come to think of it, I've seen you carting packages out of the house. I remember stopping you in the passageway one day. You were furtive then. I realize it now. What's this?"

"Yoost music, Mrs. Oessetrich. Please—don't touch. Yoost some old sheets of music I had before I came here."

"Humph. Loot from somewhere else, I suppose."

"Oh—oh——"

"Ugh, what a task! To think that I should ever have to resort to such degrading methods with you. Well, I see that you are clever enough to keep your clothes closet bare as a bone. Let's see, now. Oh, get up on that chair and open up those two cupboard doors above the closet. I intend to go to the bottom of this."

"Mrs. Oessetrich—those little doors I have never once opened since I am here."

"Hand me that chair. I don't believe in half-way methods."

Your lips, they were so heavy they would not lift.

To reach the pair of small doors Mrs. Oessetrich had to strain tiptoe on the chair.

"Please Mrs. Oessetrich, if you would just let me say——"

"Oh. Oh. Oh."

The little chills ran off you like sand down a dune. Cold goosefleshing chills. The small cupboard doors jerked open with a spill of things. To stand indicted before the stern irrefutable law of ownership. The indubitable right of Mrs. Oessetrich to her things. The colossal rights of ownership. Those rights had been outraged. It brought out in Mrs. Oessetrich's face the lean look of wolf.

The webby lovelinesses of Paula's. Chiffon with its pollen-like power to cling to a woman's flesh. Articles that had been jammed up there quickly. To stand there and gaze was to turn the eyes into blisters. The cream lace boudoir cap of Mrs. Oessetrich's, for which there had been a topsy-turvy search one Saturday morning, tucked up there behind one of Paula's little fluted silk negligees. The blue fox scarf that Ermangarde had been finally forced to decide she had left in a taxicab. A gold and vermilion batik scarf of Olga's. Stacks of unworn white gloves, Paula's narrow size. More of the filmy things. Peach-colored gowns with the rills of Valenciennes. Things. The scalding wrath of Mrs. Oessetrich over her silk rag-a-tags. Her inalienable right to them.

To stand branded with the puniness of desire for them. To stand there blanched to the very color of her teeth before Mrs. Oessetrich, whose face had begun to narrow until the nose sharpened like the blade of a knife. The shame . . . you could scarcely breathe. . . .

"So! These fur-lined bedroom slippers of mine that I haven't even missed. Silk stockings. Bath salts. Sachet.

You stupid, luxury-loving girl. You of all people! A great coarse peasant girl who seemed utterly impervious to creature things. But you have not taken all this for the sake of the things themselves. You have carted it out of the house. You are in league with someone. With whom?"

"No. No."

"Miss Ermangarde's French batiste blouse! More sachet! My silver shoe buckles. Why—why this is a case for the police."

"Mrs. Oessetrich, you would not——"

"Up here alone is stored several hundred dollars' worth of my possessions. What quantities you must have carted away without my knowing it. Come here, you. Stand there and look me in the eye. How long has this been going on?"

"I—don't—know——"

"You don't know. Well, I advise you to find out and be pretty quick about it. Maybe the police can help you to remember. This string of lapis lazuli and carnelian beads. Do you realize that it in itself is worth several hundred dollars?"

"Dollars . . ."

"Yes, dollars and don't dare let on that you did not know the value of them."

"Dollars. Let me pay in dollars. Mrs. Oessetrich. I'll give it back in dollars."

It was impossible to fumble down into the petticoat pocket quickly enough. The fingers were so numb and did not seem separate.

"See, Mrs. Oessetrich, if only you will please be so kind. Dollars. More than two hundred. I will pay for the things with dollars."

"Stolen money, too, I suppose. Thank goodness, my vaults have been safe from you."

"No. No. Saved money."

"Money cannot buy exemption from punishment for crime."

"Mrs. Oessetrich, here, if you will please to take it—my Liberty Bond——"

"You must accept your punishment like anyone else. Our penal system is to protect society from such as you."

"Take what I got."

"Why should I? You are a thief. I do not know why I even listen to you."

"You do—because——"

"Because I am a foolish, sentimental woman, my children to the contrary notwithstanding."

"Please——"

"I am a weakling for permitting you to prevail upon me. You swear to me that you are in league with no one."

"Oh, I do. I do."

"What was it that I saw you carrying out of the house that day I stopped you——"

"——for Helga—at the hospital——"

"I don't seem able to deal with you as you deserve. There is something about you—what is it?"

"Let me pay, Mrs. Oessetrich—see—money, and my bond."

"Put what you have down there on the table."

"Here it is."

"I shall take it and give it to the Red Cross. It is your restitution. You should be made to pay a harder one. Now you leave my house. Get out your valise or whatever you call the bag that you brought your things in. Open it and let me see what is in it. More loot, no doubt."

"No, Mrs. Oessetrich, there is nothing but——"

"Open it, I said."

"There."

"What is that green chiffon? Where did you get that old fashioned thing?"

"It's mine! Someone gave it to me."

"Ugh, fuzzy old evening wrap. Well, you didn't get that here. Now pack your things. What is this? A book. *The Cathedral Under* ——"

"No. No. Don't touch that book. It is mine."

"What are you doing with that volume of Rollo Farley in your bag? You must have stolen that from Miss Ermangarde's desk. Why that book is almost her bible. How dared you!"

"No! No! No! I tell you, no! Mine! Don't you! That book, Mrs. Oessetrich—is mine."

"I am convinced now that you are vicious. Don't you dare hold my arm that way. Put down that book or I shall telephone this minute for the police."

"I——"

"Put it down! How dare you ransack even our books. Give me that book. You are not fit to touch it. You! *The Cathedral Under the Sea!*"

"You don't know——"

"I know that if you do not put it down immediately I shall call the police."

"Please——"

"Immediately, or I'll——"

"There."

"Now pack your things. I'll be waiting for you down in the kitchen. You cannot leave this house without I take a final look into your belongings. I am actually ill from this outrageous scene. Now pack. Remember, just that pile of thick ugly things on the table there. I'll be waiting . . come down the rear stairs. . . ."

It was hard with all her fingers swollen thumbs, to cram the things into the bag and the chills seemed to run down off her spine just like sand. The stiff, unwieldy sailor's union suits. When they were folded over once, they rose up solemnly in the bottom of the bag and had to be weighted down with shoes. The striped, clean-smelling flannel petticoat. The cake of hard brown soap. The bit of Bulgarian embroidery. The green of Mrs. Farley's evening wrap. It crowded over the top. Ocean green. To close your eyes a moment and feel that spread of ocean green. The tears ran down and suddenly they too were ocean. Things. Things. Things. Mrs. Oessetrich's things. Helga's. Olga's. Ermangarde's. The green thought of ocean flowed over and wiped them out and left the old stark un-cluttered silence. And to sit in that silence the second before you pinned on your disk of a hat was to gather back strength.

The silence that still seemed full of the mewlings of Mrs. Oessetrich over the things. Things. Helga who had loved them and had never felt the green thought of ocean flow over and obliterate them.

The book was not a thing. It was a dear hurt heart lying forbidden there on the table. It throbbed, when you held it up against your cheek. It grew warm with the tears, the hot searing tears of degradation that flowed out finally into that calm wide sense of ocean.

"Bertha—you—up there, why are you so long? Hurry down here the rear way and see to it that you pack only what strictly belongs to you."

The book belonged. It belonged as warmly and as closely as

heartbeat. To leave it lying there on that table would be to leave a heart. Then Bertha grew sly. So sly that the carpet-bag closed without even a click of a hasp over the volume of *The Cathedral Under the Sea.*

To tiptoe down the front flight of stairs, the bag in one hand, carefully away from the banisters, and her little purse of loose change in the other, was like walking on cushions. The carpet rose so roundly to the step. There was not so much as a creak and even though the dreadful chills were running off her spine again, just the lifting of the front door by the handle as it swung in, saved the little squeal of its hinges and with Mrs. Oessetrich's voice rising again from the rear of the house, the door closed again, noiselessly, with Bertha on its outer side.

Annie was gone. It was a shock to come upon the house standing eyeless there, with iron shutters across the windows and the front stoop removed. A produce company used it for a warehouse. A crane jutted out of one of the second story windows that had been converted into a sliding door.

Change. The city swirling and sucking in the days had sucked in Annie and the lodging house with the sour halls. It felt strange coming down to face the warehouse with the crane hanging out. It had some hay clinging to it as if it had not quite licked its chops. There had stood Annie's lodging house, lean as a witch.

Quicksands. You could imagine the building, story by story disappearing to the subtle suction, until only the dirty roof remained and Jocko with a stiff, terrorized tail. And Annie. She would have gone down last with her hands waving and protesting. They would be the very last above the sands, Annie's hands, with the fingers that were the shape of potatoes. Annie's strangling hands—even Annie—love of life. . . .

Front Street banged along. Down toward Bowling Green the produce firms stood banked up in front with the boxed vegetables and fruits. Frozen smells with the green coming softly through the mild February day. Bang. Bang. Trucks over cobblestones. One of them stood backed to the curb while a negro with a red cave for a mouth flung crates of fruit, the yellow light of the oranges showing through, across the sidewalk to another negro who caught them on the fly. Bang. Bang. Trucks over cobblestones. Sh-h-h. Sh-h-h. Trucks over quicksands.

At Bowling Green the fan of the sea came in. The carpetbag, even though she shifted hands as she lugged it, began to cut. There was a bench close to the railing.

When you sat down and leaned over, you stared right down into the face of the harbor. To sit down there with a sigh, your back to the city and your eyes to the sea, rested you and made that terrifying day seem to recede.

The silly, terrifying day of the carnelian beads.

The puny little day on the edge of the ocean. Presently it would pass out with the tide. As Annie's day had passed out, the day of the carnelian beads and the cream lace boudoir cap would roll into that immensity out there clothed in fog. The beauty, through the fog, of that immensity!

She kept dreaming into it. Even that night when she finally found a bed, up three flights in a cubby-hole of a filthy tenement on Desbrosses Street, she kept dreaming into it. That pyramid of immensity out there that was built out of days.

A certain phrase began to run along the weeks.

*She's too old.   She's too old.*   She's too old.

At first it gripped her breath and made her heart shy back in a hot sort of flush.   She's too old.   She could read the phrase on the lips of clients as they discussed her at the desk with the Bohemian who conducted the employment office.   Sometimes when she applied at homes with the slip from the agency, they told her point blank.

"No.   No.   We don't want a middle-aged woman.   Tell them at the agency to send us a young girl.   You're too old."

"But——"

"I know.   You look like a strong, honest woman, but you're too old."

After a while the phrase began to rock.   To have a cadence. It even lulled.   It made it suddenly easy to sit in the back row of the office and wait until the younger girls were accounted for.   It was like sitting out of the crowd in a shady spot and watching the troubled barterers in a market place.   They hurried so and cared so and their eyes were all crowded with self. While you sat back against the wall and waited, you could imagine those faces all in one.   The faces of the barterers.   The faces of those who could be eager over the carnelian beads.   A long, lean, composite face, with a nose like a scimitar and the eyes that were full of self, so close together that they almost seemed one.

You sat in the back row along with the charwomen, because you were old with your hair and your skin and your bones and the zest in your arms.

Clients with the eyes full of self that were so close together that they almost seemed one, did not know that to be young with your heart was to be a garden surrounded by the high gray walls of the flesh.

They saw only the high gray wall of the flesh, the tired shoulders, and the white wing in the hair.

There was no evading it. Bertha was getting older with her skin and her hair and the zest in her arms. Day work tired her terribly, because it was mostly scrubbing. Sometimes when she returned to the cubby-hole in Desbrosses Street the entire surface of her body gave off a singing sensation.

It was a mean room without a place to wash, but there was a public sink in the hallway of each of the tenement floors. Sometimes Bertha did a furtive thing. The tin basin in her room was so small. You could only slap the face with water. Often when the halls were quiet of the squalling of children and the black skull of a house seemed to sleep, Bertha, in her bare feet, stole out softly to the sink and slipped down her chemise.

If she bent down double under the faucet the cool water poured over her back. She could feel the smoothness of her flesh with the evenness of the flow. At first it sent a delicious shudder through her right up into her throat, and then it flowed so clean and so pure and so cool. It was like being as still as a mountain with a rill running down it. The water slid off her white back and around up under the warmth of her breasts. It dripped down into the sink with green little forest noises. They helped the ache, these furtive rinses, and sometimes when her feet were great swollen pads, she let the water pour over them too. It was easier then not to lie awake of tiredness.

The fact was to be faced that even day work was no longer easily obtainable. Sometimes the janitors and the superintendents of buildings passed her by for the next. "She's too old."

Without the little hitting friendliness of her savings in her petticoat pocket, that was a little terrifying. The room in

Desbrosses Street was a dollar a week and there were strict fire laws against cooking in the rickety old building over gas jets or alcohol lamps. The quick lunch rooms, even the meanest of them, made heavy inroads on the day's pay. At best they were dreadful, fume-fogged places, where the fried foods clung to the cold plates on rims of grease and the coffee was the color and consistency of clay-bank. Often it seemed to Bertha that it simply would not go down. The warm slush of it in her mouth. To close the eyes and gulp until the tears sprang, accomplished it. It was easier to bear than the knife-pangs of hunger which could come slashing down on Bertha. They cut her in two. Bertha dreaded hunger. It made her shamble when she walked. It lifted the top off her head. It cut.

Sometimes, that rather terrifying year, even though you were the first to report at the agency, there was only work three days in the week. To be a little hungry was not so bad if you stayed in the room on your cot. That was what Bertha did on the idle days. Stretched out there, the hunger gnawed up and down her great body like a rat and would not let her sleep. But it was easier lying there. The top stayed on your head.

There was the peasant of her for you. Strong hot foods. Meats. Sour rye bread with a tight and heavy mesh. Pea soup so thick that it poured from the pot in clumps. Without them the pull died in her legs and the lunge from her arm sockets. The concocted foods of the lunch room, the gray-looking stews, and custards with the ooze of water on top were pallid on her tongue.

All that winter, while on three days' earnings she must live for seven, and the reefer jacket grew horrible of the patches that the fabric could no longer hold, the blades kept slashing. The hunger blades.

Sometimes in washing down a corridor the floor began to wave, or walking home or standing in the crush of a street car, you could never foretell just when, that dreadful top-of-your-head feeling; that lightness that would make you want to sway —loose-kneed—down—down. And then that little singing sensation, like a kettle boiling, that you felt against your windpipe. The nervousness of that. It was not easy to feel light-headed and cold and pursued by that little singing irritation in your throat, and still plunge a high power arm into the pail and fling out a wide and soapy fan of wet.

Bertha suffered that winter after a fantastic fashion. The days seemed etched on glass. Thin cold flat days. Like the window pane when you awoke in the morning with the wild mountain scenery frozen to it. The unreality of those days. One after another after another, as if you could put your fist through and crash them.

The idle days stretched on the cot with that incessant little sensation of the boiling tea kettle along your throat. Sometimes the hours became a little crazy with tilting walls and sagging ceiling. Sometimes it was like lying on the under side of a wave. The perversity of a bare spot on the wall where the plaster had crumbled and a lath or two grinned through! Sometimes it became the amber tunnels of Jocko's eyes, through which you ran along lovely opalescent floors calling—calling—and all the motes in the amber were faces. The faces of boys frozen into the translucence. The face of the boy in the window that she had not looked upon. The faces of boys. Boys. She did not glance at them as she ran calling, but there was one face among the many down in the beautiful drown of the amber—a dear, dear one. She did not look. She couldn't. Couldn't. But the streamer of her hair with the wing of white in it,

drifted past his face as she ran calling—calling—Rollo—no, not
Rollo. Rollo was out there on the hill. Rollo was dead. That
was not the name. Willie had known the name of the boy.
Silly Willy who had felt the dig of his heels into his haunches.
Felix! That was the name. It snapped like a little coin purse
when you said it. Felix. Of course! Felix, son of Rollo.

A windfall came along. In one night she earned sixteen
dollars. It happened this way.

On a Saturday morning at the agency the front row emptied
itself before eleven and the younger girls, many of them on tall
heels, went out jauntily, a little impudently, with their slips of
paper. So the back row came out suddenly in its horrific sort
of frieze. The frieze of the scrubwomen. Old women with
sucked-in faces like the swirl of water down a drain hole.
Women with white jade faces. Women with veiny noses and
cheek venules and lips that the muscles would not hold into
place. Women with eyes about as lifeless as gelatin. Women
with dead breasts.

Bertha sood out. Just as surely as an old horse sags to
sway-back, Bertha's shoulders were down, for good, but her
eyes were blue with water and sky. Mediterranean bays.

That is why, because her gaze seemed to project her in full
relief out from the frieze, and the front row was already
emptied, Bertha was selected. Delsher's had sent down for a
cloakroom attendant for a ball that evening.

"Here you! You're too old for that kinda job, but I can't
give 'em what I ain't got. Report there at nine to-night and ask
for Gerard, the steward."

*You're too old. You're too old. You're too old.*

Delsher's was in Fifty-eighth Street near Fifth Avenue. An awning jutted out over the sidewalk and the little striped cave was all lit with electric bulbs. A puff of hot scented breath came out even at the service entrance. Flesh. Warm, scented, excited flesh. That odor always hung over Delsher's. From ball to ball to ball. The unfastidious fact is that Delsher's smelled like a jungle. Young, excited, breathing flanks.

There were cloakrooms on each floor. Passing along, you could see the ballroom. The enchanted lake of floor, sly with wax. The jungle bowed back from it with a gesture of palms with enormous fronds and the crystal hanging moss of the side lights, and the tree stripes of great gilt pillars. Mirrors caught at the effect and tattled it on. Sometimes you could see the same tapestry and gold chair repeated six stately times.

Bertha's allotted cloakroom was gray. The dressing tables had gold pointed roofs and there were long aisles formed by the coat racks. It was very simple. You exchanged a brass tag for a dazzle of field-of-ermine or of cloth-of-gold.

The shrill, young-fleshed beauty of the old-eyed girls as they began to arrive. They stepped out of the splendid surf of the wraps, breastless as boys, and with wise scarlet threads for lips. The insolence of them with their bobbed, flaring heads that made their necks look slender and nervous. The fine fettle of young horses with docked tails and pink lightening of nostrils.

It was bewildering. The young herd of them rushing in. The perfumed dust. You saw them through the astonishing fog of cigarette smoke and face powder and fur and chiffon. The brocades had a way of clinging to Bertha's hands. They almost had to be ripped away from the flesh. Cutting, nasty sensation. The little splitting sounds of the satins along the roughened fingers. Then there were the corsets. They stepped out of

them. Tiny, boneless, pink satin urns. A half animate feeling
as you laid them away, still warm from the ripple of ribs and
the excited breathing.

The heat rose in waves and the powder began to taste in a
soft scented mud that lay along the tongue and back into the
throat. The walls had a little sway to them as the wraps
mounted and mounted. The brass checks. You could scarcely
hand them out fast enough. Slashing bareness of shoulders.
Slim things with V's of nakedness down to the waistline in
back. More and more of the discarded, pink, slim little corsets
and more and more of the confluent planes of torsos gliding
under chiffons. That odor of jungle. The excited released
flanks.

You leaped! It was the first crash of flesh-shuddering music.
The naked undulating V's. A contortion ran along the cloakroom, as if everyone had moved on little running muscles and
yet not advanced. You shivered almost ecstatically at that.
Eyelids. The white flash of them lowering. Sudden slitted
eyes. Insouciance of the docked heads. A tree shake through
the cloakroom. Only it did not begin at the heart. It lay to the
flesh. The shivering, shimmying flesh. . . .

That gelatinous room. It nauseated. It seemed to be moving
away on the running muscles and yet not moving at all. It made
you a little sick, the motionless motion. There was nothing to
clutch. The insidious horridness of it. The slitted eyes.
The wise red threads for mouths. The ripple of torsos.

You sat down in the emptied cloakroom finally. You remembered the lancinating pains in the ambulance. Mothers of men,
was it for this? You seemed to remember again—you seemed
to remember—sweat and love and solitary childbirth on wide
moors. Swing of the grinning scythes and the women who toil

and who bear and who weep, and the wide-legged men with the necks like tree boles. Peril of solitary childbirth on wide moors. Mothers of men—was it for this. . . .

The crashing and the jazzing never ceased. Where one band left off another took up. Syncopated wilderness of a night. The saxophones screamed into the jungle. Corsages died into the heat and cloyed it up. The strange new breastless girls with the docked heads and the naked V's for backs swarmed past the door with the men whose shirt fronts had gone a little awry and whose irreverent eyes slid toward the V of back and the willful rippling of the torsos under chiffon.

It was not easy to keep awake. The velvets and the furs of the wraps crowded up the heat so and the tongue was all slippery with the fine scented powder. That maniac, the saxophone! The smoke began to sting Bertha's eyes. She commenced to doze in the miasma. They started to drift in again. Some of them a little drunk. One with a broken shoulder strap and the mark of teeth on the knowing little knoll of her shoulder.

You were tempted, sewing the strap across that tender bit of flesh, to spank it. The petted peacock flesh of the new generation squalling its emancipation in naked backs and tipsy eyes and wriggle of insinuating torso.

The tipsy eyes. The cloakroom began to crowd up with them. The new eyes of the new youth. They were clear enough, but brilliant with the hard shine of blades. The cutting, slashing blades of mowing machines. The mowed-down little gardens that sometimes ⟨bloom in young girls' eyes. Bold, unveiled, inquisitive eyes, these. Impudent eyes, without illusion, without fear, but without the mist of wonder.

It was strange, the young men with the awry shirt fronts

who passed the door, looked into the new eyes of new youth without illusion, too, and without reverence and without the mist of wonder. The new eyes of the new youth. New eyes but old lusts. The mowed-down wastes of the garden. The star flowers that sometimes bloom in women's eyes and make them madonna-like. They were mowed down by the impudent steel blades. Cool, clear, matter-of-fact eyes as real as Pittsburgh.

The burning raging hours. There was no end. Crash. The gale of jazz that shook the torsos. Crash. The rumble of jungle. The odor of jungle.

There was a young man stretched out on the couch in the hallway just outside the cloakroom. He was dreadful. Bla. His mouth was a mere roving rhomboid in the fleshiness of his face and his eyes silly pools. One of the girls held his head on her lap and played with his hair. Slick clumps of polished hair. She had a startled lovely face, shaped like a heart. A cigarette hung between her lips and she talked through it. Once she reached into the young man's waistcoat pocket and drew out a silver flask about the size and flatness of a hand and tilted it to her lips. A stream oozed sidewise and down along her neck. The young man lifted that four-sided mouth of his and kissed the trickle.

You held yourself tight against the nausea of that.

Bertha, standing and looking at them with the deep blue channels of her eyes, a silent sort of peasant tower.

"Who's your friend, the Woolworth Building, *Chérie?*"

"That's not the Woolworth Building, Jerry my only, that's Grant's Tomb. Can't you tell by the dome?"

"I'll dance with you for that."

"Then make haste, Lochinvar. I'm growing awfully wobbly on my toddle toddle-toddlers."

The wild horse of a night plunged on. The figures of the trampled-down girls. The cloakroom was strewn with them. They were on the sofas and some as limp as dolls propped up against chairs. Bare arms and silk legs strewn at the haphazard angles of sawdust dolls. You stepped among the debris of them.

The maniacal laughter of the jazz. You began to feel a little mad with it yourself. Your brain was one of those Coney Island devices for noise. Raz-z-z-z daz-z-z-z. The terrible sting of fumes against your eyeballs. The rising simoon of the heat. The flung bare, beautiful necks there—about—everywhere—and the wise impudent lips. You stepped among the slim forms and propped them up and straightened out the sawdust legs and ordered the tossed loveliness of chiffon down over the legs. Raz-z-z-z daz-z-z-z. It helped as you pushed through the fumes, to try and swing out on the short quick beats of the brain, far away from what the hands did.

Somewhere, you tried to think—raz-z-z-z daz-z-z-z—somewhere, Lake Como's twilights are deep purple. Slow purple like the widening wine stain on a tablecloth. Raz-z-z-z daz-z-z-z. To lean out into that thought. It was like opening a window. Slow twilights. The standing forests with folded arms. To lean out—raz-z-z-z daz-z-z-z.

One girl asleep in a chair with neatly closed but fumy lips had to be picked up as if she were a little bag of sachet, crammed into her wrap and handed bodily to one of the young men with the irreverent eyes. He left a dollar bill on the counter that separated the cloakroom from the corridor. That was the beginning. Until dawn the coins and a few more dollar bills showered there. There was a china saucer for catching them in one of the dressing table drawers. Bertha did not know that.

At four o'clock the jazz sort of reared itself up on its hind legs, neighed enormously, and stopped like a great fantastic, fabled horse, frozen there on his dancing haunches with horror at his bray.

The strange silence began to pour. It pressed on the eardrums. It sang. A ringing silence as full of shuddering little atoms as a brass gong after a beating. You tiptoed through it, picking up oddments of a glove, a ribbon, a comb. The exhausted air was full of fog. There were three thickness of brocade across the window and the sash was hard to budge.

Finally, with all the strength of her, Bertha jerked it open. A wet cool dawn blew in. You scooped your hands into it and laved it over your face. Cool dawn that had traveled over wide and brooding silences. You fell on your knees beside the open window and drank it in as it pinkened.

It was time to go, but there was still one coat left on the rack. A lovely one of pink silver and silver fox. The money made quite a wad in Bertha's petticoat pocket. It was pleasant while you waited, to walk about the room to the friendly hit-hit. It made the rising day seem kindly. The little ducts in her mouth were running. The hit-hit meant tripe stew for breakfast.

Bertha standing there in the ruins of that cluttered bejazzed night, her silhouette against the new day. . . .

A vacuum cleaner started to whine on a lower floor. The coat of pink silver began to tarnish against the day. Voices. The girl with the heart-shaped face and one of the young men with the patent leather hair and the irreverent eyes. There had been so many of them. Hundreds of them passing and repassing that door. You wanted to laugh at the identical procession of them. A shirt front for a shirt front. An eye for an eye. A silhouette for a silhouette. Hundreds of the lean-faced young men. They had passed and they had passed until there was only the one left. He was leaning up against the door frame in an easy and insolent hypotenuse with his hands plunged into his pockets and crawling about in there, and his easy face none too steady, with the mouth off on its rhomboid every so often.

"*Chérie,* I adore you."

"Jerry, you darling villain."

"Get your wraps. I'll run down and get mine. Here's a dollar for the Woolworth Tower."

"Grant's Tomb, darling."

"Hurry along, there's a girl."

"But Jerry—I——"

"Darling, haven't my two hours of eloquence upon the subject convinced you that no one will ever know?"

"But the family—Jerry, and Father is so—so——"

"Will you leave all that to me, *Chérie?* Do you trust me enough? You'll be home tucked in your little bed by the time your maid comes in to draw your curtains. I want you, *Chérie,* with me—to-night—my rooms—for an hour only——"

"Jerry."

"I'll be back with my coat . . . wait, sit here, darling. . . ."

"Oh, Jerry——"

"No, no—no nonsense—say to me, 'Yes, Jerry darling.' Say it pretty, so I can kiss it off your lips."

"Yes—Jerry darling——"

The wrap of pink silver. She slid into it like a star into

a cloud. It was hard to tear your eyes off the pale, frightened beauty of her. Somehow you wanted to keep her. Close. Close to your bigness. To make her listen if she would, to the calmness, to the great calm tick of your heart. Your eyes, you could not take them off. You stood there drawing on her wrap for her. But your eyes. You could not tear them off. Bertha, standing there big and pale and tranquil against the daylight.

"You! Let go, please. What are you looking at?"

"I—why, miss——"

"You think I'm drunk. I'm not."

"No."

"I won't be looked at like that. You hear me? I won't."

She began to cry. Tipsy little tears that ran down to the point of her heart-shaped face.

"You! I won't be looked at like that. I hate it. I won't have it. I want to go home."

"Go——"

"Tell him—the young man—tell him when he comes that I've gone. Tell him I left the message. I've gone home. I—you—I hate you for staring like that. I won't have it. I want to go home. . . ."

She gathered the shimmer of wrap all about her and ran down the right-hand curve of the staircase. You could follow the shimmer of her through the mirror. The shimmer—the whine of the vacuum cleaner.

The empty cloakroom, it was the color of cloyed grease. Presently he came.

"Where——"

"She's gone——"

"Gone where——"

"Gone——"

"Hell," he said and started toward the right staircase.

"No. No. Wait. She'll be back in yoost a minute. Wait here, she said."

"Oh." He sat down a little unsteadily.

She closed the window so that the heat crowded up again. Tiptoe. Her movements about the room had a slow sedative rhythm. Tiptoe. There was a corsage of double Parma violets kicked under a table and dying into the heat. She picked it up and placed it on the table at his elbow. Slow tease of perfume. His eyelids began to wave like an old green frog's. Finally, he slumped over sidewise. Asleep.

Bertha, tiptoeing out, with her lips lifted back off her shining square teeth.

It was sun-up when she came out into the street. Even the city can be sweet with morning. She strode through the tender light, the bold, reassuring hit-hit against her leg. There was a certain Quick Lunch Room on Lexington Avenue. Tripe stew. The juices along the sides of her tongue were running. . . .

The half-days were humiliating. They were the crumbs from the agencies. Almost invariably they fell to the frieze of the charwomen. One day for the first time one of these part-time allotments fell to Bertha. Fell like a clod of fear. She took it and went out with her shoulders round, and the slip of paper clutched in her dread smitten fingers.

It was as if you had passed a milestone. An old stump of a milestone all worn down and shaped like the last tooth of one of the scrubwomen.

The morning's work was in an automobile showroom on Fifty-ninth Street near Columbus Circle. Polishing brass railings and the mirrors nailed to the floor underneath the motor cars to reflect their lowermost perfections. A soft morning of mousy little rubbings along smooth surfaces. At two o'clock the workaday was finished. A sun-drenched spring day swam over the Park and along the streets that were running with new thaw. Women wore bright hats and overshoes. What snow remained had great gaps in it that widened, and everywhere little rivulets were hurrying toward the gutters. It was pleasant just to stroll.

At Carnegie Hall on Fifty-seventh Street the motor cars were dense and the bright hats were bobbing. Traffic ran toward the great building in spokes. Up from the subways. Down from the elevated trains. Along the side streets. Out from the motors. Concert crowds. Bertha knew. Madam Gerbhardt had once given her the tickets to the Ukrainian Chorus.

The crowd hit into you from all sides. You began to elbow. The broad steps were crammed and everyone's face was uplifted. Two policemen swung benign clubs. This was a kidglove crowd with a scent and a rustle to it. Once the swirl tightened so that no one could move, but everybody swayed. The well-bred little squeals of the women. The firm, wellclad arms of the men forging ahead for them. Slamming of motor doors. Slow pouring upward of the crowd on the steps. The eager, fluty voices of the women. . . .

The swirl held Bertha like a vise. The women, ever so slightly, and kindly enough, veered a little from the contact with her worn old reefer. It was horrible in the spring light. Like a scab. You had to hold yourself away from it by breathing in. Bertha could do that until it almost seemed a mere box, with herself quite slimly and fastidiously down its center.

Something curious happened. A child caught down in the jam had his face crushed up softly against the reefer. His mother slid in a quick hand between his cheek and the contact.

"Daddy," she said, "see if you cannot lift Junior over on your side. Don't touch, Junior. Ugh, darling, not nice. Come over on this side with Daddy—don't touch lady's coat."

She was as snug as a plover and as plump. Sweet fleshed. Something eupeptic about her. Something about her. . . .

"Go over to Daddy and Brother Ben," she said and veered. The veering women.

The father lifted the child. His smile was very white in a brown face. Liver spotted eyes. . . .

"Come, Junior Boy," he said, "away from there. Here, Mother, you come too. Away."

It was the Musliners. The firm pat tight little group of them. You watched them edge up the steps with the crowd.

It was the spring made you hate that reefer. So with simulated unconsciousness you looked over the heads of the veering women as you tried to force your way through. And over the heads of the veering women you saw a picture. A lithograph pasted on to a panel beside the entrance. It stood out like the spot cast by a sun glass. It riveted the eye. Willy-nilly the crowds jammed around. Bertha with her big hands and wrists hanging bare in a huddle in front and her gaze sucked up against the lithograph in the panel.

The spot that stood out as if cast by a sun glass was a head. It leaned out over one shoulder and then everything was black, like a silence, until farther down over the keyboard of a piano were two hands. You wanted to cry. Such ineffably tender hands. Why—why the white hands at your heart! There they were. And that head leaning over one shoulder out of that background of silence. That luminous, tawny-looking head with the long tender cheeks and the eyes that looked tranced with the music of the chimes goldily. Who? The name ran in script across the corner. Charvet.

Ah, Charvet. That evening at dinner. Madam Gerbhardt. Moon-haunted. To be moon-haunted was to live with an opal mist about the heart. . . .

It was so hard to move. The eyes held so. They held, with that feeling of suction. . . .

"Move on."

There was still something of the sixteen dollars in that petticoat pocket. Friendly little wad. It burned. It made your body glow suddenly like a hot coin. An excoriating kind of heat that made your lips feel cracked and your eyes glossy.

The crowd bent up the steps. There was a long line before the box office. It moved up inch by inch, and Bertha, suddenly a part of it, moved too. The wad was tied into a handkerchief and it had to be bitten open with the teeth.

"Ticket please."

"Admission only."

"What?"

"Standing room only. One dollar."

"Yah. . . ."

You slid in through a baize door. The auditorium was dim and enormous and the waiting silence all arched up like a cat's

back. The stage was so far—off somewhere beyond the inter-vening sea of all the soft breathings. You could see a little, if you tiptoed to peer between the heads. The piano. A curve of black. The white hands. The ineffably tender hands. Heart flutters that had flown out there. Someone rammed in ahead, pressing you there against the wall.

The shelving slipping beach. The white keys ran down it with the purr of surf. You could feel the floor of sand mov-ing out subtly from under your feet. The floor that led under the sea. . . .

Bertha standing pinioned there to the wall with her hands caught up and crowded to her breast by the crush of the standees and her throat flexed outward and beating. It was like bleeding. As if the melodies of her heart were arteries and that running of the keys out there the precious bleeding of them. It was like that. Oh, it was. . . .

The tears came out in a dew along your eyes.

It stepped down the keys in heartbeats. You could scarcely keep back. You knew that cry. It had lain in your heart for so long. There it was on the outside of yourself, strewn along the keys. You were free of the hurt of it—where it had lodged like a knife in the plushy case of your heart.

The bleeding out of all the little inner turmoils. The dammed-up ecstasies. The music of the chimes goldily. The glad releases. The rilling beauty. The white hands at your heart. Just by tilting yourself up tiptoe you could see them flown out there above the keys. The white flutterings. To be pinioned there against the wall all of that afternoon with your hands caught up against your breast and the arteries of your heart uncocked and flowing. . . .

The applause beat itself out and then began all over again. It died down and then, on the momentum of a few little scattered claps, rose again. The crowd loosened and moved down the aisle, blackening and jamming around the platform. The cramming against the wall eased up. You could hurry, too, if you wanted.

But is was enough, just to remain there against the wall with the eyes closed and the throat flexing. She could no more have moved—down there—those white hands—the white hands at her heart—down there—fluttering. She could no more have moved. . . .

It was enough to be standing back there against the wall weak and glad.

It did not matter that her eyes somehow could not open to see the face of Felix Charvet down there beyond the opal mist, the face with the chimes tranced so goldily in the eyes and the long, choir-boy cheeks that were lit with their first faint down.

It did not matter, now that she felt so glad and weak and bled free of those lovely torments that were without dimension . . . it did not matter that she was never to know that Felix Charvet was Felix—son of Rollo.

It was frightening to see the houses board up and the exodus of the families set in. Summer. Truck loads of perilously piled trunks. Nonplussed cats mewling at sealed doors. Handbills collecting on stoops in little snow drifts.

The agencies began to crowd.

The room in Desbrosses Street was as black and as narrow as a flue and all day it drew in the heat and all night long breathed it out. There was a window, but it opened upon a brick wall that you could touch without leaning. The darkness seemed to embalm the heat. Dreadful furry thickness like the fuzz on the tongue of a fever patient.

Sometimes at night, Bertha dragged herself to the sill and crouched on the floor with her cheek to it. The wall breathed like a flank. If you looked straight up there was a bit of sky about the size of a quill. On certain nights a star wandered into it. It made Bertha laugh to see it. Like a wise eye to a keyhole. Until she fell asleep Bertha gazed, eye to eye.

But this very slit of a room was the reason why it was frightening to see the houses board up. Its rental was a dollar a week and with the exodus to the country even part time work with the families, scarcer and scarcer.

Once she did jump a week and the agent who collected each Saturday into a dirty canvas bag with a drawstring showed a tooth at her. A sort of fang and the more terrifying because she had thought his gums were empty.

One day an innkeeper engaging a staff for his back street little hostelry in Asbury Park debated between Bertha and a great green Swedish girl who spoke no English, but whose lips hung down like ripe plums.

For the life of him he could not decide. Bertha sitting back in the frieze kept saying something that was her little prayer.

"Please make him," she kept saying—"please make him."

The bald spot on his head was all crimson and beaten from the sun. It must have taken a good warm sun through clean salted air to do that. Asbury Park. Please make him. Please make him.

"You're too old," he said finally and turned to lay his hand on the Swedish girl's hip.

*You're too old. You're too old. You're too old.* The phrase was so sly. It ran after you like a shadow. It would never let you be.

But that same day there came along a week of half-days at Coronation Point Inn. Airing rooms preparatory to the opening of the season. Prying closed windows from their winter stripping. Swabbing floors and unswathing the wrapped bedsteads which were hung slightly from the floor, against winter dampness.

Oh, but it was pleasant. Coronation Point stood on a terrace and overlooked a curve of bay. You took a subway to the end of the line and then a surface car and then you walked fifteen minutes through sun-shot leafage that speckled the road and made it dance. Chipmunks made precious noises scuttling over leaves. Orioles the color of the batting of an eye flashed through. Tit-a-weet of cock robin. And smells. The damp lush ones of sun making moist places steam and the green ones of stems when they are snapped in two and bleed. The green smells came from a little tramp stream of new water without even a bed for itself which ran through the grasses. It had a trill. It made the morning a hurrying loveliness. Quick, delicate, tumbling thing—sometimes on the homeward walk, Bertha took off her shoes and stockings, stooped for a handful of skirt and waded in against its tiny tide. The toes bit down and the mud squnched up. . . .

Where the woods left off, the highway and hot little wooden houses took up. Then it *was* hot! Trudging along toward the surface car, motors tore along that macadam road, so that it was best to walk on the little rim of cinders at the edge. That was the worst of the half-day at Coronation Point. The half pay and the walk back to the surface car through the blazing noon.

Sometimes in front of the occasional frame houses there were wooden planks. They eased the feet of the burn from the macadam and before a shanty that had been rigged up as a gasoline station, an old overturned chassis, rotting there through sun and storm, was at least a resting place.

A hot, bald-faced little shanty-town squatting there on the

bare clay stretch beyond the surface cars. You could see the tracks shining in the distance like forceps and on clear days the minarets of the city. Children and hens wallowed themselves out dust-baths in the patches of yard before these houses. The women were slattern. But sometimes there were neat corrugated truck gardens. Ruffles of lettuce. Lattice work of peas. Ridged potato patches like the roof of a mouth. Tough, good-smelling gardens. Just to trudge past them could set the knife blades of hunger to slashing in Bertha.

There was a bake shop farther along. A dilapidated little packing case of a building, with a brood of dirty children wallowing in the back yard and a weedy truck garden that had somehow been eked out of the clay.

### MEYERBOGEN'S BAKERY.  LUNCH ROOM.
### CROTON'S ICE CREAM SOLD HERE.

Its breath was so sweet. The fragrance of hot bread. You could smell it as you came along the road. It teased at Bertha's faintness. It made the noonday road turn into a garter snake that rippled. The swimming, buzzing bread-scented haze. One day, because it was unendurable to wait for the three o'clock tripe stew in the city, which must serve as lunch and dinner, she turned in.

A mat of flies clung to the screen door and buzzed off as she opened it. There was a table near the door with a mustard pot on it. The bread and rolls on the counter were covered with pink netting. The proprietor served. He was enormous. A white apron girded his middle. His white cap was awry on his curly head. You saw him through a fog of flour. Great fellow, most of the objects in the shop shook as he walked.

The T of chandelier that hung down in the show window of tilted loaves of bread. The coffee mugs on the shelf. A stack of saucers.

"Veenie sandwiches, five zents. Baked beans, five zents. Gorned beef hash vid boached egg, fiveteen."

"Beans."

"Goffee?"

"Yah. . . ."

The noonday buzzed with the flies and the broken little shouts of the children. It was hard not to doze as she waited. Once her head did fall forward.

"It's a hot day," said Meyerbogen the baker, and set down a brown dish of the beans with a pale cube of pork on top.

"Yah."

Suddenly it was hard to eat. Even while her nostrils flared with the need of the strong hot food the heat was full of disks, spinning little juggler's plates and the shouts of the children were so far away—so far——

"Here—quick! You going to vaint? No. Don't. Here—drink——"

"I—where——?"

"It's all right. You god a liddle stroke from the zun. Here, sit while I fan you."

The noonday drone swam back again. It was good to feel it, hot and buzzing and full of the shouts of the children.

"I'm all right," she said, and shook herself like a spaniel, and looked up at Meyerbogen with the blue channels of her eyes.

"You're all right, sure, now," he said and went off on his waddle about the business of unstacking buns from a wooden tray which a helper had just brought up from a basement.

But the lunch. For the life of her the beans would not go

down or the cup of the light tan coffee. That was terrible.
To feel all warm again and free of the chill of cold sweat and
back safely once more in the drone of the noon and the lunch
spread out on the clean wooden top of the table, untasted.
Waste. The half days made one calculate so. Inevitably the
slashing blades of hunger that cut through and through the
great organism of Bertha would begin to champ again, a little
later and the day's food allotment was already spent down to
the last penny. Slowly and against a restricted throat she began
to swallow the coffee.

Presently Meyerbogen sat down on the chair opposite.

"It's a heat," he said and the fog of the flour rose up off
him.

"Yah."

He was like a great milk-fed baby. Pink polished cheeks.
Tight, spring-tight curls and fat hands with dimples. And the
enormous girth of him! He swayed back from himself for all
the world like a tenor drinking in breath for Pagliacci's sob.
And, ridiculously enough, he was almost dainty.

His big white throat was soft, and when he laughed he
shook from head to toe, and the cloud of flour exuded as if
someone were beating him with a baby's cornstarch bag.

"You lost your abbidite?"

"Yah—a little——"

"Take your time——"

"The heat——"

"Yah—yah—the heat—my woman—she died on me in heat
like this." He looked off toward the roadway and screwed
up his face. There was something about him actually of a
baby about to cry.

"Yah——"

"Meningitis," he said—"down two days——"

"Oh—oh——"

"A good woman. Never down with child more than three days—and then in two days—meningitis—gone——"

"Oh—oh——"

"Five of them needing her. From two years old to ten."

"The children?"

"Yah—we had it neat like a pin here once. Now look!—I had a good woman——"

"Oh."

His great baby face was still screwed and resolutely out toward the road.

"Zummer," he said cryptically, "is zummer. It's good but not too much——"

Foolishly you could have cried for him. Big baby.

"Some zinnamon buns? Just hot from the ofen."

"No."

He waddled out on the porch and began carrying a sack of flour around the side entrance. You could hear him wheeze and the white haze was everywhere. Gradually it was pleasant to be eating. The coarse, strong food—the steam of it was appetizing, and after the first forkfuls appetite came back.

Clank. Clank. One of the children wandered in. Oh, how your heart leaped back, wounded. He had a poor little leg in a brace that clanked. A fat baby, too, only it was as if the father resembled the child and not the child the father. A dirty baby. A not nice baby. Eggy. With a smeared and too-large little girl's dress hung on him and horrid, dirt-ground underthings. He was lugging something. A man's ground down and discarded shoe that he must have found in the roadway.

"Shoe," he said and held it out toward Bertha.

"Ugh, dirty," she said, and made a grimace.

"Dirty," he said, and made an identical grimace with his already dirt-grimaced face, and took the shoe by thumb and forefinger and threw it out of the door.

That was adorable and made you want to pinch the dirty little cheek.

"Lady?"

She lifted him up and sat him rather gingerly on the knee of her neat skirt. The brace bit through and down into her flesh. It was heavier than the child. Cruel. Sickening.

"Baby."

"Lady."

Meyerbogen came in. There were lines of perspiration running down his face.

"Chimmie," he said, "go back out in the yard. Get down off the missis. Here's a zinnamon bun."

"It's all right."

"He's dirty. I can't ged help in the gountry."

"Yah—dirty."

"I'm dirty," said Jimmie, and looked up at her with his clear eyes shining in their smeary sockets. The brace cut in.

"I'll wash him."

"Ach—blease——"

"Where is the——"

"Ach, no, but you ain't so good yourself with zunstroke——"

"I'm all right. Where?"

"Back there."

"Come, Chimmie."

Clank. Clank.

Incredible disorder of that room behind the shop. The fantastic confusion of a chair sitting crazily on a carpet sofa. A red hen had wandered in through a hole in the screen door. The dishes of what seemed many a breakfast were stacked on the table and half covered with the flung-up edges of the red tablecloth. Flies. There were swiss curtains at the windows, but they had dried on their poles into strings. A pet tortoise hung halfway up one. Boys' caps and flung off aprons and half a basket of new dug potatoes. A broken high chair. Dumped-out coffee grounds. Sack of grass seed. A child's slate hung on the wall with this chirography in the nonsense hand of boyhood.

It made the disorder suddenly not so terrible. It made you want to laugh.

Poor little Jimmie. He was so dirty. The smudge ran deep down into his pores and he cried at the rubbing. The brace was hard to lift off. Meyerbogen knew the device and did that, and the welts on the plump curving leg were so deep that you kissed them.

"He can ged all right. The doctor says he needs to be shown two hours every day how to walk so he don't throw his little leg out. I don't ged the time."

You kissed them again, the red fiery welts.

"I can ged all right." That was his way. The little mimic!

There were no towels and Meyerbogen ran downstairs into the basement where the baking ovens were, for some flour sacks, but while he was gone, Bertha found a clean bed sheet and rolled Jimmie into it.

He came out as round and as plump as a mushroom.

"O-o-o-o-o."

"O-o-o-o-o."

Patty-pat-pat up and down the bare back.

The children came trooping in. Three of them in dirty little steps. Oscar and Petey and Essie. Meyerbogens all. Dumpy. Thick. Sturdy. The girl had two beautiful brown braids that she could sit on. Oscar and Pete were just shaved, like little convicts.

"We gotta house-girl. We gotta house-girl."

"Shut up. It's only a gustomer gifing us help."

"I'll stay. I do day work."

"Ach, if you knew how I need help. I'll pay good."

There was a clean dress found for Jimmie. Almost immediately he fell asleep and the chair was lifted down off the carpet couch so that Bertha could stretch him out there. The children drifted off. You could hear the pleasant treble of them all through the somnolent afternoon. Thin, high incessant talk of children. Meyerbogen was downstairs baking. Once he called up for one of the large tin trays from the shop. Bertha carried it down. It was clean and full of the sweet hot breath down there in the basement, and one of the two helpers kept stoking the roaring ovens. Meyerbogen, leaning back from himself, enormous and flour-dusted and pink in the face. He lunged at the dough with a rolling pin; flattened it to

a mat, flopped over the mat, lunged. The smell was strong.
Full of life. Firm sweet bread. It was the realest smell of all.
Almost with dimension. Bread.

"It's no blace down here in this heat for you. Go right
back. You had a touch from the zun."

It was hard to know where to begin. The four tiny bedrooms up under the hot eaves were wrathy-looking with confusion. The tossed children's beds. What had once been neat
enough carpets had rents in them where children's feet had
skated. More of the once dainty curtains had sagged on their
rods. The room where the boys slept was filled with the
bulk of an elaborately contrived aeroplane. You had to climb
around it to get at the window to open it. There was not
enough fresh bed-linen but finally Bertha found a chest of it
tucked away in a small slanting garret over the back porch.

A neat, old-world trunk full of coarse, carefully laundered
linens, some with cotton crochet. Homely, strong things that
the wife of Meyerbogen must have hemmed, crocheted, laundered, and packed away. They made all the tumbled-looking
beds in that house seem suddenly cool, as if the mother of the
Meyerbogens had laid a placid hand suddenly on the hot tossed
brow of her household.

And Meyerbogen's room, with the great solemn walnut bed
and the wardrobe that just grazed the ceiling. The wife of
Meyerbogen had given life four times on that ugly brown bed.
She must have been a strong woman. An odor still hung over
the room. The green and milky sweetness of cows' breath
when they lick their calves. Something had happened to the
mirror over the dresser. It had come unscrewed and stood
with its face to a corner. There was a chair rigged up beside
the bed with a bit of looking-glass as jagged as lightning

propped up against it and a razor and a shaving mug stiff with old suds beside it.

Great baby of a Meyerbogen. It must have made him red to bursting to stoop to shave. Bertha found out the trouble with the mirror against the wall. Its screws were threadbare. It was not easy to stand on a chair and unhinge the top ruffle of mill-work that made the wardrobe just graze the ceiling, and take out its screws and lean it against the wall and drag back the mirror for mounting on the dresser. It was a man's job, and a great pox of sweat broke out as she hoisted and screwed. It was astonishing, though, how it seemed to quiet the room of its state of confusion. That adjusted mirror and the made bed. There was little hope to do more in that afternoon than to untie the strings of swiss curtains from someone's attempt to get them up out of the way, and pin up one of the neat "splashers" that came out of the trunk behind the washstand. It was especially designed for there. An oblong of white crash with a little girl and a little boy embroidered in red and underneath in scrolled red script, "Good Morning."

It made the room begin to shine.

At long intervals the screen door to the shop slammed and the bell tittered. You could hear Meyerbogen lumbering up the cellar stairs. The house shuddered. Or sometimes one of the children ran around from the side yard across the wooden porch, slamming the kitchen screen sharply.

By late afternoon the beds were at least fresh and made and the dishes washed and a clean red cloth laid out on the table. Four hours of hoisting, scrubbing, straightening, that had scarcely made their dent. The red hen still clucked among the stove cinders and would not remain shooed out. And Jimmie. Constantly in and out through the hole in the screening he

was lurid again with dirt. The crusty dirt of damp little
hands and clay and unsavory objects about the yard.

"Chimmie, you bane all dirty!"

"Chimmie bane all dirty." Clank. Clank.

There was something about that little way of repeating your
phrases. You held him very closely. The brace made him so
heavy.

Meyerbogen was generous.

"Here is three dollars! You done a big day's work in a few
hours."

"Oh no——."

"Oh yes. Could you, blease, come to-morrow all day?"

"I got morning work promised at Coronation Point."

"To-morrow afternoon, then. Part time like to-day?"

"Yah——."

"Dot's good. You can stay for zupper now, if you want."

"Oh no—no——."

The shy inexplicability of that. She wanted to stay for supper. She wanted to putter over the stove with Essie. There
was a great dish-pan of greens with the dirt from the garden
still brown against their roots on the sink, and a ham end.
Chimmie's low little body down there about her knees. The
boys tussling out in the dust. It was pleasant there in that
room with the new red tablecloth. The late sun slanted in
through the screen and one step down led right out into the
weed-ridden kitchen garden with the thin leafage of the peas
stuck on sticks against the pinkening sky.

"You live in the city, not?"

"Yah."

"It's a long way."

"Yah."

"I bay carfare."

"Yah."

"You won't dissaboint—to-morrow?"

"No."

"Dot's good. I need help, blease. It's a confusion——"

"I'll come."

"Good night."

"Good night.'"

The sun was gone. The road back to the city was like a long gray river and the light on the forceps of car tracks had died.

The bread. Every noon of that week as you came down from Coronation Point Inn, the smell ran out a little ways to meet you and the treble shouts of the children and once Essie with her pigtails, came flying.

"Bertha's here. Bertha's here."

Why, that was a greeting! The words ran down your spine. Bertha's here.

"Say, oughtta see. Chimmie fell off the counter and shinnied his nose."

"Oh Essie——"

"It bled."

"Oh——"

"Papa couldn't make it stop. Papa can't do nothing. Blood makes him sick."

"Oh, Chimmie, Chimmie. Where is he?"

"There he is, laying out in the road. Get up, you. Papa will get you. Automobile will get you."

"Oh, Chimmie, you got hurt?"

"Chimmie got hurt. Look."

Clank. Clank. There was a great wad of cotton across his nose, held there precariously with strips of adhesive plaster. The brace that made him twice too heavy. And now his shinnied nose. You pulled back the cotton. It stuck and already some of the grime from the smeared little face was under.

There was a long siege of washing with the warm water from the basin that Essie held, and Pete tore off the hem of one of Meyerbogen's clean handkerchiefs and Oscar stood by with the vaseline.

So! The little dressing on Chimmie's nose was neater and flatter and cleaner. It made you glad, the neat little flatness and cleanness.

"Now, Chimmie's well."

"Now, Chimmie's well."

The children ran off. There were the curtains to be hung. They had been washed and ironed the day before and lay out, waiting.

Meyerbogen came around the side of the house with a sack of flour on his back. The white fog made him dim.

"You, Bertha?"

"Yah."

"Dot's good."

"Yah."

"Want lunch?"

"Yah, but I can fix it——"

"No, I'll fix. Veenie sandwich. Baked beans. Gorned beef hash with boached egg."

"Beans."

It was pleasant at the little table in the bake shop. The motors spun past and left a little trail of quiet after the whizz. The mat of flies clung to the screen door but could not force in. The bread. The sweet rich smell of it from the ovens beneath. The beans were fragrant too.

Meyerbogen sat down opposite. His knees were very short and very wide apart and his great paunch threw him sway-back, so that he could not see them. Pouf! Out came the little fog of flour when he sat. His spring-tight curls and his eyelashes were all gray with it. Pouf! Out came a little fog when his hand struck the table. A short hand as dainty as a woman's and all bleached and soft from knuckling into the dough.

"It's a heat," he said.

"Yah."

"Want some mustard?"

"Yah——"

"Chimmie shinnied his nose."

"You didn't know how to dress it."

"Blood goes against me——"

"Yah——"

"Want some mustard?"

"I got some."

"You fixed it good."

"What?"

"Chimmie's nose."

"Yah——"

"It takes a woman. I can't keep help in the gountry. Since my woman is—gone, I got only confusion."

"They don't need me no more at Coronation Point."

"If, blease, you could come by us.  There is a good room for you upstairs and——"

"By the week, you mean?"

"By the month.  By the—always, if you would blease.  I can pay. . . ."

"Yah. . . ."

"It ain't easy to find such a woman like you.  The children, they like you.  There is dot something about you—they know it always first.  Children do."

"I can come."

"Dot's good.  Oh, dot is very good.  The confusion, it's bad.  I need a woman.  You.  We would treat you like one of the family."

"Yah——"

The drone of high noon.  The treble of the children.  The little shining of the beads of sweat on Meyerbogen's nose.

He began to shamble out.  Presently you could see him walking around the side of the house, bent, with a sack of flour on his back.

Family.  A snug kind of a word.  Like a new reefer that buttoned you in up the front.  Only the buttons this time were Chimmie's eyes.  Family.  A snug kind of a word.

There were the curtains to be hung.  They were very starched and stood away from the windows, and more than ever the rooms began to shine.

The dining room was the best.  The red tablecloth helped and a potted petunia, revived a bit with watering, stood in the center.  The red rooster was a trial.  Finally, you had to sit on the floor and shir together a piece of red calico and hang it for a curtain across the lower half of the screen.  For some

reason the tortoise chose that to cling to now. Four times
he had to be returned to his place under the stove. Petey's
tortoise was named Pete. Once when Bertha exclaimed at
him, for clinging to the new red curtain, Petey himself came
running.

"Want me?"

"Not you. I meant Pete under the stove."

"Gimme piece of bread and apple sauce?"

"Here."

"M-m-m-m."

His shaved yellow head. You ran your hand around and
around its bristliness and could feel his temples munching.

"Ouch."

"Don't run so hard, Petey."

"Aw quit. What you taking that down for? That's my
slate, with my drawing on it. Give me."

"I yoost want to wipe down the wall, Petey, I'll hang it
back."

"Give me. Where's my slate pencil?"

"Here."

He curled himself up in a corner. You could hear the soft
stalkings of the pencil across the slate. The walls had to be
brushed down with a broom with a cloth tied about it. They
were very dusty.

"Watch out, Petey."

"M-m-m-m."

"Petey, get out of the dust."

"Lookie. Haw, lookie. Here we are. The whole family.
I got you in this time—haw, lookie!"

There they were. The Meyerbogens as Petey had drawn

them, only there was something that made your heart catch
on its beat.

PAPA    ESSIE    ME    OSCAR    JIMMIE    BERTHA

*The Meyerbogens*

"Why Petey, that's me, on the end.  Why Petey——."

After he had gone like a streak through the door with his
bread and his apple sauce, she hung it back on the wall.  Carefully.  The Meyerbogens.

Chimmie had to be dressed and walked up and down the
room without his braces and drilled not to curve out his leg.
He cried because that hurt, and after she had helped him up
and down for a cruel twenty minutes, he fell asleep.  Then
there was the sink drain pipe to be poked out.  Essie was
such a little girl and of course she had let the grease clog it up.
Squnch.  Ugh.  It was not so bad if you turned your head. . . .

Meyerbogen was coming up the stairs.  You could tell by
the little vibrations.  They ran up the wall.  The dishes shook.
He carried a tray of cinnamon buns.  You could almost hear
their soft hot breath and get the whiff of the currants.

"Bertha, is dot you?"

"Yah. . . ."

"Dot's good," he said, and went into the shop with the tray of hot buns.

The day began to slant. There were potatoes to be dug. The screen snapped as she went out with the dish pan, and the red calico curtain swung. The clayey earth gave forth grudgingly and showed up hard and yellow through the green. But the peas ran up the sticks gayly and there was an arbor that was all spangled with tiny green grapes that were no bigger than buckshot. Presently they would swell and purple and soften. The way to press wine out of grapes was with the feet. The bare, white toes.

Bertha's toes were hurting in her bluchers. The warm clay came burning through to them, making them climb and wriggle. It was easy to kick off the shoes and slide down the stockings. The soft, naked earth. Its warmth ran up her legs in a lightning of gooseflesh. Her toes bit down. White spatulate beauties, she could lift up little dredges of clean dirt with them.

To be bled free of the torments of the ecstasies. To sit there in the wide, westering light with the flat, eager faces of the toes down tasting earth, the good earth, peasantly. Breathers. Suckers in of the little vibratory messages.

Gladnesses here with dimension. The treble shrilling of the children. Pretty leafage of peas up a stick. Clank. Clank. Chimmie must be awake. Meyerbogen disappearing around the house with a sack of flour on his back. The tawny smell of the bread. . . .

THE END